# The critics love Jennifer Echols

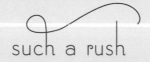

"A twisted love triangle that had us scratching our heads and biting our nails. In short, a real page turner! You'll love it if you're looking for a summer read that's loaded with drama. . . . An emotional story—complete with funny, sarcastic characters and mean-girl confrontations—that you're sure to enjoy."

*—Seventeen*

"I've come to expect certain things from Jennifer Echols's writing: candid characters, passionate chemistry, and equally poignant and hilarious moments. *Such a Rush* has all of this and much more."

*—Lost in the Stacks*

"Perfectly flawed but relatable characters. . . . Knee-weakening, steamy scenes."

*—The Readers Den*

"A brilliant lead, hot twin boys, and airplanes! What's not to love?"

*—The Overflowing Library*

"Fantastic . . . a must read for contemporary romance fans."

*—Book and Latte Reviews*

"[A] blend of romance, interesting characters, witty dialogue, and dramatic intrigue. . . ."

*—The Reading Date*

Other romantic dramas by Jennifer Echols

*Love Story*

*Forget You*

*Going Too Far*

Available from MTV Books

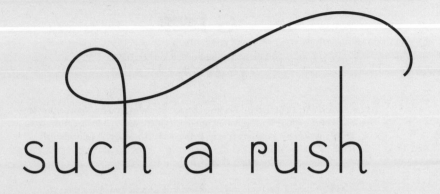

# such a rush

## Jennifer Echols

Gallery Books

 BOOKS

MTV Books

New York   London   Toronto   Sydney   New Delhi

Gallery Books
A Division of Simon & Schuster, Inc.
1230 Avenue of the Americas
New York, NY 10020

First MTV Books/Gallery Books paperback edition December 2012

For information about special discounts for bulk purchases, please contact Simon & Schuster Special Sales at 1-866-506-1949 or business@simonandschuster.com.

The Simon & Schuster Speakers Bureau can bring authors to your live event. For more information or to book an event contact the Simon & Schuster Speakers Bureau at 1-866-248-3049 or visit our website at www.simonspeakers.com.

Designed by Ruth Lee-Mui

Manufactured in the United States of America

1  3  5  7  9  10  8  6  4  2

Library of Congress Cataloging-in-Publication Data is available.

ISBN 978-1-4516-5802-6
ISBN 978-1-4516-5805-7 (ebook)

*For my dad and my son,*
*whose love of flying inspired this book.*

# one

September

In each South Carolina town where I'd lived—and I'd lived in a lot of them—the trailer park was next to the airport. After one more move when I was fourteen, I made a decision. If I was doomed to live in a trailer park my whole life, I could complain about the smell of jet fuel like my mom, I could drink myself to death over the noise like everybody else who lived here, or I could learn to fly.

Easier said than done. My first step was to cross the trailer park, duck through the fence around the airport, and ask for a job. For once I lucked out. The town of Heaven Beach was hiring someone to do office work and pump aviation gas, a hard combination to find. Men who were willing to work on the tarmac couldn't type. Women who could type refused to get avgas on their hands. A hungry-looking fourteen-year-old girl would do fine.

I answered the phone, put chocks under the wheels of visiting airplanes, topped off the tanks for small corporate

1

jets—anything that needed doing and required no skill. In other words, I ran the airport. There wasn't more to a small-town airport than this. No round-the-clock staff. No tower. No air traffic controller—what a joke. Nothing to keep planes from crashing into each other but the pilots themselves.

My reception counter faced the glass-walled lobby with a view of the runway. Lots of days I sat on the office porch instead, taking the airport cell phone with me in case someone actually called, and watched the planes take off and land. Behind the office were small hangars for private pilots. In front of the office, some pilots parked their planes out in the open, since nothing but a hurricane or a tornado would hurt them when they were tied down. To my left, between me and the trailer park, stretched the large corporate hangars. To my right were the flagpole and the windsock, the gas pumps, and more of the corrugated metal hangars. The closest hangar was covered in red and white lettering, peeling and faded from years of storms blowing in from the ocean:

**HALL AVIATION**

**BANNER TOWING: ADVERTISE YOUR BUSINESS TO BEACHGOERS!**

**AIRPLANE RIDES WITH BEAUTIFUL OCEAN VIEWS**

**ASH SCATTERING OVER THE ATLANTIC**

**FLIGHT SCHOOL**

In August I had watched the tiny Hall Aviation planes skim low over the grass beside the runway and snag banners that unfurled behind them in the air, many times longer than the planes themselves. By listening to the men who drank coffee and shot the shit with Mr. Hall on the office porch, I'd gathered that Mr. Hall's oldest son was one of the banner-towing pilots. Mr. Hall's twin sons my age were there to help

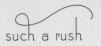

such a rush

too some Saturdays, piecing together the movable letters to make the banners. Alec was smiling and blond and *looked* like the nice, wholesome guy Mr. Hall seemed to think he was, whereas Grayson was always in trouble. He was slightly taller, with his hair covered by a straw cowboy hat and his eyes hidden behind mirrored aviator shades. I couldn't tell whether he was gazing at me across the tarmac when I sat on the porch by myself to smoke a cigarette, but I imagined he was. My whole body suddenly felt sunburned even though I was in the shade.

They were gone now—the twins an hour and a half up the road to Wilmington, where they lived with their mom, and the oldest son back to college. The tourists had left the beach. The banner-towing business had shut down for the season. It was the perfect time to approach Mr. Hall about a lesson. Hall Aviation brochures were stuffed into plastic holders throughout the office for visitors to take. I knew the high price for a lesson without having to mortify myself by asking Mr. Hall in person.

But saving the money, and screwing up the courage to go with it, had taken me a whole month. I'd finally marched over to Hall Aviation and banged on the small door in the side of the hangar with the *oo* of SCHOOL painted across it. When Mr. Hall hollered from inside, I'd wandered among the airplanes and tools to a tiny office carved out of the corner. I'd sat in the chair in front of his desk and asked him to take me up. He'd given me the worst possible answer by handing me a permission form for my mother to sign.

She hadn't been home when I'd walked back from the airport that night. I had lain awake in bed, trying to figure out the right way to present the form to her. She still hadn't come home when I'd left for school that morning. All school day, I'd worried about what I would say to her. I could point out that flying was a possible career someday. She talked like that

3

sometimes, told me I would make something of myself. I was afraid her support would disappear when she found out I'd been saving money for an extravagant lesson instead of giving it to her.

The scraggly coastal forest out the school bus window still seemed strange now that I'd spent a month in Heaven Beach. As the bus approached the trailer park, I hoped against hope my mom would be home and I could get this over with. Even if she said no, at least my torture would end.

I slid one hand down to touch the folded permission form through the pocket of my jeans. My cash for the flying lesson was wadded beneath that. Losing the money at school would have screwed me, but I'd been afraid to leave the money or the form in my room, where my mom might find them if she got desperate for funds, like she did sometimes, and started searching.

As I moved my hand, I felt Mark Simon watching me from across the aisle. He knew about my money somehow. He could tell that's what I had in my pocket from the way I fingered it, and he would take it from me. That was always my first thought. I'd had a lot of things stolen from me on a lot of school buses.

But I forced myself to take a deep breath and relax, letting go of my gut reaction. Mark wasn't that poor. He was riding this bus because he worked for his uncle at the airport after school, not because he lived in the trailer park. And as I glanced over at him, his look seemed less like larceny and more like lechery. He thought he'd caught me touching myself.

I was getting this kind of attention lately, and it was still new. Back inland near the Air Force base, the last place my mom and I had lived, I'd flown under the radar. I wore whatever clothes she found for me. I'd always hated my curly hair, so dark brown it might as well have been black except in the brightest sunlight. It tended to mat. I had broken a comb in it before. Then one glorious day last summer, I'd seen a makeover show on TV that said curly girls needed to make peace with their hair, get a good cut, use some product, and let it dry naturally. I did what I could with a cheap salon on my side of town and discount store product. The result was much better, and I'd made myself over completely in the weeks before we'd moved.

At my new school, my makeover had the desired effect. Nobody felt sorry for me anymore because my mom wasn't taking care of me and I didn't know how to take care of myself. I took care of myself and I looked it. The downside was that I'd gotten stares like these from boys like Mark, which prompted girls to label me a slut and stay away from me. But I knew what I was. I held my head high. Exchanging sympathy for pride was a fair trade-off.

Until I actually found myself entangled in a boy's come-on, and then I wasn't so sure. Supporting himself against the back of the seat as the bus rounded a bend, Mark crossed the aisle and bumped his hip against mine, making me scoot over to give him room to sit down. He glanced at my hand on my pocket and asked, "Can I help you with that?"

If he'd asked me a few months ago, I might have said yes. He didn't have that solid, handsome look of older boys at school who'd gained muscle to go with their height. But for a gawky fifteen-year-old, he was good looking, with sleepy, stoned eyes that moved over me without embarrassment, and dark hair that separated into clumps like he wasn't showering every day because he stayed out late drinking and nearly missed the bus in the morning. He was the type of guy I always found myself with, the adrenaline junkie who talked me into doing things for a rush that I wouldn't have done on my own.

He reminded me of my boyfriend from the trailer park near the Air Force base, who apparently hadn't minded that my hair was matted as long as he got in my pants. He'd convinced me to do it with him in the woods at the edge of the airstrip, with airplanes taking off low over us, exactly where they would crash if something went wrong. Through the sex and the rush and the sight of the streamlined underbellies of the planes, something had happened to me. And I had wanted more of it.

But when I told him I was moving to Heaven Beach, he took up with my best friend the same day. I was through with boys "helping me with that," at least for a while. I glared at Mark as I stood up in the narrow space between the seats. "Move. I have to get off."

He grinned. "Like I said, I can help you with that."

Now I got angry. A nice boy from a good family, or even a not-so-nice boy like Mr. Hall's hot and troubled son Grayson, wouldn't make a comment loaded with innuendo to a nice girl from a good family. If I were stepping down from the bus at the rich end of town instead of the trailer park, I wouldn't have to watch every word I said to make sure it wasn't slang for an orgasm. God. I tried to slide past him.

"Come on, Leah. Why are you stopping here? Why aren't you staying on the bus with me until the airport?" His words were a challenge, but underneath the bravado, I could hear the hurt. I shouldn't push him too far and let him know I was avoiding him. For hurting his pride, he would make things worse for me at school if he was able.

"My mom likes to see me between school and work," I flat-out lied. No way would I tell him the truth. He would mess things up just to get a rise out of me. The days I'd made the mistake of getting off the bus at the airport with him, he'd followed me into the office and lingered there, asking for brochures, asking for maps, threatening to set the break room on fire with his lighter if I didn't pay him some attention, until he finally had to mosey over to the crop-duster hangar or get in trouble with his uncle.

The bus squeaked to a stop on the two-lane highway and opened its door to the gravel road into the trailer park. Ben Reynolds and Aaron Traynor stomped down the hollow stairs. If I didn't make it to the front in the next few seconds, I'd miss this stop. I'd have to walk through the airport with Mark and backtrack to my trailer. I would die if I found out when I finally made it home that I'd missed my mom.

I banged into Mark again and said as forcefully as I could without the five people left on the bus turning around to stare, "Move."

Hooded eyes resentful, he shifted his knees into the aisle, giving me room to slide out. As I hurried up the aisle, he called after me, "Smell you tomorrow." A couple of girls tittered.

I felt myself flushing red. I did not smell. He probably did, judging from his hair today. But people expected me to smell. All he had to do was say the word at school, and everybody would believe it. In my mind I was already going through my closet for what to wear tomorrow, making sure it looked as hip and stylish as I could manage on no budget at all.

I took the last big step down to the road and squinted against the bright sunlight as the bus lumbered away. Ben blocked my path into the trailer park. His fingers formed a V around his mouth, and he waggled his tongue at me. Aaron stood behind him, laughing.

Training my eyes on the cement-block washateria that served the trailer park, I started walking. The TV said you should ignore bullies and they would stop harassing you. In practice this worked about half the time. The other half, you

ended up with two tall boys shadowing you through a trailer park, their fingers taking little nips at your clothes, like dogs. But today the advice worked. Aaron picked up a handful of gravel and threw it at Ben's crotch, then took off running. Ben chased him. They faded into the trailer park.

I felt relieved until I touched the permission form in my pocket again. *Please be home.* Now that the confrontation with my mother was imminent, my stomach twisted. Suddenly I was not in such a hurry. Anyway, if she happened to be home, she couldn't escape me. There was only one road into the trailer park and one road out. I dragged my feet around the washateria to the side where the mailboxes were set into the wall so they were harder to break into, and unlocked ours with my teeth gritted. I had been checking the mail since I was ten because my mom never did. I'd been the bearer of bad news for the last three evictions, and I always expected that business-size envelope. There wasn't one today, only junk, which I dumped in the trash. The nicer sections of Heaven Beach placed recycling bins next to the trash cans. The trailer park did not recycle.

*Please be home.* I fished my cigarettes out of my purse and lit one, relaxing into the first rush of nicotine. Back in our last town, my boyfriend had snuck cigarettes to me. Now that I had to buy them, they were a huge ding in my paycheck. I had tried to quit, but they were the only thing I looked forward to every day besides watching airplanes. *Please be home.* I entered the dark opening in the woods. Gravel crunched under my feet. Country music blasted from a trailer even though all the windows were shut. At least I knew someone was home. If Ben or Aaron came back, I could call for help if I needed it. Of course, my mom had called for help plenty of times in trailer parks when no one had come. *Please be home.*

I reached our lot, rounded the palmettos, and stopped short. A car older than me, faded red with a blue passenger door, was parked in the dirt yard. My mom didn't have a car. A shirtless man with a long, gray ponytail edged out of the trailer, onto the wobbly cement blocks stacked as stairs, holding one end of the TV that had appeared soon after we moved in last month. We were being robbed again. Nicotine pumped through me and made me dizzy as I turned to run for the country music trailer.

Then the man was backing down the stairs, and my mom appeared in the doorway on the other end of the TV. I didn't recognize her at first. She'd been a bleach blonde the last time I saw her a few days ago. Now she was a bright redhead. I knew it was her by the way she walked.

I exhaled smoke. The man must be my mom's boyfriend. She'd said we were moving here to Heaven Beach because he was going to get her a job at the restaurant where he worked. But she hadn't gotten a job yet, and he hadn't come over while I was home. I'd begun to think she'd made him up. Sometimes we moved because a boyfriend said he would get her a job. Sometimes this was what she told me at first, but I'd find out later we'd really moved because she'd owed someone money.

She must have been telling the truth this time. A TV was the first thing she asked for from her boyfriends because she knew I loved it. It kept me company. It was also the first thing to get pawned because it was worth so much cash and was easy to carry. The refrigerator had been pawned only once.

"Hey, hon!" my mom called to me. "Open that door for Billy, would you?"

I opened the driver's door of the car and leaned the seat forward so they could wrangle the TV into the back. They had

a hard time of it, cussing at each other. The TV was almost as big as the backseat itself. They propped one end inside. My mom held it while Billy sauntered around the car. While she was bent over like that, it was obvious her shorts were too tight, but she still had a great figure for a mom. She *should* have, since she was only thirty.

Finally she straightened, left the door propped open for Billy to slide into the driver's seat, and turned to me. "You look so pretty today! Give me a hug."

I walked into her embrace and felt my whole body relax, just like after my first puff on a cigarette. At the same time, I held my lit butt way out so it wouldn't set her hair on fire. I wasn't trying to hide the cigarette. I'd gotten over my fear of her seeing me smoking. I'd thought at first that she'd be mad, but she'd walked in on me smoking a couple of times and hadn't said a word.

She squeezed me and let me go. "I'm sorry we have to take the TV. Billy needs to make a car payment."

This was either a lie or just stupid. Who would make payments on this car?

"It'll only be for a few weeks," she said, "until he gets paid."

Also a lie or stupid. Pawnshops didn't work this way. They would give Billy so little money for this TV and charge him such high interest to retrieve it that I would never see it again. Besides, if he didn't have enough money to live on now, this was not going to change the next time he got a paycheck. I'd been through this scenario with my mom and her boyfriends enough times to predict the outcome. I was never sure whether she didn't know or didn't care or simply saw no way out.

She flinched and her eyes snapped skyward as a plane roared overhead. The trailer park was at the end of the airstrip

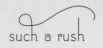 

where the planes landed. The prickly forest shielded the trailers from some of the noise, so the planes could sneak up like this. The unlikely piece of machinery suddenly appeared overhead and loomed in the sky as if by magic, slow enough to look like it ought to fall, loud enough to vibrate the corrugated metal of the trailers. Adrenaline rushed through my veins, like nicotine but better.

"God, I hate those fucking airplanes," my mom said. "Billy's going to get me that job soon and we'll move someplace nice, I promise."

"Okay," I said with no emotion. She said stuff like this all the time. Occasionally she really did get a job, but the longest she lasted was a month. I watched the plane until it dropped behind a stand of pines. Even after that I could hear the engine, and I looked in the direction of the airstrip where it had gone.

"Wait a minute," my mom said. "*You* have some money you could give to Billy."

My cigarette had burned down to the filter. I took a drag anyway as I turned back to my mom, concentrating on *not* glancing down at my pocket where all my money was. Exhaling smoke, I asked casually, "From the airport? I don't make very much. They take out taxes. And I'm already paying the power and the water."

The afternoon light glinted weirdly off the creases in her heavy blue eye shadow as she considered me skeptically. "You work there every day after school and all weekend long."

"Actually . . ." I was horrified at how easily the lie came out. "I'm not working half the time I'm there. They won't give me enough hours. My boyfriend works there, and I hang out with him."

"Really," my mom said, raising her penciled eyebrows. "What's his name?"

Mark. Mark was the obvious answer, but I couldn't bring myself to tell that fib. Before I knew what I was saying, this came out: "Grayson Hall. His dad owns the airplanes that tow the advertising banners at the beach."

"I hate those things," she said. "But a boy like that, maybe he'll stay in school and amount to something."

"Maybe," I said, feeling sick.

"Sheryl," Billy called from inside the car. "This year."

"See you soon, hon," my mom said. She air-kissed her fingertips and blew the kiss to me, then shuffled around the car, kicking up dust, and got in on the other side.

Waving to the car as it disappeared into the forest, I realized I was still holding a dead cigarette. Normally I would have taken it inside, made sure the fire was out, and deposited the butt in the trash. Today I tossed it onto the dirt along with countless butts from my mom and everyone who'd ever lived here, then climbed the cement blocks and went inside the trailer.

The wall where the TV had been looked bare, even though it wasn't. Before the TV had appeared, my mom had hung my first-, second-, and third-grade school photos there in frames. Fourth grade was the year she started saying the school was gouging her and the pictures were highway robbery. My newly exposed smiling faces watched me as I passed through the combined den and kitchen. I escaped down the hall and into my bedroom, where I opened my dresser drawer and pulled out the trailer lease agreement. My mom threw stuff like this away. I tried to snag it from her first. Sometimes having the paperwork helped when a landlord wanted to kick us out. This time it would help me forge her signature.

I pulled the permission form out of my pocket and unfolded it. For something to press down on, I drew the

magazine off the top of my dresser: last month's issue of *Plane & Pilot,* which I'd borrowed from the airport office. I hadn't thought much about it at the time. I liked to read the articles in bed at night. They kept me company. I'd always intended to take the magazine back. Suddenly I felt like a thief.

And I wasn't done. Watching my mom's signature on the lease, I copied the *S* in *Sheryl* onto the permission form. It wasn't a perfect imitation. My hand shook. But Mr. Hall wouldn't have her signature on file for comparison like the school did. I copied *heryl.* I was going to get in trouble for this. It would come back to haunt me, I knew. I copied the *J* in *Jones.* The alternative was to stay on the ground and never go up in an airplane. I copied *ones.* Go ahead and fork over my last dollar to my mom so she and Billy or whoever her boyfriend was that month could fund a party with my money, he could get a new fishing rod and a shotgun, they could pawn it all for beer money or for crack if he was one of *those* boyfriends, then try to win the money back at the Indian casino in North Carolina. I underlined *Sheryl Jones* just as she did, like an eighth grader still in love with her own signature.

I pocketed the form. With the magazine under my elbow, I locked the trailer door behind me and walked to work. I skirted just beyond reach of my neighbor's chained pit bull, prompting the dog to bark and lunge maniacally at me. As I popped out of the forest, into the long, wide clearing, the barking was drowned out by an airplane engine. The World War II Stearman biplane that Mark's uncle once used for crop dusting was coming in for a landing.

Mark had told me that his uncle, Mr. Simon, had bought three Air Tractors just recently—the ugliest planes I'd seen at the airport yet, with ridiculously long noses and harsh angles, painted garish yellow. Now that Mr. Simon used those

monstrosities for crop dusting, he'd converted the biplane back into a passenger plane so one of the crop-duster pilots could give tourists a joyride.

The biplane was beautiful, the huge motor in the nose balanced by the long wings above and below. It looked like it had soared out of a time machine. I watched it sail downward and held my breath for the crash—but planes always seemed to me like they should crash. None of them had actually crashed while I'd been a witness. The biplane skimmed to a smooth landing and slowed. I tripped and realized I'd stumbled out of the long grass and onto the asphalt tarmac.

Way in the distance, the men of the airport lounged in rocking chairs on the office porch. Mr. Hall. The Admiral, an actual retired admiral who looked anything but in his cargo shorts and Hawaiian shirt. Mr. Simon, looking exactly like the owner of a crop-dusting business in overalls and a baseball hat from an airplane manufacturer. Another retired Navy guy— Heaven Beach was a popular place for them to settle. The jet pilot for one of the local corporations. As I drew close, several of them turned to watch me.

As I reached hearing distance, *all* of them watched me, and they fell completely silent. I was sure they were staring at the copy of *Plane & Pilot* under my arm. I hoped my elbow covered the label with the airport address. I stepped under the awning.

Mr. Hall said, "Hello, Leah."

"Hello, Leah. Good afternoon, Leah," came a chorus of voices.

I grinned blankly, staring past them at the runway, as I backed through the glass door.

The town sent one of their maintenance guys, Leon, to take care of the airport when I wasn't around. He put chocks under airplane wheels just fine, but he didn't have the greatest

telephone skills, and I'd made him promise never to touch the files because I wasn't a hundred percent sure he could read. I took the keys and the airport cell phone from him. After he left, I listened to the messages he'd let go to voice mail. As I called a man back about renting a hangar and went over the lease agreement with him, my skin caught on fire. If I got caught forging my mother's name on Mr. Hall's permission form, I couldn't very well claim I was only fourteen years old and didn't understand what was legal in paperwork and what wasn't.

I tried to forget it and play friendly airport hostess as I greeted a millionaire jetting in for a weekend vacation with his family. I called the town's only limo service to come pick them up. I made fresh coffee in the break room. I wiped the whole office down, even the empty rooms. After the old men left the porch and I was pretty sure nobody was watching, I slipped the copy of *Plane & Pilot* back onto a table in the lobby.

For the last hour and a half the office was open, I sat in a rocking chair on the porch in the hot afternoon, watching the occasional air traffic. The office was set slightly ahead of the straight line of hangars. Beyond the brick corners of the building, I couldn't always see who was prepping a plane to go up. I loved when an engine suddenly roared to life, startling me, and the plane taxied to the end of the runway. It revved its motor, then sped toward me and lifted with no additional noise at all, like a car driving up a hill, except there was nothing underneath but the runway and then grass and then trees and then—I couldn't see where it went.

At two minutes until closing time, I lit a cigarette. Mr. Hall's truck still sat outside his hangar, but he might close up and go home at any moment. Then I would lose another night of sleep and go through this whole ordeal again tomorrow. I

had told him I would be back today with my signed permission form, but maybe he didn't believe I would get my mother to sign it. And he would be correct. *Please don't leave.*

Exactly at closing time, I stubbed out my cigarette in the urn of sand outside the office door and walked over to the Hall Aviation hangar. I'd learned the hard way yesterday not to bang on the outer door, because this just annoyed Mr. Hall. The screech as the door opened was warning enough for him. I walked on in. Beyond the shadows of the airplanes, he looked up from his desk inside his bright glassed-in office in the corner and swept his hand toward the empty seat.

I dug in my pocket for the money and the permission form, unfolding them and handing them over as I sat down.

He set them aside without looking at them. "You're back."

"Yes, sir." Why had he placed my money and the form to one side? Did he already know the signature was a fake? I forced myself to calm down and concentrate on his face, as if I actually wanted to have a conversation with him.

He was in his late forties, like the parents of fourteen-year-olds ought to be. I could tell his hair used to be blond and curly like Grayson's, but it was turning white, and he'd cut it so short that it looked almost straight. I could also tell he used to be hot like Grayson. The traces of a strong chin and high cheekbones were still there in his weathered face, but he seemed to have gained a lot of weight quickly. His face was misshapen with it now, and the roll didn't sit right around his gut.

"I figured you'd be back," he said. "How are you liking your job over at the office?"

I loved my job. It was the best thing I'd ever done. But I knew that would sound weird and overeager. Basically all I did was sit on my ass over there. I said, "It's going okay."

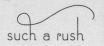

"The airport old-timers have a joke about you."

He meant the men who talked on the porch. I stiffened, bracing to get made fun of even here at the airport, where I had felt relatively safe.

He rumbled on, "We're remembering something that happened fifteen years ago, and somebody will say, 'Ask Leah.' Get it? You do such a good job and know everything that's going on. We've never had anybody like you running the office before."

"Oh, ha-ha," I said. The joke wasn't funny, but he was trying to pay me a compliment. Which was ridiculous, because anybody could have done the job I was doing if they'd cared. Though, come to think of it, maybe caring was the secret ingredient.

"Why do you want to be a pilot?"

I opened my mouth. This was a test, and I shouldn't hesitate with an answer. The truth was, I didn't understand the question. I was here for one lesson. One. Maybe in my fantasies over the last month, I *had* pictured myself with a job as an airline pilot, in a dark blue uniform, with my hair tucked and sprayed into submission under a neat brimmed hat, standing in the doorway to the cockpit and greeting passengers as they boarded, all of them looking me up and down and mistrusting a small woman, but deciding to give me their confidence because of the uniform and the vast airplane that was all mine to fly. At least, that's how I pictured an airline flight starting. I'd never flown before. I'd only seen it on TV. Maybe my fantasy was stupid.

On a sigh I said, "I like airplanes."

He raised his white-blond brows at me, not helping me at all, waiting for me to continue.

I swallowed. "I've always lived near the airport."

"Really?" he asked, furrowing his brow now, confused.

"Not this airport," I clarified. "Other airports. I move a lot. The last one was at the Air Force base, and I got closer than I'd ever been to an airplane. I can't stop thinking about it."

This he understood, nodding slowly.

"When I moved here, I got the job at the office. Now I'm not just hearing the airplanes and seeing a flash of them above me through the trees. I watch them take off and land. They look like they shouldn't be able to fly."

He laughed. Though he cut himself off quickly, pressing his lips together, I could tell he was trying not to grin. "Let me tell you something, Leah. Years ago, this place was crawling with kids wanting to be pilots. There were four folks doing your job, two in the office and two on the tarmac. That rabbit warren of empty rooms you're in charge of was full of business. But since 9/11 and the bad publicity about airports and a couple of recessions, not as many people want to take flying lessons."

I nodded. The office with all its nice furniture and no people did smack of more exciting days gone by.

"We old guys, not just here but across the country, talk about getting young people excited about flying again. What we say is this: Most people hear an airplane in the sky and think, 'There's an airplane,' and go back to what they were doing. A few folks look around for the airplane, try to figure out what kind of plane it is, and watch it from the time they spot it to the time it disappears on the horizon, maybe after that. Those kids are the ones who will be pilots." He pointed at me. "I knew that about you. I've just been waiting for you to show up." He reached for my form.

He was telling me I was some kind of Chosen One. Yet he expressed this opinion with a self-satisfied, know-it-all air that

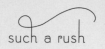

ticked me off. I suddenly understood why, when he'd yelled at Grayson for handling the banners wrong last month, Grayson had yelled back.

Mr. Hall eyed me over the top of the paper, then looked at the form again. I forgot my annoyance. Panic took over as I realized he was examining the forgery.

He set the form almost all the way down on the desk. It drifted the rest of the distance to lie on piles of other paperwork. He said, "I'll give you a lesson on one condition."

That I go back and get the form signed by my mother for real this time? This would be better than having me arrested for forgery, yet neither was the answer I wanted. My stomach turned over as I waited for him to finish.

"Quit smoking," he said.

I sucked in a breath, surprised that he would care whether I smoked, and that he would even know—though I probably reeked of it. My mother certainly did after she'd lit up.

Then I was relieved that he hadn't mentioned my mother's signature. Then annoyed that he was getting in my business. "*I* am paying *you*," I pointed out. "You can't make me quit smoking."

"You can't make me take you flying." He grinned at me, rubbing it in.

Then he leaned forward like he was letting me in on a secret. "I'm doing you a favor. It took me thirty years to quit. Okay?"

I nodded. I didn't have any choice.

"Then let's go." He jumped up from his chair like a kid. Maybe he really *had* been waiting for me to come in.

I followed him as he wound between and under the planes packed into the hangar like puzzle pieces. Finally we reached a white plane, larger than the others, a four-seater. We circled

it as he pointed out things that could go wrong with it and that I should be looking for before I flew. He sent me up on a stepladder to stick a glass rod into the wing to check the fuel level.

"This seems awfully low-tech," I said, resistant to these chores if they were busywork, like everything in my definitely-not-college-track classes at school. "Don't airplanes have a gas gauge in the cockpit?"

"They do," he said. "I've just showed you a bunch of things on this aircraft that can break. Don't you think a gas gauge can break?"

"I guess."

"'I guess' will get you killed."

I recognized the tone he used to reprimand Grayson. He didn't have to use it on me. I turned around on the stepladder and looked down at him.

Seeming to realize he'd mistakenly snapped at me like someone he loved, he held up both hands, explaining himself. "If the gas gauge were broken on your car and you unexpectedly ran out of fuel, what would you do?"

"Pull over." I didn't know, really. I could get my learner's permit when I turned fifteen in a month and a half. But with my mom gone all the time, I doubted I would ever learn to drive.

"That's right," he said. "And if the gas gauge were broken on your plane and you unexpectedly ran out of fuel, what would you do?"

"Crash?"

I had meant this as a sarcastic joke, but when he folded his arms, I realized that's *exactly* what would happen.

From then on, I did what he told me without complaining and tried to remember everything he said. There was too much information, especially now that I realized my life would be

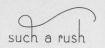

riding on it, lots of other lives too, if I actually became a pilot. My little fantasy of nodding to passengers as they boarded my airliner seemed naive now. I would hide my misgivings from Mr. Hall, get through this lesson, and never come back.

He showed me how to pull the enormous front doors of the hangar open to the afternoon breeze. Then he told me to help him push the plane out of the hangar. I thought *he* was kidding this time—the two of us pushing this heavy airplane around. But come to think of it, I'd seen men pushing small planes on the tarmac. They must be lighter than they looked. I shoved from behind, he tugged on a contraption made to steer the front wheel, and the plane was rolling by itself onto the tarmac. We climbed into the plane, which wasn't as luxurious as I'd pictured, with thin upholstery like a cheap car. We plugged bulky headsets into the dashboard so we could hear each other when we spoke into the microphones.

"Clear!" he yelled, his voice like gravel. He pressed a button. The propeller spun so fast it disappeared. The powerful vibration shook my seat. He drove the plane down the tarmac, past the hangars, and turned around. The trailer park was directly behind us. The other end of the runway was far off. My heart raced.

"Now we check the controls," he said, his voice tinny in my headphones. "Don't just look at these dials. Your brain can stay asleep that way. Touch each one and make sure it's working." He made me touch all the black circles in the high dashboard that curved in front of us. Then he showed me how to use the steering wheel—when he moved his, mine moved the same way—and the foot pedals. We looked out the windows to make sure the parts of the airplane were doing what the controls told them. I felt sick, and then my headphones filled with static. Something had gone horribly wrong.

21

Mr. Hall reached over. With calloused fingers, he bent my microphone a few millimeters farther from my lips. The static had been my own hysterical breathing.

"Ever read *The Right Stuff*?" he asked. "Heard of Chuck Yeager?"

"No." I tried to utter the syllable casually, but I sounded like I was strangling.

"Chuck Yeager was an Air Force test pilot. First man to break the sound barrier, back in 1947. Other pilots were amazed at what he was willing to risk his life to do, and even more amazed at how calm he stayed while he did it—at least, that's how he sounded. Airline pilots all use the Yeager voice when they come over the intercom and speak to the passengers, right?"

"Right." I had no clue.

"And we use the Yeager voice on the radio too, no matter what kind of trouble we get into. Cracking up where the public can hear would be bad for business. Use the Yeager voice and say this."

I repeated his words, information about the airport and our plane so other pilots in the area wouldn't crash into us when we took off. In my own headphones I sounded like I was six years old. Any second, pilots and mechanics would come streaming out of the hangars like ants to pull the rogue toddler out of the cockpit.

"Now," Mr. Hall said. "You were telling me that you like to watch airplanes, and they look like they shouldn't be able to fly."

"Yeah. And that was even before I knew what I know now."

Out of the corner of my eye, I saw him shift, turning his shoulders toward me. I faced him too, for the first time since we'd been packed close in the cockpit. He tilted his head to one

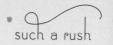

side, considering me, his weathered face impossible to read. But his voice was kind as he said, "There are lots of mistakes you can make. Pilots make them, and pilots die. Obstacles will kill you. The weather will kill you. But, as I'm about to show you, the airplane is your friend. The plane wants to fly."

"If it has gas," I said dryly.

"The gas is going to get the engine up to fifty-five knots—sixty-three miles an hour—but that's all we need. Once we have air moving that fast over and under the wing, the shape of the wing creates lift. The airplane is an amazing invention. Watch."

He faced forward. The engine moaned. We were racing down the runway before I realized it was too late to bail out.

"I'm not doing anything," he said. Sure enough, his hands were off the steering wheel, fingers splayed, as we drew even with the Simon Air Agriculture hangar and rose into the air. "Lift. It's all in the way this fantastic machine is constructed."

We shot over the trees at the end of the runway and kept rising. I hadn't realized how vast the forest was, unbroken in that direction as far as I could see. The plane slowly banked, and we circled back over the airport. I'd never realized how long my walk was from the airport office to the trailer park. I had thought it was fairly short because there were no trees or buildings marking my place beyond the last hangar, but the flat grass was deceiving. It was a long way.

Then we buzzed the trailer park. The directions of the roads and the narrow spaces between the trailers seemed different as I looked down on them. But this eagle's-eye view was the true view, I realized. The view I'd had my whole life, at trailer level—that was the disorienting perspective. I was able to pick out my own trailer because of the position of the long metal roof in relation to the dark palm tree next to my

bedroom window, which was taller than the trees around it. And the next second, when the plane had gained more altitude, I could see the ocean.

"Oh my God!" My own voice was loud enough in my headphones to hurt my ears. I had forgotten about the Chuck Yeager person who always spoke calmly. I thought Mr. Hall might reprimand me, but he just chuckled as I stared out the window.

Heaven Beach was, after all, a beach town. Other residents went to the ocean every day. I had known the ocean was there. I just didn't get to see it very often. It might as well have been a million miles away from the trailer instead of two. And now, there it was, rising to meet the sky, dark blue crossed with white waves. I could see whole waves, crawling in slow motion toward the shore.

"Now you take the yoke," Mr. Hall said.

Yoke. Not steering wheel. Lifting my head from the window, I put my hands on the grips and squeezed. My fingers trembled.

"You won't kill us," he assured me. "My controls double yours, remember? If you make a mistake, I'll pull us out. Just do what I say, and you'll be flying. First, for safety, we have to make sure only one of us is trying to fly this thing at a time. I'm transferring control to you. I say, 'Your airplane.' You say, 'My airplane.'"

"My airplane," I whispered.

"Press your right foot pedal—gently first, to get the feel of it. That will turn us."

I did what he said. The plane veered away from the beach. I was flying. I was seeing everything for the first time and maybe the last. All of it at once was overwhelming. I stole a look back over my shoulder at the ocean, fascinated by this beautiful

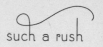

piece of the Earth that everyone else enjoyed and that was so close to where I lived, yet completely out of my reach.

We flew—*I* flew—over the high school, and the discount store out on the highway. They looked exactly alike, just a flat black roof, a huge rectangle with smaller squares hanging off here and there for the gym or the garden department, and silver cubes of industrial air conditioners on top. I wouldn't have been able to tell the school and the store apart if it hadn't been for their huge signs out front, which from the air were tiny.

Since Mr. Hall had told me to head back inland, I'd been afraid the flight was about to end. But now he instructed me to point the plane back east toward the ocean, then north. We flew up the coast to little beach towns where I'd never been. Civilization petered out and nature preserves took over, with wide rivers snaking through swamps to the sea. We flew all the way to Cape Fear in North Carolina—my first time out of South Carolina, ever. The buildings of downtown Wilmington were visible on the horizon when Mr. Hall said, "We could land and see my boys, but I don't think they'd appreciate that. We'd better go back. I can fly in the dark, but you can't. That's a lesson way down the road."

I followed his instructions and turned the airplane around, probably the widest turn possible for this small plane. When I was flying straight back down the coast again and relaxing my death grip on the yoke, I asked him, "Why don't you see your sons more?"

"I was just kidding about that," he grumbled. "Alec and Grayson live with their mother, and Jake is in college."

The roar of the engine filled the cabin while I thought about what I was really trying to ask him. Finally I said, "It seems like they would be in Heaven Beach every chance they got, wanting to fly with you."

"That's my fault," Mr. Hall said shortly. "I made a mistake."

I shouldn't have asked, and now our conversation had gone awkward. I racked my brain for something to say, some question to ask about flying or the airport or anything except his sons.

"A very, very bad mistake," he said. "I've been trying to make up for it, but some things you can't make up for." He shifted in his seat and stretched his arms above him, which for him might have meant he was trying to escape whatever bad memories haunted him, but for me meant he was nowhere near saving us if I moved the yoke the wrong way, and I had better keep the airplane steady.

"*Man,*" he exclaimed, "what a pretty day to fly."

I flew us all the way back to Heaven Beach. Then he made me say, "Your airplane," and he took over. But he talked me through the landing, telling me every move he made and why. The plane touched down so smoothly that I knew we were on the ground only because I heard a new noise, the wheels on the runway. He let me drive the plane to Hall Aviation—*taxi* it, rather—and showed me how to power it down. We pushed it back into its place in the hangar.

As I was hauling the big metal door closed, I heard him say, "Well, hey there." A middle-aged lady slipped through the side door. She was dressed in a trim jacket and wore a carefully teased hairdo, heavy makeup, and flowery perfume, like she'd just gotten off work. He kissed her on the cheek and led her by the hand over to me.

"This is Sofie," he told me. "Sofie, meet my new student, Leah."

"Hello, Leah." Sofie held out her hand with glossy red nails.

I wasn't sure what to do. My only experience with polite adults was working for them in the office for the past month, and they hadn't held their hands out to me. I guessed I was supposed to shake her hand, which I did.

She let me go and grinned at me. "Look at that big smile! You had fun up there."

"Yes, ma'am." Funny—people commented on my face a lot. I was pretty, apparently. I could also pull off a very convincing go-to-hell expression. But nobody ever said anything about my smile.

"Same time next week?" Mr. Hall asked me.

I felt my smile melt away. "Uh." I wanted so badly to fly again next week. If he'd let me, I would have flown again tomorrow. Better yet, right now. But saving the money for a second lesson would take me more than a week.

Almost immediately he said, "We're in the off-season and business is down. I'm running a two-for-one special. Next week is free."

"Cool." This was charity, I knew. I took it without arguing.

"We're headed to dinner," he said, jerking his thumb over his shoulder. "Want to come with us?"

I glanced at Sofie, who still grinned at me. She didn't mind me tagging along on their date. I minded, though. I'd blown almost all my money on the lesson, and I couldn't let them pay for my food. That was too much charity at once. "Thanks so much," I said, "but my mom probably has dinner on the table waiting for me by now." I almost laughed at my biggest lie of the day—further from the truth than my boyfriend Grayson, more outrageous than a forgery—and hurried out the side door.

On the sunset walk home, I stopped to unlock the office and snag my bottle of water from the reception counter. I'd

never understood why someone would pay soda price for water. Or for soda, for that matter. I bought one bottle of water, took it home with me each night and washed it and refilled it, and replaced it only when the peeling label threatened to give away my secret. But not today. I did buy a pack of crackers from the machine in the break room. Sometimes when my mother appeared at the trailer, she stocked the refrigerator for me. I doubted she'd done that today, since she was out of money and she'd been so focused on the TV. My stomach rumbled at the thought of the real dinner I'd passed up with Mr. Hall.

As I walked past the dark Simon Air Agriculture hangar, I popped the first cracker into my mouth. I craved a cigarette instead. But I had become a pilot today, and now I had something real to look forward to.

# two

Three years later
December

My afternoon behind the counter at the airport office had been eerily quiet. Suddenly I jumped and the pages of my newspaper went flying. The weather app on the office's cell phone beeped crazily. With a glance at the phone, and a glance outside at the sky, I shut off the noise and speed-dialed Hall Aviation.

Mr. Hall answered, "Merry Christmas, Leah."

The bad news I'd been about to give him stopped in my mouth. He was still my flight instructor, and starting next April he would be my boss. We were all business. But Grayson and Alec were visiting him over Christmas break, and Jake was home on leave from Afghanistan. When I'd walked over to Hall Aviation to fly practice runs in the past week, the hangar had been full of boys teasing and shoving each other, and warmth. I heard the same uncharacteristic warmth in Mr. Hall's voice now.

I hated to tell him. "The weather service just issued a wind

advisory. A storm's coming in. Isn't Grayson still up? You need to get him down."

The phone beeped. Mr. Hall had hung up on me.

I used the phone to navigate to the weather forecast. The radar showed a wide, wicked storm moving in fast from the Atlantic.

Setting the phone aside, I glanced toward the big windows facing the runway. Grayson, Alec, and I had all turned eighteen and earned our commercial licenses in the past few months, so Mr. Hall could finally employ us instead of random college-age pilots over spring break and during the summer. For days we'd taken turns flying the ancient planes as Mr. Hall taught us how to snag the long advertising banners and fly them down the beach and back. I'd gone up on my lunch hour from the airport office, and Grayson had climbed into the plane after I'd climbed out. From here behind the reception counter, I'd watched him take off. I hadn't seen him land.

Judging from Mr. Hall's rude ending to our call, I'd been right. Grayson was still up.

I swallowed my heart, then gathered the scattered pages and went back to reading the newspaper, a delicious luxury I swiped daily from the waiting area and examined between odd jobs if I'd already digested the month's *Plane & Pilot* cover to cover. In the past couple of years, I'd made friends with a new-comer at school named Molly. The great thing about Molly was that she wasn't embarrassed to be seen with me, so she saved me from being a complete outcast. The bad thing about her was that she was a normal girl in a normal home with a normal family. By comparison, she made me more aware of how far I was out of the mainstream. Through my friendship with her, gradually I was finding out exactly how much my life differed from hers, Grayson's, the life of almost anybody who

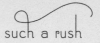

was my age. My mom had never subscribed to any magazine or newspaper. I turned the newspaper page to the obituaries.

Something flashed past the windows. I sighed with relief. Grayson was landing. I hadn't heard his engine because small planes were hard to hear indoors, at this distance from the runway.

But when I put down the newspaper and walked to the window to make sure he'd landed okay, I saw it wasn't a plane at all. The flash I'd seen was Alec and Jake running past the office, closer to the end of the runway where Grayson would land. Mr. Hall chugged more slowly behind them.

This was not a good sign. When one of us hooked a banner, someone else watched to make sure the rope and banner unfurled correctly, nothing got tangled, and no parts fell off the airplane. But we didn't regularly watch each other take off or land. If even Mr. Hall was hurrying down the runway for Grayson's approach, Grayson was in trouble.

I adjusted a dial in the wall so the common traffic advisory frequency would play on the speakers outside. When Grayson announced over the radio that he was getting close, we would hear him. Then I zipped my thin jacket, the only coat I owned. It wouldn't protect me from today's cold, but I had to see what was going on. I pocketed the office phone and stepped through the door outside.

The icy wind hit me in the face and blew my curls into my eyes as if the elastic holding them in a ponytail weren't even there. The blue sky was still visible, but a bank of ominous gray clouds swirled over the trees. A few puffs scuttled overhead, their shadows racing along the ground faster than a plane. On one side of the office, the rope clanged against the flagpole over and over in the breeze, a strike and a hollow reverberation like a church bell. I should lower the flag for

the day before the storm came. The orange windsock high on its pole stood straight out, perpendicular to the runway. The crosswind was strong and frightening.

Several yards away, the Halls stood in a line, each squinting at the sky in a different direction, looking for Grayson. I'd seen Alec and Jake often in the past few days, but never standing together, and I was struck by how much alike they looked now that Alec was eighteen, even though Jake was five years older. Same muscular build and bright blond hair, except Jake's hair was cut ultrashort for the military. Same open, friendly face and easy stance in old jeans and sweatshirts and bulky hiking coats, hands on hips, model-handsome without trying at all. In the face, they looked like a picture Mr. Hall had shown me of their mom.

Self-conscious to the point of blushing, I walked over to stand beside Mr. Hall. Alec was my age and I should want to stand next to him, not his middle-aged father. The truth was, after three years at the airport, I still didn't know Alec, Jake, or Grayson very well. They came to Heaven Beach only for summers and holidays and occasional weekends. I knew them mostly by watching them while I sat on the front porch of the office and they loitered outside the Hall Aviation hangar. They competed with each other and insulted each other. Fights broke out occasionally, with one of the boys throwing a punch at another before the third brother shouted for their dad and pulled them apart. The glimpses I got of them filled my mind for days afterward. I would have given anything to join them and feel like part of their gruff, dramatic family. But there was a standoffishness about them, like they resented me for butting in.

Then, around this time last year, right before Jake deployed to Afghanistan, Mr. Hall had told me to come over for my flying lesson as usual. As I'd crossed the asphalt and approached

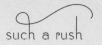

the door in the side of the hangar, I'd heard the boys' voices echoing inside. I didn't want to anger them by interrupting them, but I thought it was best to walk in like I belonged, just as I always did. So I pushed the door without knocking.

As the door was opening, I couldn't see them, but I recognized Alec's voice. "Do you think he's doing her?"

"Good God, no," Jake said.

"Of course he is," Grayson said. "Why else would that stingy bastard give away flying lessons for free?"

The door swung all the way open and banged against the metal wall like a gunshot. All three of them jumped and then turned to stare at me: Alec sprawled in a lawn chair, Jake leaning against the nose of the red Piper, Grayson with both hands in the engine.

I stood there for a moment more, processing, trying not to jump to conclusions. Maybe they hadn't meant what I thought they'd meant. Maybe they hadn't meant Mr. Hall. Maybe they hadn't meant me.

Yes, they had, I saw in the next instant. Jake looked at the cement floor and shook his head like it was a damn shame I'd heard them, but he didn't really care. Alec, wide eyes on me, started to get up from his chair. Grayson kept staring at me across the airplane engine, gaze cold, daring me to deny it.

I had not denied it. I'd turned away from the open door, never looking back even when I reached the airport office. I'd told Leon that he could go back to his regular job because I didn't have a flying lesson that day after all.

In the year since then, I'd never skipped another lesson. Flying was too precious. But I'd avoided Mr. Hall's sons every other way I could. They hadn't acted differently toward me. Jake had been in Afghanistan. Alec and Grayson had given me a polite hello when they absolutely had to, and had held

open the door of the airport office for me when I was carrying a box of files, like southern gentlemen, or southern boys
whose father had threatened them within an inch of their lives
if thcy didn't act like gentlemen, same as always. Maybe they
had wanted to apologize but had missed the moment, and now
bringing it up would be even more awkward than letting it lie.
It didn't matter, anyway, when we didn't matter to each other.

But *they* mattered to *me,* I realized as Jake and Alec scanned
the sky. They viewed me as a stranger, but I viewed them as
my heroes in a one-sided relationship, like a television drama
I looked forward to every week and pined for when my mom
pawned the TV.

My heart pounded at the thought that one of them was
about to attempt a very ugly landing.

"I can't believe this," Mr. Hall muttered beside me.

"I know," I said.

"I've been checking the weather all day. I wouldn't have
sent him up if I'd seen this coming in so fast."

"We're on the ocean in the winter," I reminded him.
"Storms are going to blow in that you don't see coming."
Whatever happened to Grayson—my stomach twisted—I
didn't want Mr. Hall to blame himself. Though he would.

"That's right, Leah." Mr. Hall nodded. "That's good. You
have to be better than me."

*You have to be better than me* was one of his favorite lines and
the most often repeated by his sons when they imitated him
behind his back. I hoped Grayson really was better than his
dad, and better than me too. I doubted I could have landed in
that wind.

Static sounded over the loudspeaker, then Grayson's dead
calm voice, unflappable as Chuck Yeager, announcing his in-
tention to drop his banner.

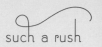

Mr. Hall must be so proud of Grayson right now, but he didn't show it. He just crossed his arms and scanned the sky.

"There he is." Alec pointed. Now we could see the plane, a tiny dot above the trees, and hear it, a low buzz underneath the wind.

Mr. Hall's handheld radio crackled down by his side. Then came Grayson's smooth voice again. "Is the crosswind still bad?" Even though this wasn't the airport's frequency but the one Hall Aviation used to communicate with its pilots, it was still public, and Grayson still had to stay calm. In his natural state, he was nothing like Alec and Jake, not calm at all. I imagined every curse word that filled the cockpit when he turned the radio off.

Either that, or he enjoyed the danger, the rush. Grayson was like that.

Mr. Hall glanced at the wind sock, then brought the radio to his mouth. "Affirmative, it's still bad."

Long minutes passed while we watched the dot make its way down the length of the runway, the banner now visible as a streak behind the dot. He reached the base of the runway and announced himself smoothly over the loudspeaker, then turned to make his final approach and announced himself again, exactly as Mr. Hall had taught us. The plane descended, roaring closer.

After three years of watching countless banner pickups and drops from the airport office, I still found the sight shocking: how tiny the plane was, how long the banner, how tall and vivid the red letters. The banner he was towing, which he and Alec and I had been taking turns towing all week, was left over from the summer: SUNSET SPECIAL 2 FOR 1 BEACHCOMBERS. I'd been worried Beachcomber's would blame us when customers asked for a special that the restaurant hadn't run since last September. But there *were* no customers in December, at least none who would see the banner from the deserted beach on a blustery day.

SUNSET SPECIAL 2 FOR 1 BEACHCOMBERS came closer and closer to us, dwarfing the plane. Grayson didn't have to land. He only needed to get near enough to the ground to drop the banner safely, but he was having trouble even with that. The nose of the plane pointed diagonally toward us, rather than straight down the runway, to combat the wind. The left wing rolled up suddenly as Grayson lost control. All four of us watching made a noise.

He straightened the plane as it roared even with us. He was close enough that I could make out the straw cowboy hat he always wore, but nothing else through the windows reflecting the clouds.

"Drop drop drop," Mr. Hall shouted, not into his radio but into the wind.

On cue, the plane pitched up, climbing to a safer altitude. The banner hung in midair for a moment, then drifted slowly toward Earth. At least, that's what it looked like at first. The four of us realized at the same time that it was coming toward us, just as Grayson commented over Mr. Hall's radio, "Maybe y'all should move."

Alec and Jake dashed one way around the airport office. I ran and Mr. Hall jogged the other way. The seven-foot-tall banner rippled toward us like a snake, impossibly fast for its size, and *smack,* the metal pole at one end hit the office's glass door.

Wincing, I rounded the building to the front again and examined the glass. Amazingly, the pole hadn't broken it. Now the pole scraped along the concrete floor of the porch, dragged by the banner going wild in the wind. Alec and Jake were rolling up the banner from the other end, which had wrapped itself around the far side of the building.

"That's some wind," Jake shouted. I'd known Grayson was in trouble when I saw the Halls running. But if I'd had any

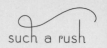

lingering doubts, this sealed the deal: the fighter pilot home on leave after a year flying dangerous missions in Afghanistan, worried about the wind.

"He could land at another airport," Alec called to his dad.

"I looked up the storm on radar," I told Mr. Hall. "It's a monster. Grayson won't be able to fly past it. To do him any good, the runway would need a different heading." That way, he could land into the wind, rather than the wind blowing across the airplane and tossing it off course. Community airports flashed through my mind, airfields up and down the coast where I'd practiced touch-and-go's, landing and taking off repeatedly.

"Florence," Mr. Hall and I said at the same time. He brought the radio to his mouth again. "Florence has a couple of strips with different headings. Why don't you fly on over there? We'll come pick you up, and tomorrow we'll go back and get the plane."

"Florence is seventy miles away," came Grayson's voice. "I don't have enough gas to make it."

"Roger," Mr. Hall told the radio. He glanced at the wind sock again.

Alec and Jake had wrestled the unwieldy banner into a big, sloppy roll and plopped it on the porch, behind a rocking chair and against the wall, where it wouldn't blow away. We all walked out to stand on the tarmac again and watch the plane fly parallel to the runway, then turn. Grayson would go through the same motions as on his first pass, but this time he would land.

Or try.

It wasn't right that he fought through this alone. He and I had no bond, but I would have been the one in the plane instead of him if I hadn't taken my turn first. Raising my voice

over the wind, I told Mr. Hall, "Seems like there's some advice you could give him."

Mr. Hall shook his head. "I've taught all of you correctly. Whether you learned it correctly or not, I don't know. That kid never had the sense God gave a goat. He probably thinks this is fun."

True, Grayson was the live wire in the family, the adrenaline junkie who would do anything on a dare, who'd gotten in trouble in the past year for smoking, drinking, weed, speeding, skipping school—Mr. Hall had spilled it all to me while we were flying. Mr. Hall worried constantly that his ex-wife couldn't handle raising Grayson on her own. Alec got in trouble only for refusing to rat Grayson out. But I doubted even Grayson enjoyed trying to land the plane in this windstorm.

Worried as I was, what Alec was going through must have been ten times worse. Grayson and he looked nothing alike, and they'd never seemed close. Alec was closer with Jake, glomming onto Jake really, and Grayson was off by himself, getting into trouble. But Grayson and Alec were still brothers, and twins. I wasn't surprised when Alec crossed one arm on his chest, propped his other elbow on that arm, and put his hand over his mouth.

What did surprise me was that Jake put his arm around Alec's shoulders.

Over the loudspeaker, Grayson calmly announced his approach. The red plane dropped out of the sky, skimming twenty feet above the runway, then ten.

I squinted and struggled to stand against a cold blast of wind. On that gust, the sound of the tiny engine drifted across the field to us. The motor suddenly roared in a higher pitch as the plane jerked to the left. Grayson was using the stick and the rudder pedals to fight the wind. I was fighting it too,

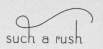

sympathetically, my hands balled into fists, arms tense, toes curling in my shoes. And holding my breath.

The plane made several more agonizing darts this way and that, wings jerking up and leveling off. Finally he was one foot off the runway, inches, then none. The plane landed as straight and level as if the wind were calm.

Mr. Hall said, "Perfect."

The plane was still rolling fast when the wind swept under it and tipped one wing up to the sky, the other down to scrape the asphalt.

"Damn it," Mr. Hall barked. I made a noise too, something between a yelp and a scream, and Jake pressed one hand against Alec's chest to keep him from running across the field. There was nothing we could do for Grayson, and nothing he could do either. Helpless, while someone chanted "No no no no no," we watched the wing tilt as far up as it could go without the plane turning upside down. The plane seemed to be sinking then, the wind tiring.

That's when a gust caught the tail instead and spun the still-rolling plane all the way around backward in a ground loop, exactly what we'd all been afraid of and exactly why most people didn't fly these old-fashioned planes anymore. The wind spun the plane all the way forward again, then lobbed it at the trees.

Now we were running. Jake and Alec shot past me. I hoped they knew how to help Grayson when they reached him. All I could see was the bright red plane propped at an odd angle against the dark tree line. I concentrated on the tarmac under my feet, then the uneven ground where the grass hadn't been cut since October, then the runway, with my usual bottle of water sloshing hard in my jacket pocket the whole way. As I got close, I remembered I had the phone in my other pocket. I pulled it out to dial 911.

But all three of the boys emerged from underneath the wing: Jake first, then Alec, then Grayson. They were laughing.

I stopped on the asphalt. My lungs burned so painfully that I almost bent over and braced my hands on my knees, but I didn't want to do that where the boys could see me.

I turned to yell back to Mr. Hall that Grayson was okay. He saw the boys too and slowed from a jog to a walk. He put his hand over his heart.

As I walked down the short, grassy slope to where the airplane was lodged and the boys stood, Jake said, "I wish the Admiral had seen it. He would have recommended you for an aircraft carrier." Jake worshipped the Admiral for his combat record.

Grayson knew how special this compliment was. It showed in his grin. "Oh, pshaw, it was nothing." Even his eyes laughed, which looked strange to me. I rarely saw Grayson without his aviator shades and his straw cowboy hat. They must be lost in the cockpit.

"I wish we'd filmed it," Alec said. "I wish you could have seen it yourself, Grayson. It seriously looked like you were about to lose it, what, three, four times?"

"Six or seven times," Jake said.

"I don't have to see it," Grayson said. "But if we can get the tractor to haul the plane back onto the runway and it checks out, I'll go again."

Jake and Alec hooted laughter. Alec said, "That's exactly what I was thinking: 'Grayson is probably enjoying this.'"

"That's what Dad was thinking too," Jake said. He slipped into the imitation of Mr. Hall that all his sons could do so well. "'That boy probably thinks this is fun. He never did have the sense God gave a goat.'"

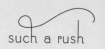

Their laughter quieted as Mr. Hall passed me on the grass. Grayson still smiled, but the laughter had left his eyes. He waited for his father's verdict.

I held my breath for the second time that afternoon. When something went wrong at Hall Aviation, it was usually Grayson's fault, because he forgot a chore or blew it off. But Mr. Hall tended to blame him even when the problem was Alec's fault, or Jake's fault, or Mr. Hall's own fault, or nobody's fault at all. I had wanted to tell Mr. Hall this before, but it was not my place to say.

Mr. Hall slapped Grayson's shoulder, then moved his hand to the back of Grayson's neck. "And that, son, is a ground loop."

They all burst into laughter again, Mr. Hall included. Grayson said sarcastically, "Thank you for the insight, Father."

"Let's see what kind of damage you did to her." Mr. Hall walked around the wing tip lodged in the grass, heading for the nose. Alec and Jake followed him, but Grayson stayed where he was. Now that they weren't watching him, his blond brows knitted. He looked at the plane, then at the sky, and bit his lip.

I whispered, "Are you really okay?"

His gray eyes widened at me, as if he hadn't noticed me standing there until now. He whispered back, "Actually, I think I'm going to hurl."

"I'll cover for you."

He stared at me for a moment more, like he didn't trust me. Then he turned and jogged toward the trees.

I followed Mr. Hall and the boys around the wing and peered over their shoulders as they turned the seemingly undamaged propeller by hand, testing it. I waited until they noticed Grayson was missing.

"Grayson? Where's Grayson?" Mr. Hall called.

41

I glanced back at the wing. "Uh-oh, the gas tank has rup-
tured."

"What?" Mr. Hall bellowed. He and Alec and Jake moved
from the propeller to crowd around the wing. I pointed to a
scrape as if I thought this indicated structural damage to the
tank. They poked at the wing, ran their hands along it, fingered
the joints. After a few long minutes, Mr. Hall looked up at me
like I'd lost my mind.

I felt Grayson's shadow return behind me. "I guess not," I
said.

All of them straightened and discussed the findings. Grayson stepped toward them without comment like he'd been
hanging around the other end of the plane the whole time.
The consensus was that the plane was hardly damaged at all,
but they wanted to tow it back to the hangar where they could
get a better look before the rain came. Without glancing at
Grayson, I handed him my bottle of water. He took a swig
while the rest of them were talking and spat it on the grass.

They all turned and sauntered back toward the hangar.
Their laughter rolled back to me against the cold wind. It
wasn't like the boys had forgotten me, because I was never part
of their family anyway. I was nothing to remember. But Mr.
Hall had forgotten me completely, as if I hadn't been standing
next to him while we witnessed the wreck.

That was only fitting. All three of his sons were with him at
once. That hardly ever happened anymore. It was Christmas.
And Grayson was safe.

Without breaking his pace, Grayson looked back over his
shoulder at me and mouthed, *Thank you*. He turned around
again without waiting for my answer.

A month later, back in Afghanistan, Jake would die in a jet
crash. And Mr. Hall's heart couldn't take it. A month after that

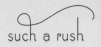

he would follow Jake to the grave. So in the end I was glad they had this one last family afternoon together, and I wasn't loitering around the Hall Aviation hangar, polluting it.

The phone rang in my back pocket. Still watching the Halls walk away, I brought the phone to my ear. "Heaven Beach Airport." My voice shook. I held the phone at arm's length and took a deep, steadying breath. Then I started again. I said into the phone, evenly and all better now, "This is Leah. How may I help you?"

# three

April

The Admiral's dead calm voice came over the radio on loudspeaker, announcing to other pilots in the area that he was nearing the airport. The moan of his engine drifted to me on the breeze, but the plane was too far away to see.

I sat in one of the rocking chairs on the porch of the airport office, ready to run onto the tarmac and place chocks around the wheels of the plane after the Admiral landed. But mostly I was preoccupied with staring past my newspaper, past the gas pumps and the flagpole, way up the tarmac at the Hall Aviation hangar. This was the first day since Mr. Hall had died that I'd seen Grayson's truck and Alec's car parked there. They must be starting spring break of their high school senior year, like I was. They would spend their free week going through Mr. Hall's things, his papers and gadgets and inventions and equipment and four airplanes, preparing to sell them off and pocket the dough. They didn't need to work

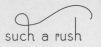

for him to earn college money anymore. They could take it all and run.

Which was unkind of me to assume. It must be hard for them to sift through their dad's stuff, hard even to be in the hangar without him or Jake either. More than once during that long Saturday at work, I'd thought about ambling over and peeking in on them to see if there was anything I could do.

Memories of Mr. Hall's funeral stopped me. The Admiral and his wife had taken me with them to the funeral home. The Admiral's wife probably made the Admiral ask me whether I needed a ride. Much as I hated accepting obvious charity, if they hadn't driven me, I wouldn't have been able to go. Molly had a Valentine's date. I wouldn't have asked her to break it for me.

At the funeral home chapel, and later at the graveyard, I stayed close to the Admiral's wife, like we were family. The Admiral sat up front because he and Mr. Hall had been such good friends, and he was the one who had found the body. So he was next to Alec and Grayson, and neither of the boys ever looked around at me.

They should have. They could have come and asked me earlier today about Mr. Hall's ridiculous filing system. I would have saved them hours of work. But they wouldn't ask, and I wouldn't offer. I'd shared one glimmer of a friendly moment with Grayson four months before when he crashed the Piper. That didn't matter now. I couldn't shake the sound of him saying more than a year ago, *Why else would that stingy bastard give away flying lessons for free?* If I stepped inside the hangar, they would think I wanted something.

As I gazed across the tarmac, Grayson opened the door in the side of the hangar. Though he and Alec were twins, there was no mistaking them for each other. Alec was beautiful,

smiling, easy. Grayson was tall, muscular, and a mess, an eighteen-year-old version of Mr. Hall.

By the time Mr. Hall died, he was fifty pounds overweight, his hair nearly pure white like the Admiral's, his face lined with regret. But the whole three and a half years I'd worked at the airport, a photo of Mr. Hall as a slender fighter pilot had lived at the bottom corner of the bulletin board in his office. His hands were shoved in the pockets of his flight suit. One side of his mouth was cocked up in a lopsided grin. He leaned forward as if any second he would lose patience with the guy holding the camera and grab it away.

On this warm spring day, Grayson wore a T-shirt, cargo shorts, flip-flops, and his usual straw cowboy hat and mirrored aviator shades, but his air of quick impatience was the same as his dad's. He managed to convey frustrated energy across the tarmac, though he was only banging the hangar door open and retrieving something from his truck. Or, after an hour of work, he was knocking off for the day. Later Alec would complain that he kept working doggedly while Grayson goofed off. The argument might escalate into a shouting match that I would witness from the porch. At least something in their family would still be normal.

Wrong. Grayson passed his truck and kept walking toward me. Or not toward *me* but toward the building I happened to be sitting in front of. He wanted hangar rental records or flight plans from the office. But he would have to pass me to get inside. He would have to say hello or pretend I wasn't there, one or the other, on our first encounter since Mr. Hall's funeral. My fingers ached from gripping the edges of the newspaper so hard out of a strange anger I hadn't even realized I felt until today.

Grayson and Alec had not been here for their dad. Not

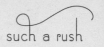

to form a family with him for the past three and a half years, not to help him through Jake's death at the end. I had been here when they weren't. I had been here *because* they weren't. Not in exchange for being Mr. Hall's girlfriend, but maybe in exchange for filling in as his daughter, he had let me fly his planes. Since he died, I'd lost my free ride. It would have taken me twenty hours working at the airport to earn one hour's rental in someone else's plane. For the two months since his death, I'd been as grounded as the day my mom dragged me here to live in Heaven Beach. And now Grayson and Alec would sell Mr. Hall's planes off.

The instant I had that idea, I was sorry, and my stomach twisted into a hard knot. I couldn't guess at Mr. Hall's motives, but I'd liked him because he was kind to me and funny, not because he gave me something I wanted. I felt guilty for putting the loss of him and the loss of my flight time into the same depressing thought. The guilt brought tears to my eyes.

Then I was self-conscious that Grayson, only twenty paces away now, would think I was pretending to mourn his dad. Casually I touched my fingertips to the inside corners of my eyes to remove the tears.

But I shouldn't have worried what Grayson would see when he looked at me. My rocking chair was three feet from the airport office door, yet he didn't glance in my direction. Somehow he made swinging the door open and stepping inside the building a huge commotion, as he always did, though he said nothing and carried nothing in his hands. The door automatically hissed shut behind him. The only noises left were the warm Atlantic breeze whispering in the long grass that lined the single airstrip, and the rope clanging against the flagpole.

Jennifer Echols

I had wanted something from him. Even expected a confrontation. To be ignored was a sentence without a period. Like Mr. Hall's death out of the blue.

Grayson burst out the door again, startling me. The newspaper ripped in my hands. I hoped he hadn't heard.

But if he had, who cared? He would stomp back across the tarmac to the hangar without looking back, whether I watched him or not.

He surprised me again by sitting in the rocking chair beside mine and handing me a bottle of water from the machine in the break room. I was afraid he'd seen my worn bottle on the counter and was hinting I needed a new one—but through my paranoia about looking poor, at least I could still tell when I was being paranoid. He was paying me back for the bottle I'd given him the day he crashed. Or he was just being nice.

He settled back in his chair and folded his long legs to prop one ankle on the opposite knee, flip-flop hanging from his toes. With his elbows up and his hands behind his head, he looked like the Admiral and the other pilots who sat out here in the afternoons and watched planes take off and land and told dirty stories, stopping in midsentence when I walked by. I wondered whether he was imitating them consciously.

Over the loudspeaker, the Admiral announced his final approach.

Out of habit, Grayson and I gazed past the two-seater and four-seater planes parked on the tarmac, across the grass rippling white in the spring breeze, toward the end of the runway. The Admiral's plane was visible now, sinking fast over the trailer park.

Grayson said, "So, Leah."

Carefully I folded the newspaper. There was no way Grayson could know I felt self-conscious about it. I was

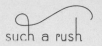

overreacting. I tucked the pages under my thigh anyway, and I said, "So, Grayson."

"I know my dad promised he would hire you to fly for him starting this week," Grayson said. "Nothing's changed since he died."

I let my head fall back against my chair and watched him, looking as bored as I could behind my own mirrored aviator shades, while I puzzled through what he was saying. *Everything* had changed since Mr. Hall had died.

Then it dawned on me what Grayson meant. Shifting forward with my elbows on my knees, I asked, "You're going to try to run the business? You want me to fly for *you*?"

"I'm not going to try," Grayson drawled. "I *am* going to run the business. And yes. You had a business agreement with Hall Aviation. I expect you to honor it."

The crack about honor got under my skin. I had no honor? I couldn't be trusted?

But he didn't seem spiteful. He met my gaze—I assumed, though I didn't know for sure, since there were two pairs of aviator sunglasses between us. Slowly rocking in his chair, he watched me watching him. Without seeing his eyes, I couldn't read a thing in his face. There was nothing to learn from his hard jaw dusted with a few days' blond stubble, his straight nose, or the straw cowboy hat I'd seldom seen him without. I got the impression he was doing exactly what I was doing, remaining calm like a professional pilot, waiting for me to make a comment so he could size me up and redirect his argument.

For some reason, he really wanted me to fly for him.

I glanced toward the end of the runway, where the Admiral was landing just in time to save me from this uncomfortable conversation. As the white Beechcraft touched down and sped across the asphalt, waves of heat made the plane seem to ripple.

I dismissed Grayson with, "I've already got a job. Not for this week, but starting in the summer."

"No," Grayson said. "You're supposed to be working for me this week *and* in the summer." His voice rose over the engine noise as the Admiral taxied closer.

"Working for your dad," I corrected him. "I didn't dream you'd reopen the business. I haven't heard from you until now. What was I supposed to do, wait around for you just in case?"

"You could have looked up my number and called me," he shouted above the racket.

"Even if you'd offered me a job, that wouldn't have meant you'd come through," I yelled back. "You'll fly for a week, change your mind, and blow it off to go surfing. Just like you always did."

The Admiral cut his engine. *Just like you always did* rang against the brick wall behind us. I cringed at the volume of my own ugly words.

Luckily, I had an escape. Leaving the torn newspaper in my seat as if I didn't care about it and didn't plan to steal it at the end of the day and take it home with me, I headed for the Admiral's plane. I grabbed three heavy sets of chocks from a rack just beyond the porch.

"This time is different," Grayson called after me.

My left arm could handle one set of chocks, but I'd taken two in my right hand so I wouldn't have to go back to the rack and face Grayson again. My right arm might pull out of its socket with the weight. I hoped he'd give up on this ridiculous idea and go back to his hangar by the time I secured the Admiral's plane. I knew Grayson was grieving and I didn't want to upset him, but there was no way I could afford to give up the summer flying job I'd been promised in exchange for this job he'd made up.

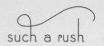
I tried not to groan with relief as I dropped the first set of chocks at the front wheel of the plane and kicked the wooden blocks into place around the tire. The plane's gyros whined, still winding down, as the Admiral opened his door.

"Nice flight?" I hollered in my friendly airport voice.

"Beautiful." The Admiral stepped down from the plane and reached toward me for the second chock. "Perfect. Unlimited ceiling. Beautiful day to fly."

I felt a pang of jealousy that he could fly and I'd been grounded for two months, followed swiftly by the ache of losing Mr. Hall, who loved to say, "*Man,* what a pretty day to fly." But I just handed the chock to the Admiral and kept up the polite conversation like I didn't hurt at all. "Where'd you go?"

"Touch-and-go's in Darlington, then over in Orangeburg."

I nodded, put chocks around the third wheel, and hooked a cable to the side of the plane to secure it to the tarmac. When I straightened, the Admiral was staring at Grayson, who still rocked on the porch.

"What's Grayson doing here?" the Admiral asked me quietly.

"Reopening the banner-towing business, he claims."

"Really." The Admiral didn't use the incredulous tone I expected. His tone sounded more like . . . admiration. He'd walked a few steps toward the porch before he turned around and called, "Thanks, Leah."

I gave him a little wave of acknowledgment, then rounded the plane and bent to secure it to the tarmac on the other side. But I listened for what the Admiral said to Grayson, and I watched them from under the curls in my eyes. I expected Grayson would keep rocking in his chair, sullen, and the Admiral would lean over him and say a few soft words of encouragement I wouldn't be able to hear. But Grayson stood

with his hand extended to shake the Admiral's hand before the Admiral even reached him.

The Admiral grasped Grayson's hand and simultaneously slapped him on the opposite shoulder. "Good to see you back."

"Thank you, sir," Grayson said. He might even have been looking the Admiral in the eye. Like a business owner at the airport, not just the son of one.

The Admiral's voice dropped lower, his words more private, and I felt almost guilty for overhearing the end of his speech: ". . . good men."

"Thank you," Grayson said again.

"Let me know if there's anything I can do." The Admiral disappeared through the glass door into the office. After using the bathroom and buying a pack of M&M's, which his wife did not allow in the house because of her weight struggles, he would get into his Infiniti parked on the street side of the building and drive home to their condo on the swanky end of Heaven Beach, where they would take an ocean-side stroll together before dinner. It seemed so foreign. I couldn't imagine being retired. Or having enough money to do what I wanted.

Grayson rocked slowly in his chair again, waiting for me to finish tying down the plane.

There was just so long I could dawdle over a metal hook attached to a ring sticking through the asphalt. I stalked back toward Grayson, but if I had any idea of slipping past him into the office without continuing the argument, he ruled that out. "Who is your other job with?" he demanded, stepping into my path and towering over me.

This was none of his business, but I felt bad about the *Just like you always did* comment. I felt worse now that the Admiral had been so nice to Grayson. I was trying to get rid of Grayson as politely as possible. Without stopping, I walked around

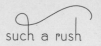

him and opened the door. "I'm flying a crop duster for Mr. Simon," I said over my shoulder before I swung into the office. I hoped now Grayson would take no for an answer, and he wouldn't follow me inside.

He was right behind me. "Leah." He trailed me all the way across the lobby, down the short hallway, to the open doorway that led behind the reception counter.

Turning around at the threshold, I took off my sunglasses, tossed them on the counter, and eyed him. He seemed to get the message that the area beyond the doorway was my private territory. He walked back down the hallway, into the lobby.

But instead of leaving, he leaned over and rested his elbows on the counter like he was there for a long discussion. "Leah," he said in a coaxing tone. "What do you want that job for? Every organic fruit you've ever bought and eaten will be negated times a thousand with each pass you make spreading chemical filth over a field."

I'd never eaten an organic fruit as far as I knew, except maybe at Molly's parents' café. I wondered if they tasted different and whether I would be able to tell. I definitely hadn't bought one. My mom would die twice if I paid that much for a banana. Grayson and I were from different worlds.

"You'll spend all day every day breathing that crap," he said. "Aren't you worried about your health?"

I laughed. "Yeah. That's why I'd rather spend my summer flying an airplane built this century."

He gaped at me in mock disapproval. "We keep up the maintenance on our planes. We have to. You know the FAA says any plane has to fly like it did when it was built."

"Yours were built in the 1950s."

"It was a very good decade for airplanes. It never bothered you before. And you're completely trained in banner towing.

You didn't pay anything to learn it. Isn't Simon making you pay for training? A lot of those crop-dusting jackasses will charge to teach you how to do it. They'll promise to hold a job for you. You drop thousands of dollars for training and then your job mysteriously disappears."

I stared at him like he was an alien life-form. On what planet did an eighteen-year-old girl living in a trailer park have thousands of dollars to drop on *anything,* much less crop-duster training? I said, "No, I'm not paying for it."

One of Grayson's eyebrows tilted up sharply behind his sunglasses. "How'd you manage *that* arrangement?"

I thought I heard something ugly in his tone, but I didn't want to call him on it without being sure. I asked innocently, "What do you mean? It's not strange. I paid your dad for flying lessons and rented his airplane for a long time." The rental and lessons had been cut-rate, but I *had* paid for them. Mr. Hall probably knew I wouldn't have taken them otherwise. "He only let me use his plane for free after I agreed I'd fly banners for him. Pilots take care of each other."

"No, my *dad* took care of *you,*" Grayson corrected me.

I'd thought so too. His dad had been kind to me because he'd missed the three sons who hadn't lived with him full-time for years and years. And I was not above turning this around and using it against Grayson if he wouldn't leave me alone. I didn't want to. I had more respect for his dad than that. But I absolutely was not going to let Grayson guilt me into working for him, only to close up shop and abandon me when it was too late for me to start over with another job flying this summer.

Exasperated, I asked, "Why do you want *me* to fly for you? There will be ten college guys hanging around at the beginning of the summer, begging you to hire them."

"I can't wait until then," Grayson said. "We have contracts. My dad scheduled banners this week because he knew you and Alec and I would be on spring break. I need you tomorrow."

I put my hands on my hips. "That is kind of short notice, Grayson."

He opened both hands. For the first time he looked like the Grayson I'd known from a distance for three and a half years, the one who tried to talk himself out of trouble. "We only decided a few days ago that we were going to reopen the business."

"Exactly," I said. "You're starting it on a whim, and that's how you'll end it. I can't work for a whim. In case you hadn't noticed, I need an *actual* job."

"Right." He folded his arms across his faded rock band T-shirt. He was tall and slim, and it wasn't until moments like this that I noticed how muscular he was. His biceps strained against the sleeves of his T-shirt. But this was no time to admire his body. His body language told me he really was back to the Grayson I knew. He felt cornered, like his dad was shouting at him. Next came a counterattack.

"Tell me more about your *actual* job," Grayson said. "You've talked to Mr. Simon about it, right?"

"No, I talked to Mark," I said, suspicious. Grayson was driving at something. Granted, Mark was not the decision-making person in charge of Simon Air Agriculture, but he wouldn't have told me I could fly for Mr. Simon this summer without checking it or okaying it. Would he?

Grayson nodded. "Mark told me this morning that he's shacking up with you."

I put several fingers to my mouth, something between shushing him with one finger and covering my mouth with my hand in horror.

55

A toilet flushed and then whooshed louder as the Admiral opened the bathroom door. I stood there with my hand to my mouth, watching Grayson fill the space in front of me with his own mouth in a hard line. I hoped the Admiral hadn't heard what Grayson had said. The Admiral and I weren't close, but I'd always assumed he thought I was a nice girl. Grayson thought I was *not,* I realized. I listened for the Admiral as I puzzled through it:

Mark was at the beach with his friends right now, but he'd flown a crop-dusting run that morning. (The Admiral's footsteps sounded from the bathroom back to the break room.) Grayson's truck had been at the Hall Aviation hangar early that morning too. (The Admiral fed coins into the vending machine.) Hall Aviation and Mr. Simon's crop-dusting business used the same mechanic. (The Admiral's M&M's fell into the chute with a *clank*.) It was plausible Grayson and Mark had run into each other and talked.

"See you tomorrow, Leah," the Admiral called in his normal voice, not the tone of someone who'd overheard what Grayson had said to me.

"Yes, sir," I called back. As the front door of the office opened and shut behind me, I continued to watch Grayson and think. It was *not* plausible that Mark had walked up to Grayson and blurted that we were living together. "Did he *say* that?" I asked Grayson incredulously.

"Yes."

"Did he *phrase* it that way?" After the initial shock of Grayson knowing more about me than I wanted him to know, I realized I didn't need to ask. Of course Mark had phrased it this way, because Mark was turning out to be kind of an asshole.

I only hoped that's *all* Grayson knew, because there was more to the story. For years I'd stuck to my policy of avoiding

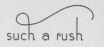

Mark and boys like him. That became easier when Mark turned sixteen and stopped riding the bus, and easier still when he graduated from high school last December, a semester late. He worked at the airport every day, but mostly in the mornings and early afternoons when I was still at school. I might hear him announce himself over the airport frequency and watch him land an ugly Air Tractor, but our paths rarely crossed.

Last week, he'd come into the office, hunting up some records for his uncle. I'd mentioned I was out of a job with Mr. Hall and wondered whether Mark's uncle was hiring crop dusters. I didn't want to deal with Mark at work every day, but I would suffer through it for a flying job. To my surprise, he'd said yes. I'd been so happy and never more relieved.

Then he'd asked me on a date. I'd hesitated at first, but after a few minutes of flirting, I'd said yes to that too. I'd had a boyfriend when I was fourteen, but I'd never been on a date. Though my relationship with Mr. Hall hadn't been romantic at all, his absence left a hole in my heart that I was hungry to fill. And a somewhat greasy fifteen-year-old Mark had grown into a decidedly sexy nineteen-year-old with a nervous edge.

My mom had been home when he'd brought me back from dinner that night. Usually I was so happy to see her, right up until she took the TV or some food or a pile of clothes away with her, like she was using the trailer only for storage. This time I was terrified he would mention to her that I was a pilot, or that I was working the whole time I was at the airport, not hanging out with my fake boyfriend Grayson Hall. And I didn't trust Mark enough to ask him to keep quiet.

So I was almost relieved at the turn the conversation took. Mark told my mom that his mother had kicked him out of the house. He hadn't mentioned this to me before. My mom

offered to let him stay with us—by which she meant he could stay with *me*—for a few days until he found another place to live, if he would help her with rent. I was already helping her with rent on top of paying the utilities. Basically she was arranging for us to take over the lease from her. He might not have agreed to this if he'd known she was leaving that night with the TV. She told me she was pawning it for cash to take to the Indian casino in North Carolina. That was the last I'd heard from her.

Technically, Mark and I *were* shacking up. But that implied we were doing it, when we weren't. True, I had ached for him at first. I'd been staying away from boys for so many years, and the shift in how I saw him was new and exciting. But that night when my mom had left and Mark brought his stuff inside the trailer, he'd also brought beer. He'd drunk too much to go through with it. Each night after that he'd been too drunk or stayed out too late with his friends. And now that he'd lived with me for a week, the thought of him was vaguely nauseating.

But this was *way* none of Grayson's business.

I still couldn't read Grayson's expression with his eyes hidden. He hadn't taken off his shades when he came into the office. But when I asked him how Mark had phrased our living arrangement, Grayson arched one eyebrow again.

"I don't know what you're getting at," I said. "No, I haven't talked to Mr. Simon about the job, because Mark is the one who's taking me flying in the Stearman every day this week. He's showing me the ropes and giving me a taste of what I'll be doing by myself in the summer. I asked off work from the airport and everything."

"In the Stearman?" Grayson's eyebrow stayed up.

"Yes," I said. "We can't go in one of the Air Tractors. They're one-seaters."

"I've personally heard Mr. Simon tell my dad that he would never let Mark take anybody for a ride in the Stearman."

I didn't doubt it, since Mark was a live wire. But I said carefully, "Did you overhear this on the office porch? A lot of bullshit flies around on the porch." Mr. Hall had said many negative things about Grayson on the porch too.

Grayson got my meaning. His eyebrow went down. Then he asked pointedly, "Mark's taking you flying every day this week? But not today?"

"No," I said impatiently. "Starting tomorrow."

"What time tomorrow?" he pressed me. "Have you set a time?"

We hadn't set a time, and frankly, I'd begun to worry. Mark had promised me when we first talked about it that we'd start flying together on Monday morning, but here it was Sunday afternoon and he hadn't mentioned it again. He was getting drunk at the beach. And I'd been afraid to bring it up—afraid that if I said the wrong thing to Mark, the job would disappear.

Which was pretty much what Grayson was telling me. Mark had told me a lie so he could move in with me.

I was frightened. But I couldn't show Grayson this, so I tried to be furious instead. "Why can't this be a transaction between pilots? In your mind, why does it have to be dirty?"

"You tell me," Grayson said bitterly, removing his elbows from the counter and straightening to his full height. "That's how you work. I used to envy the rare people you smiled at when you pumped their gas, like they'd done something special and earned a reward. But now I realize you were smiling at them because they'd given you something you wanted. A big tip. Flight time. You wouldn't smile at someone without good reason."

I hadn't thought he noticed whether I smiled at him or not.

There was a possibility here. A spark. I'd always viewed
him as Mr. Hall's black sheep son, impossibly cool and way
too good for me, passing through. Finally, here was a hint of
reciprocation of the crush I'd pretended not to have on him
since I was fourteen.

No. Mark might have fooled me. I wouldn't let Grayson
fool me too. Cheeks burning, I said sternly, "Grayson Hall.
The second you feel cornered, you fly off the handle and
say anything that pops into your head. You've always gotten
away with it, and maybe you still will, but that's not a good
interview technique for potential employees. If there was *ever* a
chance I would fly for you, you blew it the instant your mind
fell into the gutter."

My anger drained away. My fingers hurt from gripping the
countertop. Grayson's mirrored shades still stared me down
like nothing was behind them.

Then he bit his lip. "I need you," he said in his nicest tone
so far.

"Tough."

He put his fist down on the counter. Not hard. Just *there.*
He balled it tightly and relaxed it.

He took a long, deep breath. His broad shoulders rose and
fell with it.

And then, without another word, he turned and left the
office. He crossed the porch and disappeared in the direction
of the Hall Aviation hangar, where I couldn't see him out the
lobby windows.

All the tension whooshed out of the room behind him.
Without it, there was nothing left to hold me up standing. I
collapsed into my desk chair and took a few deep breaths. I
felt like I was going to lose it, but Grayson might be hanging

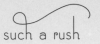

around outside. Alec might. Mr. Simon might. I couldn't lose it here at the airport. I had to get home.

I locked up for the day, shut off the connection between the radio and the outside loudspeaker, and put the cell phone in a drawer. When I'd first started working here, I'd stayed until eight some nights because being alone here was better than being alone at home. My supervisor from city hall made me stop because I was running up the light bill. He didn't know I needed a handout, and I wasn't going to tell him.

Locking the porch door from the outside, I couldn't help one more glance at the Hall Aviation hangar. Grayson's truck and Alec's car were still parked outside, and they'd opened the wide door facing the runway as if they actually planned to bring an airplane out and power it up. I didn't care. I would fly for Grayson Hall over my dead body.

# four

I turned my back on Mr. Hall's hangar, water bottle in my hand, newspaper under my arm. Carrying my treasure, I walked most of the length of the airport, into the grass at the end of the strip. Where the chain-link fence turned a corner, I lifted the loose end of the wall of links and ducked underneath, onto the trail through the trees.

Most neighborhoods would be busy this time of day with the bustle of parents pulling in from work and greeting their kids. The trailer park would be busy later, at a partying hour. Right now it was quiet. Not a lot of people here had a regular job. A few of them were still sleeping off last night's binge. For once, drinking the world away didn't sound like a bad idea.

I walked just out of reach of the lunging pit bull. At my own trailer, I balanced on the cement blocks while I unlocked the aluminum door that had been kicked in four times since we'd lived here, three times by burglars, once by my mom's ex-boyfriend Billy. After locking the door behind me, I walked

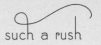

through the creaking hall, slumping lower and lower like I was coming in for a landing, and crashed into my bed.

One of Mr. Hall's Pipers roared overhead. Over the years I'd grown to love the sound of planes approaching the runway and just clearing the treetops above our trailer. I prided myself on listening closely enough that I could identify the type of plane without looking. Today I felt like my mom, cringing and cursing at the racket and burying my head underneath the pillows.

The newspaper crackled underneath me as I curled into a ball and hugged my knees. Maybe Grayson was right and I really didn't have a job with Mr. Simon. When Mark had told me I could fly for his uncle, I'd felt like a heavy weight had been lifted from my chest. Mr. Simon could train me on the specifics of crop dusting. I didn't want to fly a crop duster my whole life, but I could work my way through college by taking courses during the off-season and flying during the growing season—and I would rack up a huge portion of the flight hours I needed for my next certification. It had never occurred to me until Grayson brought it up that Mark was lying.

But of course he was lying. I heaved myself up from the bed and trudged back into the combination kitchen and den. A blanket lay rumpled anyhow on the sofa where Mark had slept last night. All his worldly possessions were piled in the corner where he'd dumped them when my mom first said he could stay: garbage bags full of clothes, several rifles, and a plant light for growing marijuana indoors. He had not *told* me he grew marijuana, but boys his age did not grow tomatoes. Mark had told me what I wanted to hear in exchange for the prospect of sex and a free place to stay. He hadn't forked over any cash to help with the rent, and now I doubted this had ever been his plan.

Both hands pressed to my mouth, I tried very hard not to panic. I knew the airport up, down, and sideways, and there were no other jobs.

On the bright side, I was all set to graduate from high school in a month and a half. I was one step ahead of my mom. And I hadn't gotten pregnant. Two steps ahead of my mom. And I had a commercial pilot's license.

With no paid experience as a commercial pilot. And my only solid reference was dead.

I longed for Molly. Even if I'd had a phone, I wouldn't have called her. I refused to be that needy friend. I mean, I *was* that needy friend, but I sure as hell wasn't going to whine on the phone to her and make it worse. Sometimes she dropped by, though, and took me for a drive. I listened to her talk about her problems, and maybe after a while, when there was no way I could be accused of taking and taking and taking without giving, I might mention one of *my* problems. That wasn't happening tonight. She and her rich friends were at a beginning-of-spring-break concert. Even if I'd been able to afford it, I wouldn't have gone. Her friends didn't like me.

Molly or no Molly, moping would do me no good. The thing that bothered me most about my mom was that every time something went wrong, she went through the same motions, expecting different results. I needed to think out of the box.

But my mind was empty of ideas, my stomach empty to the point of nausea. For breakfast I'd eaten a pastry from the machine in the airport break room. For lunch I'd had a pack of crackers. In the back of my mind I'd been thinking Mark would have returned from the beach when I got here. But if he did show up soon, I wouldn't ask him to drive me to the grocery store now. Not after what Grayson had told me. And the

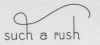

closest convenience store was a two-mile walk, which hadn't seemed so bad on other days but loomed tonight like the distance to China.

I opened every kitchen cabinet and found salt, cayenne pepper, and one beef jerky stick that had expired two years ago. It must have come with us the last time we moved. That was pretty bad, when your beef jerky expired, because it was manufactured to last through the apocalypse. The refrigerator held ketchup, mayo, and one unopened case of beer, which Mark had deposited when he'd come in late last night.

I opted for a beer. I sat with it on the couch, in the dip hollowed out in the cushion by one of my mom's weightier boyfriends, and stared at the wall where the latest huge high-def miracle of a TV had been until earlier this week. My first-, second-, and third-grade photos stared back at me.

The beer smelled like vinegar and tasted like dirt. I felt a lot better after I drank it, so I had another.

I was on my third beer and feeling completely rejuvenated when Mark's truck turned from the highway onto the gravel road through the trailer park. I didn't have superhuman hearing. The trailer walls were thin and let in everything. I knew it was him by his favorite country band blaring from the open windows. My gaze shifted from my school photos on the wall to Mark's pile of shit on the floor.

Suddenly I was seeing it through Grayson's eyes, or Molly's. There was a reason I never let Molly in the trailer.

I didn't want Mark in here with me either. But he *lived here*. The den/kitchen walls collapsed around me like the shrink wrap Mr. Hall had used to package gadgets and tools for storage.

I jumped up and jerked open the door. The sun was low behind the trees, but the sky was still bright compared with the

murky trailer. I took my shades from the neck of my T-shirt and put them on, then started down the stairs.

I'd never drunk much. I didn't want to flow into the same crowded pool as all the people around me and drown. Two and a half beers was quite a bit for me—obviously, or I wouldn't have forgotten I was still holding one—and I worried about my balance as I descended the wobbly cement blocks. I felt my face color at how Grayson would stare in revulsion at a cement-block staircase outside a mobile home.

Then I felt a new wave of embarrassment that I was obsessing about Grayson. Mark would see my flushed face, think I was even drunker than I was, maybe try to take advantage of me. I was very thankful I was wearing sunglasses and he wouldn't be able to see my eyes.

The music came closer and closer, inciting the pit bull to riot, until Mark's enormous pickup truck with roll bars and fog lights weaved across the gravel road and stopped right in front of me. A couple of bare-chested guys from school waved to me from the payload. I waved back halfheartedly.

Mark slid out of the driver's seat. His friend Patrick was in the passenger side. Patrick didn't fit in with these guys. He was wearing a shirt, for one thing, and the shirt still had both its sleeves. Sometimes I wondered what he was hanging around Mark for. Pot was a good guess.

A girl sat in the middle. Her hair was bleached blond and her roots were black. Not every girl looked good as a blonde. I had learned this lesson from observing my mother. The girl wore one of Mark's plaid shirts, tied beneath her big boobs in a tiny bikini. Judging from what I'd seen at school before Mark graduated, she fit his usual taste in girlfriends. Which was not a compliment. And which did not say a lot for me, either.

"Leah!" he exclaimed, rounding the hood of the truck,

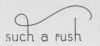

staggering a little. I shouldn't have worried he would notice how soused I was. *He* was drunker than *me*. He slurred, "What are you doing home?"

His use of the word *home* made me cringe. His question made me mad too. "This is when I always get off work," I said. He would have known this if he didn't stay out so late partying every night.

But I looked past him at the girl in the front seat. She'd scooted away from Patrick now that she had more room. Which meant she wasn't with Patrick. And Mark hadn't wanted me to see her. He'd thought I would be gone.

Shocker: I didn't care. Things had not been great between Mark and me, but I was shocked at how relieved I felt to see this girl wearing his shirt. A few girls at school had found out he was staying with me. They'd told me how lucky I was that my mom let my boyfriend stay with us. They had no idea.

Mark staying with me was not fun. It felt crowded. I'd dreaded walking home from the airport at night. I'd wanted him to drive me to get dinner tonight, because I was hungry, but also because that was an excuse not to get too friendly again in the long expanse of time before bed. He went out partying but he always came back. He never went away completely.

Strangest of all, although Grayson had not come through the chain-link fence to the trailer park and likely never would, his gaze had followed me. I was seeing everything through his eyes now. I had no chance with a boy like Grayson, but he had ruined Mark for me.

Mark was staring at the can in my hand. "You didn't get into my beer, did you? I just bought it last night. That's what we stopped by for."

This rubbed me the wrong way, probably because there

was nothing else in the fridge. "You told my mom when you moved in that you would help with rent. You haven't helped with shit, so I took three beers and we'll call it even." My angry words made me even angrier and gave me the courage to add, "I want you to move out."

"What?" Mark glanced over my shoulder at the girl in the truck, then turned back to me. "Why?" He was very drunk. There was no more denial. He started backpedaling immediately. "Aw, Leah, c'mere." He pulled me into a hug.

I lingered in his arms for a moment, relaxing with my cheek on his hot, sunburned shoulder. I hadn't realized how badly I'd needed a hug.

The girl's cackle rose above the country music and the noise of the idling truck.

I pulled away. "I want you to move out," I repeated.

"Your mom said I could move in!"

"My mom isn't here."

He rolled his eyes. "Is this about flying? You think I was lying because we haven't talked about it again. I'm going to take you up."

Would I let him continue to stay with me if he promised I could still have the crop-dusting job? I wasn't sure. "When?" I pressed him.

He frowned at me. "When, what?"

"When are you taking me up? Last week you said tomorrow."

He shook his head, then blinked a few times as if shaking his head had disoriented him. "Tomorrow's not good."

"Tuesday, then," I insisted.

"Tuesday's not good either. Later in the week, though." He put his hand on my arm. "I can tell you're mad, and you've had a few." He glanced at the beer can in my hand

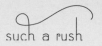

again. "I'll spend the night with Patrick"—by which he meant his new girlfriend—"and you and I can talk about this tomorrow."

"No," I said. "We will not talk about this tomorrow. You can't go with that skank ho and expect to stay here. Period."

He gaped at me, outraged. "I've been staying here a whole week, Leah, and you haven't given it up. Most girls understand that if they don't want to give it up, that's fine, but their man is going to get it somewhere else."

I put my chin in my hand and tapped my finger like he was a wildcat and I was a biologist truly perplexed by his behavior. "No," I murmured, "I did not understand that. Sorry."

He jerked his thumb over his shoulder at the truck. "I'm telling you, she doesn't mean anything. She was just for today."

"How does that make it better?" I didn't know why I was asking. The idea that a man was having a one-night stand rather than an affair made it all better for some women, my mother included.

"Leah, please." He stepped closer. I shouldn't have looked into his dark eyes, but I did. They almost melted me. The hot breeze teased a lock of dark hair back and forth across his tanned forehead as he said, "I've wanted to get with you for so long. Back when we were kids and we rode the bus together, I used to dream about you. You wouldn't give me the time of day. I'm so stoked we're together now. I don't want to lose you over something like this." His hand touched mine. "Okay?"

His lashes were long. His eyes were warm. He looked adorable when he coaxed me. It would be so easy to tell him he could stay. He would want to wrap up his day with his friends (and that girl), and then he would come home to me.

Which sounded exactly like my mother's life in miniature. Her boyfriend didn't mean it when he screwed that other woman. It wouldn't happen again. Sure.

"No," I said. "Get out." I was shouting now, and that was a page out of my mother's life too, getting in a screaming fight with a man outside my trailer while a pickup idled in the dirt yard. There was no way out for me, whatever I did. The alcohol was kicking in for real now. The sky between the palms turned a funny color.

"Baby," Mark growled, sliding his hand across my shoulders.

I shoved him away. "Why can't people take no for an answer today? Get your stuff and go on. Anything you leave, I'm throwing in the garbage." I couldn't do this, of course. It was illegal. My mom and I had been evicted enough times that I knew the law.

Mark might have known the law too, but the wheels turned slowly behind his eyes. Even if I didn't throw away his stuff, I might go through it now that I was angry, and there was something in it he didn't want me to find, weed or worse.

"Fine." He stomped across the yard toward the trailer. A cloud of dirt billowed around his feet. He mounted the cement blocks two at a time. The cloud of dirt reached me, and I turned away to avoid inhaling it.

"Leah," Patrick called over the music and the engine noise and the pit bull. He crooked his finger at me. I walked over and leaned against the passenger door, peering at the girl, mildly curious. She'd pasted a silhouette above her left breast before she spent her day in the sun. Now she'd peeled it away to reveal a white Playboy bunny in the middle of her tan.

"What's the holdup?" Patrick asked me.

"I'm kicking Mark out."

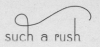

Patrick's eyebrows shot up. Not one eyebrow, like Grayson's expression of skepticism. Both eyebrows. "What for?"

I switched into trailer park voice. Polite airport voice was gone now. The Admiral would not recognize me. "Mark brought this whore here and thought I wouldn't find out he's doing her. He can't stay here. The trailer is set to self-destruct when it senses an IQ that low." This wasn't true, considering some of my mom's boyfriends.

The girl leaned toward the window. "What did you call me?"

I was about to clarify it for her when Patrick interrupted us. "Ladies, ladies." Normally boys like Patrick encouraged a good catfight, but he was sitting between us and was probably scared of getting scratched. To change the subject, he asked me, "Where's the beer?" His eyes slid to the can in my hand. "Did you drink it all?"

I set my sunglasses on top of my head and looked him straight in the eye. "If you ever mention that beer to me again, I will retrieve it from its supersecret hiding place and shove the entire case, can by can, up your ass."

Mark kicked the door of the trailer open so hard that it banged against the metal wall. He started down the cement blocks with the case of beer on his shoulder, the garbage bags of his stuff in the other hand, and the rifles underneath his arm.

Patrick leaned nearer, as if he had a secret. I bent my head to hear him, so close now that the breeze blew my curls across his cheek.

"Mark really likes you," Patrick said conspiratorially.

"He has a funny way of showing it," I said in the same tone, mocking him.

"I mean," Patrick whispered, "he may not be that easy to get rid of."

"Don't even talk to her." Mark handed the case of beer to one of the boys in the payload, then swung the trash bags over the side without warning the other guy to move first. "Hey," the guy protested. He drunkenly slid off his seat on the wheel well.

Mark pointed at me. "You can kiss that job with my uncle good-bye."

I shrugged. I wholeheartedly agreed with Grayson now. Probably there had never been a job. Even if there had been a position open, Mark wouldn't have the power to give it and take it away. His mother had kicked him out and his uncle hadn't taken him in. That's how close Mark and his family were. Funny that I had ever convinced myself this summer job was waiting for me, just by wanting it so badly.

He rounded the back of the truck. As he slid behind the steering wheel, the girl called across Patrick to me, "Serves you right. You need to learn how to treat a man."

"If I ever see you again," I told her, "I will beat you like a dog." I was no more violent or tough than the next person, but talking big scared most people away as effectively as smacking them. I had learned this through trial and error at school. I thought I'd made my point, because her eyes widened at me before she remembered to scowl.

Patrick just winked at me, though. Then the engine revved. The music rose to a deafening level even for a trailer park. The truck whipped forward, then back, then forward, then back, in a drunken, poorly executed more-than-three-point turn. It had ground up enough dust to coat me before it finally sped down the narrow road through the trees, the pit bull barking at its highest pitch to sound the alarm.

I crossed the bare dirt and settled in a plastic chair near my bedroom window, under the tallest palm. There were two

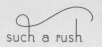

chairs. A stump between them served as a table. On this stylish
side table was a small margarine tub filled with cigarette butts
and rainwater. I never would have let this mess stay here if I'd
known my mother or Mark had made it. I didn't hang out in
the yard, because of the pit bull.

But it didn't bother me as much as it normally would have.
I popped my neck, shook out my shoulders, took a long swig
of delicious cheap-ass beer, and relaxed into the plastic chair.
I gazed at my home of corrugated metal. It had been parked
here so long that palmettos grew out from under it, and it was
coated in a thin green film of moss or lichen or something.
Whatever it was, it grew a lot better on the trailer than it did
in the dirt yard. I listened to the music of the pit bull. I set my
beer down on the stump, crossed my legs like I was having a
tea party, and pondered the fact that the boys I knew had everything and I had nothing.

An airplane roared overhead, one of Mr. Hall's Pipers. I
looked up just in time to see the yellow one pass across a patch
of blue sky between the trees. Grayson must be flying, or Alec,
or some new dope they'd hired instead of me. An advertising
banner stretched way behind the plane, but I couldn't read
what it said from underneath.

As the engine noise faded, the pit bull's barking filled the
empty space. The dog had reason this time. Someone knocked
on the door of the pit bull's trailer. And then Grayson was
yelling over the barks, asking the owner where Leah Jones
lived.

I waited for the fight-or-flight adrenaline spike to pass.
Better to sit tight than to attempt an escape into the trailer.
If Grayson turned, he might see my movement through the
palm fronds and catch me more quickly. Even if I did make it
through the door unseen, he would find me eventually. And

73

when I opened the door, he would see inside. Outside was bad enough.

So I eased my sunglasses from my hair back down to cover my eyes, held my breath, and felt thankful Grayson had missed Mark and his crew by several minutes. Grayson hadn't even located me yet, but I squirmed in his sights.

Maybe he wouldn't find me after all, I began to think as he gave up on the pit bull owner and knocked on the door of another trailer. Good luck with that. The trailer park wasn't known for its block parties or ice cream socials. As residents of three and a half years, my mom and I were some of the longer-term neighbors, yet I doubted a single person here knew my name, except the boys I was acquainted with through long years of hoping they would leave me alone on the bus. It was spring break, so they would be at the beach. If I sat here quietly, maybe Grayson would knock on a few more doors, give up, and go away.

But from our talk a few hours before, I knew Grayson wanted me to work for him. He wanted it badly for some reason. He wouldn't go away until I talked him out of it. In the past year, I'd had a run-in with Ben Reynolds when he got off the bus with me, followed me home, and wouldn't go away. I hadn't let him in the door, so he'd found a heavy branch in the woods and walked around the trailer, banging the club against the metal walls as he went, around and around until I thought I would go insane. I'd had no way to call for help. My mom had let the bill go unpaid way too many times for us to have a phone.

"Leah Jones," Grayson said to a man across the road.

"Is her mother's name Patsy?" the man asked.

"No," Grayson said. "It's Sheryl."

The fact that Grayson knew my mother's name set off

tornado sirens in my head, but I didn't know what they meant. I just listened through the trees as Grayson made his way down the row of trailers. Nobody had heard of me. On his fourth or fifth try he got wise. Now I was not just Leah Jones. I was Leah Jones, walks down this path to the airport every day, tiny eighteen-year-old girl, "dark hair like this." I pictured the motion he made with his hands as he pantomimed the explosion of my curls in the coastal humidity.

"Oh, I know what girl you mean," said a woman. "She lives right there."

For thirty seconds I expected Grayson to walk past the palm fronds that framed the road, into my yard. I still jumped when he did appear because he was so shockingly out of context. He crossed the dirt to my chair, kicking up hardly any dust with his flip-flops, and stood right in front of me.

I looked up at him. He was a lot taller than I remembered.

He stared down at me like a stern state trooper, eyes inscrutable behind his sunglasses. His straw cowboy hat mashed his blond curls against his head, and a drop of sweat trickled from his hairline down his cheek. "Can we talk?"

Politely I inclined my head, inviting him to sit in the other plastic chair. Behind my own sunglasses, out of the corner of my eye, I caught another glimpse of the makeshift ashtray and wished for a cigarette, any distraction to fumble with.

He sat down and slapped a mosquito on his arm. "Does your mom know you fly?"

It seemed like an innocent question, a friendly conversation starter. I knew better. After three and a half years of basically pretending I didn't exist, Grayson had not come through the fence and searched for me just to have a casual chat.

"Of course she knows," I lied, staring now where he was pointing. He'd taken a sheet of paper out of his pocket and

unfolded it on his thigh. My mother's ironically neat and upstanding signature, underlined with a flourish, was at the bottom of the form Mr. Hall had wanted her to sign when he started giving me flying lessons.

Grayson's broad fingertip tapped the paper, denting the signature, which seemed more delicate with every strike, as if every tap were a hammer blow, until it dawned on me what he meant. I had forged my mother's signature on that form, and somehow he knew.

I grabbed for the form.

Before I could touch it, he snatched it away and held it above his head. "I have copies," he said. "In fact, I mailed one home to Wilmington, so don't bother."

Slowly I sat back in my plastic chair and tried to wipe the emotion off my face, whatever it was—surprise, fear, horror, blind panic.

He relaxed too. He brought the form back down to his thigh and smoothed the wrinkled paper with his palm as if it were the original Declaration of Independence. "I'm sure this signature looks exactly like your mother's. You signed it carefully. I have a lot of experience forging my mother's name on report cards, and even I wouldn't have noticed this if my dad hadn't marked it with a sticky note." With his thumb and middle finger he thumped the yellow square hanging off one side of the form. An arrow drawn on the note pointed to the forgery. "Like he suspected what you'd done, and then decided to let it go."

"There's no way you could prove that," I said quickly. "You'd have to pay for a handwriting expert or something, and the FAA doesn't care. Nobody cares that much about me."

"*I* care about you, Leah," he said sarcastically. "But luckily, I don't have to hire a handwriting expert *or* report you to the FAA. All I have to do is show this to your mother."

# five

I sucked in a breath. Then realized that sucking in my breath had revealed to Grayson just how right he was, and how much I *did not* want him to involve my mother. "She's out of town," I said as evenly as I could. "Good luck finding her."

"She'll be back," he predicted. "But if not . . . My dad just died. For the moment, I'm loaded. I'll hire a private detective to find her."

I blinked at Grayson. He was so handsome, and sitting so close in his chair, that my heart went into overdrive. I blinked again and he was the devil, sent here to seek out my every hope and crush it, my every fear and make it come true. I had never found my mother when she went missing, but I had never tried. I imagined it would be easy for a professional. A private detective would be friendly with the police, and my mother's boyfriends were usually on parole.

"What would she do if she knew you'd forged her signature

so you could start taking flying lessons at such a tender age?" Grayson asked.

She would kick me out of the trailer for forging her name and—more important to her—for lying to her about where my money was going. The trailer wasn't much, but I had a month and a half of high school left, and nowhere else to go. Molly would offer to let me stay at her house. Her parents wouldn't understand. Rich parents didn't kick their children out. Molly's folks would assume I'd done something truly awful and that I was a bad influence on her. They would make sure Molly stayed away from me. That would be the end of our friendship. And then—

"Would your mother pitch a fit at the airport office?" Grayson prodded me. "My dad's dead. There's nobody for her to sue. Does she understand that? I'll bet she would try to lay the blame somewhere. Everybody at the airport would get dragged into it—everybody still alive who could have written you recommendations for jobs and flight schools and college in the next few months. You *were* planning to go to college at some point, right? You'd have to, if you want a job as an airline pilot."

He had me there. College was not an option for me right now. Every dime I hadn't given over to my mom, I'd blown on flying. I'd been counting on flying for Mr. Simon and saving up money for junior college tuition. After a few semesters, I would use my stellar new GPA and glowing recommendations from Mr. Simon and the Admiral and everyone else I knew at the airport to get a scholarship to a decent college that offered an aviation degree. But if Grayson ruined those recommendations for me—

"You know what else you need to get that airline pilot job?" Grayson asked. "Good moral character."

He'd done his homework to blackmail me. He was quoting the FAA rules for an airline pilot's license. I'd never known what "good moral character" meant, but I was pretty sure it ruled out forging my mother's name to take flying lessons.

"All right," I said through my hand, which I'd clapped over my mouth at some point while he was talking.

"All right, what?" he prompted me.

"All right, I'll work for you."

"Great," he said calmly, like he didn't think it was great at all. He just folded my entire future, sticky note and all, and shoved it back into his pocket.

"For how long?" I asked weakly.

He shrugged like he hadn't thought about it. But his words betrayed him. He'd thought about this a lot. "Definitely this whole week of spring break. Most weekends after that, because Alec and I will be coming over from Wilmington to fly too. Not the next weekend after spring break is over, though. That's our high school's prom. My dad didn't schedule any banners then, like he expected Alec and me to want to go."

He turned his head toward the road as if listening for something, but the pit bull had stopped barking.

Grayson went on, "And after school lets out for the summer, we'll reevaluate."

I took a swig of beer, considering. Grayson would drive the business into the ground way before school let out. So I would fly for him this week. He would go back to Wilmington. The following weekend, his dad had given him the excuse of the prom to skip flying. There would be more excuses after that. Grayson and Alec would not come to Heaven Beach again, at least not to fly. They'd stay in Wilmington and forget all about me, and it would be like none of this had ever happened.

In the meantime, I could start looking for another job flying. I hadn't expected the crop-dusting job to drop in my lap. The imaginary crop-dusting job. Maybe an actual job would come up too. My prospects looked brighter than they had an hour before, when I'd buried my head under the pillows. Honestly, I didn't want to fly for Grayson, but my spirits *were* lifted at the thought that I would finally fly a plane again. Or maybe it was the beer. I took another long pull and set the can down on the stump.

"I want you to pay me at the end of every workday," I said.

Grayson's brows went down behind his shades. "Why?"

"This is a day-by-day operation. I don't want to walk over there one morning and find out you've packed up and run back to Wilmington without paying me."

"That's not going to happen," Grayson said so firmly that I almost believed him. "But sure, if that's what you want, I'll pay you every day. And there's one more thing." His fist gripped and relaxed. "I need you to date Alec this week."

I laughed shortly. The alcohol rushed to my head and heated my skin in the warm evening. I couldn't make sense of what Grayson was saying. "You want me to what?"

"Date Alec."

*Date Alec?* All day I'd fought my long-standing crush on Grayson. The idea of dating Alec, who was so different from Grayson, was a one-eighty, and I felt dizzy with the turn. "I haven't even seen Alec since the fune—" Even drunk, I was able to stop myself, almost.

"Come to work tomorrow morning," Grayson said as if I hadn't spoken. "Flirt with Alec. He'll ask you out. You're local and it's spring break, so it should be easy for you to show him a good time."

"Grayson, that's nuts!" I was yelling now, and the pit bull

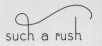

barked viciously in response. I lowered my voice. "Why in the world would you want me to date your brother?"

"I can't tell you," Grayson said simply.

"Then I'm not doing it," I told him just as glibly.

"Then I'll hire someone to deliver this forgery to your mother when you're not around to stop it." He leaned forward to stand up.

"No!" I exclaimed. "Sit down."

He seemed to be watching me as he eased back into his chair.

"I'll do it," I said, "but you have to tell me why."

"No."

"Grayson!" His name set the pit bull off again. I whispered, "Is it for something illegal?"

"No."

"Or something else that will screw up my commercial license?"

"Nothing like that," he assured me. "It will get you *out* of trouble, because I'll give you back this form and all the copies I made."

And I would burn them. "Why do you think Alec's going to ask me out just because I flirt with him? He hardly knows me."

"But *I* know *him*," Grayson said.

I shook my head. "Alec would not go out with me." He might never have seen my trailer, but he knew. Everybody at the airport knew.

"Yes, he will," Grayson said. "I've seen you in action. That *oh, you're a big strong man* thing you do. Do that."

I was tired of Grayson basically calling me a slut. "Why do you keep telling me I have to sleep with people to get a job? It's a fourteen-year-old boy's wet dream about how the business world functions. Grow up."

Even though I couldn't see his eyes, I could tell my words had finally affected him. He shifted backward in his chair like I'd slapped him.

Then I realized where I'd gotten that "grow up" line. From Mr. Hall himself. It was his favorite thing to yell at Grayson when he forgot to lock the hangar door or left a banner out in the rain. Mr. Hall didn't mind yelling it across the tarmac for the Admiral and the other pilots and me to hear. *Grow up, son*.

"I said I want you to date him, not sleep with him," Grayson said sharply. "If you assume you're going to do everybody you date, that's your problem."

The palm tree above us swayed violently in the breeze, and my feet ached, two things that should not have gone together. I had been flexing my feet in my flip-flops as if pressing the foot pedals in a plane, stabilizing it against the buffeting wind.

"And"—his voice was soft now—"you're a beautiful girl. If you show the slightest interest in Alec, he'll want to go out with you. I know I would."

My skin prickled with goose bumps, a chill in the hot April evening. My brain knew Grayson didn't have the crush on me that I'd imagined when he got mad at me at the airport that afternoon. He wouldn't have asked me to date his brother if he'd been interested in me. But my body didn't know this, or didn't care.

"Tell me why you want me to do this," I said, quietly this time.

"It's for his own good."

I laughed, because that was a ridiculous thing for Grayson to say. Grayson and Alec were twins, *exactly* the same age, yet Grayson sounded like their father.

Grayson didn't laugh. And as I watched him, he bit his lip nervously, gripped and relaxed his fist, kept himself barely

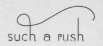

under control. Convincing me to date Alec mattered to Grayson. A lot. Almost as if he *were* trying to do something for Alec's own good, for once. As if someone needed to fill those shoes now that their father and their older brother were gone.

I understood why Grayson had recruited me for this job rather than sending the smoother Alec, and why irresponsible Grayson seemed to be the one in charge. For some reason having to do with the business and their dad's death, Grayson was manipulating Alec.

If I could figure out why, I could blackmail Grayson right back.

I swallowed. "So you're saying *I'm* for Alec's own good."

Grayson looked me up and down. He moved his head enough that I wouldn't miss the tilt of his hat, and the provocative meaning behind it. "Ridiculous as that sounds, yes. Trust me, I have an excellent reason. You trust me, don't you, Leah?"

"I thought I had made it very clear that *no.*"

"And Alec can't know I told you to do this. If he finds out, I will make your life as difficult as I possibly can."

Not if I made *his* life difficult first. I let out a frustrated huff. "Is this all because I didn't say yes to your job in the first place?"

"No. I was always going to ask you to do this too. But when you didn't say yes in the first place, you made me mad, and I went and found something to hold over your head. Now I'm not asking you. I'm telling you." He took off his straw cowboy hat. I saw his hair so seldom that it always surprised me: how blond it was, almost as light as Alec's, and how curly, whereas Alec's was board straight. Grayson's hair reminded me how young he was, even though he was acting like a boss, a manipulator, a god.

He passed the back of his wrist across his sweating brow, then put his hat back on. "You kicked Mark out, right?"

I frowned at Grayson. "What? Why?"

"Because you're out here drinking beer. Let me guess. You asked Mark about the crop-dusting job. You found out he made it up, like I said. So you broke up with him. Is that what happened?"

I ground my teeth together, squeezed my eyes shut behind my shades, anything to keep from sobbing in front of Grayson.

"Hey, Leah, seriously." His voice was soft and sweet like the spring wind. "He didn't threaten to hurt you or anything, did he?"

I put one hand up to my temple, which had begun to ache. "No, but thanks for asking."

Grayson nodded. "We talked about you for a while this morning. I thought he was lying to you about that job, but I don't think he could fake the way he feels about you."

I took the bait. "How does he feel about me?"

"Very strongly."

I flared my nostrils in distaste. "I think he could fake that," I muttered. "He was cheating on me anyway."

"Doesn't matter with Mark," Grayson said. "My mother warned me about girls like you."

I sighed the longest sigh. "Girls like what, Grayson?"

"Girls with crazy boyfriends. She says girls like you are bad news. I need to know whether you really are. I want my brother to fall for you, but I don't want to get him killed."

The back of my neck prickled with danger, something the pit bull did not sense for once, because he was silent. This was the second time today someone had warned me about Mark. I didn't know him that well, honestly. He hadn't gotten violent when he left. But I knew he'd repeated his final semester in high school because he'd been suspended so many times for fighting.

"Last year we played a pickup basketball game at the

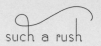

hangar," Grayson said, "and I beat him. Later that afternoon when we were both trying to land, he cut me off."

"In the *air*?" I asked.

"Yeah. He didn't announce himself. He came in right underneath me. It could have been bad. Of course, nobody was outside watching. I should have told my dad, but he would have blamed it on me and told me to grow up." He balled his fist and tapped it on his knee. "I wanted you to work for me, Leah, but I also didn't want you to take a job where you'll be around that guy."

"You said there *was* no job."

"There isn't," Grayson insisted, "and if you double-check with Mr. Simon about it, you're going to be embarrassed. Anyway, you have a job now." He closed the distance between our chairs and stood over me again. "Tomorrow morning at seven."

My stomach was doing flips. I reached for my beer on the stump.

He snagged it before I did and poured the rest on the dead palm fronds behind my chair.

"Hey," I protested.

He crumpled the can in one fist. Then he crossed the yard, jogged up the cement-block stairs, and swung through the aluminum door.

"Grayson!" I yelled. But I didn't run after him into the trailer. The only thing worse than him rooting around in there was watching him while he did it, and seeing his expression of pity. I kept my eyes on the door, and waited, and wished for that beer back.

He leaned out the doorway. "Where's the rest of the beer?"

"Gone," I said. At the beach. At a party. At Patrick's brother's house, where Mark and that girl were getting it on in the basement, having a lot more fun than me right now.

Grayson ran down the steps and jogged across the dirt to stop in front of me with his hands on his hips. "No more drinking tonight."

I opened my hands to show him they were empty.

"Seriously. No hangovers. I've told Alec too. We're not crashing any planes this week." He crouched in front of my chair so he was on my level and we faced each other. "I'm going to leave now. Will you be okay?"

I didn't know what to say. I couldn't even process anymore. My brain was too overloaded with Grayson, acting like himself but a million times worse because he was dragging me into his impulsive bad ideas this time; and Grayson, acting protective like a father.

When I said nothing, he reached forward and put his hand on my knee.

Electricity shot up my thigh and made my heart pump painfully.

Maybe Grayson felt the jolt too. He took his hand away. I could see my own shades reflected in his sunglasses, my dark curls sliding around my face in the breeze, my frown.

I finally guessed, "Yes? I'll be okay."

Satisfied, he stood. "See you bright and early," he called as he crossed the gravel road and disappeared up the path. The pit bull lunged insanely.

I didn't sit there long. Or maybe I sat there for a very long time. I was drunk. Twilight settled over the trees. But my heart raced. Although Grayson had left the trailer park, his gaze remained. I was seeing everything through his eyes again. I saw myself sitting alone in the dark, my knees pulled up to my chest in the plastic chair, watching the dust sparkle and slowly settle in the dusk, listening to the pit bull strain against his chain.

I moved back across the yard, into the trailer, and locked the door behind me, muffling but not shutting out the pit bull.

Inside, I retrieved my newspaper and I settled on the pitted sofa, facing the wall where the TV had been. I hoped to lose myself so the day would effectively be over, and I would have no time between now and seven a.m. to worry about what would happen tomorrow with Alec and Grayson. But right away, my stomach growled. The walk to the convenience store didn't seem so far now. I didn't dare walk there at night. Heaven Beach had an upscale resort end and a flophouse end. The trailer park was on the flophouse end, and whenever I walked along the highway after dark, men stopped their trucks to ask me whether I was working. Since boys seemed slow to take no for an answer today, I chose not to tempt fate. My stomach groaned in protest.

After a while, I jumped and dropped the paper at a shockingly loud knock on the aluminum door. "Who is it?" I hollered.

"Delivery."

It was too much, a takeout order misdirected to my door when I was starving. I stomped across the trailer and flung the door open.

Startled, a Chinese guy backed down one cement block, nearly fell, and stepped up again. He held a big white bag in front of him like a shield, printed with red Chinese characters. "Delivery," he repeated.

I inhaled one long, heavenly noseful of Chinese spice before I said, "Not mine." I started to close the door.

"Compliments of Hall Aviation." He shoved the bag at me and hopped off the cement blocks. "Don't forget! Be there seven a.m. sharp!"

I watched his car disappear down the gravel road. Then I

stared through the dust where his car had been, past the yard with the bellowing pit bull, at the path through the trees to the airport. I'd forgotten this when I was saying unkind things to Grayson, and kicking Mark out of the trailer, and threatening to shove beer cans up Patrick's ass. But when I was a little girl, my mom always told me to be nice to everybody, no matter what they looked like or how they treated me, because I never knew who might be an angel God had sent to Earth in disguise.

Despite the fact that Molly lived on the upscale resort end of town, she deigned to be my friend. She didn't mind that I lived in a trailer park. But she didn't seem to consider it an actual home, either, or to think other people lived here. Around eleven I recognized the rhythm of a rock song tapped out in sharp beeps from her electric car.

That is, she didn't *mind* that I lived in a trailer park, but she did *care*. She might even have sought me out. Her parents had run an architecture and interior design business in Atlanta. Now they had "retired" to the beach (they were way too young to retire, in their midforties like everybody's parents except my embarrassingly young mother) and opened a café that was constructed to look weathered in order to appeal to vacationers on the rich end of town. From the peacenik stickers in the window to the organic menu, their café shouted bleeding-heart liberal. They had taught Molly to reserve judgment and value difference.

And Molly had learned well. The instant she'd moved to town two years before, she'd become the crusader of our high school, lobbying the lunchroom for vegetarian choices, organizing cleanup crews to keep the nearby bird habitats free of garbage. She was no pushover, though. When she thought I was trying to steal her boyfriend, she found me in the hallway

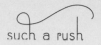

between classes and, within hearing of everyone, told me what she thought of the school slut.

But when she saw the way the other girls joined in to bully me—that's when, ironically, she befriended me. So in a way, she was using me. I was her Different friend. She gave herself brownie points for hanging with me. But she didn't see herself in this light. And I hadn't told her, because it would be like kicking a puppy. I was glad that she'd picked me for her cross-cultural experiment, instead of somebody else from the trailer park, like Aaron Traynor, who would have convinced her to try meth "just once," or Ben Reynolds, who would have screwed her.

I threw on some clothes against the cool spring night, locked the door behind me, and dashed out to her. I was so happy to see her that I almost hugged her across the front seat of the car, but I didn't dare ruin our friendship with a blatant show of my affection. Our bond had started with our mutual respect for each other's toughness, sense of humor, and utter lack of sentimentality, and that's how it would stay. I said, "Hey, bitch."

"My God. You disgust me. You look like you just rolled out of bed, and I swear you're prettier than me even with all my swagga." She ran her hand down her side and out, presenting some part of her outfit—the low-cut top, maybe, or the miniskirt, or the platform shoes. She was no prettier and no less pretty than any rich girl at our high school.

I said, "I think it's my hair."

"You always think it's your hair." She looked over her shoulder to back the car across my yard and didn't flinch when the bumper hit one of the plastic chairs, tipping it over. She turned forward again and tore out of the trailer park at fifty miles an hour.

"Good concert?" I asked.

"Please. I couldn't wait to ditch those silly chicks I went with. I've been dying to tell you. At breakfast I finally connected with the coolest guy at the café!"

"If he's so cool, why are you with me instead of him?"

"Smart-ass. I had the concert. You know I never break a commitment. And he's working early tomorrow." She stomped the brakes at the entrance to the highway and looked both ways before pulling into traffic, at least. "But tell me what you need to tell me first."

"No, you go ahead."

She stomped the accelerator and the car hissed toward town at top speed, which luckily wasn't very fast or we both would have been dead when she first got her driver's license. Then she glanced at me. "No, *you* go ahead. Something big's happened. You look like you're about to pass out."

I told her everything that had happened with Grayson, and with Mark, and with Grayson again, leaving out the Chinese food, because that would sound like begging. Molly wasn't allowed in the trailer, and she'd never opened the usually empty refrigerator.

She interjected a lot of "Wait a minute. You mean your friend Mr. Hall's sons? Twins are so sexy!" and "He wants you to do *what*?" and "That ass!" which referred to both Mark and Grayson. Though I should have been accustomed to it by now, it was pretty strange to hear filthy language coming from her lips. She was naturally sunny and rich and innocent looking—a lot like Alec, actually—and she'd worn very heavy, glittery eye makeup to her concert, which she thought made her look older but actually made her look about twelve, with huge eyes like a cartoon character.

"I know," I said. "I don't understand how Grayson did it.

I went into our talk thinking of myself as a pilot. Somehow I came out as the airport whore."

Molly laughed so hard that I thought she would run off the road because I had said "whore." Molly was easily amused by smut. Therefore, our conversations tended to be very dirty. I liked to hear her laugh.

When her giggles died down, I said, "You know I'm not a whore." I was double-checking, actually. I had a bad rep around school, but that's because the new girl at school was an easy target. After three and a half years here, I was still considered the new girl. Molly hadn't lived here as long, but she'd blended in better. The new girl who lived in a trailer park was a sitting duck.

Molly cut her eyes sideways at me. "I know you're not a *practicing* whore. But Mark Simon living with you? Even for just a week? I'm so glad you got rid of him."

"Me too," I said.

"Did you end up doing it?"

"No."

"Gah!" Molly exclaimed. "I'm so relieved. I tried to be glad you were finally going to get some, but Mark Simon is not the crazy I would have picked out for you. Girls were talking about you. I mean, more than usual. That was out there, living with a guy when you're only eighteen and you haven't even graduated yet."

*It wasn't like that,* I almost told her. But I'd said this to her all week: *It's not like that.* I sounded like my mother trying to explain a few of her military boyfriends to me. Why do you stay with him when he hits you, Mama? *You don't understand. It's not like that.*

"Do you think I gave Mark the wrong idea without meaning to?" I asked. "I never meant that I would do him in

exchange for a job. Do you think Grayson is right, that I'll look at Alec and he'll fall at my feet?" What I wanted to ask was whether Mr. Hall had befriended me for the wrong reasons, like Grayson had said a year ago in the hangar, which seemed like a lifetime ago now. But I didn't ask that. I didn't want to know the answer.

She took a long breath, considering. "I do think you turn on a very sexy act around men when you need something, and you may not realize you're doing it. Obviously you don't realize it if you're asking me about it."

"Give me an example."

"Ryan." Ryan was the boyfriend Molly and I had argued about when we first met.

I hated it when she brought Ryan up. She didn't know the whole truth about what had happened. The fact that I'd hidden it from her made my stomach twist even now. But my fib had landed me this beautiful friend. I wouldn't let her go. So I continued with the tough act she loved so much. I said, "Oh, I realized I was seducing Ryan all right."

She cackled at our oldest joke. "Okay, another example. You've gotten in one million fights at school, and you've been called to the principal's office one million times, but you've never been suspended."

"That's because I don't start the fights," I said self-righteously.

"Maybe not," Molly said, "but that's not what those other girls and their friends are telling the principal, yet they're getting suspended and you're not."

"So you *do* think I'm a whore," I said grimly.

"No. You're not doing the principal. The rumors about you aren't true. But they're not random, either. Think about it. Do you own a T-shirt that doesn't show your cleavage?"

I put both hands over the deepest part of my V-neck.

"And then there's Mark living with you," she said. "You're not a whore. You're a chick who hasn't exactly grown up with every advantage, and you've learned to use what you've got. You don't do it on purpose. It's second nature. You act girly and helpless and make men think you're harmless."

I swallowed.

"Leah. You look like you're going to pass out again. I'm not helping."

"Sure you are," I said brightly. "You're a candle in my window."

I meant for her to laugh at this, but she stared out the windshield, tapping one finger nervously on the steering wheel. "So, about these Hall boys. Are you in love with Alec?"

"What? No." As I said this, we passed the convenience store. I was always amazed how little time it took to drive here when it took forever to walk here.

"Are you in love with the one who thinks you're a whore?" she asked.

I snickered at the way she'd put it. Then I realized I shouldn't be amused, because the way she'd put it was pretty accurate. "Grayson. No." My skin tingled as I said his name, which was just stupid.

"I can't put my finger on it, but you're in love with somebody."

I fished in her purse at my feet, found a clove cigarette, and lit it. "I've been watching them from afar for a while. The twins, and their father who died, and their older brother who died. I guess I've fallen a little in love with all of them." One puff and the cigarette was making me sick. Mr. Hall was looking over my shoulder, telling me to put that garbage out. I stubbed it out carefully in an empty paper cup in her cup holder.

"So you're nostalgic for their lost family, and you feel sorry for this guy. You're making excuses to yourself for his poor social skills. But you can't forget he's blackmailing you into dating his brother. Worse, he's blackmailing you into doing this dangerous job flying."

"Well, I don't know that it's a dangerous job. Before Mr. Hall died, I actually wanted that job."

"When Mr. Hall was running the show, yes. Now he's not. With this inexperienced eighteen-year-old dude running the place, it'll be even more like suicide than it was before."

"I wouldn't call it suicide."

"You've described it to me, Leah. You're flying this little tin can of a plane pulling this long, heavy banner it was never made to pull. And you're fighting with the controls the whole time to keep the plane from stalling and plunging you to your death."

"Technically, all of that is true, but a pilot wouldn't phrase it so dramatically. If we did, we wouldn't be pilots very long. Because that sounds like some crazy shit."

"Exactly. And you said they've stripped all the instruments out of those little planes so they're light enough to carry the banners. You're flying without instruments, and that's not dangerous?"

"They don't take out *all* the instruments. The ones they've taken out, you don't really need unless it's cloudy or dark. I mean, yes, they'd be nice to have, but you don't *need* them."

Molly turned to gape at me.

I realized what I was saying *did* sound kind of lame. "Yes, I can hear myself," I said. "Was that your next question? Yes."

"Well," she said, "since you love these guys so much, and you swear the job isn't 'that' suicidal"—she took her hands off the steering wheel to make finger quotes—"I don't see what

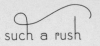

the problem is. I mean, I understand your concern about the good moral character thing and your mother finding out that you forged her name. You're just trying to keep your head down and your nose clean until you can get out of Heaven Beach."

"Right." We passed the grocery store. The few times I'd walked here to shop, the bags had pulled my arms out of their sockets, just like the heavy chocks on the tarmac, as I hiked back to the trailer. But if I could have driven here, I would have plopped the bags in the trunk and forgotten about them until I reached home. Yes, I was amazed at this miraculous invention called a *car*. On pretty much every drive Molly took me on, I was tempted to ask her to stop and let me get a few groceries. I never asked, though, and it never occurred to her.

"And maybe you have a little problem with authority—" Molly said.

"Who, me?"

"—so Grayson telling you what to do gets on your last nerve, especially when it involves whoredom."

"Correct."

"But if his business is going to be as short-lived as you say, can't you just ride it out and then go back to your airport job on the ground? I don't see why you're so upset at losing the crop-dusting job with that jerk. You've flown before but you've never had a *job* flying. Why do you need one now?"

"Because every type of pilot's license has an age requirement, plus a requirement for the number of hours you've flown."

"And a pesky requirement for good moral character."

"That's only for the airline pilot's license. But yeah, that's exactly what I'm up for next. For my commercial license I had to turn eighteen years old and log two hundred and fifty hours.

At first I had to rent Mr. Hall's airplane to get those hours. Airplane rental isn't cheap. If he hadn't started letting me use it for free, I wouldn't have that license by now."

"I see."

Now we were passing the library. I checked out one or two books per visit so they wouldn't be too heavy or bulky on the walk home. That way I always had a stack. I'd seen Molly check out a whole stack before. At once. And put them in her car.

"For the airline pilot's license," I said, "I have to be twenty-three years old, and I need to log fifteen hundred hours. Now that Mr. Hall is gone, that's another twelve hundred and fifty hours of renting an airplane. Plus, if any airline is going to hire me, I need a college degree. How am I going to pay for all that in the next five years, Molly?"

"Hell if I know."

"I'm going to get a job flying. Then I fly for free. I fly a *lot* and log a lot of hours. And I get paid more than minimum wage."

"But if you *can't* get a job flying," she said, "maybe you keep your airport office job, work on your hours and your degree, but do it more slowly, as you save up your money. You don't *have* to get that license the day you turn twenty-three."

"True." But if I didn't get it at twenty-three, I would never get it. That life was too hard, always looking to the future and never living in the now, saving for an impossible goal. Thirty years later I would *still* be working in the airport office for minimum wage. There would be a rumor that I had been a pilot once, but most people wouldn't believe it, looking at me.

"Yeah, I understand now," Molly said.

Really?

"Maybe Alec and Grayson's company won't go under like

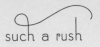

you so gleefully expect," she said, "and you can keep your job with them for a long time."

"And continue to be the airport whore."

"It's a dirty job but somebody's got to do it."

We'd reached the beginning of the motels. Because we were still on the flophouse end of Heaven Beach, the signs out front boasted ridiculously low room rates, and the pools were small and stained and green.

I said, "Tell me the rest of your story, which is not nearly as interesting as my story. You finally connected with a guy at the café, and he had to go to bed. Aw."

"Aw." She poked out her bottom lip sympathetically.

"Will you see him again?"

She took in a slow breath and exhaled before she spoke, as if considering her answer. Which was not like her. "I think he's going to be really busy this week."

"But you were all excited about him a few minutes ago. You drove over to my mansion at eleven o'clock at night to tell me about him." As I uttered the words, I realized they probably weren't true. Maybe the boy didn't even exist. Molly always had an excuse like this—she *had* to see me so she could tell me about a cute boy, or a dorky thing her mom had done, or something she'd seen on TV—but a lot of times when she came over, she was really checking on me, or getting me out of the trailer for a little while. Or casually driving me back to the café and feeding me, as if I didn't know what was going on. I played along.

"I *was* excited about him," she said, "but he seems awfully vanilla next to your whore story."

"He does. Let's trade places." Now *I* was the one speaking before I thought. I sounded ungrateful and jealous and bitter. Which I was, but nobody wanted to hear that. I opened my mouth, thinking hard, forming a genuine apology.

She opened the console between us, brought out a white paper bag, and set it in my lap. "Warm chocolate croissant."

"Oh!" My cry of ecstasy at a pastry was so heartfelt and genuine that I burst into laughter.

She glanced over at me with her eyebrows raised like she was worried about my sanity.

"Shut up." I tore off a big bite of flaky croissant filled with gooey chocolate sauce and stuffed it into her mouth, purposefully smearing it across her cheek. "Mmph," was all she said. Her mouth was full, and her dad's chocolate croissants were that good.

And we were right to silence each other with food. It was better that we never apologized to each other. Then we'd be admitting that we were wrong and we owed each other something. That's where people got into trouble.

"Look, genuine whores." She nodded out the window at a couple of teenage girls crossing the street in front of us, both with bad blond dye jobs, both in ill-fitting, low-cut T-shirt dresses exposing the real or fake tattoos on their chests. One girl wore cheap heels and one was barefoot.

"How do you end up like that?" Molly asked me, not the whores.

I didn't know whether they were really whores. There *were* plenty of whores on this end of town. But there were also lots of trailer park girls from farther inland, vacationing at the beach. Those girls and the whores looked about the same. Peering at these specimens, I decided they were tourists because they seemed happy.

As Molly pulled through the intersection, I changed my mind. The girls had reached the corner and were shouting at cars.

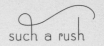

Talk about trading places. I wouldn't even be trading if I were in those girls' place. I would be taking a very small step. A girl ended up like that by growing up like me. She made the mistake of tangling with the other people around her. And she never ducked through that fence to the airport.

Not that it seemed to be doing me much good at the moment. I'd resisted working for Grayson. I was alarmed at being blackmailed. I resented having to throw myself at Alec. Yet in the end, I'd given in, hadn't I? I wasn't much better than those streetwalkers.

But the thought of reporting to the Hall Aviation hangar in the morning sent a little thrill through me. I would fly again for the first time in two months. Such a rush! I would get involved in Grayson and Alec's game with each other. It was like starring on a TV reality show where I'd probably be publicly humiliated—but that was better than watching the show on TV at home, or not being able to watch it at all when the TV went missing and the trailer fell silent.

And I would see Grayson again. He needed me. He was using me. He didn't have a crush on me, yet I could still feel his hand on my knee. Watching the whores shrink in the side mirror as Molly sped down the street, I put my own hand on my knee and rubbed my thumb back and forth, feeling that rush all over again.

# six

I concentrated on that rush of feeling, relying on it to push me along, step by step, up the path through the trailer park, into the orange sunlight of early morning, across the long, wet grass that stuck black seeds to my ankles. I would see Grayson. I would fly a plane. Those were reasons to keep walking toward Hall Aviation and the beginning of my charade with Alec.

I'd fretted over what to wear: something innocent that Alec would like? He probably dated cheerleaders who wore pink and slept with teddy bears. Or something super-whorelike to make an ironic point to Grayson? At the tail end of fifteen minutes of trying on clothes, then standing on the toilet and leaning way over to see my torso in the mirror above the sink, I decided I'd better not risk angering Grayson and driving him to spill everything to my mom. I'd worn what I would have worn if everything were normal, everybody were still alive, and I was working for Mr. Hall instead of his son. Admittedly,

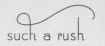

hmmm, this was kind of whorelike after all, short shorts with a sexy cropped T-shirt cut to fit loose, which I would take off in the plane to reveal my bikini top underneath. The plane wasn't air-conditioned, and the cockpit would heat to a hundred degrees up near the sun.

Where the tarmac started, I veered toward the pavement to step out of the cold grass. Huge hangars sat to my left, one of which was Mr. Simon's. I passed it warily, looking through the vast doorway while trying not to look like I was looking. I didn't want another confrontation with Mark this morning—or ever. Men shifted inside the hangar, but I didn't recognize Mark's quick movements. I doubted he could have made it in this early if he'd continued the bender he'd been on last night.

Recalling all the shit I'd been through in the past week with him, in a sex-for-flying exchange I hadn't fully understood, I decided I couldn't do this all over again with Grayson and Alec. Yet I kept walking, my flip-flops trailing dew across the asphalt embedded with white shells. I needed to lose these cold feet before I reached the Hall Aviation hangar. I didn't want to flirt with Alec. He was crazy handsome, but I'd never been attracted to him like I had to Grayson, and the thought of flirting with him made my stomach hurt. I reminded myself I hadn't flown in two months, and my whole future as a pilot was on the line.

As I passed the airport office, I picked up my pace. The yellow Piper already sat on the tarmac in front of Hall Aviation. The small side door and the wide front doors of the hangar were open to the morning, and the strange beat of alt-rock spilled out. I'd always kept my eyes and ears open when I went into the hangar and the boys were there. They played interesting music, wore T-shirts for bands I'd never heard of, and

read books that were making the rounds at their high school but would never travel as far as Heaven Beach. I felt silly for looking up to the boys. They were from Wilmington, not New York City. I was from the armpit of the tourist industry, though, and it was all in your perspective. I kept my eyes and ears open around Molly for much the same reason. Her old friends in Atlanta were always clueing her in on the latest. She still was not as cool as these boys.

I stepped through the side door, on high alert. But the boys both sat in lawn chairs in front of the red Piper and had their heads bent to breakfast in boxes on their laps. I felt a pang of jealousy mixed with hunger, all one and the same for me when I hadn't eaten breakfast. With the prospect of Alec asking me out on a date that night but no iron-clad plans for dinner or a ride into town, I'd carefully hoarded the Chinese leftovers. I dared not waste them by gorging myself on them for breakfast.

"Heeeeeeey!" I called in a parody of some girl who was not being blackmailed and was naturally sweet and gave a shit about other people. I walked toward Alec and put my arms out.

Startled, he set his breakfast aside on a nearby tool bench and stood to hug me. He was just as handsome as I remembered him, his hair bright blond, his face round and friendly. He didn't beam at me, exactly, but the default setting on his face was a half-smile, and he managed that for me. "Hey, Leah!" he exclaimed, wrapping both arms around me and squeezing briefly. "Long time no see."

Then I turned to Grayson, who wore his shades and straw cowboy hat in the gentle light of morning. I didn't want to hug him or touch him. I was angry at him for manipulating me. But in that moment, it seemed strange to hug Alec and not him, especially when Alec must know Grayson and I had

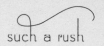

talked recently. How else would Grayson have hired me? I prompted Grayson, "Heeeeeeey!"

He looked up at me without moving his head. For a split second he glared at me over his sunglasses.

Then he set his breakfast aside too and stood. "Heeeeeeey!" he replied in an unenthusiastic imitation, more resigned than sarcastic. He came in for a hug and slid his hand very slowly across my bare waist where my T-shirt rode up.

His hand trailed heat and seemed to take forever, though its passage across my skin was one motion with his body coming closer, moving in for the hug. His other arm curved around my back, and he brought me in tight within his arms for a fraction of a second before letting me go. He backed into his chair again and picked up his breakfast.

As an afterthought, he slid another takeout box from a table, handed it to me, and gestured for me to take a seat on the empty sofa.

And I was still standing there, dazed, wondering what the difference had been between Grayson's hug and Alec's, and fighting my attraction for the boy who meant to sabotage me.

I eased down very carefully onto the sofa. I'd always been wary of it because dust rose when anyone touched it. The boys and Mr. Hall had never seemed to give it much thought, probably because fifteen years ago, way before the divorce, when they all lived here in Heaven Beach together, it was in their den. Only after I'd sat down did I notice the logo on the takeout box in my hands. "Oh! This is from my friend Molly's parents' café. Do you guys know Molly?"

Grayson shook his head without looking at me.

"Tall? Auburn hair? Probably some inappropriate glitter on her face at seven in the morning?"

Alec shook his head without looking at me.

Giving up, I opened the box, and *oh,* a ham-and-egg biscuit waited inside with a cup of cold fruit and a warm chocolate croissant. To have been so hungry and so bereft while walking across the tarmac, and now to be presented with Molly's dad's warm chocolate croissant, not as warm as the one in Molly's car last night but still flaky and gooey enough . . . it was so good that I knew something bad was about to happen.

I gazed at Grayson in his lawn chair and tried to catch his eye to thank him for the food, but he was absorbed in his own croissant.

I dug into my breakfast before my reverence got weird, like I was at church. "I'm so excited about flying!" I exclaimed between bites. "I haven't flown in a while."

Both boys stopped chewing and looked up at me. I hadn't mentioned Mr. Hall's death. I hadn't needed to. For the past two months I'd gotten used to walking around in my own space, where I was the only person who had known Mr. Hall and missed him. But when I'd stepped into the hangar, I'd entered an alternate universe where other people were thinking exactly like me.

If Alec was going to be convinced to ask me out, I needed help out of this awkward situation. I thought Grayson would help me—interject a comment, something. But he just stood and wandered into Mr. Hall's little office in the corner.

After chewing and swallowing, Alec finally said, "I hadn't flown in a while, either. I took one of the Pipers up last night and flew some banner practice runs, just to make sure I could still do it."

"I heard you," I said. Then I wished I hadn't said this, because I was reminding him that I lived in the trailer park.

This time Grayson did rescue me. He came back from the office, handed me a clipboard with forms attached, sank down

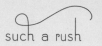

into his lawn chair, and took a long sip from a large paper coffee cup with his eyes closed.

I looked down at the W-4. "You're taking out taxes?" I couldn't hide the dismay in my voice. As a pilot, I'd be making three times as much per hour as I'd made when I was the airport gofer. In my mind I was already socking that money away without giving up a fourth of it in taxes.

"Surprise. It's the law," Grayson said, picking up his takeout box again.

"I know," I said. "I just—"

"Didn't think I was smart enough to figure out how to withhold taxes?"

I couldn't believe he was picking a fight with me when he'd said he wanted me to go out with Alec. But he was looking at me very intentionally with angry accusations in his gray eyes.

I muttered, "Didn't think you'd bother." I tore off a big hunk of my chocolate croissant and stuffed it into my mouth, half-afraid he would take my breakfast away.

Alec tried to ease the tension this time. "Grayson's been studying the taxes. Reading a book on business tax law for idiots. They make a great pair." He slapped Grayson on the back.

Grayson grimaced. At first I thought Alec had slapped him so hard it hurt—but even if he had, Grayson wouldn't have shown pain. These boys didn't play that way.

Then I realized Grayson *was* showing a sort of pain. It wasn't the slap on the back but Alec's words that had hurt him. Alec had implied that Grayson was an idiot and irresponsible. Grayson would have embraced this characterization five months ago if it had gotten him out of a chore for Mr. Hall. And now it hurt.

When Grayson didn't laugh or slap Alec back, Alec leaned forward and looked up into Grayson's face, trying to meet his

eyes. Suddenly Alec gave up. "I'll ask Zeke if he needs help with the banners and then get going." He rose from his lawn chair with the default smile on his face. "I'll see y'all at break."

My mouth was stuffed full. I swallowed quickly. "Bye, Alec!" I called brightly, but by then he'd disappeared through the wide door facing the runway. I turned to Grayson. "That was not successful," I said quietly. "You're not helping."

He glared at me. "What do you want me to do? Get you a room?"

I was on the edge of standing up, throwing my half-eaten breakfast in the garbage, and stomping out of the hangar. To hell with Grayson, and Alec, and my career as a pilot, and food. I could swallow a lot of insults, but not directly to my face. That was too much like a threat, and it called for an immediate reaction, like someone kicking in my trailer door.

Seeing the look on my face, he widened his gray eyes at me. "I'm sorry. I shouldn't have said that. I didn't get a lot of sleep last night."

"Then you need to get more," I said, "and stop insulting me for doing *what you are making me do.*"

"You're right," he grumbled. "I meant to say that I don't expect him to jump you the first time you walk into the hangar. It might take a few days for him to ask you out. A few hours, at least. Possibly in a more romantic setting that doesn't smell this strongly of avgas." He took another bite, proving that the smell of fuel didn't bother him any more than it bothered me, then nodded to my breakfast. "After you finish, you can take the orange Piper up. Fly for about two hours and then come in for a break."

"I might not need one that soon," I said. I wasn't sucking down coffee like Grayson was, and I was used to spending hours in an airplane without a pee.

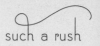

"Take one anyway." Grayson's voice rose like he was angry at me for talking back.

I swallowed my resentment along with my biscuit. Mr. Hall would have kept tight control over me when I came to work for him too. But Grayson was not Mr. Hall. Grayson didn't know this job much better than I did.

"Remember," he said, "in an emergency, drop the banner over an unpopulated area. What matters most is," he touched his thumb, "other people," he touched his pointer finger, "you."

"Then the airplane, then the banner," I finished for him. "I know, Grayson. You and I learned this at the same time. You don't have to repeat it to me."

He squeezed the armrest of his lawn chair so tightly that his knuckles turned white. "If I don't repeat it, who's going to?"

The hangar wasn't empty. It contained the lawn chairs, the sofa, lots of filing cabinets and worktables and equipment, the red Piper, the orange Piper, and the white four-seater Cessna. But the hangar seemed huge and empty as Grayson's voice rang against the metal walls. Any other time in the past three and a half years, I would have known he was imitating Mr. Hall. Now I knew he wasn't. As my skin went cold, I wondered whether he heard how much he sounded like his dead father.

An engine started just outside the hangar, Alec in the yellow Piper, taxiing away. That loud rumble canceled out Grayson's echoing voice. Grayson talked over the noise. "Nobody can crash this week, do you understand? If anybody crashes, all of this is for nothing. You can complain, Leah, but at some point—at *this* point—*I* am in charge, *I* am blackmailing *you,* and *shut up*." His gray eyes were narrow and his jaw was set. He'd backed down and apologized to me after his comment about getting a room. He wasn't backing down this time.

He stood. "Ready?"

He wasn't asking me whether I was ready. He was telling me I was. I stuffed the last of the biscuit into my mouth, threw away my garbage, and followed him over to the orange Piper. Automatically I took my place at the wing, like I'd done a million times with Mr. Hall. When I saw Grayson had control of the guide on the back wheel, I pushed the strut. One good shove got the plane rolling out of the hangar, and it didn't take much strength to guide it all the way out onto the tarmac.

In the distance, Alec was taking off. A lone figure in the grassy strip between the tarmac and the runway struggled with a hook on a rope between upright poles. A long banner stretched out behind him and rippled in the morning breeze. Zeke, Alec had said, but I didn't know this person. I didn't want to ask Grayson about him when we were both in this mood, but I had a right to know who would be setting up the banners I was risking my life to snag with an airplane. "Who's Zeke?"

"Somebody the unemployment office sent," Grayson called from behind the tail. His voice betrayed none of the emotion we'd let slip a few minutes before. "I don't have high hopes for him."

"That's not reassuring," I said. "But gosh, if you figured out how to hire a guy from the unemployment office? You *are* running this business."

Grayson half-turned to me, a warning, not sure whether I was making fun of him. I wasn't sure either.

"I just made a phone call," he muttered. Then he patted the tail of the airplane fondly. "Check this one out really well before you go. We haven't taken it up yet, so it hasn't run since . . . my dad died."

Only a slight hesitation let me know he felt a stab of pain

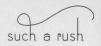

as he said the words. I felt the stab too and wished he'd left the sentence hanging. But I was impressed that he'd gotten it out.

He slipped back into the shadows of the hangar.

With a sigh, I turned to my airplane. And immediately cheered up. I was about to fly again.

But first I had a lot of things to check. I walked all around the plane, running my hand along the fuselage, looking for anything broken. I checked the oil. I pulled the towbar on the back of the plane, checked the ropes and hooks for towing the banners, and brought the hooks into the cockpit so I could throw them out the window at just the right time. I went back into the hangar, my eyes straining in the dark after the bright sunlight, and felt blindly in a toolbox for a dipstick. Grayson was in a far corner of the hangar, rummaging around the red Piper, and didn't say anything. I went back out and checked the gas. Then I hopped up into the seat and started the engine—my pulse raced with the roar—and taxied over to the gas pumps.

One of Mr. Simon's Air Tractors was parked there already. I hoped Mark wasn't in it. But of course he would be. That was my luck. As I drove closer, I saw I was right. Mark climbed out of the cockpit very slowly, like he was hungover. No surprise there either.

He glanced over at my plane. I faced the sun, and I hoped he hadn't seen me behind the glare off the windshield. He might not know I was flying for Grayson. I could shrink behind the controls and let him pump his gas and taxi away before I got out, thus avoiding another shitstorm altogether.

Settling back to wait, I pulled off my shirt and opened one of the windows to circulate the air in the already hot cockpit. Even though it was only the middle of April, it was summer. The trees across the runway were in full leaf. The grass where

Zeke wrestled with the banner was green and long, waving in the breeze like it was tapping its foot, waiting for somebody to wake up from a long winter's nap and cut it. Really the summer lasted here from April until October, at least. It was strange that the town filled with spring breakers in March, when the weather was so fickle, warm one day and wintry the next. It was strange that the town cleared of tourists in the warm September and October, when the gray tide rolled onto the tan beach under a blue sky without giving it much thought, unimpeded by drunk college students and dangerously sunburned children and obese tattooed exhibitionists. Summer in Heaven Beach went on whether people noticed or not.

I opened the other window. Along with warm air, the heavy scent of honeysuckle rushed in, and the growl of Alec's plane. He dropped out of the sky and dipped low over the grass, headed for the banner pickup between the poles. The sight was frightening. He looked like he was going too slow to remain airborne. But I knew from experience that this was what a banner pickup looked like, and there was no getting the human eye used to it. The nose pitched up sharply. The engine groaned. The plane slowed even more, perilously close to losing lift and dropping like a stone. The banner, which had been all but invisible sleeping in the grass, protested being roused. It wiggled and thrashed and finally, when it couldn't resist any longer, unfurled to its full length and height in a diagonal line behind Alec's still-climbing plane: 4$ COCKTALLS LIV BAND CAPTAN FRANKS LOUNG.

Wow, Zeke couldn't spell. If that episode back in the hangar was a sample of how Grayson would act for the rest of the week—an awful lot like his father—he was going to blow a gasket.

I turned back to Mark, who was knocking his head

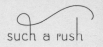

repeatedly against the gas pump. Something wasn't right—something other than Mark. I had pumped enough gas into airplanes that I could tell. Then I realized what it was. I jumped out of the cockpit. "Mark, whoa, whoa, whoa!"

He kept his forehead on the gas pump but turned to look at me. "Back so soon? I knew you'd change your mind."

I stopped the gas pump, carefully took the heavy nozzle out of Mark's gas tank, and hit the button for the electric motor to coil the hose back up. Quickly I checked the area for sparks, small fires, anything else unusual. While Mark watched, I uncoiled the grounding clip, pulled it across the asphalt, and attached it to the tailpipe of the crop duster. "Didn't your uncle teach you never to pump gas without grounding your airplane first? You could cause a spark and blow the whole place up."

"That never happens," he said.

Which was true. But only because everybody was grounding their airplanes before they pumped gas, except him.

"Do you understand what I'm telling you?" I insisted. "A spark that ignited the underground gas tank would take half the airport with it."

He grinned and shrugged. "Some way to go. Boom! At least it wouldn't hurt." He cocked his head to one side, then closed his eye like moving his head had hurt. He eased his head back to its normal position. "What are you doing in that dead guy's plane?"

The confrontation was inevitable now. Better to have it while nobody was watching. "I'm flying for Hall Aviation."

"No!" he shouted.

I shrank back at the violence of his reaction.

The next second, the violence was gone, and he gave me a charming smile. "Come fly for my uncle! I'll take you up . . ."

"When?" I prompted him.

"Soon. Patrick's having a party tonight. Come with me and we'll talk about it."

"Take that 'blond' friend of yours." I made finger quotes around her bleach-blond hair with black roots. "I have to get to work."

He must have been in a lot of trouble with his uncle and very late, because with only a few more pointed looks up and down my body, he taxied back to Mr. Simon's hangar.

Standing in the cockpit doorway and hauling the heavy hose on top of the wing, I gassed up my own plane on the Hall Aviation account, then carefully retracted the hose and the grounding wire. My heart sped faster and faster as I cranked the engine again, slipped on the headphones, and taxied to the end of the runway.

Here I paused, going through Mr. Hall's checklist in my mind. The hand controls and foot pedals moved the flaps and the rudder the way they were supposed to. I put my finger on every dial in the instrument panel in turn, making sure each was working. The meter confirmed I had a full tank of gas. The altimeter worked. Finally I ran up the engines and checked the magnetos. The plane vibrated like it would shake to pieces, but all three Pipers were like that. There wasn't much else I could do to find out whether the plane was working properly short of flying and crashing.

Pressing the button to broadcast over the radio, I announced my departure into the mike at my lips. My childish voice in my own headphones surprised me every time. I sounded nothing like a pilot.

Remembering what Grayson had told me about Mark's vindictive landing after a basketball game, I looked around for Mark. He'd parked the crop duster in front of Mr. Simon's hangar. The rest of the airport was clear. The skies were clear.

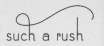

I looked a second time, because the only people saving me from crashing into another plane were the other pilot and me.

I turned from the taxiway onto the runway for the first time since the day Mr. Hall died. The wind was calm. Taking off wouldn't be hard. I had done it a thousand times. The butterflies in my stomach weren't from fear. They were from anticipation.

The hair on my arms stood up. I squeezed the controls to brace myself so I wouldn't shiver with the chill of wanting. Normal people got that feeling when they quit smoking cigarettes. I had gotten it then too.

Normal people did not get that feeling when faced with danger.

Here it came. I sped the plane down the runway. All I had to do was keep it fast and straight. The shape of the wings and airspeed and physics did the rest. The plane wanted to fly.

Suddenly it soared. The view out the front of the windshield changed gradually, so it was hard to tell how high I was. But out the side window, the plane separated from its shadow on the asphalt like Siamese twins cut loose from each other. The ground rushed away. The trees, so towering and textured before, flattened into uniform treetops like a field of grass. As I turned the plane, the ocean two miles away glinted into view. This time I couldn't suppress the shiver of pleasure.

I announced my banner pickup into the mike, cringing at the sound of my baby voice. No wonder the boys had made fun of me and Mark hadn't taken me seriously. I wouldn't hire a pilot who sounded like me, either. My anger drove me to throttle the plane higher than I needed to as I dove for the grassy strip beside the runway. Lining up with the posts where my banner waited, I raced along the ground, the plane almost meeting its twin shadow again.

At the Hall Aviation hangar, Grayson stood with his arms crossed, watching me.

At the Simon Air Agriculture hangar, Mark stood next to his plane with his hands on his hips, expecting me to fail.

I threw my first hook out the window.

Held the altitude steady.

Trusted my own instincts and the feel of the airplane, like Mr. Hall had taught me, trying not to overthink. Just feel.

The poles passed under me. I had no way of knowing whether the hook hanging from my plane had snagged the bar on the end of the banner. Not yet. I waited for the feel of it, refusing to lose my cool just because two boys who had never believed in me were staring me down.

When the plane had traveled a long way from the poles—too long, it seemed—I felt it. The engine whined higher and the entire plane resisted forward motion, as if it were a paddleball stretched to the end of its rubber band and bouncing backward. I throttled down to give the plane more power to tow the banner. I pulled the controls to point the nose up into heaven, a climb almost steep enough to stall. The banner anchored me to the ground with its weight. The plane shuddered like it would tear apart.

# seven

The engine groaned. But I kept going up. The shadow of the plane fell away in the grass. An invisible hand gave me a boost when the end of the banner left the ground, as if severing that last tie to the Earth was all we needed to propel us forward and up. I glanced down at Grayson, tiny on the ground now.

He wasn't standing with his hands on his hips anymore. He was standing with his hands on his head, like something had gone wrong. He put one hand down and then brought a dark shape to his lips—Mr. Hall's radio. His voice came over the frequency Hall Aviation used. "Leah. Zeke can't spell."

"Affirmative," I said into the mike. "He couldn't spell for Alec's banner either."

"Motherf—" Grayson clicked off his radio before he cussed over the public airwaves. But he was still talking animatedly to himself on the ground. He reared back with one hand like he would pitch the radio down the tarmac. *Don't throw the radio, Grayson.*

115

I'd flown far enough that I couldn't see him anymore when he came back over the frequency. "Leah and Alec, both of you come in and drop your banners so we can fix them. Keep an eye out for each other."

As I made the turn at the end of the airport, I could see Grayson again, looking across the tarmac at Mark. Mark was calling something through his cupped hands.

I concentrated on my flight again. Every flight might be my last, now that Hall Aviation and my job there were balanced so precariously. I circled the airport, dropped my banner, circled the airport some more while watching for Alec so I didn't crash into him, and at a signal from Grayson finally dipped down to pick up a correctly spelled banner that he'd supervised. I headed out to sea.

Even though the cockpit was hot with the unrelenting sun shining in, and the air was muggy with the scent of my sunscreen, my chest expanded and I finally felt like I could breathe as I flew over the ocean. The Atlantic lapped the Earth so close to my trailer. I could always feel it there, pulsing and cleansing two miles from me. But I rarely saw it now that I never flew. I caught a glimpse only if I got a ride somewhere and we happened to drive by it in the daytime. Now here it was, laid out for me farther than I could see in three directions. I couldn't even make out its true color for all the sunshine glinting off every wave, like the whole expanse was made of molten gold.

When I'd reached a safe distance from the shore, I turned and flew parallel to the beach. Swimmers wouldn't venture this far, so if I dropped the banner or crashed the whole plane into the water, I wouldn't kill them. But I was close enough to the beach that vacationers could read the banner from the sand.

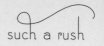

I flew past the flophouse end of the beach first. Garishly painted high-rise hotels crowded each other here. The actual flophouses were across the beach road where I couldn't see them, with no ocean view. I couldn't make out details of individual people, but I knew from experience that these folks on the beach were the whores, the girls from trailer parks inland who could easily have been mistaken for whores, the tattooed exhibitionists, the privates in the military with their huge young families, way too many children for one man to support on such low pay. The vinegar scent of beer and cigarette smoke and occasionally marijuana wafted on the air here, even around the children, even at eight in the morning. The party for these people started early and went on all day since they could only afford a night or two in a hotel, and then they'd have to go back home. The few times I'd spent a day, this was where I'd been taken.

As I flew toward the nicer end of town, the folks on the sand thinned out. The bright high-rise hotels shrank into smaller brick hotels farther apart, then thinned further into complexes of condos with shared pools, then individual mansions where each family had a pool all their own. This section of the beach went on for the longest. There was probably one person vacationing here for every hundred on the flophouse end. I could pick out these individual people. They walked along the beach at great distances from each other. Or they took their children out very early so they wouldn't get sunburned in the heat of the day, and watched them closely so nothing bad happened to them. Unlike at the flophouse end, these children did not have to take care of themselves.

All the while, I looked out for other planes. The Army base sometimes sent Chinook helicopters skimming across the water and frightening the tourists. The Air Force base sent out

F-16s. Occasionally a Coast Guard plane or helicopter would scoot past, on its way to save someone, or just cruising the beach like I was.

And then there were Alec and Grayson, flying in the same pattern as me. I heard Alec announcing over the radio that he was dropping his banner, circling around, and picking up a correctly spelled one. Then Mark took off to go on his crop-dusting run. I was surprised he announced himself according to protocol, considering what Grayson had told me about Mark using his plane as a weapon. Then Grayson took off and circled back for his banner.

Grayson, Alec, and I knew the sequence by heart because Mr. Hall had drilled it into us. We flew out to the ocean and made a slow turn at a safe distance from the shore, always keeping other people in mind. We headed from the flop-house end of the beach to the ritzy end. Where the population thinned to the point that there were a lot more birds than beachgoers and hardly anybody would see the banners, we made a slow, wide, careful turn, always aware of the heavy banner that the plane was not built to drag behind it.

We flew back down the beach the way we'd come, even farther from the shore now to avoid a collision with each other. It seemed impossible, but we had no radar, nothing to tell us another plane was coming except our own eyes, and planes weren't as visible head-on as they were from the side. Where the commercial section of the beach ended in a nature preserve and the crowds disappeared, we made another slow turn for the ritzy end again. That was the job, until we headed back to the airport for a break or lunch or a different banner.

Each time I passed Alec's plane, I thought about ways I could talk to him when we took a break around ten, excuses I could use to get into a conversation with him. I didn't really

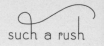

believe that I could land a date with him like Grayson wanted. But as long as I looked like I was making an effort, I figured Grayson would have no cause to complain, and he would stay off my case until the business folded and he went away.

Every time I passed Grayson's plane, I thought something completely different. Anger at him first. Then sympathy for the swirl of emotions he was obviously suffering through, all of them negative. In my experience, Grayson was wrong most of the time. But he felt very deeply, and I supposed that was why I'd always watched him. He said and did what I wanted to say and do but couldn't because I knew my place or I knew better. My sympathy for him didn't disappear just because he was using me.

Mostly their planes were too far away for me to see except as pinpoints in the sky. I concentrated on flying. I watched the few instruments for trouble. I listened to the engine, because a change in the pitch of its hum would be my first clue something had gone wrong with the plane or the banner. I relaxed into the rush of flight, my fingers and toes tingling with adrenaline at the knowledge that nothing but lift held me a thousand feet in the sky, and nothing below me could break my fall.

The truth was, this plane was not mine. It was tethered to the airport as surely as the pit bull was anchored to its trailer. But if I ever wanted to, just for a little while, braving dire consequences such as prison, I could head out over the Atlantic. Down to Florida. Up to New York. Wherever I wanted. I wasn't going to do it, but the thought that I *could* made me smile.

Around ten, Alec announced over the radio that he was dropping his banner at the airport, then landing his plane. I gave him a few minutes so I wouldn't crowd him, then headed in after him. Landing was a lot harder than taking off. The

plane wanted to fly. It didn't want to land. The asphalt rushing to meet the plane was potentially a more violent situation than the asphalt falling away underneath it. My eyes never stopped moving: over the instruments, all around me in the sky, on the ground, making sure Zeke was off the grassy strip before I roared across it to drop the banner. He couldn't spell worth shit and he might not have the sense to get out of my way, either.

The runway was clear. I lost altitude exactly like I was landing but without decreasing my airspeed. It was important that I get as close to the ground as possible before dropping the banner so it didn't float away on the wind and wrap itself around an expensive piece of equipment or knock somebody in the head with the heavy pole like it had knocked the glass door of the airport office last December. I didn't need help with this. I had done it a hundred times in practice and I operated by feel. Still, I heard Mr. Hall yelling in my head, *Drop drop drop.*

I dropped the banner and pulled the plane into a safe climb, unlike the dangerous half-stalling climb of a banner pickup. I would leisurely circle around the airport and land. The wind was calm, the weather clear. There was no reason to feel shaken. Mr. Hall's ghost was not in the cockpit in the seat behind me. I hadn't heard his voice in my head, only the memory of his voice. Yet my hands trembled on the controls.

I'd expected to have a reaction like this if I ever flew in the Cessna again, since Mr. Hall had so often ridden beside me, teaching me. I hadn't thought I'd react this way in one of the Pipers. Though he could have instructed me from the backseat, that would have added too much weight to tow a banner. He'd coached me on this kind of flying from the ground, over the radio. Especially dropping a banner.

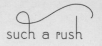

And especially landing the lightweight Piper with its tendency to spin in a ground loop. As I announced my final approach over the radio in my babyish voice, he would be standing on the tarmac with his radio—

And there he was.

No, that was Zeke, the banner guy who couldn't spell. He stood on the tarmac, watching my landing. I willed away the new, unwanted rush of adrenaline. No matter how ideal the conditions, flying was never safe, and I had to concentrate on landing this plane. I pushed Mr. Hall and the alarming sight of Zeke out of my mind as I lowered the plane to the asphalt and felt the gentle meeting of runway and rubber tires through the foot pedals.

The plane slowed to a crawl on the runway. I turned it and taxied toward the hangar, looking out all the while for Grayson landing behind me, or Mark landing. Wrecks happened on the taxiway as well as in the air. But the runway was clear. Zeke had moved to the grass, where he wrestled with the banner I'd dropped. I parked the plane outside the hangar, next to Alec's yellow Piper, and cut the engine. The propeller in front of me transformed from a circular blur back into a propeller. Silence flooded the cockpit.

I winced at the sudden rush of emotion now that the adrenaline was leaving me, and I squinted to keep from crying. I couldn't cry in an airplane out here on the tarmac. Pulling the headphones off my ears and over my thick hair, I opened the cockpit door and stepped way down onto the asphalt.

As I hurried through the dark hangar, Alec called "How was it?" from a corner. I couldn't see after the bright sunlight outside, and with tears crowding my eyes. "Good," I called back, still headed for the restroom in the back. With Alec in the hangar and Zeke on the runway and Grayson still up in

the air, the bathroom should be empty, but with my luck, it would be occupied. In that case, I didn't know where I would put these tears.

I could hardly see the doorknob in the shadows. I turned it and stepped into the pitch-black room and flicked on the light and closed and locked the door behind me and collapsed against the door. I could not make a noise. I shoved my fists into my eyes and screamed silently about everything I had lost.

Why couldn't Mr. Hall be here this week, running this business like always? His life had been small—coffee, corned beef sandwiches because he had grown up in Pennsylvania and still had a taste for Yankee delis, flying—but his life had been nice, and I had enjoyed sharing it with him. It wasn't fair that he'd had his son taken away and then died alone in his condo and waited half a day for a friend to find him.

That thought choked a noise out of me. I wrapped both arms around my waist and squeezed the air out of my chest so I wouldn't have any noise left in me to scream. I wished Mr. Hall were here. I wished I'd never felt I needed to let Mark into my life. I wished Grayson weren't forcing me to fake feelings for Alec. I wished I could fly without relying on anyone. Or relying only on Mr. Hall would be okay, if I could just have that back. I missed his gruff voice, his kind words, his powdery-smelling old-man cologne closed up in the cockpit with me. Dizzy with despair, I set my forehead against the door.

Someone knocked. I felt like I'd been shot in the head. I jumped even higher than I had when the delivery guy had knocked on the door of my trailer the night before.

"Leah," Alec called. "Open up."

"Just a sec." Glancing in the mirror above the sink, I saw there was no way to disguise that I'd been bawling my eyes

such a rush

out. I ran water into my cupped hands anyway and splashed it over my face.

"Come on, Leah," Alec called. "I feel the same way."

I paused with a paper towel halfway to my face and considered my red-rimmed eyes in the mirror. I wouldn't convince him to ask me on a date while I looked this way, but I had a hard time caring when I felt like death. I unlocked and opened the door and walked into his arms.

"Shhh," he said, stroking my hair as I sobbed into his T-shirt. "I cried yesterday, the first time I went up. Grayson had gone to talk to you about working for him. I was alone so it was okay." He squeezed me gently. "You can hear my dad yelling at you, can't you?"

I nodded against his shirt. "Sorry. I'm getting you all wet." He felt shitty enough about his dad. I didn't mean to make things worse for him. The last thing he needed was to comfort somebody else. I put both hands on his chest and pushed away.

"Nah, I probably got my sweat all over *you*. Too hot for this." He stepped away from me and pulled his T-shirt off over his head.

The back of the hangar was dim after the bright sunlight and the bright bathroom, and my eyes seemed to jump around in the dimness, unable to focus completely on his smooth skin, his muscled chest and arms, his compact body.

"I'm going out for a smoke," he said. "Want one?"

I did. It would be a great way to bond with him and take another step toward him asking me out, but I couldn't. I'd promised his dad that I would stop smoking. I *had* stopped, and I didn't want to be tempted now, when I felt weak. "No thanks," I croaked. "I'd better stay in here and cool down."

He reached out and rubbed his hand up and down my bare

123

arm a few times, soothing. In the dim light, he was monochromatic, his skin and blond hair the same color.

I followed him into the main part of the hangar. While he kept going out the wide door to the tarmac, I stopped in front of an electric fan and let it blow on my bare stomach. The sweat underneath my bikini top turned cold.

"Good job, Leah," Grayson called over the noise. "Nice acting."

I was too stunned and hurt and angry to speak, but not too angry to look for him. He was in Mr. Hall's tiny office, typing on a computer keyboard, gazing at the screen. He didn't even care what horrified expression passed across my face.

The words *I quit* formed on my lips. Also, *You are cruel.* I took a breath to say them.

An alt-rock song, strange and tinny sounding, sang in his office. He picked up his phone and watched the screen for several seconds as if he thought it might change.

"What's wrong?" I asked. I didn't want to care, but his face had gone white, like someone else had died.

He looked up at me in surprise. He'd forgotten I was standing there, though he'd lobbed an ugly insult at me ten seconds before. Whoever was calling owned all his attention. He shook his head almost imperceptibly—at me, maybe, but I wasn't sure. He finally put the phone to his ear and managed a "Hi, Mom!" that sounded a lot more cheerful than he looked.

I turned my body so the fan cooled my back. My ears were out of the wind, though, so I could hear him as he said, "No, everything is good. The plan is good. He's not making things any easier, but he's doing what I told you he'd do."

Nonchalantly I turned my head in the darkness so I could see Grayson in the bright office. Normally he acted comfortable with his tall body. He took up a lot of space when standing. Sitting, he spread himself out over a chair and the surrounding area. But as he sat in the chair behind the desk in the office, he looked half his size, knees drawn close, ankles crossed on the floor, one arm hugging himself, head down and cradled in the palm that held the phone. "Alec told you that?" he asked.

I didn't want to get in his business. The more I did, the more he was likely to get in mine, which was how I'd gotten in this mess in the first place. But I was so alarmed at how he looked that I watched him unabashedly now, waiting for a different angle so I could glean some information about what had gone so horribly wrong that he curled into a tight ball.

He glanced up at me, and I thought I was busted.

But he couldn't see me very well, out in the dusky hangar. Almost as soon as he looked up, he looked down again, reabsorbed into the conversation, as if I weren't there. "I'm doing everything I can. I'm doing some other things you don't know about."

To keep Grayson from blackmailing me, I'd been hoping for a way to blackmail him right back. Here it was. Whatever Grayson was trying to get Alec to do, their mom was in on it. I felt sure I was the part of the plan Grayson hadn't told her about. She was a middle-class mom, after all. She'd been married to Mr. Hall once upon a time. I couldn't imagine that she would approve of Grayson forcing me to date Alec, no matter what the reason was. All I had to do was threaten Grayson that I would tell her, just like he'd threatened to tell my mom about me.

But as I thought this through in my head, I realized there were big holes in my plan. I had no way to get to Wilmington to talk to this lady. I could steal Grayson's phone, punch the speed-dial marked *Mom,* and call her. Then a strange girl

would be calling her to say her middle-class son had black-mailed me to date her other middle-class son, months after the deaths of their father and brother. She would call the police. When the cops cruised to my address and saw where I lived, they would arrest me for extortion. I lived in a trailer and people assumed the worst about me.

"Love you too. Bye." He clicked off the phone and stared at it in his hand for a few moments. Glanced at his watch. Scooted back the chair with a rattle of ancient casters and walked out of the office. Stopped short when he saw me standing there.

While he was on the phone, he had forgotten *again* that I was there. He'd even forgotten about insulting me down to my very bones.

He realized I'd overheard him on the phone with his mom.

He was afraid he'd given away why he wanted me to go out with Alec.

He went back over his words, calculating whether or not he was safe.

I saw it all in his face, surprisingly easy to read when he wasn't wearing his shades—which was probably why he wore them so much, like his whole life was a poker game and he was trying to prevent himself from telling his hand. I just wished I really had overheard something that gave away his secret. I still didn't have a clue.

I spun on my flip-flop and headed farther into the hangar to refill my water bottle from the fountain, hoping the whole time that he wouldn't hurl another stone at me. I wasn't sure I could take it. Then I escaped back outside to my airplane.

# eight

Grayson had lunch delivered to the hangar. My empty refrigerator must have given him a shock, and he wanted to make sure I didn't faint in flight and crash his plane. *We're not crashing any planes this week.*

While we ate, I made another attempt to flirt with Alec where Grayson could see. Alec was friendly as always but hard to flirt with. I tried to talk to him about the alt-rock music I loved so much blasting from a speaker in the corner. He said it was Grayson's. Alec tried to explain to me that he preferred country music but his player didn't dock with the contraption they used in the hangar. Soon I would have to admit I'd never owned a contraption, a player, or a computer, and I had no idea how to download music. Grayson spent most of the hour in Mr. Hall's office, poring over ledger books.

Late in the afternoon, I let Grayson and Alec land first, hoping they'd want to pack up for the day and get out of there, and they would hardly notice me. As I came in for my own

landing, scanning the runway, I did a double take as a figure crossed the tarmac. Mr. Hall was my first thought—the same disorienting shock I'd received that morning. Then Zeke. But Grayson had sent him home for the day after we snagged our last banners. Because I'd been thinking about Grayson and Alec, they passed through my mind. As I came closer, though, I saw it was Leon, who was manning the airport office for the week while I was flying. He held up the airport's cell phone.

I didn't get phone calls. My mind spun to the only possibility: my mother was in trouble. She'd gotten in trouble before. But when she did, she didn't call me at the airport, because I couldn't help her. She only let me know through a friend of the moment or a begrudging ex-boyfriend who stopped by the trailer that she wouldn't be home for a few more days.

I taxied my plane to the hangar and cut the engine. I didn't want to answer the phone. But sitting in the cockpit and hiding from the phone would be weird. I opened the door and took it. "Thanks. I'll bring it back over," I told Leon, who was already retreating.

"Good riddance," he called over his shoulder, like the conversation he'd had with the person on the other end of the line had been difficult.

I glanced at the screen. A local number. "Hello?"

"What did he have to do, FedEx the phone to you?" Molly demanded. "I've been waiting for five hours. Jesus! Did Alec ask you out yet?"

"No," I said, relieved the call was from Molly and nobody was in jail. "All's well that ends well."

"Nah, I've got an idea. Why don't you and Alec bring the one with a rudder up his ass, what's his name?"

I giggled. "Grayson."

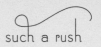

"Right. Bring Mr. Happy and we'll all go to the club to-night. That way, you and I will get some spring break. Grayson will see you're dutifully trying to screw his brother. I'll be there to chaperone and make sure nothing happens and you stay safe from these perverts."

"Um." It sounded good in theory. I actually felt better just thinking about leaning on Molly throughout the night. Nothing these boys threw at me could be so bad if Molly was around.

Grayson came out of the hangar then. His final flight must have been broiling. Like Alec, he'd stripped off his T-shirt. His muscles were tanned and hardened—not from working hard, but maybe from playing hard, as Mr. Hall had told me. Mountain climbing with his friends whenever he could get away. Playing basketball for his school whenever he wasn't benched for mouthing off to the coach. His wavy blond hair blazed almost white in the bright sunlight, darker around his ears where it was wet with sweat and kinking into tighter curls.

He'd forgotten to put his shades back on when he came outside, so he squinted almost blindly at me and tripped over something as he made his way to my airplane. Strange that I felt I was suddenly seeing him more clearly than I ever had, now that he couldn't see me at all. Blinking, he opened the cockpit door, handed me something, closed the door, and headed for the hangar. His skin shone with sweat.

"Um," I said into the phone again. A catastrophic vision formed in my mind of Grayson and Molly at the club, hook-ing up.

But Molly was having a little fun and getting me out of a tight spot, as usual. She had no designs on Grayson.

Of course, she had not seen him. Yet.

"Um."

"So you've said," she broke into my thoughts. "Just vote yes. Isn't this better than going out with Alec alone, if he ever asks you? What if he's a horndog? He already thinks you're the airport whore, so where does that leave you? Flat on your back, missy."

I laughed then. Maybe this date would work out after all. It was hard to stay depressed about my situation while talking with Molly, who couldn't imagine having problems like mine. "Yes. I don't know how to introduce this date idea to these boys, though."

"Give the phone to the sane one. Alec. I'll take care of it. I'll convince him I'm a vivacious airhead and he has to follow along with my schemes."

"Don't get too far out of your comfort zone."

"Ha."

"And listen," I said. "You can't let on to Grayson that you know what he's making me do. He is dead serious about this shit. I respect his ability to screw me over."

"Roger that."

"Hold on." I hopped out of the cockpit and followed Grayson across the strip of white sunlight, into the shadowy hangar. I couldn't see, but I heard water running. The farther I walked into the hangar, the more clearly I saw Alec bent over the industrial sink, pouring water over his head with a hose. "Alec?"

"Hey." He felt around for a nearby towel until I handed it to him, and he straightened while scrubbing his hair dry. "What's up?"

"This is hard to explain, but my friend Molly is on the phone and she wants to talk to you. I mean, everything about my friend Molly is hard to explain. Here."

He'd been smiling already. His eyes smiled too as he held

out his hand for the phone and put it to his ear. "Hello, Leah's friend Molly."

I wanted to hear what he said, but it seemed awkward to stand there and listen in. As I wandered away across the hangar, I looked down and saw I'd been holding something in my other hand the whole time. While I'd been sitting in my airplane talking with Molly, Grayson had come out to give me a check for my first day's pay.

He was in Mr. Hall's office again, the overhead light spilling into the darker hangar. I didn't want to follow him in there and have this conversation with him, but I had to. I shuffled to the doorway and knocked gingerly on the doorframe.

He looked up from his computer but didn't gesture for me to come in. I walked in anyway and sat in the empty chair. "Thanks for the check. Could you cash it for me?"

"*Cash* it for you," he said, not even a question, just a restatement of my statement, which he found ridiculous.

"The airport cashes my checks for me," I said in my defense. "I can't get to the bank very often." Even when my mom spent time at the trailer with a boyfriend who had a car and we could run errands, I didn't ask them to take me by the bank. I didn't like to remind my mom I earned money. Then my paycheck would never make it into my account.

Without another word, he took a pen out of a cup on the desk and handed it to me. I endorsed the check and gave it back to him. He opened the desk drawer with the cash box. While he counted out the amount of my check, he asked, "What do you do with your money in between trips to the bank? Stash it in your mattress?"

"I have a better hiding place than that," I said, "but I can't tell you what it is. You might tell Mark, since the two of you are so chummy."

One of his eyebrows went up. Now that he wasn't wearing his shades, I saw the full meaning of that expression in his face. Disdain for trash. "You're afraid he'll steal your money, but you dated him?"

"I've dated for less," I said pointedly. "Or at least tried to get a guy to ask me out. I don't understand why it's not enough for you to blackmail me. You keep insulting me too. I *do* have a limit, Grayson, and you're trying hard to find it."

He held the stack of bills out to me, complete with a few coins on top. "I saw you talking to Mark this morning."

I pocketed the cash before Grayson could take it away. "I'm not allowed to talk to Mark now? He hadn't grounded his airplane when he was pumping gas. He was about to blow the whole airport up."

"That sounds about right." Grayson stared at me from behind the computer like he was waiting for me to leave.

Looking for Alec, I glanced through the dark hangar to the bright sunlight shining on the planes outside. "Your brother's on the phone with my friend Molly. We're going to a touristy dance club in downtown Heaven Beach tonight."

Grayson frowned at me like he was fifty-two years old. "Do they serve alcohol at this club?"

"Yes, it's eighteen to get in, twenty-one to drink."

"Do you have a fake ID? You and Alec can't drink," he said quickly.

"So you've said."

"You can't be hungover and fly," he went on as if I hadn't spoken. "And you can't stay out late. We start work at seven again tomorrow morning."

"Molly knows that already."

He bit his lip, looked longingly at his computer like he

would rather spend the night with it than go out. Then he said, "I'm going with you."

"We already figured you were going with us like a double date from hell. Molly thinks we're two girls going out with two hot guys. She has no idea we all hate each other."

Grayson sucked in his breath, watching me, like he was going to say something.

He let out his breath in a huff. "Come help me get the airplanes in."

Alec was just hanging up with Molly on a long laugh. The three of us pushed the Pipers back into the hangar, fitting them around each other. The hangar seemed huge with only the Cessna in it, but very cramped when filled with four airplanes.

After calling good-bye to Alec (but not Grayson), I stopped in at the airport office to give the phone back to Leon, then hiked back to my trailer. Took another shower and stood on the toilet again, leaning way over to glimpse the only clubbing dress I owned in the mirror. I wanted Grayson to know I was trying to look cute for Alec.

As I examined my smoky makeup and cheap dress, jealousy of Molly came creeping back. She would be wearing a sexy clubbing dress her mother had bought her at a boutique on a shopping trip to Atlanta. It would not be the worst thing in the world if Grayson fell for her. I loved Molly, and although I was very angry with Grayson all over again for the way he'd treated me about cashing the check, something about him made me watch him, keep track of his whereabouts, wish the best for him. Maybe I should wish for him to be with Molly.

But my stomach reminded me I hadn't eaten since lunch and twisted in knots at the thought of Grayson unexpectedly

falling for Molly tonight. No matter how well I wished them, I didn't want them together.

My gaze drifted from my makeup to my hair hanging in wet ringlets. Drying it curly with a diffuser, as usual, would take ten minutes. Blowing it out and straightening it with my thrift store flat-iron would take forty-five—which is why I never did this, though straight was the style at school.

But I had forty-five minutes before the boys picked me up. Picturing Grayson's first glance at Molly with her long, sleek auburn hair shining in the sun, I fished underneath the sink for my fat round brush.

Arms aching from holding the brush and the dryer over my head, I was sitting in one of the plastic chairs outside the trailer when Alec pulled up in his car. I hadn't wanted to get all dusty, or to sit listening to the pit bull while I waited. But waiting outside was better than having him climb the cement blocks and knock on the door. I crossed my legs and let my skirt ride way up my thighs, hoping this would prove a distraction from the lichen-covered trailer. Then I hopped up and skipped across the gravel before he could turn the car off.

Grayson, looking down and thumbing his phone, climbed out of the passenger side. He glanced up at me—and squared his shoulders, taking a longer look at me than he'd intended.

Though I'd obviously gotten his attention, he didn't comment on my hair. He said nothing at all. He left the car door open for me and slid into the backseat.

Fine. I eased onto the front seat he'd vacated and told Alec, "Hi!"

"Hey!" Alec exclaimed with a brilliant smile. "Wow, your hair is so different! You look beautiful."

"Thank you!" I didn't want him to look too closely at his surroundings as he turned the car around, but I couldn't think

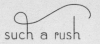

of anything else to say. After spending all day at the same risky job, we still didn't seem to have much in common. I settled for tugging my skirt down—just a little—drawing attention to my thighs. Then I pulled my strangely smooth hair over one shoulder so it wouldn't hide my cleavage. I flipped down the sunshade and checked my perfect makeup in the mirror, like an idiot. I watched myself grin, and I glanced over at him.

He was staring at my cleavage. Score! Then, pulling to a stop at the highway and waiting for traffic to pass, he looked around us and made the only comment he could think of. "Hey, a real washateria! I didn't know those still existed. Maybe I'll walk over from the airport and wash clothes sometime."

*You lame-ass.* I interrupted his pitiful attempt to make conversation with the trailer park girl before he embarrassed himself further. "It's broken. All the dryers have been broken for a while. The last washer broke last week."

"Why don't you ask the owner to fix it?" he asked in the logical tone of someone who'd never had a landlord.

"The owner doesn't care," I explained patiently. "I'm the only one still doing laundry here. Everybody else goes to the washateria closer to town, by the library."

"Why don't you go there too?"

"Because I don't have a car."

He tilted his head back, half of a nod, considering. He lowered his chin again as he asked, "But why do *they* go there, when this one is so much closer?"

"Because all of the washers and dryers are broken." I wasn't sure why I found this discussion so annoying. I had discussions like this with guidance counselors sometimes, and with Molly more frequently, and my explanation of why I did things a certain way always came out bitter. Rich people didn't want to hear bitter.

Alec pulled onto the highway. I looked out the window at Heaven Beach passing by. I saw it so rarely that I never got tired of looking, even on the flophouse side of town. The hour was late for beachgoers and early for partygoers. But it was spring break, so the sidewalks were crowded with sunburned, tattooed, half-naked people sipping frozen cocktails from huge plastic cups. The scent of frying food drifted through the windows, and the smell of coconut tanning oil that only people who'd never heard of cancer would use.

Grayson's phone made a sound directly behind me. He probably had a message from a girl he wasn't blackmailing.

Alec made a comment occasionally. Unlike Grayson, he knew how not to be rude. But when we were halfway to Molly's, even he was running out of words. He reached forward and turned up the volume on the car radio, which was tuned to a country station.

Soon we reached the nice end of the beach. I'd been here before, mostly eating at the café with Molly or crashing at her house for a few hours. I hadn't gotten used to it. It looked like beach towns on TV, not real life. If I hadn't just ridden in the car for twenty minutes, I would have thought we'd arrived in a different country. The palms were the same species, but spaced out, aligned, planted on purpose. The buildings weren't made of corrugated metal. They were rock and stucco with thick foundations, built to withstand hurricanes. There was grass and it was green. The sprinklers were on at several condo complexes we passed. The sprinkler streams weren't always directed correctly. Water sprayed across the wide sidewalks and into the street.

The sound of water beating on the hood startled Grayson. A *thunk* sounded behind Alec's seat. Grayson bent over, his T-shirt riding up his tanned back, feeling around for his phone.

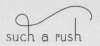

"Is that your friend?" Alec asked me as he pulled into the parking lot of Molly's café. Her long, sleek hair was not as long and sleek as mine. But her dress was low-cut and obviously expensive. It's hard to explain the look of expensive, but there was something about the way the fabric fell exactly right. She wasn't model pretty, but she looked like a model in her glam dress, standing outside the expensive new café built to resemble an old beach shack. At least, she looked like a model while she wore a pensive expression, shading her eyes to gaze down the road for us. Then she recognized me in the car, and she waved frantically, like I might not see her standing there. Her boobs jiggled.

I didn't dare glance behind me to see whether Grayson was a witness to this.

"In the flesh," I told Alec dryly.

He got the joke, I guessed, and he laughed.

She skittered over to the driver's side in her high heels and knocked on Alec's window until he opened it. "Hi! I'm Molly!" She shook his hand.

"I'm Alec," I heard him say. I couldn't see his face, but he sounded like he was grinning, and she certainly was grinning back at him.

Then she opened the back door and bounced onto the seat. "Hi! I'm Molly!" She held out her hand to Grayson.

I didn't want to see this, so I faced forward as Alec pulled back onto the road. But I listened as Grayson said, "Nice to meet you, Molly. I'm Grayson." He sounded like he was smiling too.

"The boss man!" she exclaimed.

Grayson chuckled. It was the first time I'd heard that sound in months.

"Hi! I'm Molly!" she said again. Something punched me in the shoulder. I realized she was talking to me.

"So I heard," I said, shaking her hand over the seat. But I smiled at her and tried to telegraph to her, *I'm glad you're here.*

"You must be Rapunzel. My God, girl, your hair is longer than Francie's!"

I took my hand back. She'd inadvertently insulted me, linking me with her rich friend who hated me most. I wasn't so proud of my hair achievement anymore.

Oblivious, Molly turned to Grayson again. "You know this club has a dress code. No unwashed pilots."

Grayson and Alec both burst into laughter. It was amazing how alike they sounded when they laughed.

"Do I smell that bad?" Grayson asked.

"You don't smell," Molly said, "but you look like you've spent the past week outdoors."

"Do I look like I just hosed off my head?" Alec asked, watching her in the rearview mirror. I wanted to tell him to keep his eyes on the road, but I just grinned along with their good times.

"Mebbe," Molly said in a funny voice that was an imitation of something.

"We're headed to shower and change, if that makes you feel better," Alec called.

"You're showering for me," Molly said, "but you weren't going to shower for Leah? I guess everybody knows what a dirty girl she is."

Behind me, Grayson cleared his throat.

Alec looked over at me and smiled. "Really?"

I shook my head and opened and closed my hand like Molly's yapping mouth. In truth, I was so happy to have her yapping, comparing me to her friend Francie, even making jokes at my expense. It beat country radio and silence.

"And here we are." Alec parked the car at a beautiful condo,

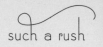

white stucco and Mexican tile surrounded by bright green grass and palm trees. "It'll only take me a sec to shower and change." He asked me, "Do you want to come up?"

"Is this . . ." I faltered.

"Where my dad lived," Alec said, confirming what I was thinking.

And where he'd died. I couldn't go in there. But I didn't want to be rude to Alec, or make Grayson think I wasn't following instructions. "I'll just wait for you," I said with a big smile.

Alec frowned, but all he said was, "I'll be right back." He left the engine and the air conditioner running as he hopped out of the car and jogged up to the building.

"What's up with that?" Grayson asked me from the backseat. "Don't tell me you've never been here before."

# nine

I looked over my shoulder at him and had absolutely nothing to say to that.

Molly peeked at me from behind Alec's seat. "God, Grayson, what's that supposed to mean? She hasn't looked at me that way since she and I first met two years ago. And when we first met it was *not* good."

I almost laughed, but I couldn't. Grayson's words weighed my face down, my whole brain.

Finally he said, "While we're waiting, I guess I might as well go ahead and change too. I'm just across the street." He opened his door.

"What do you mean, you're across the street?" Molly asked. "There's nothing over there but beach and shacks."

He grinned at her. "I'm in a shack."

"You *are*?" Molly yelled. "I want to see!"

"Okay, come on."

He and Molly both got out of the car. I wasn't sure

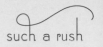

whether I was supposed to go with them or wait for Alec. Grayson might get mad at me if I didn't wait. He might lob another insult at me. But I wanted to go. It seemed a little too easy right at that moment for Grayson and Molly to pair off and have private time at his shack of some kind. The thought of this made my stomach hurt worse than the thought of kissing Alec.

Molly peered through the windshield at me and motioned with her head for me to follow her.

At the same time, Grayson startled me by opening my door. "Come on, Leah. Alec will know where we are. Get the key."

Carefully I turned off the ignition—I figured this worked the same in a car as in a plane—and slid out after them.

We started across the street, but Molly stopped dead on the center stripe and gaped up at the sky. "Wow, look at that sunset!"

It wasn't a pretty sunset. The colors were as expected: violet clouds, bright orange and pink underneath, against the pale blue sky. But the clouds were high cirrus, wispy, and crossed with the contrails of F-16s, a colorful glowing mess. I said, "It looks like God barfed a rainbow."

"So sentimental," Grayson said under his breath.

Molly shrieked laughter. "Charming." She swung her glam purse on its long strap and whacked me in the ass. "So, Grayson, why do you have a condo *and* a shack?"

"This property has been in my family a long time," he said. "The highway follows the original Native American trail." He pointed north, where the road disappeared under wide-branching water oaks. "Right here it runs so close to the ocean that you're not allowed to build a house on the beach side, but you can build a shack. My grandparents moved here from Pennsylvania when beachfront property was a lot cheaper.

They owned a shack plus a house. Later they sold the house, which was demolished to build condos. They kept one condo unit, and they kept the shack."

"Sweet!" Molly said. "You must be loaded."

I couldn't believe the comments Molly got away with sometimes. Maybe it was her matter-of-fact delivery. Or maybe, in this case, Grayson liked her.

Whatever the reason, he just smiled at her, almost shyly in the streetlights. "Not anymore. My dad sank most of that money into the business. Banner towing doesn't pay all that great."

"If your family is from here," Molly said, "did you live here before your parents got divorced?"

I cringed. I guessed, sometime in the two years Molly and I had been friends and I'd crushed on the boys, that I'd told her about their family situation. I didn't want Grayson to know this.

He didn't seem to notice, though. Again, Molly got away with that nosey question. "Yes," he said, "we lived here."

"You must know a lot of people at our high school," Molly said. "We'll probably run into them when we're out partying this week. It will be so weird, like a class reunion!"

I was still puzzling through the idea that all of us were going to be partying together all week—or maybe Molly just meant herself and Grayson—when he laughed. "I didn't know *you* until today."

"I just moved here two years ago," Molly said. "My purpose in life is to keep mean girls away from Leah."

"Mean girls don't like Leah?" Grayson asked, looking around at me.

"I think it's the hair," I said.

"You *always* think it's the hair," Molly said.

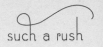

"It's all I've got."

Grayson looked at me again. This time his gaze traveled from my hair down, and he let me see that he was looking. What he meant by this was that he thought I was beautiful, it was *not* just my miraculous hair, and we shouldn't get distracted from our true love by the pesky detail that he was blackmailing me into dating his brother.

Right. I hung back and let him and Molly walk together up the wooden ramp to the shack. I'd never had a chance with Grayson anyway. All I wanted to do was fly. I needed to remember that or I was going to get myself in even more trouble.

The shack was so tiny that I was thinking Molly and I should stay outside while Grayson showered. But Molly followed him right through the door, exclaiming, "This is so cool! You can hear the ocean. When you wake up in the morning, it's *right there.*" She must have thought I was going to hang outside myself, because she stood in the doorway, put her hand behind her back, and wiggled her fingers at me, coaxing me in. I didn't want to cause a scene or seem weird, so I stepped into the shack behind her.

"It's pretty cool," Grayson agreed, looking around. The shack was made of weathered, smoothed boards on the ceiling, walls, and floor. A futon took up one wall, a surfboard leaned against another, and a mountain bike hung from hooks in the ceiling. An air conditioner took up half of one window, but it was off, and the sound of the ocean filled the tiny room.

"I guess the condo has stuff you're missing here," Molly said. "Like a kitchen. Why did one of you take one place and one of you take the other? It seems like you guys would want to be together, whichever place you chose. You're not getting along?"

"You could say that." Grayson opened his hands. "You know, our dad died recently." This time he didn't hesitate as he said it.

Molly nodded, oblivious to what a touchy subject this still was. She sounded like she was consoling an elderly neighbor on the death of his even more elderly father, a natural and expected ending, as she said, "Leah told me. I'm sorry."

"And our older brother died," Grayson said. "We've been through bad times before, but never without our brother. He was . . ." Grayson splayed his fingers and looked through the wooden ceiling toward heaven for an explanation. ". . . the leader. The peacekeeper. Alec and I didn't realize that until we talked about running this business together. We have no idea how to get along. We can't even order a pizza without being at each other's throats."

Grayson changed as he said this, from an angry, bullying boy into a kind young man with a horrible problem. He looked taller in the small room. The bare bulb cast dark shadows under his eyes.

Molly had been the one to draw these feelings and this truth out of him. I'd known him three and a half years. Molly had known him five minutes.

She made a joke of it. "Good thing you and Alec are living apart this week, then. And I in my infinite wisdom insisted that we should go out together."

"It's okay." He dismissed the problem with a wave designed to make her feel better, something he would *never* have done for me. He told her, "We don't have Jake, but at least we have someone to run interference so we don't need to talk to each other. We have you. And you." He finally looked at me.

His expression turned uneasy as he read my face. I don't

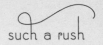

know what he saw there—my stupid jealousy of Molly, maybe, or my sense that he'd betrayed me in confiding all this to her instead of me, when he and I had never been friends in the first place.

He jerked his thumb over his shoulder. "I'll just be a minute. Make yourselves comfortable. Or try." He disappeared into a bathroom carved into the corner.

"Come on." Claustrophobic in the shrinking room, I pushed Molly all the way through the shack to another door that opened onto a porch.

Weathered stairs led down to a hundred yards of clean sand pitted with dry footprints. Beyond that lay the dark blue ocean. "Want to walk down there?" I asked her.

"God, no. I've been at the beach all day. Sick of it." She sank behind me into a wooden lounge chair and closed her eyes. I waited for her to tell me her opinion of the boys. She was meeting them for the first time, and they were hot. Their suffering made them dreamy. She would want to tell me this and scold me for keeping them to myself all this time. But she didn't say a word. She must be very tired from her long, hard day of lying on the beach.

I turned for the ocean again, inhaled the clean scent of it. Folding my arms on the porch rail and setting my chin on my arms, I watched the white waves slowly roll in. Like everything, the ocean looked completely different in person than it looked from the air. Hypnotized by its beauty, I forgot where I was and why. I jumped when Alec put his hand on my bare shoulder and asked, "Ready?"

Grayson's insistence that we have an early night worked out well. When we arrived at the club, we could still get in the door. The place was already packed, though, mostly with

strangers, lots of them seedy, and a few seniors from my high school, all of them drunk.

I was in a mood to break my no-drinking rule again because of the stress I'd been under that day and the situation I was in with these boys. But Grayson took up residence at a graffiti-covered pillar, watching all of us for bad behavior. So Molly and I danced to the throbbing beat under the spinning colored lights instead. Alec played along with us, doing an unembarrassed white boy dance. Molly asked Grayson to dance three times. He refused. She tried to send me over to ask him. I wouldn't go. I was having a lot of fun dancing with Molly and dancing with Alec, who was acting like a not-too-interested boy/friend, something I'd never had before. I didn't want to ruin it by dragging Grayson over—or having him turn me down.

Finally we took a break. Grayson had ordered food for everybody. When I opened my billfold to give him money for it, Alec frowned at me and shook his head. We found an empty table a group had just vacated on the crowded deck outside, overlooking the ocean. Molly went back inside to grab a strawberry daiquiri using her cousin's old ID. Alec whispered that he'd get me a soda.

Which left Grayson and me snacking alone at the table, if you could call it alone when we were surrounded by four hundred and fifty people. I expected him to insult me over the noise. But he watched the crowd with a half-smile on his face, a lot like the half-smile Alec wore most of the time. On Alec it was the default setting. On Grayson it meant he was happy.

I leaned across the table and said, "You're back."

"What?" He jerked his head toward me, surprised that I'd spoken, losing part of the smile.

"You seem like yourself again," I explained. "The way

you've been acting, I thought the old Grayson was gone forever."

He nodded. "I think he might be," he said slowly. "I mean, if I were the type of person who talked about himself in the third person. I think he might be."

"You think he might be gone forever?" I asked. "Or you think he might be back?"

"Gone."

That one word sank deep into me like a hot rock disappearing into a snowbank somewhere up north. I noticed again how tired he was, how he sat low on his stool, broad shoulders hunched, with dark smudges of fatigue under his gray eyes. I felt lost on his behalf. I felt lost myself. As we shared a look of understanding across the table, the drunk spring-breakers and colored lights faded on one side of us. I was more aware of the blackness off the railing on our other side, a black sky and a black ocean we knew were there but couldn't even see.

"I'm sorry about Jake," I blurted.

Grayson didn't take his eyes off me. His only reaction was a little tic of his jaw.

"I talked to your dad every day about what happened to Jake, but I never told you. I guess I never saw you again until your dad's funeral. And . . ." I could feel my cheeks burning, but now that I'd started, I couldn't stop until I'd blabbed everything. ". . . I'm sorry about you and Alec. I wish you'd tell me what exactly is going on between you and why I have to date him. You spill this whole story to Molly when you've just met her, but I've been right here the whole time and you treat *me* like the stranger. Less than a stranger. Like the enemy. What did you mean when you acted incredulous that I'd never been to your dad's condo?"

Grayson's lips parted. He watched me for a moment before

he found words. As he spoke, his voice was so quiet that I could barely hear him over the music. "I was talking to *you* about Alec and Jake."

"You were looking at Molly," I accused him.

"I was talking to you." He looked down at his half-eaten food. "Sometimes it's hard for me to look at you. Just like it's hard for me to be here. At the shack, at the condo, at the hangar."

I understood now. He associated me with the tragedy of his family. He would take what he thought he needed from me in order to save Alec. That's all I was good for.

Molly cackled somewhere in the crowd. I couldn't make out what she was saying. As she and Alec emerged from the throng, the first word I understood was, "Cocktalls!"

"I was telling Molly about Zeke losing the spelling bee today," Alec explained, sliding me a soda and slipping onto the stool beside me.

I grinned at him. If I concentrated hard enough on joining his light-hearted conversation with Molly, maybe the tension between Grayson and me would ease, and I would be able to breathe again.

"I can just see the tourists on the beach," Molly said, "squinting up at the sign. 'Cock . . . talls.' They probably thought it was for real. Some new drink invented by the tourist-trap bars on the boardwalk. They would be bubble gum flavored! They would come with a piece of bubble gum on a toothpick as a garnish instead of a lemon!"

"Spoken like the daughter of restaurateurs," I said, trying to get back into the swing of her banter.

"Those misspelled banners cost us a lot of time in the air," Grayson grumbled.

I could see why he wasn't laughing. The contracts Mr. Hall

had made with these businesses specified that we'd fly their banners for a certain number of hours a day. When Alec and I dropped our banners, we circled above the airport, waiting for Zeke to spell everything correctly. Then we picked them back up, but we had to tack that many minutes onto the ends of our flights. Grayson had paid me a little overtime in my check. I hadn't minded, but Grayson had minded very much.

"Did you talk to Zeke about it?" I asked Grayson. I didn't see what good that would do, though. A bad speller was a bad speller, and there was no spell-check for banners.

"I fired him," Grayson said. "I can do it myself."

"And not fly?" Alec stopped laughing for the first time since he'd sat down. "You have contracts for three planes in the air."

I puzzled over Alec phrasing it that way: "*You* have contracts," rather than "*We* have contracts." The business belonged to both of them now.

Grayson didn't seem to notice the way Alec had put it. "I'll take some extra time between my flights to get the banners ready," he said. "After you two are up in the air, I'll go myself. I'll have to fly longer to make up that time." Fly longer, and work longer. He was talking about his eight-hour day stretching into ten, probably more since he was doing the paperwork.

Molly's voice broke into my thoughts. "Who was in charge of the banners when your dad was still around?"

I watched Grayson and Alec for their reaction, the wince that passed across both of their faces when someone mentioned their dad. I saw it flit across Grayson's, even in the flickering colored lights from the bar.

Alec didn't hesitate. He leaned forward and told Molly, "Grayson and I took care of the banners. We couldn't get our commercial pilot's licenses until we turned eighteen last October, so we haven't been allowed to fly for money until now."

I pointed out, "You also watched the takeoffs to make sure nothing fell off the planes when they snagged the banners. If Alec and I are already flying, who's going to do that for you, Grayson?"

Grayson glanced at me with no expression on his face and squeezed his fist into a ball.

"Hire me," Molly piped up.

"Yeah!" Alec exclaimed at the same time Grayson asked "What?" and I said "No."

"I can spell," Molly said. "I can drag these banners around if they're not hugely heavy, right?"

"You're hired," Grayson said.

I glared across the table at Molly, but I couldn't catch her eye. Not knowing what she was up to made me very nervous. She wandered into her parents' café to help out only if she happened to wake up early enough and was bored. She could definitely work at the airport instead of the café if she wanted to. But why would she want to? The work would be dusty and hot with a side of gas fumes. I couldn't imagine what good she thought she could get out of this job, unless she intended to meddle in my business with the boys. And I couldn't let her do that. My flying career was too important. I couldn't let her give my secret away to Alec, accidentally or otherwise.

"Wait a minute," I chimed in. "Grayson, I don't think this is a good idea. You just met Molly. There are things about this job that she won't be used to."

"Like what?" she challenged me.

"Labor," I said.

"Oh," she said with a threatening laugh, "I will cut a bitch."

I kicked her underneath the table, warning her that she was making me look bizarre and unglamorous to Alec. "Not in front of the children."

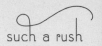

"You're hired," Grayson told Molly again. "But whatever kind of drama we've got going on when we're on the ground, we're not doing anything that affects what happens in the sky. There is no crashing at Hall Aviation. That means no hangovers. No drinking." He slid Molly's daiquiri toward the middle of the table.

"Hey!" she cried. "It's spring break! Just one drink?"

"None," Grayson said firmly.

"But I'm not flying," she pouted.

"You're aligning the banners correctly," he said. "You're watching the airplanes to make sure nothing falls off. You're spelling."

She stuck out her bottom lip and fluttered her eyelashes at him.

He laughed. "You can have *one*." He slid the daiquiri back to her.

"Thanks, boss. Want a sip? It'll loosen you up a little."

"I'll pass. Loosening up wasn't my goal for the night. I don't get involved with my employees."

I'd been watching this whole exchange in horror. At first they seemed to be flirting. But I doubted he would have made this comment about his employees so flatly if he'd wanted to make a move on her.

She wasn't offended. She laughed straight through it. "Why are you the boss of this outfit instead of Alec? Are you older?"

"We're twins," Grayson and Alec said at the same time.

"I knew that!" Molly exclaimed. "I totally forgot! You're nothing alike."

"Yes, they are," I said. This wasn't true, but I was feeling territorial again. Molly got along with the boys so much better than I did, and she didn't even care about them.

"No, we're not," the boys said at the same time. They

looked at each other across the table. Grayson smiled, and Alec laughed. I got the feeling they hadn't laughed together in a while.

"How did you and Leah become 'friends'?" Grayson asked Molly, making finger quotes.

I grinned at him and spoke up. "I stole her boyfriend."

"You *tried*." She reached across the table and patted my arm soothingly.

"What really happened?" Grayson asked.

I looked to Molly to answer this. She didn't know what had really happened. I did, but I wasn't going to tell her. We were friends now, and that was all I wanted. Honesty wasn't worth the trouble.

"I'd just moved to town two years ago," she said. "I snagged the hottest guy at school, right? And the next thing I know, all these chicks are telling me that Leah Jones is after him so I had better watch out."

Alec chuckled. Grayson said dryly, "She's that kind of girl, is she?"

"Apparently," Molly said, giving me a brief glare as she always did when she mentioned Ryan. She was still resentful about him. "If I'd been at my old school in Atlanta, I might have let it go and watched how things went. But I was at a new school and I felt like I needed to lay down the law so girls wouldn't mess with my property." She moved her finger in the air as she said this in a poor imitation of some kind of gangland gesture, which was even funnier coupled with her blue glittery clubbing eye shadow. "So I confronted her about it."

"Girl fight!" Alec exclaimed.

I giggled, because Alec was funny. Patrick anticipating the same thing outside my trailer last night hadn't been funny at all, probably because it had been a lot closer to the truth.

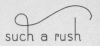

Grayson watched me without laughing. "What did Leah do when you confronted her?" he asked Molly.

"She was *funny*," Molly said. "Can you believe that? Everything I tried to serve her, she dished right back to me. I realized that I wanted to be friends with her more than I wanted to go out with that hunk of burning love."

That's not what had happened with Ryan. But I let her go on thinking so, since she liked viewing me as a tough girl from the hood. She might not want to be my friend otherwise.

However, I didn't appreciate the way she characterized the argument, like she'd decided we would be friends, and therefore we were. Like she'd chosen me over Ryan. Like she'd adopted a kitten from the pound. I certainly felt that way when she picked me up and took me to her parents' café for dinner, but I hated the way it sounded now that these boys were listening.

"So you've always been a heartbreaker," Alec said at my shoulder, low enough that Grayson and Molly couldn't hear, and close enough that I felt his breath across my skin. I turned to him. He watched me with that half-smile on his lips, looking into my eyes.

For the first time that night, I got the feeling that we were more than friends. Grayson might have put a halt on being paired with Molly, but Alec wasn't putting a halt on him and me. I held his gaze, gave him my sexiest smile, and tried my best not to panic.

By order of Grayson for everyone to get a good night's sleep, we left not long after. First we drove through gates draped with flowering tropical vines and dropped Molly off at her parents' beachside villa. If there'd been any question remaining about whether Grayson wanted to be more than friends with

her, it was answered here. Alec waited until she went in the front door to drive away, but Grayson stayed in the car.

Next they drove me home. Alec explained that Grayson was still in tow because he had some work left to do at the hangar. Alec would drop him off. Grayson would drive his truck back to his beach shack later. I wondered whether this was really why, or whether Grayson had engineered this excuse to watch Alec and me from the backseat and make sure I held up my end of our dark bargain.

Alec was handsome and so sweet, a super-nice guy. I kept reminding myself of this as he drove closer to the trailer park. The pain in my stomach grew worse, even though I had a belly full of bar food and wasn't hungry for once. There was no way out of what was coming, but I gave it a try anyway. As he turned onto the gravel road and dust billowed into the headlight beams, I said, "You don't have to walk me to the door."

He didn't answer. The silence stretched into awkwardness, without even a noise from Grayson's phone in the backseat to break it.

Finally Alec asked, "Why not?"

I didn't have an answer for that. I made up one. "It's not much of a door."

"Of course it's a door, and I'm walking you to it." He parked the car, cut the engine and the lights, and got out.

He was walking around the car to open my door for me. I didn't have much time. I turned around, looking past the seat's headrest, and said, "Good night, Grayson."

He was already looking straight at me when I turned around. "Good night," he said with absolutely no expression on his shadowed face or in his voice.

I didn't know exactly what I'd wanted from him. Jealousy?

Maybe a declaration of *No, Leah, don't do it! I'm calling the whole thing off!* Whatever I'd wanted, this wasn't it.

"I like your hair better curly," he said in the same flat tone.

Before I could ask him what he meant—*he* liked my curly hair, or he thought *Alec* liked it better?—Alec opened the door.

Heart racing, I got out of the car and stepped into a thick cloud of barking from the pit bull. Alec followed me across the yard and up the cement-block stairs. I didn't want to kiss him, but there didn't seem to be any way around this now. I met his gaze and tried to telegraph to him that, sure, I did want to kiss him, but his brother was watching us, and moreover, hello, was *he* horny with that pit bull barking his head off?

Alec didn't seem to get my meaning, though. I was afraid I'd screwed things up by accidentally implying that I didn't want to kiss him at all. I almost explained the whole thing to him: *I don't want to kiss you outside my trailer with a pit bull barking in my ear. It's too much like my nightmares about my marriage someday.*

But he did understand. He half-smiled down at me. "Tomorrow night I'll make sure we're alone."

There would be a tomorrow night? This was good—Grayson couldn't complain that I wasn't holding up my end of the deal—yet my face burned with the possibilities. I was frightened that Alec would want to do more than I was willing to do.

He bent toward me. I went rigid, anticipating his kiss, and tried to relax. Maybe he felt me go stiff, or maybe he didn't really want to kiss me either. For whatever reason, he hesitated, and swallowed.

Then he came in the rest of the way, pushing both his hands back into my hair. His lips met mine.

He was kissing me. But not very dynamically. The kiss was awfully chaste for a couple of legal adults on spring break. I

didn't want him to think I was a prude, but I didn't want to encourage him, either. Or, I did, but just enough for Grayson to see I was encouraging him.

And for Grayson to eat his heart out.

So I slid my hand into Alec's hair and pulled him closer.

He broke the kiss and started again. I felt his tongue against my lips, but he didn't press inside. It was like kissing a middle school boy who'd heard about kissing but had never done it himself.

I didn't correct him.

He pulled back and slid his hands out of my hair, or tried. One finger got caught in a layer underneath that had kinked in the night humidity, defying the flat-iron.

"Ow!" I squeaked.

We both laughed.

"Sorry. Hold on just a sec." He squinted at my hair in the moonlight and used his other hand to extricate the finger that had gotten caught. As he released me, I glimpsed the hand that had been snagged and saw he was wearing Mr. Hall's Air Force ring.

"Good night," I said too quickly. "Thanks. I had fun." I turned my key in the lock, escaped through the door, and closed it behind me before we could get into another scrape. And before I could gaze into the yard, checking to see how closely Grayson had been watching.

The odor of mildew hit me in the face and made me breathe shallowly. I never noticed it unless I'd been away for a while. The trailer was rotting underneath, where I couldn't reach it, and there was nothing I could do.

Standing there with my back to the door, listening to the pit bull barking and Alec's car starting through the thin aluminum, I was overcome with fatigue. I wasn't sure I could negotiate another night of Alec kissing me and Grayson look-ing on.

But Molly would be at the airport tomorrow. Molly made things easier for me, just by talking out her ass.

And I would get to fly again. Whenever this farce didn't seem worth it over the next few days, I had to remember I was doing it to keep my wings and fly.

# ten

As I walked over to the airport in the morning, I kept an eye on Mr. Simon's hangar. I didn't want to resolve anything with Mark. If I could just avoid him for the rest of my life, that would be perfect. I was in luck for once. His plane wasn't visible through the tall open doors of the hangar. He'd arrived a lot earlier today than he had yesterday—possibly because he'd gotten in trouble with his uncle the day before—and he was already up.

Alec taxied the yellow Piper past me, waving to me from the cockpit. I waved back. Then I veered toward Molly, who stood in the grass between the runway and the taxiway, struggling to fold the huge red banner letters into the fabric sleeve that held them in place during flight. The morning breeze carried her scents of sunscreen and bug repellent. Walking nearer, I noticed that, though she might be chemically prepared for this job, she hadn't dressed for it. She wore her blinged-out sunglasses, a stylish straw hat, diamond hoop earrings—the diamonds might have been real—and cute beach clothes. The heavy-duty work gloves Grayson must have given her made her hands look like robot claws.

She didn't approve of what I'd worn, either. With one mechanical hand, she gestured to my slouchy T-shirt layered over my bikini top. "I see you dress up for work."

"How's the labor going?" I joked.

"Laboriously." She wiped her brow with her wrist and put both hands on her hips like she was winded already. She didn't laugh like she should have. I wondered whether I'd offended her last night with my comment about her laboring. That didn't make sense, because Molly didn't get offended.

I couldn't apologize to her, though. We didn't operate that way. So I simply asked, "Why'd you want this job?"

"To watch over you and protect you from these animals, of course."

That didn't make sense, either. She should have been jumping up and down and squealing right now and telling me how hot these boys were and I was crazy not to do both of them at once right there in the hangar.

"Did you have to kiss Alec last night?" she asked.

"Yes." I tried not to sound suspicious as I asked, "Did he tell you that?" I doubted he'd dished to her at the hangar this morning about taking me home last night.

"I just figured," she said. "I've got something planned for tonight that may be more of a distraction so we can keep him off you. I okayed it with the boys already. We'll eat dinner at my café. If we start there, my parents will be less likely to inquire in too much detail about the drunken orgy we'll be attending later. Francie Mahoney's parents have taken her little brother to Disney World. Alec and Grayson used to live here in town, so they'll know a lot of people at her party. Maybe

Alec will hook up with his old flame from third grade, and that will get him off your case."

"Oh God, no." My words were drowned out by an engine. Alec raced past us on the runway, the yellow Piper sailing into the air.

When the roar had faded, I said, "Anything but that." Most people in my high school hated me only in passing. A few rich girls would walk all the way across the hall just to make a nasty remark about my curly hair, if they thought of a good one and could get a friend to go with them as a witness and bodyguard. Francie was one of those girls. I'd tried to tell Molly this about her friends repeatedly, but she didn't believe me. They were on their best behavior while she was around. They called me a sack of shit the instant Molly left the room. And Molly didn't have PE with us.

"You don't want Alec off your case?" Molly asked sharply.

"Of course I do," I said, "as long as Grayson doesn't mind."

She shifted her weight and blew her bangs out of her eyes with a big sigh. "I'm trying my best to help you, but it's not *always* about you. It's *my* spring break of *my* senior year too, and maybe *I* want to go to this party."

And maybe *I* didn't have to go just because *she* was going. I almost told her this. But she'd already convinced the boys this should be our outing of the night. I couldn't back out now, stand Alec up, anger Grayson. I would have to go.

She knew why I didn't want to. She knew I had to go anyway. Her understanding of my situation and sympathy for my plight lasted right up until she got tired of it and turned her back on me.

Which wasn't a fair assessment. We'd been friends for a couple of years, and I couldn't recall that she'd done anything like this to me before. Of course, there hadn't been boys involved before, not since the beginning and Ryan. I hadn't been blackmailed into dating someone before. We were in new territory and all bets were off.

"Look, we'll talk about it later, okay?" she said. By which she meant that we would *not* talk about it and we were going to the party that night. "Alec's already in the air. I have to get this banner hooked up. You go get your breakfast. My dad made a strawberry Danish for you, the kind with the Hawaiian raw sugar on top."

That got me headed for the hangar again, and it wasn't until I was halfway there that I realized she'd pointed me in that direction by baiting me with food, like I was a puppy. I didn't know what to think about this girl I'd assumed I knew so well, suddenly set down in this place I knew so well, and acting like it was hers instead of mine, and these boys were hers.

But Grayson wasn't hers. He'd made that clear last night. And he was standing outside the hangar, alternately glancing at his phone and gazing into the southwest corner of the clear blue sky. When he turned in my direction and saw me coming, he stared at me, or let me *think* he was staring at me behind his shades. Though the morning was cool, I felt sweat break out across my skin, whether his gaze was real or not.

But as I finally reached him, he was business as usual. "Watch out for the weather today."

I tried to shake off the shivers he'd given me and act like a pilot. "You mean the storm system coming up from the Gulf?" I'd noticed it on the weather app when I used the airport office phone to talk to Molly the day before. The storm was angry, and its tornadoes had already torn up some towns in Mississippi. "It's nowhere near us yet. It probably won't get here until tonight." It hadn't even reached my mother, at a casino over in the mountains.

"Last Christmas, Dad had been watching that storm all day," Grayson said, "and suddenly there was a wind advisory way before we thought. I don't want anybody to get caught. Radio me if you run into turbulence you weren't expecting. And if you see dark clouds, don't wait for me to radio you. Come on in."

I shrugged. I was all for caution, but he was being a little ridiculous. Shell-shocked from his own crash, I thought.

"Your breakfast is inside," he said, nodding back toward the hangar. "When you're through eating, before you check your plane and go up, could you take my truck and drive a banner out to Molly? That will save her some time. She can spell, but she's going to have trouble keeping up with us at first." He held out his keys to me.

"I can't do that," I said.

"I'm telling you," he said, "just do it before you go up. I'm keeping track of your hours and I'll pay you overtime if you run over. No problem."

"I can't drive," I said.

He pulled his hand back in surprise, keys jingling. "What do you mean, you can't drive?"

I meant that nobody had ever taught me to drive, and it didn't matter anyway because I didn't have a car. But I wasn't going down that road again. I was still pissed about trying to explain the washateria to Alec last night.

"You mean you can fly a plane but you can't drive a car?" Grayson asked. "That's crazy."

I chopped my hand across my throat. This had been Mr. Hall's way of telling us to kill the engine. I meant for Grayson to stop quizzing me on my home life. I'd had enough.

He balled his fist and squeezed until his hand turned white.

"Okay," he said on a sigh. "Sorry. Go have something to

eat." He rounded the corner of the hangar and started his truck himself.

I walked into the darkness and feasted on strawberry Danish and eggs and ham, stuffing food into my mouth like a starving dog now that nobody was watching. The day continued to get better from there. I never missed a banner pickup, and I took three long flights up and down the sunny beach. By the third flight, the wind had picked up, but the storms were still a long way off, nothing to worry about yet.

Mr. Hall would have thought it was beautiful. In a Grayson-like outburst, he would have exclaimed, "*Man,* what a pretty day to fly!" and then settled with me in the cockpit for the ride. This time I hardly teared up, thinking of him. His memory made me happy.

My morning break didn't coincide with Molly's because she took a break while I flew, and she spelled out my new banner while I took a break. But she ate lunch with the boys and me. Things didn't seem weird between us like they had when I'd talked to her alone that morning. Like the night before, she carried the conversation and took a lot of pressure off me. I decided there was nothing wrong with her after all. Early that morning she'd just been overwhelmed with work, maybe, or disoriented at waking up before ten on a school holiday.

I didn't take my afternoon break with her. When I taxied to the hangar, Alec was sitting outside with his back to the corrugated metal wall of the building, smoking a cigarette and watching Molly struggle with the banner Grayson had just dropped, tiny across the field. I didn't want to sit outside and be tempted to smoke, but I thought I should be sociable since apparently Alec and I had another date that night.

"Welcome," he said as I walked up. He patted the asphalt

beside him like it was a plush seat. Giggling, I sank down. He offered me a cigarette and I shook my head.

He exhaled smoke away from me. "Beautiful day for flying," he said, squinting into the sky. "Grayson's already freaking out about the weather."

"I think he's nervous about the wind since his wreck last December," I said.

"Is that what you think it is?" Alec asked. "I thought he was just being an overbearing ass."

Weirdly, I wanted to jump to Grayson's defense. He *was* being an overbearing ass, and not just about the weather. But somehow, while it was okay for me to think this, it wasn't okay for Alec to say it.

Before I could open my mouth, Alec's phone rang. He slipped it from his pocket, glanced at the screen, and grinned. "My mom."

I put my hands behind me on the hot asphalt to push myself up. "Do you want me to—"

"Oh, gosh, no, sit down." He pressed a button on the phone. "This is your favorite son speaking. How may I help you?"

Even though he'd told me he didn't need privacy, I felt uncomfortable listening to his end of the conversation with his mom. I knew he and Jake looked like her, but the photo I'd seen of her had been decades old. As I pictured her now, she was a pudgy woman with cotton clothes like sacks and the same haircut she'd had in high school because it was easy and there was no reason to bother anymore, now that her eldest son was gone, and her husband was gone, who had cheated on her, and whom she had always loved.

I was basing this assumption on nothing. She might be slender and stylish with a professional job, a lawyer, suffering

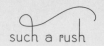

the loss of her son and sorry about her ex but already moving on, because her own life was important too. Either way, she was none of my business. I would never meet her. I'd cheapened this lady's mourning with my nosey musings. I tried to relax and shut her out, but when I sat back against the corrugated metal building, I was shocked at the heat and sat up straight.

Alec eyed me as he spoke. "No, it's going great." He pivoted the phone so he could still hear the speaker but the mouthpiece was away from his mouth, then took a drag from his cigarette. He moved the phone back and said, "Yes, really." Smoke curled out of his mouth and around his lips. He moved the phone away again and exhaled in a quick huff that his mother wouldn't hear. Then he said into the phone, "Mom. Mom. Mo-*ther*. Why don't you believe me?"

Grayson was landing his plane. A gust inflated the wind sock on the tower and knocked Grayson a few feet off course, but he straightened up in time for the landing. Perfect.

Alec laughed into the phone. And even though he clearly had been bullshitting his mother about how things were going, his laugh sounded genuine. It started as a low manly rumble and ended in a higher cackle like a little boy, cracking up and not caring how he sounded because the joke was that funny.

While laughing, he'd moved his mouth away from the phone again so he didn't hurt his mom's ears on the other end of the line. He took the opportunity to suck in another quick drag from his cigarette before he told her more somberly, "That's Grayson's problem. You'll have to ask *him* about that."

They chatted for a few more minutes about the weather, it sounded like, and the temperature of the ocean, and whether the beach was crowded, while Grayson taxied his plane closer.

Finally Alec said, "I will. Love you too. Bye." He pocketed his phone.

"Your mom called to check on you?" I asked. "That's sweet." I said it like I was teasing him, but I really did think it was sweet. My mom didn't call to check on me.

Alec nodded toward the approaching red Piper. "Checking on Grayson. There's something wrong with him."

"Of course there is," I said. "Both of y'all have been through so much in the past few months."

Alec sucked in smoke and huffed it out his nose. "Yeah, Dad died and Jake died, but I'm still the same person I was at Christmas. Grayson isn't. He had to go to counseling for impulse control when we were kids. They taught him to grip his fist really hard to keep himself from doing or saying something he'd regret later. Like this." He made a fist and squeezed until his hand turned white, just like Grayson did. "Mom and Dad would make him do it at the dinner table when he interrupted the conversation or tried to steal all the rolls. He would *never* do it unless they made him. And nine years later, have you seen how often he's doing it?"

He shouted these last words as Grayson parked his plane next to ours. The engine cut off. Grayson jumped down from the cockpit and strode across the tarmac toward us.

"Put that garbage out," he told Alec, sounding exactly like Mr. Hall. Not his imitation of Mr. Hall, but Mr. Hall himself, annoyance and superiority behind those gruff words.

"You're such a hypocrite." Alec's comment was harsh, but his tone was mild. As he said it, he stubbed out his cigarette on the asphalt and stood. He tossed the butt into the trash can at the corner of the hangar, then walked back to me. "See you on the other side." We bumped fists, and he jogged toward the yellow Piper without another word to Grayson.

Grayson sat beside me in Alec's place. "*You're* not smoking, are you?" he grumbled.

166

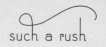

"Not anymore. Your dad made me quit."

"Really?" Grayson seemed surprised. "Why?"

Alec started his engine. I waited for him to turn his plane and taxi toward the far end of the runway, engine noise fading, before I explained. "Your dad said it took him thirty years to quit and he was going to save me the trouble. This was back when I was still paying him for lessons. I told him he couldn't tell me what to do, and he refused to take me up unless I quit."

Grayson said knowingly, "You could have faked quitting."

"He would have smelled it," I said. "My hair is large and aromatic." For emphasis, I ran one hand through my back-to-normal curls. Grayson wouldn't have believed my real reason for quitting: I had made a promise to Mr. Hall, and therefore I had kept it.

"Do you ever want one?" Grayson asked.

"No. Sometimes I think I do, and I start one, but it's been more than three years since I finished one. I didn't want to sit out here and watch Alec smoke, but . . . no, I don't want one." Something in Grayson's hungry tone made me ask, "Do you?"

"Yes. I'm like"—he inhaled deeply through his nose—"ahhhh, secondhand smoke."

"When did you quit?"

"Saturday."

"God!" I exclaimed. "No wonder you've been acting that way."

Tiny on the opposite end of the runway, Alec took off. Molly lost her hold on a banner and chased it through the grass on a breeze, which was picking up ahead of the approaching storm.

Finally Grayson said, "Alec and I both were smoking more because of the stress, I guess, and it got out of hand. We agreed

to quit because thirty years of smoking was part of what killed Dad. Alec's having a harder time than I am."

"That's weird," I said. "I would think *you'd* have the harder time."

"Why?" he asked flatly.

"Alec says there's something wrong with you. You've changed."

A new engine started up. In front of the airport office, the Admiral was getting ready for his afternoon flight.

Grayson said quietly, "I changed that day I crashed last December. I'd never been scared before. Never. I've been scared ever since." He sounded so uncharacteristically solemn that I turned toward him.

He still didn't look at me as he continued, "I understand cause and effect now. Life was more fun when I didn't, but I can't undo it."

At the far end of the runway, the Admiral had finished his run-up of the engines. He raced forward and sailed into the air, sweeping toward us and then away, headed for the sun.

"There's something wrong with Alec, though," Grayson said. "I'm doing all the brainwork for this business. It's like him to be worry-free, but it's not like him to trust me."

His phone rang in his pocket. He drew it out and glanced at the screen, then answered it. "Hello, this is your favorite son. May I help you?" His imitation of Alec was dead-on, both the words and the teasing tone of his voice.

I didn't offer to walk away and give Grayson privacy for his phone call with his mom, like I had for Alec. I wanted to hear this.

His tone returned to normal: a pleasant voice. A radio voice, as in a DJ rather than a pilot, not too high or deep,

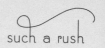

friendly with just a hint of the sarcasm under the surface, waiting.

"Everything is going great," he said. He didn't have a cigarette to fidget with like Alec had, but I heard him playing with a rock, tapping it on the hard tar beside him. "No, that hasn't been a problem, because I planned it out before, remember?" The rock tapped faster as she said things he didn't want to hear.

Finally he tried to interrupt her. He was imitating Alec again. "Mom. Mom. Mom. Mo-*ther.* The business is running just as smoothly as when Dad was here."

I looked at him incredulously before I realized what I was doing.

His eyes darted to mine and away. He reared back and hurled the little rock he'd been tapping. I followed its trajectory across the sunny tarmac. It sailed a long time, bounced on the asphalt, and kept going. I couldn't see where it went.

"Okay," he said. "Love you too. Bye." The instant after he pressed the button to end the call, he turned to me and said angrily, "It *is* running just as smoothly as when Dad ran it, because when Dad ran it, it didn't run smoothly at all."

He probably suspected again that I'd figured out his secret by listening to his conversation with his mom. I hadn't. All I could hear was how worried he was. About what, I had no idea.

"I didn't say anything." I stood to duck inside the hangar and snag a drink before taking my last flight of the afternoon. "By the way, thanks for feeding me today. And yesterday." I paused. "And Sunday night."

He shrugged. "I'm just doing what Dad would have done."

"He fed his pilots?"

"Yes, because they were hungover."

Alec and I were *not* hungover. Grayson had made sure of that. He was just ensuring I had enough to eat after he peeked inside my empty refrigerator. I didn't want to discuss this any more than I'd wanted to tell him I couldn't drive. But I didn't want him to think I was naive, either. I was about to tell him I knew why he was feeding us.

He tilted his head to one side, the blond curls beneath his cowboy hat moving against his shoulder. "You looked really beautiful last night. I do like your hair better now, curly, but it was pretty last night too."

"Ha-ha," I said.

"And you look sexy when you dance."

I put my hands on my hips. He probably thought I was trying to look sexier. I put my hands down. "I told you yesterday. It's enough for you to make me date Alec. You can't insult me too."

He gaped at me. "I'm not insulting you. How is that insulting?"

"You're being sarcastic." I wasn't sure whether this was true.

"I'm *not* being sarcastic."

"Well, you can't make me date Alec and then compliment me, either," I said.

"It's not a compliment. It's a fact. You looked beautiful last night, and you looked great dancing."

This was how things had started with Mark a few weeks ago. We'd been talking in the airport office about a job flying with his uncle, and suddenly he was asking me out.

Except that Mark had not been blackmailing me.

And when Mark had told me I was beautiful, I'd felt flattered. I hadn't experienced this rush of pleasure through my body, my face flushing, my skin tingling like sunburn in the heat. I hadn't fallen for Mark's line like I was falling for Grayson's. I hadn't felt stupid.

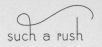

"Are you coming on to me?" I asked sternly.

He lowered his shades on his nose and looked over them at me, his big gray eyes serious. "Considering your reaction, I guess *not.*"

"You can't come on to me and make me date Alec."

He pushed his shades back up so his eyes were hidden. "I have to make you date Alec."

"Then stop talking to me."

"Okay." He took a deep breath and tapped his tightly balled fist against his mouth.

The airport was eerily quiet, no airplane noises at all, no traffic noises this far out from town, just bugs screaming in the long grass.

Finally I said, "Exhale."

He let out his breath in a long sigh, his broad shoulders sagging with it.

"You're having a hard time," I said gently.

He nodded, gazing at the sky.

"I'm sorry." I closed the two steps between us and put my hand on his shoulder. When he didn't flinch or shrug away, I rubbed his shoulder in a comforting way. I *meant* the gesture to be comforting, anyway, but I was distracted by how hard and muscular his shoulder was. And then I noticed that chill bumps popped up on his skin.

I was so confused about what he intended. But if I'd asked him for a straight answer, I doubted he could have given me one. He was confused himself.

It was time for me to fly, and there was no room for confusion in the cockpit of an airplane. Sliding my hand from his tight shoulder, I grabbed my drink from the hangar, then walked to the orange Piper. Grayson sat there watching until I took off.

# eleven

This time I didn't bother to stand on the toilet and check my look in the mirror over the sink. My sympathy for Grayson had faded. Now I was only fed up with him for coming on to me but making me date his brother. Fed up with Alec for playing along. Fed up with Molly for dragging me to this party. Also, I'd already worn my one clubbing dress and rinsed it in the sink. It hadn't dried yet. Whatever I wore next would be inappropriate. If Molly was going to force me to a party where the girls would call me trash, and Grayson was going to treat me that way, I would dress the part.

I chose a pair of shorts that were too small a couple of years ago and obscene now that I'd grown a few inches taller. Molly, who had good fashion sense except for the glitter, would have told me that if I was showing that much leg, my top should be more demure so the whole outfit wouldn't be overkill. I went for overkill with a tight, low-cut knit shirt. I ventured into my mother's catastrophe of a closet for a pair of stilettos.

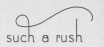

I wasn't waiting for the boys outside my trailer this time. I listened for Alec's car, then made my grand entrance down the wobbly cement-block staircase, watching their expressions. I couldn't read them, really. They both stared at me open-mouthed. Alec said something without taking his eyes off me. Grayson said something back. He jumped out of the front seat, left the door open, and slid into the back. Normally he would have focused on his phone again immediately, but he watched me cross the yard.

I slid into the car beside Alec. My shorts rode even higher on my thighs. You're welcome.

I was so exasperated with everybody that I hadn't even thought the whole night through. But when I walked with the boys into the café, suddenly I was embarrassed. Molly's mom and dad hugged me as warmly as always. To judge by their reactions, I might as well have been wearing footed flannel pajamas. I was embarrassed anyway. It was almost like dressing this way for a flying lesson with Mr. Hall, which I *never* would have done.

And then, when Molly walked from the kitchen into the café, she cackled. "Jesus Christ, girl, you really *don't* want to go to this party."

"What do you mean?" Grayson asked her.

I was afraid that she would come out with the words *airport whore.* But she let it go, pressing everyone for what we wanted for dinner. I was glad she'd gotten my message, at least. If she was going to drag me to her rich-girl party, I was going to make her wish she hadn't.

We took our gourmet organic food, which always tasted a lot better than it sounded, outside into the ocean breeze. The deck was empty because most of the tourists had eaten already. If we'd been on the flophouse end of town, the beach would still have been full of tourists, many of them staggering and

sunburned to the point of hospitalization. Such things didn't happen here on the magazine spread end. Only the sandpipers trotted across the beach. A stray toddler chased them. Behind that, his mother ambled along, half watching him in this safe environment, not the least bit afraid of him encountering a cigarette butt and picking it up to eat it.

At first, the noise of a plane was hard to discern from the noise of the surf, growing and fading on the wind. The engine's growl loomed louder. On the horizon down the beach, I recognized the Coast Guard Super Hercules from the station in North Carolina. It had passed me in midair earlier in the day. I had announced myself over the radio because it was coming so fast and I didn't want it to run me down or get its propellers tangled in my banner.

Coming back in my direction now, materializing out of nothing, the plane was gorgeous and classic: orange and white with four propellers and a huge tail. It flew so low over the beach, and its wingspan was so wide, it looked like an alien spacecraft hovering over the planet, something that shouldn't have been able to fly with human technology. It drew even with us and I put my hands over my ears. It passed us and I turned to watch. It was gone surprisingly fast, blocked out by the roof of a mansion as the beach took a slight turn. I could still hear it, though.

Disappointed that I couldn't see it anymore, I turned back to the table. Alec was turning back at the same time. Grayson's eyes stared where the plane had disappeared. Molly focused on her plate, munching salad, unaware that we'd been distracted.

I remembered what Mr. Hall had told me when I first asked him for a lesson: the kids who watch planes are destined to be pilots. And I envied Molly. She heard a plane and thought, *Hmmm, a plane,* and went back to eating without even

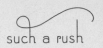

registering, instead of looking around desperately and wanting a piece of the action. She wasn't driven toward a life that was out of her reach.

But envying Molly was a dangerous road for me. I knew better than to go down it. I turned to Alec and opened my mouth to change the subject.

"Why did you want to start flying in the first place?" Molly spoke before I could, looking at Grayson. So she *had* noticed us watching the plane.

Grayson gazed at her for a moment like he hadn't quite realized she was talking to him. It shouldn't have been a personal question, and Molly was not rude for asking it, but it *was* a personal question for Grayson.

Finally he said, "It's such a rush. I mean, it's exactly the kind of thing I love to do."

"Adrenaline junkie," Alec broke in, explaining Grayson to Molly.

Grayson kept talking as if Alec hadn't spoken. "Flying is perfectly safe if you do everything right. If you make one mistake, you could easily die. I've made a lot of mistakes in my life—"

Alec laughed.

"—so I couldn't believe my dad was letting me do this, and I felt lucky." As Grayson said this, his gaze drifted toward the sky again, where the Super Hercules had disappeared. Now he looked back at Molly. "I still do."

She nodded shortly and turned to Alec. "What about you?"

Alec shrugged. "I've always been around it. I can't remember a time when my dad wasn't flying, or when Jake didn't want to fly. Grayson and I were always hanging around Jake, wanting to do what he did and fighting with each other to see who could do it first."

It was mostly Alec, not Grayson, who wanted to be like Jake. I glanced at Grayson to gauge his reaction. He was looking at the sky again.

"But that sounds like you don't really want to fly," Molly told Alec. "It sounds like you fell into this, and if you'd fallen into something else instead, that's what you'd do."

Alec frowned at her. "Isn't that true of any family business? I mean, is the guy who inherits the shoe factory thinking to himself, *This is where I belong, and this is what my whole personality and all of my talents are pointing me toward*? Or is it the luck of the draw? I can't imagine doing anything else." He turned to me. "How about you? Why did you want to start flying?"

A sudden gust of wind picked up a pile of recycled paper napkins on the table. I slapped my hand down on them to keep them from blowing over the deck rail to litter the sand. People cared about stuff like that on the nice end of the beach.

And I puzzled through what Alec wanted to know about me. Molly had asked Grayson why he wanted to fly. She had asked Alec. We were going around the table, yet I'd expected to be left out.

"Not because of family," Alec prompted me, "but maybe because of location, since you live near the airport. It's convenience for you, just like it's convenience for me."

"It's not convenience for me." I tried to prevent the words from coming out sour. I was on this date with Alec right now because I wanted so badly to fly. This was not what I'd call convenient.

"Then what is it?" Molly asked.

"Convenience got me over to the airport," I acknowledged. "A job was available within walking distance of where I lived. Curiosity drove me to take that first flying lesson. And then I was hooked."

"But why?" Alec seemed genuinely curious.

I paused, looking straight into his blue eyes—by mistake, really. I was used to glancing at Grayson and seeing nothing but aviator shades, with my own shades hiding my eyes so he wasn't sure I was looking. Two people could do that when one was working for the other, or one was being blackmailed by the other. Two people couldn't do that when they were on a date. Alec and I were supposed to be connecting, looking into each other's eyes on purpose.

And I saw his innocent expectations there. He was asking a simple question. We were getting to know each other. This was what normal teenagers did.

I told him, "It was the first time in my life I felt like I was in control." I paused, like he would get some profound meaning from that short statement.

He didn't. He only nodded for me to go on. But his open blue gaze had grown a little wary. On a date, you shared your deep thoughts with each other, but not *that* deep. We were eating sandwiches, for God's sake.

I couldn't stop. I'd never really examined this, and now that I was, I was finding out something about myself. "I could see," I said. "For the first time, I could see what most people never saw. I could see the whole town, and how I fit into it, and how far I would have to go to get out of it. I got such a rush, seeing that. And until that plane ride, I hadn't realized how low I'd felt for years, because I didn't have a high to compare it with." My voice ended on that high note, giving away how desperate I'd felt, how frightened I now was of never flying again.

I found my fork and picked around in my salad. Without looking up, I said, "So, Molly. Why do *you* love to fly?"

Both boys laughed, thank God. Awkward moment over.

"Flying makes me yak," Molly said.

"What does your mom think about you flying, Leah?" Alec persisted. "Is she proud of you?"

I munched a bite of lettuce and swallowed. "She doesn't know I'm a pilot."

Alec's blond brows furrowed. "How could she not know that?"

"She's gone a lot," I said simply, allowing him to draw his own conclusions. Maybe she was gone on business. Ha! Or she was caring for a sick friend. I left the statement there and hoped he would leave it too.

Molly ensured that nobody would leave it there. She offered, "We've been best friends since we were sixteen, and I've never met Leah's mother."

"Really?" Alec asked, astonished. "How is that possible?"

"She is literally never home," Molly said.

"She's there sometimes," I said, rushing to my mom's defense. When Molly eyed me dubiously, I said, "Okay, she's not there much, but that's my fault. She used to take me with her on visits to see her boyfriends, or she would invite them over to stay with us. But when I was ten, we lived near the army base. She got with a guy who'd been to Iraq and had problems. He beat her. He beat his fifteen-year-old son who lived with him too. One night his son hit *me,* and then—"

I stopped. The three of them were gaping at me.

This was what they got for asking me about this shit during dinner.

"It wasn't so bad," I backtracked. "I told my mom I didn't want to go to her boyfriends' places anymore. I could stay at home by myself, and she could go where she wanted. I knew when I said it that she would be gone a lot. I didn't picture her being gone almost always." I crunched a baked potato chip.

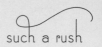

Ignoring their eyes on me, I looked past everyone at the water.

The TV said you should ignore bullies and they would leave you alone, eventually. Sometimes it worked and sometimes it didn't. Likewise, you would think rich kids would stop badgering their poor friend when she didn't melt down about her home life. But the more calmly I answered, the more they kept after me.

"What about your grandparents?" Alec asked.

"What about them?" I asked. "You mean, why haven't I gone to live with them?"

He nodded, but his eyes were getting wider. He was going to stop me and say this was too much information after all.

I kind of enjoyed telling them, "My grandparents kicked my mom out of the house when she got pregnant at fifteen. She had to drop out of school so she could get a job. Sometimes I think that experience did something to her, being thrown out on her own like that, because she'll do anything to avoid getting a job now."

"That was eighteen years ago," Molly said.

I resented the challenging tone in her voice. How dare this privileged rich girl question my story? I asked her, "So?"

"So, your mom should have gotten over it," Molly said.

"Some people have problems," I said. "When something awful happens, sometimes people get stuck."

Grayson moved in the corner of my eye. He'd been so quiet that I'd almost forgotten he was sitting there, listening to this whole mortifying conversation. I turned to him to give him my special go-to-hell face.

But he was staring at me with a shocked expression—not bad shock like Alec, as if he were horrified by my life story, but good shock, as if he'd had an epiphany.

"That explains why she doesn't get a job," Molly said. "What part of your mother's problem makes her leave you alone all the time?"

I was still so surprised by the way Grayson was acting that it took me a second to realize Molly had deeply insulted my mom. Pride took over as I turned back to Molly. "I'm eighteen years old," I said. "There's no reason for my mother to mother me. Why are you harping on this?"

"Because people deserve to be treated with respect," Molly said haughtily. "Children should be cared for. Friends and relatives should not lie to each other. And when I see that happening, I'm going to call it like it is."

My skin burned so hot that I glanced at the setting sun to make sure it hadn't caught me in its bright beam. Molly was talking about Grayson blackmailing me to date Alec. Why was she talking about this? She didn't need to make a point to *me*. She knew Grayson had me over a barrel. If she let Alec know he was being fooled, or even if she let Grayson know I'd told her about the whole arrangement, Grayson could get so angry that he'd show my forgery to my mother and everyone at the airport.

But I didn't dare telegraph this to Molly with a look. A sideways glance at Grayson let me know he was still watching me, rapt, like he was seeing me for the first time. I was almost relieved when Alec kept on with his questions.

"You've never even tried to contact your grandparents?" Alec asked. "Maybe they've had a change of heart."

Right. Like they had decided to start donating to charity: namely, me. I bit out, "Contact them, how, Alec? They live somewhere in South Carolina and their last name is Jones. You do the math."

"What about your other grandparents?" he asked.

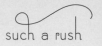

"I've never met them, either."

"What about your dad? Where is he?"

"I don't know."

There was a soft thud as someone kicked Alec under the table. He didn't get the hint. He said, "I don't mean right this second. I mean in general."

I took a deep breath. This fake dating thing was wearing me down. I needed to think about it further, really plan it all out, and invent some kind of brainless persona who could go out with Alec without exposing her heart to danger. This sharing of my own actual life was above and beyond the call of duty for this job, and I didn't want to do it anymore. Finally I said on a sigh, "I don't know that either. I don't know who my dad is."

Alec's own dad hadn't lived with him for years, but Alec had known where his dad was. His dad had paid child support and held joint custody, on paper at least. Alec, from his suburban Wilmington home in a neighborhood with paved roads and curbs and sidewalks, with a TV in every bedroom, could not fathom not knowing who his father was.

"I don't mean to be rude," he said soothingly. "I just wanted to learn more about you." He lifted his hand toward my cheek.

"No, you didn't," I said. His questions had a fishing-for-information quality about them. Either that or I was just mad now. The upshot was the same: I was tired of his bullshit. I scooted away from him on the bench. An inch, not enough to escape him if he wanted to touch me, but enough to be symbolic.

It was a gesture he read perfectly. He tilted his head at me, puzzled and hurt, just like he should be as his date drew back from him when he was trying to help. His instinct was to comfort an upset girl. And he was quickly learning not to do that

with me. So frustrating, that once in a while I had actual emotions that got tangled up with the fake ones.

"Okay," he said, giving in. "Really here's what I've been curious about from the beginning. My dad always said what great character you had, and how much drive you had to become a pilot."

"One day a year and a half ago, I walked in on you and Grayson discussing my drive to become a pilot." I meant their joke that I'd screwed Mr. Hall.

He knew exactly what I was getting at. His cheeks flushed red against his pale hair. But, typically, he pretended he had no idea. He went on, "I wondered where your drive came from."

I nodded. "Clearly not from my mother, because she's white trash."

"Oh," Molly said in warning. I wasn't sure to whom.

Alec gaped at me for a moment, then managed, "I *never* said—"

I interrupted him. "The only explanation is that my dad is a nuclear physicist. Either I inherited that drive genetically from his side of the family, or just knowing that he's a nuclear physicist gives me the motivation to make it out of the trailer park myself. It can't be that I'm just like this. That I just look around and say to myself, 'It is no fun being a sitting duck during tornado warnings, with no car to drive to the safe shelter they always talk about for people who live in unsafe places like that. It's no fun not to have food in a refrigerator, or a car to go get it. I think I'll make an effort to get a job.' No, I couldn't possibly come to that conclusion all by my lonesome."

He stood up suddenly. I flinched at the loud screech as the bench raked back beneath me on the deck. He still blushed, but the red in his cheeks had shrunk from an embarrassed flush to two small, angry points.

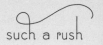

"I'm going to get a refill," he muttered. Then, almost as an afterthought, he looked down at me. "Would you like something?"

I shook my head, adamant about what I'd said, and yet ashamed at the same time.

He took his cup and stalked away across the deck, through the door to the café.

I picked through the salad with my fork again. Two days of regular meals had finally caught up with me. I wasn't ravenous anymore. I couldn't eat another bite. I waited for Molly's cutting comment, which would be that much more cutting because she made it in front of Grayson.

What she said surprised me. "Leah, Alec's not like Grayson."

"Oh, thanks," Grayson protested. "What do you mean, he's not like me? I am a nice person."

She turned and cupped Grayson's face in both hands. I would not dare do such a thing to Grayson, but Molly got away with it. She told him, "You are *not* a nice person. Shut up."

She turned back to me. "You can't be mean like that to Alec. He's such a gentleman, and he's treating you like he wants to be treated. He didn't understand he was wading into a hornet's nest with your nuclear physicist daddy and whatnot. Holy Mother of God."

I put my fork down. "You are one to talk, Miss Manners."

"I observe and adapt," Molly said. "I'm treating you like you want to be treated, but unlike you, I can turn that mean streak off. Watch and learn." She spun around, lifting her long legs over the bench, and clopped across the deck to follow Alec inside.

I needed to find something else on my plate to play with, but Grayson caught my gaze before I looked down. He said,

"Molly's right. I thought you would be good at this, but you're incredibly bad at this because you're so sensitive. I could have sent Molly in to flirt with Alec with better results than you're getting."

"If you think Molly is so great, why can't you use her, without even using her?" I asked. "Why can't she be the girlfriend Alec falls in love with over spring break?"

I expected him to give me an angry list of reasons why not. Instead, he seemed to consider my suggestion. His blond brows knitted. He took a long pull at his drink, watching me over the rim of his cup. After he set the cup down, he still stared at me like he would find the answer in my face.

Finally he asked, "Where is she going to college in the fall?"

"SCAD." When he gave me a puzzled look, I remembered SCAD was a lot closer to my high school than his. Maybe he'd never heard of it, even though the people at my high school thought it was the coolest postgraduation destination possible. "Savannah College of Art and Design."

"Then, no," he said, shaking his head. "Heaven Beach is a two-and-a-half-hour drive from Charleston. Savannah's a hair closer to Charleston. I need him to feel pulled *away* from Charleston."

My obvious next question was, "What's so awful about Alec going to Charleston?" That was the key to the whole puzzle. And yet, because clearly I had a head as big as the state of South Carolina, I asked, "How do you know *I'm* not going to college somewhere else in the fall?"

"Because you're not."

"I can't believe you!" Molly exclaimed. She and Alec were coming out the door. Laughing, she leaned into him. As they stepped outside, she looked for me and arched her eyebrows at me: *This is how it's done.*

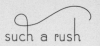

Oh, yeah? If everybody was pushing me into hooking up with this clueless boy, *I* would show *them* how it was done. I rose from the table and walked across the deck with a swing in my step, assisted by the stilettos. Ignoring Molly still touching him, I put my hand on his chest. "Alec," I whispered huskily, "I'm so sorry I was mean to you before. You touched a tender spot." I looked up at him through my eyelashes.

Out of the corner of my eye, I watched Molly remove her hand from him, staring at me with awe and new respect.

"Oh." Beet red, Alec gazed down at me with wide blue eyes, mesmerized by me. He'd completely forgotten he was standing on a deck outside a restaurant with two other people, holding a drink. "No, *I'm* sorry." He glanced down into my cleavage.

I tugged him by the arm down the deck steps, toward his car. As we walked, I glanced behind us and stuck out my tongue. Molly stared after us with her lips parted.

But my greatest triumph shocked me, and I had no idea whether it was really a triumph at all. Grayson stared after us too. His blond brows were down. His face had gone pale underneath his tan. Down by his side, he had squeezed all the blood out of his white fist.

# twelve

As soon as we reached the party, it was like my triumph had never happened. Walking to the door of Francie Mahoney's parents' mansion, Molly caught up with Alec and asked him who he remembered from her classes. She must have assumed, probably correctly, that Alec would recall these people, whereas Grayson would not, or wouldn't admit it.

"Does she know the whole school?" Grayson asked me quietly as we fell in behind her and Alec.

"Yes," I said. "Molly's so popular that she's not even worried about being popular. I've never seen a popular person before who wasn't trying really hard at it. But she's rich and smart and interesting *and* she doesn't give a shit."

"She sounds perfect."

"She *is* perfect," I said. "I want to be her. Not be *like* her, but *be* her, like in a creepy roommate movie."

He laughed, the genuine relaxed laugh I'd heard from him

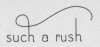

a few times. "I don't know everybody. And I didn't when I lived here, either."

"Did Alec?"

"Yes," he said as we walked through a huge front door into the party.

Molly was instantly surrounded by her friends, who screamed over her and wanted to know who she'd brought. She introduced Alec—didn't they remember him? *Didn't they?* And they did!

Didn't they also remember Grayson? Maybe not. He was acting polite enough, though, so several girls who couldn't fight their way into the circle around Alec settled for the circle around Grayson. Molly's friends hardly noticed me, which was good. Their eyes might slide over to me, but they didn't dare flare their nostrils or, worse, pointedly look me up and down. Not with Molly standing there. They went back to talking to Grayson.

I wished for a drink. I didn't particularly want to get drunk. I definitely didn't want to be hungover when I had an airplane to fly the next day. Grayson was right about that. But forced to stay here with these people, I would have preferred to nurse a beer in a corner and bond with some geek I hardly knew from history class, who was plastered. It was easier to make a good impression on plastered people. As it was, I stood in the same circle with Grayson, or sometimes with Alec, and listened to what these drunk girls had to tell them. I grinned so I wouldn't look unhappy.

After several years of this, I snuck up behind Molly and whispered that I was going to find a soda. I was parched from my long, hot flights that day. "Come with?" I asked hopefully.

"No, I'm good," she threw at me before turning back to Alec and the girls. Alec didn't even glance at me. Grayson did,

though, over several girls' heads. He probably thought I was going to get wasted. I would let him worry.

I wandered through the crowd standing on the expensive hardwood floors and lounging with their feet up on the white sofas. I'd almost reached a wide doorway that I assumed led to the kitchen when Francie Mahoney herself caught up with me. She was about a foot taller than me even in my stilettos, and she had a tall friend with her. When she took me by the shoulder and rudely whipped me around against the wall, I had to fight down the urge to run between their long legs like a rabbit cornered by dogs.

"You're here with Alec?" Francie asked me. "The cute one?"

I felt my brows go down, perplexed that she thought Alec was the cute one. I supposed I understood why she would think this. Alec had the face of an angel. A girl might think he was sexier than Grayson if she'd never seen Grayson move, walking with barely contained energy across the tarmac. "Yes," I said.

"But I heard you were dating Mark Simon," she said.

I wondered how she'd heard this. Mark was about as far as possible from popular, and her crowd did not keep up with his crowd. Only their own. "No," I said.

"Yes," she insisted. "I heard he moved into your trailer with you." She smiled at me, teeth large and white, lips glossy red, but her words dripped sarcasm. It was hard to say which part of this scenario held more derision for her: *moved into* or *trailer*.

Girls like her slept with boys. They even slept over with them when they could get away with it. But they and their boyfriends would stay at home with Mommy and Daddy until they were safely ensconced in a college dorm. And girls like her did not live in trailers.

At school I avoided these girls by arriving late on the bus so I didn't have to hang out before school, leaving early on the bus so I had no opportunity to hang out after school, and skipping lunch. It was unintentional but lucky that I'd neglected to turn in my homework throughout middle school and landed in the stupid classes, so I never encountered these girls in their college-track experience. In the unlucky event that I ran into them in the women's bathroom, I played deaf.

But at school, they hated me only in passing. Now they wanted to take me down. I was in possession of the beautiful blond boy who had stolen their hearts long ago and moved away. They didn't like it.

I couldn't tell them the truth: "Yes, I shacked up with Mark Simon, and now I'm dating Mr. Popularity from another school." Even "Yes, I *had* shacked up with Mark Simon, but now he's moved out" sounded hopelessly trashy, and "It's none of your business" would verify I had something to hide. Briefly I considered taking the offensive with "You are a bitch," but these girls would tell everyone what I'd called them without explaining what the provocation had been, which would make me seem, if possible, *more trashy.*

So I squinted at Francie and said, "I don't mean to be rude, but what have you been eating? You've got something stuck in your teeth."

She blinked at me, straightened, and inserted one manicured fingernail between her front incisors.

"Let me see," said her friend, whose name was Tara, I thought. My only interaction with her was that she had tried to trip me with her tennis racket in the locker room in PE.

"Check in the mirror," I told Francie. "It looks like gristle." I stepped past her, which I could do easily now because she was headed to the bathroom. She must have suspected I was

lying, but she wouldn't waltz away through a party without verifying that.

"Your lipstick looks like blood," Tara called after me.

I said something back to her that was a comparison between her own lipstick color and her twat. Molly would have been proud of me.

"Hey!" Francie said so loudly that I stopped, and so did everybody else around us in the grand living room.

"Don't go into that kitchen," she said. "The drinks are for invited guests only." The two of them laughed and turned for the bathroom again.

I stood there in the passageway with eight people staring at me. I couldn't continue on my path toward the kitchen, because one of these people might be a friend of Francie's, or just an asshole who would go rile her up and tell her I'd defied her order. Then there would be a bigger scene. But I couldn't slink back to hover at Molly's feet, either. Undecided, I stuck my chest out, then realized I was sticking my chest out.

I had only six more weeks of high school, I told myself. Six more weeks. Six more weeks.

And then what? If high school was supposed to have been the time of my life, what did I have to look forward to?

"God, what have you done now?" Molly hollered, catching me by the arm and dragging me into the kitchen with her. "I can't take you anywhere." She crossed the room like she owned it. At the sink she scooped ice into a plastic cup, poured me a soda, and handed it to me. Then she drained the dregs of her own plastic cup that somebody must have brought her. She made herself a soda. Looking around the kitchen, probably for Grayson, she sloshed in a generous helping of bourbon.

"Spill it," she said. "Grayson told me Francie watched you

leave and then followed you. He said it was like an old West-
ern."

I told her what had happened, expecting her to congratulate
me on my twat line.

Instead, she put her hands on her hips and said, "I don't see
why you're upset. Ten years from now, you're going to be an
airline pilot."

Without even thinking, I reached one hand to the cabinets
to knock on wood.

Molly didn't stop talking. "In ten years, do you know what
Francie's going to be?"

"A presidential candidate?"

She pointed at me. "An ignorant, frightening one? That's
good! But no. With her holier-than-thou attitude and her level
of mean, she's headed for only one thing. Pastor's wife."

I laughed.

"At a really *big* church," Molly went on, "so I don't know
what you're snickering about like you're all that with your big,
bad airline pilot self."

I nodded as if I believed her, because Molly did not like
to hear that I didn't believe her. "I should leave. It's Francie's
party, and I'm not welcome here."

"Why don't you just go outside?" Molly said this absently
while she looked over my head, waved at a friend, and moved
in that direction. I couldn't tell whether she was just trying
to get rid of me, her whiny companion at this fun party, or
whether she understood who sat outside at these parties. The
trash sat outside: the boys invited by popular girls because they
might bring weed. Maybe Molly was telling me to go out there
with the trash and box my weight.

Molly had already snatched up her drink and gone to hug
her friend. I let myself out a side door in the kitchen so I

wouldn't have to go back through the house and face down Francie again. Carefully I stepped across the lush lawn kept alive artificially by an expensive sprinkler system. The grass lay loosely across a bed of sand, not a good walking surface for stilettos. I should have watched the ground as I made my way along the side of the house, but I held my head high in case anybody was looking out a window. The storms that had been approaching all day and freaking Grayson out were finally close now. The wind tossed the tops of the palm trees. Though a gust might start cold, it ended warm on my bare arms and legs. I hoped we would get rain only, none of the tornadoes that had been creeping up the map all day.

Among the cars parked anyhow on the driveway and in the yard underneath the palm trees, a cluster of pickup trucks and the faint scents of tobacco and pot told me where the trash was. A couple of boys sitting on the trunks of cars whistled to me as I passed. I smiled brilliantly at them. As I neared the pickups, I recognized Patrick perched on a tailgate. I'd never thought I'd feel so relieved to see Patrick. Someone to talk to! I hoped he didn't bear me any ill will for threatening to shove beer cans up his ass.

Apparently not. "Hey, girl," he called as I approached. "You look niiiiiiiice."

"Ha-ha," I said, hefting myself onto the tailgate beside him.

"Toke?" he asked.

"No thanks."

"Smoke?"

"Yes," I said with relief. I took the cigarette he shook out of his pack and let him light it for me.

After one puff I knew I wasn't going to smoke it. I felt sick, and I could hear Mr. Hall scolding me. I had promised him.

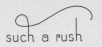

"You're making the news tonight," Patrick said. "I heard you're here with that pretty boy, Alec Hall."

That sounded about right. "You know him?" I asked.

"Played ball with him a long time ago," Patrick said. "He's not your type."

"Oh, really?" I laughed. "Who's my type, Patrick?"

"His brother," Patrick said. "Grayson? We used to be pretty good friends. You and me, we like playing with fire for some reason."

"Hm." I'd held my cigarette so long without inhaling that the fire had died out, and the wind had blown the ash away. I tossed the long butt into the cup Patrick was using as an ashtray. On second thought, I wished I'd thrown it down in Francie's driveway for her parents to find. They probably cared whether she smoked.

"Grayson and Mark are kind of similar," Patrick said. "It's like they don't have an off button, you know? It's fun to watch that fire, as long as you don't get burned."

"I don't think Grayson and Mark are anything alike," I said, watching Mark emerge from the cab of his pickup nearby in a cloud of pot smoke.

Following my gaze, Patrick said helpfully, "Oh, there's Mark now. You know what? He's still pissed about the whole thing with you, and then when he heard you were here with Alec . . . wow. Maybe you should g—"

I was already hopping down from the tailgate, my heels sinking into the sand. That slowed my exit. In two steps Mark crossed the space between us. He grabbed my bare upper arm, pulled me back the way he'd come, and pushed me into the cab of his truck.

I never stopped moving. I slid on over to the other side of the cab and reached down to open the door.

He gripped me by the arm again and pulled me back toward him across the seat so I couldn't reach the door handle. "Leah, come on. I just want to talk to you."

I stopped squirming, because pulling away from him was what hurt. I sat still and took a deep breath. I was more angry with him for pulling me around than scared of what he might do to me. He had never hurt me—other than grabbing me—or forced me to do something I didn't want to do. I'd seen men treat my mother a lot worse than this a hundred times, and I tried to remember what she'd done in this situation.

Started dating them again, that's what.

"Listen." Mark put his hand on my bare knee and stroked all the way up my thigh to my shorts. "I've been thinking a lot about what you said. I see now that you were right about Brenda. I broke it off with her, and I won't do anything like that again if you'll let me come back. I'll talk to my uncle about letting you fly for him too."

I shouldn't have considered this offer seriously. Not when he'd dragged me to his truck. But he was stoned. He didn't realize he'd hurt me.

And the more I'd thought about Mr. Simon's job over the past few days, the more I'd wondered whether Grayson had told me Mark had made it up just so Grayson could get me to work for him instead. When it was a matter of finding a cheap employee, I didn't think Grayson would stoop to that level. Now that I knew Grayson needed my help to keep Alec in town, for whatever reason, I was *sure* Grayson would stoop to that level. Which might mean Mr. Simon's job had been real all along.

"You can't move back in with me," I said. That had been the worst part of being with him. I wouldn't have gotten so angry at him in the first place if there had been less of him.

"I won't. I'm getting my own place." He gripped my knee harder. "Just come by the hangar tomorrow morning."

"I can't do it tomorrow," I said. "I've got another job."

"Oh, right," he said, "with those Hall assholes, over spring break. What kind of job is that, Leah? My uncle says they'll last another week or two without the old guy around. My uncle will hire you permanently."

He should have stopped when he was ahead. Now I was thinking about working for Mr. Simon permanently. Working with Mark. Being trained with Mark. Dating Mark under the constant threat of having my job taken away if I did something he didn't like. I'd been ready to give his job another try as soon as I could get out of this tangle with Alec and Grayson, but now I was having second thoughts.

"Come on, Leah," Mark whispered. His eyes were dark. He was *there,* when the other boys were inside the house with Molly and had forgotten me. He leaned closer to kiss me. I might have let him, except that he was squeezing my arm so hard.

The driver's door opened. Mark yanked my knee for a handhold as he was dragged out. He hit the cab of the next truck and bounced off with his fist already coming around, barely missing Grayson, who slammed him in the jaw. Boys in the surrounding trucks yelled and scrambled toward the fight.

"Hey!" I squealed, clambering across the seat. I didn't want these boys to beat each other up. Then there would be nobody left to employ me. "Grayson, Mark didn't mean any harm. He was just—"

"Get out of the truck, Leah," Grayson commanded me without looking around at me. He watched Mark. His hand was balled in a white, bloodless fist. "Go back to the house."

"Fuck off, Hall," Mark yelled, wiping blood from his mouth with one hand. "Leah, you stay right there."

Running footsteps sounded behind the truck. "Grayson!" Alec called from a distance.

Grayson didn't turn around for Alec either, but a second later, Alec and Patrick burst into the ring of boys that had formed to watch the fight. They dashed between Grayson and Mark. Alec caught Grayson from behind by both arms, spun him around, and shoved him in the direction of the house. The ring of boys parted to let Grayson through. Patrick put one hand on Mark, who slouched unsteadily against the cab.

Now that Grayson was gone, Mark leaned around Patrick and told Alec to fuck off instead. Alec stood there with his muscular arms crossed on his chest. He didn't look like a pretty boy anymore. Patrick had called him that and I had silently agreed . . . but in the face of Mark calling him every filthy name he could think of, Alec looked grim and didn't back down.

Alec turned to me and said sternly, "Go after Grayson. Make sure he gets to the car and waits for me there. You should know better than this. You have to keep him out of this type of thing or we'll all end up in jail. I'll fight Mark if I have to, but Grayson will kill him."

# thirteen

Alec shouldn't have worried. Grayson was standing behind Mark's truck with his hands on his hips, breathing hard. The instant he saw me, he stepped toward me like he'd been waiting for me. He grabbed my arm to pull me away from the fracas.

I stopped dead in my tracks. "Hey," I said.

I didn't have to explain why. As soon as I exclaimed, he realized he was grabbing me in exactly the same place Mark had grabbed me. Patrick must have told Grayson what happened. Patrick might even have gone to get him from the party. Grayson let me go immediately and spread his fingers as if consciously *not* making a fist. But he said, "Keep walking."

By the time we reached Alec's car, Alec was right behind us.

"Did you take care of it?" Grayson asked.

"Patrick talked him down." Alec turned to me. "Are you okay?"

"Sure." I'd been rubbing my arm unconsciously. I put my hand down.

Alec ran his fingers back through his hair, messing it up for the only time I'd seen, other than yesterday when he took the hose to it in the hangar sink. "Why were you talking to Mark?" He sounded exasperated with me, another first.

"I didn't want to come to this party," I said in my defense. "Y'all knew it. Molly knew it. She told you. You brought me anyway. The girl who lives here told me I wasn't welcome. I asked Molly if we could leave and she told me to go outside."

The boys exchanged a look over my head. "I'll go get her," Grayson said, obviously wanting me to have some alone time with Alec, my hero who had saved me, sort of, after Grayson saved me first. Grayson took a step toward the house.

Alec put his hand on Grayson's shoulder to stop him. "I'll get her. You're too mad."

As Alec walked toward the mansion, some boys ambled up the driveway from the direction of Mark's truck. They stared pointedly at me. Grayson crossed his arms and glared at them until they looked away.

Still watching them, he opened the front passenger door of Alec's car. "Get in."

He closed the door behind me and got into the backseat. The hot night had been cooled by the stormy breeze, but the car was like a sauna. Down the driveway toward Mark's truck, a radio blasted rap music and then quieted.

"Are you drunk?" Grayson asked.

"No," I said haughtily. "That, among other things, is a condition of my employment."

"Stoned?"

"No."

"Then why did you get within a hundred feet of Mark?"

"I didn't know he was out there," I said. "And I can't imagine why he's still after me." The massive front door of the mansion opened. Alec and Molly stepped out. The way they tossed sentences at each other and jerked their heads away, they looked like they were arguing. I wondered what Molly and Alec had to argue about.

"Have you seen yourself in those shorts?" Grayson asked me. "I'm beginning to think you really don't know."

I leaned around the headrest to face him in the backseat. "Know *what*, Grayson? That nobody will hire me just as a pilot? That all my flying jobs come with a side order of sexy times? Yeah, I'm beginning to figure that out. Not that *you're* to blame."

"God!" Molly was saying to Alec as she got into the backseat and he sat down in the front. But as soon as Alec started the engine and rolled down the windows to let the heat escape, Francie skittered out of the mansion with her minions behind her, pointing toward the car.

"Go, Alec," Grayson said quietly.

Francie's long, straight, glossy locks bounced around her shoulders as she stopped by my door and screamed through the open window at me. "What are you trying to do, start a fight and bring the cops to my party? This is why I don't invite trash." She peered past me into the car. "Molly, this is why I don't invite your trashy friend. Do *not* bring her near me again." She called across me to Alec, "You'd better be careful. You'll definitely catch something."

Her friends behind her laughed. More and more people were streaming out of the mansion to hear what Francie would say to me: all the girls who were actively mean to me in the hall and the bathroom and PE, the whole reason I never ventured to the lunchroom, and now a lot of other people too,

199

who had never given me a second glance but were realizing now who the trashy girl was that everybody had been talking about. I'd felt safe at school when those girls and certain boys weren't around. Now I wouldn't be safe anywhere.

As my world crumbled around me, I opened my mouth to insult Francie back. I had no idea what would have come out. Through long years of practice, I was pretty good in these situations, though there was no way I could hurt her as badly as she'd hurt me. Making fun of a girl for being rich didn't have the same zing as bullying her for being poor.

Before I could say anything, Molly exclaimed "Francie!" in a truly shocked tone.

But Alec drowned her out. "That is a nasty thing to say." His voice was louder than I'd ever heard it when he wasn't trying to talk over engine noise. "This town has gone to seed since I left." He hit the button to close all the windows. As a glass barrier rolled up to protect me from Francie, he threw the car into reverse to back out, then jerked it forward.

I watched Francie in the side mirror. She posed on her lawn, gaping in shock, half the school behind her. Her dear friend Molly couldn't shut her up, but an adorable boy from a different town had been able to make her see herself for what she was. Or, more likely, he'd just embarrassed her into silence temporarily.

As he turned from the driveway onto the main road, he bit out, "What did you bring Leah here for, Molly?"

"I warned y'all Leah didn't want to come!" Molly said. "I told you that's why she was dressed that way, and you didn't seem to mind *then.*"

"You didn't tell us that girl would come after her," Alec said.

"I've never seen Francie act that way!" Molly protested. "I

knew she didn't like Leah, but I thought that was because Leah can be kind of brusque, in case you haven't noticed. Did Leah tell you what she said to Francie's friend inside earlier? It was a doozy."

"That's because Francie followed Leah." Grayson was speaking for the first time. "I told you that before. It was obvious they were waiting to corner her. That's why I sent you after them."

"Well, what do you expect?" Molly snapped. "Did you think Francie would welcome Leah to the party and compliment her on her cute outfit? Leah's dressed like a hooker."

"Hey," Alec said disapprovingly. At the same time, Grayson said, "I think she looks nice."

I turned around in my seat and glared at Grayson, furious with him for manipulating me and getting me into this whole ill-fated date in the first place. "I hope you're enjoying this."

He stared back at me, lips parted, brows raised, looking almost apologetic.

I shifted my go-to-hell look to Molly. "And I'm sorry you're *not* enjoying it. You told Grayson and Alec last night that you decided to be my friend instead of sticking with Ryan because I'm so fun and brazen for a poor girl. Now you're saying you *don't* want me to dress like a whore and stick up for myself when you drag me to a party thrown by your bitch friend who hates me and calls me trash to my face every time she sees me. You need to make up your mind, girlfriend, how you like your charity case."

Delicate brows pulled low in a scowl, Molly took a long breath. She was going to tell me I was right. She didn't want to be friends with me anymore. My heart was breaking already, but I wasn't going to be used as anybody's emotional punching bag—not Francie's, not Molly's.

Only Grayson's. And only while he made me.

Instead, Molly slapped her hands over her face and burst into tears. Her sobs were loud at first. She tried to contain them, holding her breath, and ended up with a case of the hic-cups.

Grayson could have slipped an arm around her to comfort her. I didn't want him to, but that would have been humane. He chose the low road: "This is so awkward. You're still com-ing to work tomorrow, right, Molly? I told you, no drinking this week, and no drama."

"Really?" I shouted at him. "I'm about to lose my best friend and it's still about work for you?"

"*Yes,* it's about work for me," he said. "I'm your boss."

At the same time, Molly wailed, "You're not about to lose your—" She hiccupped. "Please, Leah, you're not about to lose your—"

"Molly, you would deserve it if you did," Alec muttered. I could tell from the way he was looking in the rearview mirror that he was watching her.

"And what about you, Leah?" Grayson accused me. "You didn't tell us Mark Simon would be at the party." I felt his hand on my shoulder. "You promised me he wouldn't come after Alec."

I turned around again and frowned at Grayson. "I promised you no such thing. I told you Mark wasn't dangerous."

"He came after you, and Alec and I had to save your ass. In effect, he came after Alec."

"Alec and you did not exactly have to save my ass," I mut-tered at the same time Alec said with uncharacteristic bitter-ness, "Shut up, Grayson."

We rode in silence for several minutes, except for the coun-try music on the radio, and Molly hiccupping.

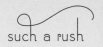

"I don't know what you girls have going on with each other," Grayson said quietly. "I think it would help if we all were more honest with each other."

Molly snorted.

I glared at her, terrified all over again that Grayson would guess I'd told her about seducing Alec. Grayson glared at her too, and Alec continued to stare hard at her in the rearview mirror.

"Pardon *me*," she grumbled.

The closer we got to her house, the more I worried. I still believed I was her charity case. But whatever her motivation for calling me a friend, I called her a friend because I was more myself around her. I relaxed more, laughed more. I wasn't willing to throw that away over one party. Our relationship was a delicate balance. I shouldn't have tipped the scales by telling her how I really felt.

At her house, she got out and slammed the car door without a word. I got out too and reached for her hand. She didn't swing it playfully as we walked to her front door, but she didn't pull away, either. On the porch, I closed the distance between us and hugged her. "I'm sorry."

"No, *I'm* sorry," she said so somberly that I believed her. "I honestly didn't think Francie would do that. And even if she did, I had no idea you cared."

Fair enough. Molly was so popular that girls never told her to leave their parties. She probably hadn't been trying to be mean to me. She simply had no clue what my life felt like, and she never would.

"I'm drunk," she said. "I'm sorry." She backed up and put her hand on the doorknob. "I will have regained some of my IQ points by tomorrow, and we'll talk."

"Deal." I laughed, so relieved that the Molly I loved was

coming back. But as I gently closed the door behind her and walked to Alec's idling car, I knew everything was all wrong. We'd never had an argument like this before, not since we became friends in the first place. Something had come between us. It had to do with the boys. And we'd broken the most important unspoken rule of our bond. We shouldn't have told each other we were sorry.

Back at the car, Alec covered my hand with his on the seat between us, not like flirting with me but like comforting a friend, and I gave him a small smile.

Grayson immersed himself in his phone all the way to the airport. We dropped him off at the hangar. He didn't climb into his truck immediately. He unlocked the side door of the hangar.

"Is he really staying here that late to finish paperwork?" I asked Alec.

"He did last night," Alec said. "Tonight he's worried about the airplanes in the storms."

On the short drive from the airport to the trailer park, I tried and failed to think of something to say. The night had been full and there was plenty to discuss, but every subject seemed touchy between Alec and me.

And I was so bone-tired. Maybe flying all day had fatigued me. Spilling my guts about my lack of a family. Unsuccessfully skirting Francie. Fighting with Mark. Nearly losing Molly. Pining after Grayson and hating myself for doing it.

"May I walk you to your door that is too an actual door?" Alec asked.

I laughed, trying not to sound nervous. I didn't want to kiss Alec anywhere, but especially not at my door. "Can we stay in the car for a minute instead? The dog will calm down eventually. If we're standing outside, he won't."

"Okay." Alec parked in the dirt clearing and turned off the engine. Into that silence, the noise of the trailer park flowed: the pit bull having a fit at the end of his chain, the wind tossing the trees and making the joints of the metal trailers screech, a couple standing in the road and cursing at each other. Staying in the car parked in the dirt yard was awkward. I should have told Alec to come inside the trailer. But I wasn't going to do that.

He cleared his throat. "I wanted to ask you something."

Uh-oh. Every time Alec had asked me something tonight, I'd wished he hadn't.

But I said, "Okay," and grinned at him, like if I grinned hard enough, the hard ball of dread in my stomach would dissolve. I hoped he didn't ask to get serious with me, physically or emotionally, because I didn't know what I would do if that happened.

"It seems like you have two modes," he said. "One is a giggly, flirty mode. The other is a no-nonsense pilot mode. They never mix or cross. You're like two different people. Did you know you do that?"

My heart raced. I tried to talk myself down from panic. Alec hadn't figured out I was putting on an act with him. He'd known me for a long time and had observed me acting different ways over the course of years.

I shook my head no. "I've been told that I do that, though." I glanced slyly over at him. "Which one am I doing now?"

"Flirty mode."

"Which one do you like better?"

"Definitely flirty mode." He grinned at me. "Come here."

The lead-up was so sweet and sexy. If I'd liked him romantically at all, I would have enjoyed his kiss. But as it was, the only thing good I could say about it was that it was fifty percent shorter than his kiss the night before.

He gave me one more peck on the lips and backed away. "Anyway, here's the reason I asked about your modes."

If I'd known he wanted to have an actual conversation, I would have drawn the kiss out longer.

"I have trouble reading you sometimes," he said. "You have these two personalities. I never know which one I'll be talking to. They get offended at different things. Then, at the café, you told us why you want to fly, and that was so . . ."

He looked out the windshield at the palm trees swaying violently in the wind.

"Honest. Finally. Maybe for the first time ever." He looked straight at me.

I shrank back.

"I jumped on that and asked you about your dad," he said. "And then, when you got mad . . . I'm really sorry about that. I thought about it later and realized that wasn't a question I should ever have asked anyone. It's just that you fooled me, because flirty Leah wouldn't have minded. Anyone can ask her anything. No-nonsense Leah minded. A lot."

I laughed. "She did."

"Forgive me."

"I forgive you."

I hoped all this forgiveness would equal a good-bye, but he still walked me to the door and gave me another kiss. A short one, and then I was inside my trailer that smelled like a basement. I removed my slutty makeup and clothes and cuddled in bed to read myself to sleep, listening to the clock-radio yammer about a tornado one county south.

I knew from watching TV during tornado warnings in the past, back in the heady, luxurious days of owning a television, that the meteorologists liked to say, "If you're in a trailer home, get to your safe place." Like there was a safe place for

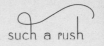

me. What was I supposed to do without a car, go outside and lie in a wet ditch, waiting for the pit bull to jerk out of his collar and tear me to shreds? This time I even turned off the radio. Why bother? A tornado probably wasn't going to hit me. And if it did, I was going to die. Hunkering next to the toilet wasn't going to change that when my trailer home wrapped around a tree with me inside it.

Most of my life was a huge effort to look like everybody else. Occasionally I realized there was no point in making the effort, and there was a certain delicious luxury in giving up entirely. This was one of those times, I decided, as the tornado sirens woke me. They were spaced throughout the town, but of course the city planners put one smack in the middle of the trailer park, because people out here wouldn't complain when it rang in our heads, much as we didn't officially complain about the airplanes screaming overhead. I lay in bed, holding on to either edge of the mattress. The wind shook a palm frond in front of the streetlight streaming through the window.

People who lived in houses said the noise of the rain was soothing. In South Carolina in the springtime, the rain pounded so hard it hurt. The sound on the metal roof of a trailer was a special kind of torture. The additional sound of a train, the tornado noise people talked about, would have given me such a rush churning through the forest.

I jerked up to sitting at a noise that trumped even the tornado siren and split the drum of the rain. Someone was pounding at the door.

I stumbled through the dark trailer, heart thumping, certain someone had gotten caught in the storm and was coming to me for shelter. Who? Nobody would come to me for help. Maybe my mom's boyfriend, Roger, had dropped her off and

she had lost her key. Or Mark was using the cover of the storm to trick himself inside. My instincts told me to pull more clothes over my tank top and boxers I'd been sleeping in, but I couldn't spare the time if someone was in trouble.

"Who is it?" I shouted.

"Grayson!" He pounded the door again, a single blow that shook the metal walls. I jumped backward in surprise, then moved forward to jerk the door open.

He was soaked, his blond hair dark, rivulets of water streaming down his cheeks, his T-shirt plastered against his chest.

"Come on." I put out one hand to drag him inside. There was an exception to my nobody-comes-in-my-trailer rule, apparently.

He hung back. "I'm already wet. There's a tornado at the edge of the county. Get your stuff and let's go."

I ran back to my bedroom, able to navigate the dark much better now that it mattered. Saving myself from a tornado hadn't been important. Now that Grayson was involved, the thought of the freight train tearing up the palm trees on its way straight for us made me sob. I shoved my feet into my flip-flops, grabbed my purse, and ran. I paused beside Grayson on the cement-block stairs long enough to lock the door. In the five seconds this took, I was already as wet as him. We jogged down the steps and through the yard, a floodplain of mud, to his truck.

The inside of the cab was a relief from the rain, but drops pounded the roof. As he ripped onto the gravel road, the raindrops turned to white streaks in the headlights. He yelled above the noise, "I called Alec to make sure he knew about the tornado. I asked him if he was with you, and he said no. I'd hoped you'd still be out with him."

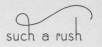

"No," I yelled back, "he's a perfect gentleman."

"That's what I was afraid of."

I wondered what Grayson meant by this. He wanted Alec to keep me out all night until the public places closed and there was nothing left to do but go somewhere private and paw each other? Did he really intend me to do that with Alec, knowing I wasn't into him?

The way Grayson was looking at me, it seemed that's exactly what he intended me to do. As he paused at the highway, he glanced at me with a dark expression. Suddenly conscious of the soaked boxers and tank top I wore, I wanted to cross my arms over my chest, but I wasn't going to let him intimidate me.

Finally he said, "It sounded like Alec was still out, though. Do you know where he went?"

"No."

"And he didn't sound particularly concerned about you. He told me he'd dropped you off and that you would hear the tornado siren and you'd be okay."

"I *would* have been okay."

"Well, you and I have different definitions of okay, as we're finding out."

He parked the truck beside the airport office, where stairs led down to the cellar door. I'd been in the small cellar before. The airport stored old records there, and every now and then I had to dig up a hangar rental contract. A lot of people had the key—everybody who rented a large hangar, so they'd have access in case of a storm exactly like this—but the last time I'd taken a peek, the cot and blankets hadn't been there.

"Did you bring these down?" I asked from the bottom stair as he closed the door at the top, shutting out half the noise of the rain.

He looked around from his high vantage point. "Yeah."

"You thought ahead." I meant this as a compliment. Mr. Hall had yelled at him countless times for not thinking ahead.

"I knew the storm was coming and I had a feeling it might blast right through here. If I'd really thought ahead, though, I would have brought you an umbrella." His eyes drifted to my tank top, which must have been see-through. He forced his eyes away.

Now that he was being nice, I *did* cross my arms on my chest. "It wouldn't have done any good with the rain blowing sideways."

The tornado siren shut off. That didn't mean the tornado was gone. The siren sounded only a few minutes at a time so everybody did not go insane.

He trod down the stairs in his wet flip-flops and kicked them onto the cement floor at the bottom. Shaking out one blanket from the cot and holding it between us like a wall, he said, "You can take off those wet clothes. I won't look, promise. I know you're cold."

Well, I just did what he said. Why not? My teeth were chattering, I faced a long night of sleeping down here, and the blanket would be a lot more comfortable than wet cotton plastered to my skin. The flirty Leah described by Alec might have dangled her wet clothes out one side of the blanket to tempt Grayson. I was no-nonsense Leah and I had to get some sleep and fly tomorrow, assuming the airport was still here then. An airport fifty miles inland had been destroyed by a tornado last month.

I stripped off my boxers and tank top, plopped them on the floor, and took the blanket Grayson was holding up. Cocooning myself in it, I lay down on the cot, facing him.

He picked up my boxers, squeezed the water into the drain in the center of the floor, and stretched them out on the stair railing to dry. That was optimistic, because the air was cool and humid here underground, in a spring storm. He did the same with my tank top.

Then he pulled off his T-shirt. The cotton clung to the muscles of his chest and arms like it loved him and didn't want to leave. Finally it popped off over his head. He shook his curly hair out like a dog, water spraying everywhere, droplets touching my face. He wrung out his shirt in the drain and hung it beside mine on the rail.

He glanced over at me and saw that I was watching him, waiting for him to take his shorts off.

He would not. Grabbing the second blanket, he hunched it around his shoulders and sank against the cement-block wall, staring into his phone.

"Is the tornado gone?" I asked.

"Yes. Looks like it was a circulation that never touched down, but—"

The tornado siren cranked up again, quietly at first so that it could have been mistaken for a motor humming, then escalating into a grating wail.

"—there are more behind it," Grayson yelled.

I waited another few minutes until the siren relaxed, its voice fading until it disappeared. Then I asked, "Are you going to stay up all night?"

He looked up from his phone and shifted uncomfortably against the wall. "If I have to. Why?"

"You've got me down here. There's nothing you can do about the airplanes. Why are you watching the weather? If a tornado comes through here, are you going to run out in the rain and stop it?"

A sad smile played at the corners of his mouth. "Good night, Leah."

I snuggled down into the blanket. My head was cold because my hair was sopping wet. My feet were cold. But curled up on itself, my body at its core was warm.

I hadn't been very aware of my body in the past few days. It was a tool to get me what I wanted. How it looked and how it performed mattered to me. How it felt did not.

Now I began to feel again. The blanket was soft against my elbows and my knees and my breasts. It was all that separated me from Grayson a few feet away, brooding into his phone, then glancing up at me with hard gray eyes.

I didn't sleep at first. I regressed into some kind of animal state in which I wished the world away and didn't want to be touched. I might have been able to sleep except that the unfiltered lights in the ceiling were on, or I dreamed they were, drilling into my head and prying their way behind my closed eyelids.

Then I knew I'd been asleep, because I woke with a start. Something was different in the dark room. "What happened?"

"The power went out." Grayson was nothing but a shadow now, sitting against the wall with his long legs bent in front of him, his phone gone dark. "It flickered first. That's probably what woke you."

I sighed and tried to relax again into my blanket, warm with my own heat. My body still tingled with the same awareness of itself and of Grayson that I'd felt when I first lay down. I must have been dreaming about him.

"Leah," he said out of the darkness.

"Mm," I answered, still half-asleep, wishing his gentle voice really was pillow talk.

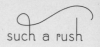

"Do you know how to scatter ashes over the Atlantic?"

That woke me up. He was talking about a Hall Aviation service. A lot of the people who retired in Heaven Beach wanted to be cremated and have their ashes scattered over the water by plane. It had been a surprisingly large portion of Mr. Hall's business. I said, "Yeah."

"Do you just dump them out the window or what?"

"No." I didn't laugh at this idea, because that's what I'd thought too, before Mr. Hall showed me otherwise. "They would blow back in the window. There's a special funnel attached to a tube. You pour the ashes into the funnel and put the end of the tube out the window. It's on one of the shelves in the back of the hangar. I can show you."

"Thanks."

The rain pounded on the door at the top of the stairs. When it began to fade again so we could hear each other, I ventured, "Do you need to do that for your dad's ashes?"

"Eventually. I don't think Alec's ready for it yet."

There it was again, the strange protectiveness I kept hearing in Grayson's voice when he talked about Alec, like he was Alec's older brother rather than his twin.

"For Jake's ashes, then?" I prompted him.

"No. My dad suggested it, but my mom wanted Jake buried at the cemetery in Wilmington. They fought even about that."

Now that I couldn't see Grayson, I could sense so much more in his tone. Loss of one brother. Love for the other. Desperation to hold together what was left of his family.

Failure.

He cleared his throat. "It's just that ASH SCATTERING OVER THE ATLANTIC is painted on the side of the Hall Aviation building."

"True."

"I don't have any contracts for it right now. But I can tell from the books that Dad made a lot of money doing it. In case someone calls about it, I need to know how so I don't look like an idiot. Any more than I already do."

Even though I couldn't see his face in the dark, I propped myself up on one elbow and gazed toward him. "You don't look like an idiot, Grayson. Everybody is amazed at what you've done for this business."

"Because I acted like such an idiot before," he said softly.

I didn't say anything. He hadn't acted like an idiot before, just like someone who didn't care very much. And that was no comfort when his father was dead.

After the silence had stretched, though, with the rain beating on the door again like someone knocking and urging me to go on, I asked him, "How did you figure all this stuff out for the business?"

"It's amazing what you can do when you actually do it. If you act like you can't take care of yourself, someone will step in and take care of you. Like my dad and Jake used to do for me, and like I'm doing for Alec now. If you act like you don't need help, nobody will mess with you. I don't need to tell *you,* though. You're the queen of that."

I laughed bitterly, thinking of Molly dragging me to Francie's party. "Grayson, people do mess with me. Taking care of yourself makes you a target. And as Molly so kindly pointed out at dinner, the people who should have taken care of me never have, because nobody gives a shit."

"I do."

My body lit on fire with a new wave of the awareness I'd felt since I'd been here. But Grayson was manipulating me. Rolling on my back and staring up at the exposed pipes in the ceiling, I murmured, "You have a funny way of showing it."

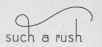

He was moving by the dark wall. For a second I thought I'd made him mad, and he would stomp out into the storm.

But then he was kneeling beside me, one hand very close to me on the cot. "Leah, I'm sorry about tonight with Mark. Patrick ran into the house to tell me Mark had grabbed you. I was afraid he'd hurt you. I may have overreacted, but"—he opened his hands, giving up—"that's just what I do sometimes. You can't hang out with Mark, okay? You'll be really sorry."

"Right," I grumbled. "You care about me so much that you shove me toward your brother."

Grayson sighed in frustration. "That's for his own good. All of this is for him."

"Tell me why," I insisted.

"I can't." Grayson focused on me and his face was full of concern. "If I told you, you'd change the way you act around him, and he would know it was all for show."

"Is he sick?" I guessed, hoping not. That would be too much for both of them to take.

"No!" Grayson said so vehemently that I believed him. "He just needs some help remembering that he's human. I guess we all do." He moved his hand from the side of the cot to my cheek.

Our gazes locked. Electricity formed in my cheek and zinged straight down, through my whole body.

He blinked slowly. Up close, his face was an elongated version of Alec's. His long, blond lashes were the same. But his eyes were completely different from Alec's innocent blue ones. They were stormy gray, swirling with heat.

Suddenly I knew why he'd been hiding behind his shades or looking down at his phone whenever I was around. Why he'd taken potshots at me yesterday for flirting with Alec, even though he was the one making me do it. He couldn't

have me. That would ruin his plans for me and Alec. But he wanted me.

We paused there on the edge. His thumb stroked my jawbone as he leaned closer. I closed my eyes.

And then we were kissing, panting, kissing again, his lips hard on mine, his hand sliding down my bare skin underneath the blanket.

Wow. Earlier that night and the night before, kissing Alec would have been nice if not for all the baggage with it. It felt good, and he acted like a gentleman. Grayson did not act like a gentleman at all. Kissing him was an adventure, a journey, a battle, every movement of his lips and hands sparking new explosions all over me.

"Oh," he said, drawing back. Then he changed his mind and kissed me again. His hand cupped my bare breast, his thumb rubbed across my nipple, and I was not going to tell him no. I didn't need to. He would make a fist and exercise the impulse control he'd been taught in five, four, three, two, one.

He broke the kiss and sat back on his heels. His hand moved from my breast to the center of my chest, over my heart. "Leah." He was breathing hard. "I'm sorry. I do care about you. Please know that. I just . . . I don't know what to say."

"Tell me I don't have to date Alec anymore."

"What?" His face hardened against me, and he withdrew his hand. "No."

"Tell me *why* I have to date Alec."

"No."

"Then fuck off." Hugging the blanket tightly around me, I rolled over with my back to him.

Much later I woke again and sat up suddenly, alarmed at the weight on my chest. The lights were still off, but I could see

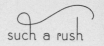

in the dim glow through the cellar window that both blankets covered me. Grayson lay sprawled across the cement floor with no blanket at all, his wet T-shirt balled under his head for a pillow. I watched his smooth, muscled chest rise and fall for a few peaceful breaths. Then I lay back down.

"Leah," he whispered. "Hey. Wake up."

As I opened my eyes, he was moving his hand away. My scalp tingled like he'd been stroking my hair.

"Get dressed," he said. "I'm waiting outside for you in the truck." He climbed the stairs in his damp clothes and disappeared through the door.

The light was back on. I slipped my own cold clothes on, wishing for the warm blankets, and followed him up the stairs. Outside it was still night. The rain had moved away, leaving a heavy white mist in its place. The airport looked ghostly and abandoned but intact. I wondered why Grayson had woken me.

"What's the matter?" I asked as I hopped up into his truck. "Did the tornado touch down?"

"Not around here," he said. "A couple of people were killed in a trailer park a few counties west of here."

Nothing unusual. A chill passed through me.

"But the storms are gone," he said, "so I'm taking you home."

"Couldn't you let me sleep through the night and then walk home?" I grumbled.

"No, Alec might get here early in the morning and see you."

"Why couldn't you tell him the truth? That you didn't want your employee to die, so you brought me into the storm cellar and slept on the floor across the room from me, and we made out for a few minutes but didn't do it?"

217

The truck bumped from the highway to the gravel road through the trailer park. He said quietly, "It would look like we did it." Gravel crunched under the tires as he stopped the truck in front of my trailer. "If I told him about it, he would figure out that I wanted to. He knows me pretty well."

Though my fingers and toes were frozen, my blood heated as he whispered this.

He sighed, dismissing the thought, back to business. "Sleep late tomorrow if you need to. I'll make up an excuse to tell Alec. Or take a nap on break. What matters most is other people—" He touched his thumb.

"Then me, then the airplane, then the banner. I know." I jumped down from the truck and crossed the dirt yard, unhealthily pissed that every time Grayson and I were about to make an actual connection, he brought up business. Or Alec. They were one and the same for him.

I tripped over the edge of a miniature canyon the rain had carved into the dirt. That was the only difference the storms had made. In Grayson's headlights, the trailer shone dully. Like a cockroach after a nuclear war, it would still be here when we all were dead.

# fourteen

"Is he really asleep?" I called to Alec, just loud enough to be heard over the drone of the fans in the hangar.

We both sat in lawn chairs. I'd just started lunch, Alec was finishing his, and Molly was outside, getting his next banner ready. I'd thought Molly would make my job flying for Grayson more fun and less awkward. She'd said she was here to protect me. Yet because of the way our meals and breaks fell, I hardly saw her. When we did speak, she acted funny, like there was something wrong between us.

Or maybe that was me, still miffed about Francie's party last night.

Grayson lay on the couch in front of Alec and me, obviously unconcerned about its dust issues. He'd been talking to us about the turbulence we'd all felt that morning now that the days were getting warmer and pockets of hot air rose from the beach. He'd closed his eyes, but he kept responding to everything Alec and I said . . . more and more slowly . . . and now he

219

looked like he had in the basement last night, his face at peace, his long body strangely relaxed.

Alec nodded. "He spent the whole night here last night, watching over the airplanes. In the one-in-a-million event that a tornado *did* touch down here, what was he going do? Hold on to one wing of each Piper to keep them from blowing away?"

Afraid to admit I'd asked Grayson the same thing last night, I shrugged. Grayson's vigil had nothing to do with the airplanes themselves. It had to do with worry, responsibility, helplessness, and the need to do *something,* I thought. And it had a little bit to do with me.

Alec stood and threw his trash in the can. "I'll see if Molly needs help, and then I'm flying. Don't wake Grayson up, even if it's time for you to fly, okay? Just let him sleep. And if he jumps down your throat later, tell him I told you so." He crossed behind me and squeezed my shoulder.

I nodded, still watching Grayson. Alec disappeared into the hot afternoon. Out on the runway, Mr. Simon's Stearman biplane passed in front of the opening of the hangar. One of his employees was taking a tourist for a ride instead of Mark taking me. The distant roar echoed around the metal walls and mixed with the drone of the fans, hum upon hum. Grayson didn't stir. I took another bite of my sandwich as I examined him.

One long leg extended off the edge of the couch, past the armrest. The other leg was folded under him. His arms were folded across his chest too, hugging himself. His face settled to one side, toward me, his features softened by sleep, his blond lashes long against his cheeks. His shaggy curls peeked from behind his head on the sofa cushions. In that moment I saw him differently: not as an American boy with a tenuous grip on the family business and his own sanity, but as a British teenager crashing after a night on the town in London, listening to some strange pop music, wearing the straw cowboy hat for offbeat fashion rather than to keep the glare of the sun out of his eyes. Tall as he was, with a long nose and elegant hands despite the engine grease that usually streaked them, he would make a good Brit.

I felt like a voyeur, watching him sleep as I ate my sandwich, as if he were a movie for my entertainment while I munched popcorn. He'd watched me sleep the night before, I reasoned, so I didn't owe him this sort of privacy.

I finished my lunch and dumped my own trash in the can. Instead of walking outside to my plane, though, I sat back down in my chair, a few feet from Grayson. I didn't think he needed protecting, exactly. Nobody would come into this hangar to attack him, not even Mark, while his uncle kept him busy. And Alec was right: I shouldn't wake Grayson. He would be angry that we hadn't woken him. Alec and I would argue that if he was tired enough to need a nap in the middle of the day, he was too tired to fly until he caught up on sleep.

I should have left him sleeping and gone back to work. Something stopped me. His chest rose and fell more rapidly underneath his protective arms and his red T-shirt. His smooth brow wrinkled ever so slightly, like he'd had the briefest glimpse into something horrible.

A plane started not far outside the hangar, Alec's Piper. The engine was quieter because he was only taxiing toward the end of the runway, not taking off. But he was so close that the noise vibrated the hangar, growling underneath the drone of the fans.

Grayson sat up in a rush, one hand gripping the sofa cushion and the other white-knuckling the back of the couch. He looked straight at me, mouth open, gray eyes wide. His sudden

movement had stirred the dust in the couch. A cloud of it twinkled around him in a shaft of sunlight streaming through the hangar door.

He asked, "My dad, and Jake. Are they dead?"

My fingers turned icy in the warm hangar. I could only imagine what cruelty his subconscious had dealt him. A family lunch, with his dad and Jake gathered around the dusty couch instead of Alec and me. A family argument that he'd hated every second of but wished he could have back again now that he understood it had been their last.

I nodded.

He closed his eyes. "Where is Alec?" he asked quietly. The noise from Alec's plane had faded as he taxied away on the tarmac, but Grayson's voice was still barely audible above the fans.

I waved toward the runway. "Flying."

Grayson winced. Swinging his legs off the couch to set his feet on the floor, he leaned over and cradled his face in his hands. "It's not fair," he murmured through his fingers.

I wanted to reach out to him. I didn't think it was fair, either, and I wanted to put my arm around him and tell him so. He'd been cruel to me in the past three days, though. He'd made it clear what he thought of me. He didn't want comfort from me.

He sobbed into his hands. Silently. I recognized the sob by the way his shoulders moved.

Just once.

In two steps I crossed the empty cement floor between us, sat next to him on the couch, and slid my arm around his back. I wasn't tall enough to put it around his shoulders. As I sat, I stirred up more dust. The air around us filled with golden sparks.

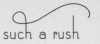

Now that I was touching him, I could tell how fast he was breathing. He tried to control it, though, refusing to let go of more than that one sob. He breathed long and deep, then wiped both hands down his face. He turned to me, eyes red and wet. "Do not tell Alec."

"I won't," I said.

He growled, "I will make your life hell."

I heard my own gasp of surprise. I removed my arm from around him and shifted back to my original chair. "You don't have to threaten me, Grayson. I said I wouldn't tell him, and I won't."

He ran one hand across yesterday's blond stubble that he hadn't gotten a chance to shave. "I'm sorry. You're right." He sniffed. "I don't think I'm getting enough sleep at night."

"I don't think you are either," I said haughtily, then stood. "I'm going up."

"Leah, I'm really sorry," he said again. His eyes pleaded with me.

I stopped thinking. Instinctively I stepped back across the divide between us and put my hand in his hair. His curls were surprisingly soft, unlike the wires on my own head. I weaved my fingers through them, down to his scalp.

This time he didn't stiffen when I touched him. He leaned his head against me and let me comfort him for five seconds.

*Then* he pulled away and stood, towering over me. "I'll be up too, as soon as I pull myself together." He headed for the restroom.

Yeah, I knew that feeling. Thinking I had a handle on the grief. Being overwhelmed with it all of a sudden, where other people could see me. Running for the restroom and wishing I could wash it down the sink. Though he'd said he was sorry,

he hadn't acknowledged he was doing exactly what I'd done Monday morning, when he accused me of acting.

I tamped down that flash of anger. Nothing like that would make sense to Grayson right now. Nothing mattered as much as what he had lost.

Grayson was the one who suggested we go surfing that night. Alec and Molly thought this was a great idea. They guessed I didn't have a surfboard, but Molly had one I could borrow. They guessed I couldn't surf, but it was easy and they would teach me. This wasn't going to happen. I was confident I could wiggle out of it somehow.

All in all, it sounded like a terrific alternative to the last few nights. We would eat at Molly's café. She would bring her boards over from her house, Alec would carry his from Mr. Hall's condo, and we would go into the ocean at Grayson's shack. With any luck, Alec and I wouldn't get much time alone. Even his kiss good night at my trailer would follow the trend and get shorter still. We would all call it a night early, and Grayson could claim some sleep.

By the time we got to the beach, the sky was bright pink with violet clouds, and the warm ocean rolled dark blue underneath it. I couldn't blame Molly and Alec for hitting the beach running with their surfboards. They slid right into the water and paddled for the horizon.

With them gone, I felt like I'd dodged a bullet. I settled the board Molly had loaned me into the sand and sat on it with my toes in the water. I didn't mind the ocean touching my toes.

The surf was so loud that I didn't notice Grayson until he was right behind me. He'd gone to pull his surfboard out of the shack. Setting it upright in the sand and leaning on it, he looked every inch a hard-bodied, sun-bleached surfer dude.

Only his words gave him away. Always plotting, he never relaxed, even at the beach. "Did they leave you?" He gazed out to the horizon. "Are you going to pout like you're jealous? That's good, but then you won't get to go surfing. Come on, plan B. We'll catch up with them." He held out his hand to pull me up.

I didn't take his hand. I said, "I can't swim."

His mouth dropped open. "You can't swim!"

There wasn't a good answer to this. He shouldn't have countered my "I can't swim" with "You can't swim!" in a disbelieving tone, like he was asking me if I was *sure* I couldn't swim?

I watched the waves and wished I could shove my whole body down beneath the sand, not just my feet.

He wouldn't let it go. "You're eighteen years old," he insisted.

I huffed out an exasperated sigh.

He couldn't hear my frustration over the ocean breeze. Or he didn't care. "Why haven't you ever learned to swim?"

Finally I looked up at him. I was surprised at how clearly I could see him in the dusk, his blond curls glowing in the sunset. I must have appeared just as clearly defined to him, and exposed.

"Who taught *you* to swim?" I asked.

He answered without thinking, "My da— Oh."

I'd never had a father. "Oh," I echoed Grayson in a dead tone.

I cringed as soon as I said it. Sarcasm was a weapon for children. I had used it a lot in grade school and middle school, and all it had gotten me was slapped in the girls' bathroom. I used it too much now. Grayson would realize, *She is reminding me she is pitiful!* and he would try to apologize. Best to let it pass. The less said the better.

He dropped his surfboard on the beach and sat beside me on my board. "Hey." His foot burrowed under the sand, the dry mound moving like a blanket, and his toes nudged my heel. "I'm sorry."

"Hooray." I gazed where Molly and Alec had disappeared, the sunset gone now, the black sky and the black ocean different from each other only because the ocean was striped with white waves. I wished I were viewing the scene from the air, where I had control.

"Next summer I'll teach you to swim," Grayson said. "This isn't the time or place, in the waves and the dark, but in the summer we'll go to the pool at my dad's condo and I'll teach you."

I didn't have anything to say to this. I just wanted him to get out all his guilt and shut up. I had no idea what I would be doing in the summer, except that it would *not* be frolicking with Grayson in the pool at his dead dad's upscale condo on the swanky end of town. I could fantasize about it all I wanted, but it would never happen.

"You can't just sit there and sulk about it, Leah," he told me. "You have to *do* something about it. Same thing with not knowing how to drive. You can't go on this way. Your world is very small."

Wearing a pained expression I wasn't able to control, I chopped my hand across my throat, telling him to shut up. I could see him dimly in the moonlight, and I knew he could see me.

He refused to shut up, though. "I'm not insulting you. I'm just saying that if someone offers you an opportunity to learn something new, do something different, get out of this town, you should take it. I even feel kind of bad about running you off Mr. Simon's crop-dusting job."

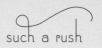

"You said Mark just wanted in my pants," I growled.

"He *did* just want in your pants." Grayson sounded out-raged. "I'm not sorry about that part. I just think you would be the world's best crop-duster pilot. You want that thrill, but outwardly you remain calm. You would never get yourself killed. Mark wants that thrill and he does *not* remain calm. He's so busy looking back at how close to the barn he flew that he forgets to look ahead of him. One day soon he's going to smack into a tree. I know this because I want that thrill too, and I don't remain calm either. Lately I've learned better than to get myself into that situation. In the original *Star Wars,* Obi-Wan Kenobi tells Darth Vader, 'If you strike me down, I shall become more powerful than you could possibly imagine.'"

I laughed at Grayson's dead-on British accent. Again, I thought he looked British, with the long nose and fingers and body of a 1960s rock star.

"Sometimes I think that's what happened to my dad," he said.

*You think he became one with the Force?* I almost asked. But I couldn't joke about his father. And I remembered what Alec had said about Grayson, that there was something wrong with him. I asked very carefully and nonjudgmentally, "What happened to your dad?"

"All he used to say to me was, 'You're going to die young. You're going to get fired from every job you ever land. You don't plan ahead. You don't pay attention. You're going to get yourself killed.' And maybe, in the end, he decided that nothing would convince me short of dying himself."

*Oh, Grayson,* I nearly gasped. I looked over at him, but all I could see was his profile outlined against the dark beach. He looked out at the ocean like he was talking to himself, not to me. I wondered if he had ever said this to anybody.

I said conversationally, not letting any of my alarm come through in my pilot voice, "Your dad died because he wasn't taking care of himself and he refused to go to the doctor, and he had a heart attack."

Grayson didn't nod or shake his head no. Keeping eerily still, he asked, "Were you the last person to see him alive?"

I winced, but he was watching the ocean and couldn't see. I said, "I've wondered about that. I did have a lesson with him the day before the Admiral found him. But sometimes after he left my lesson, he'd stop at a restaurant for dinner on the way back to his condo. Actually he went to Molly's parents' café quite a bit because it's on this end of town. But I didn't ask around. He was gone, and I guess I thought it was best to let him go." That's how I liked to think of him, hunching his coat around him, ducking into the airport office to tell me good-bye, and driving off through the winter night in his truck.

"What was the last thing he said to you?" Grayson persisted.

I thought back. "He had acted down during the lesson. As I was leaving, I asked him why lately he hadn't sat on the airport office porch with the Admiral in the afternoon like he usually did when I got to work."

"What did he say?"

"He said it had been too cold."

"That sounds prophetic, like he was willing his death to happen."

The surfboard was getting hard, and I squirmed on the slick surface, uncomfortable with this line of reasoning, in which Grayson was going to point the finger at himself any way he could. "Well, I think he'd given up," I said. "The last time he had a girlfriend, I'd just started working at the airport. She moved to Florida to take care of her mom. He wouldn't

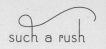

move with her because he wanted to stay close to you guys. So they broke up."

"What?" Grayson exclaimed. "I never heard of . . . What was her name?"

"Sofie."

He tried the name out. "Sofie." Then his tone turned darker. "How old was she?"

"His age. Early fifties. Or, back then, late forties."

"Did they see each other a lot?"

"She came to the airport all the time."

He frowned at me, perplexed. "How come I never knew about her?"

"You weren't around. Y'all had started telling your dad you didn't want to come stay with him, even when it was his weekend."

"That's because I was playing basketball," Grayson protested, "and Alec was wrestling. We had games and meets, and he wouldn't come see us."

"He thought you didn't want him to."

Grayson's lips parted. "Did he tell you that?"

"Yes." I wasn't going to lie to Grayson. He'd been agonizing over the details of Mr. Hall's death, and he was trying to puzzle it out. But I didn't want him to dwell on the rift between them. "I don't think it does any good to go back and second-guess this stuff. I'm just saying, different people see things different ways, and that's how he saw it. After Sofie left, you could say he let himself go. He gained more weight, and that made him more likely to have a heart attack, yes. Then Jake died, and that was hard on him.

"But Grayson." I reached out and put my hand on his knee. His skin was cool to the touch. "Your dad wasn't so cruel that

he would want to die as a message to you. And if that's what you honestly believe . . . you need to find a better way to deal with this." I rubbed his knee, just one pass, and drew my hand away.

"You know so much about him," Grayson murmured. "You knew him better than I did."

"I saw him almost every day," I explained. "Last December, whenever y'all weren't here, every waking moment I wasn't at school or at work, he was training me in the tow plane. It's funny but I think a lot of people spend less time with their own families, especially if they don't all live together, and more time with complete strangers."

It was certainly true of my own so-called family. I knew who my mother had been spending her time with last week: her boyfriend Roger. But that could have changed by now. It often did. I wondered who my dad spent time with. Could have been anyone. Anyone at all.

Grayson turned to face me, bracing himself with one hand on the surfboard and tucking his long legs beneath him in the sand. "You and I have never talked like this before. But my dad kept telling me what I'm finding out about you now."

I smiled. "You mean the chip on my shoulder?"

Grayson shook his head. "No, nothing could be more obvious than the chip on your shoulder. But my dad liked to tell this story about you. He said you were fourteen and you'd been working at the airport a few weeks. He knew you by sight from the airport office. One day you stomped into his hangar and said you wanted a flying lesson, sort of demanded it, and threw the money for the lesson down on his desk in front of him, plus tax, in cash with exact change."

I hadn't stomped. The rest was accurate. "I wanted a lesson," I said, "and wanted to take away all his excuses not to

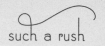

give me one. If I paid him up front in cash, he couldn't say no. Why did he tell you that story?"

"He said he knew from that moment that you had strong character and drive. You were everything I wasn't. Whenever he got tired of comparing me with Jake or Alec, he would compare me with you."

*Wow,* to be compared unfavorably with the strange loser girl? No wonder Grayson was bitter. "Did you believe him?"

"Believe what?" Grayson asked.

"That I have a strong character and drive?"

He looked me straight in the eye and said, "No, I thought he was screwing you."

# fifteen

So much for our friendly conversation. I turned to face Grayson on the surfboard. "As long as we're being honest, two Christmases ago, I walked into the hangar while you were telling Alec and Jake I was trading sex for flying lessons with your dad. You hurt my feelings, and I've thought less of you as a person since then."

He stared at me for a moment, then opened his mouth to say something.

Before he could utter more bullshit, I went on, "Men always do that to women when they feel threatened. They tell everybody the woman must be giving out blow jobs because there's no way she could be successful otherwise."

Grayson had found his voice. "First of all," he said loudly enough that he blinked when he heard himself. He looked over his shoulder to see if anyone was listening. The beach was empty. He leaned toward me and lowered his voice. "I never felt *threatened* by you. He was *my* father."

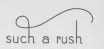

I looked down at my hands, tracing patterns in the sand, feeling ashamed all of a sudden. I'd been angry with Grayson about this for a year and four months. With good reason, I still thought. But yeah, my anger had come out as an insult to his relationship with his father, which I never intended.

"And second," he said, "you walked in on us while we were talking. I didn't know you were there, and I didn't say it to insult you. I would have no reason to do that. I hardly knew you. I was making that assumption about you because of my dad's end of the equation. My parents got divorced when he cheated on my mom. That girl was twenty-five. It was disgusting."

"Yeah, but wasn't he in his midforties at the time?"

"Yes!" Grayson exclaimed, outraged all over again.

"They were both adults," I reminded him. "Forty-four to twenty-five is a big age difference, but it's nothing compared with fifty-one to seventeen, which was how old your dad and I were last year when this entered your head."

Grayson scowled at me. "You're awfully defensive of him."

"Your father and I were not lovers," I said firmly. "Ever. You don't believe me?"

Grayson's face opened. He was less angry now but not quite ready to let go. "I believe you, but I don't see how you can say what he did with that girl wasn't so bad. *He* left *us*, not the other way around."

"Because your mom didn't want him to fly anymore," I said. "It's one thing to marry somebody and then ask them to change their annoying little habits. Ask them not to drink a six-pack every single night. Ask them not to pawn the TV. She asked him to become somebody else."

"Of course she didn't!" Grayson exclaimed. "It wasn't that she didn't want him to fly at all. She wanted him to stop doing

that as his job. My uncle had another job for him at his insurance agency."

"Can you hear yourself?" I yelled back. "Can you picture your dad working at an insurance agency? Can you picture him taking any job that his brother-in-law *had* for him? Working for somebody else? Someone in your mother's family?" I tried to calm down. To my own ears, we sounded like an old couple bickering, except our roles had been reversed. He was the wifely voice of reason, and I was Mr. Hall, flying off the handle.

But I couldn't believe Grayson didn't understand his dad's side. The point needed to be made. "And your mom may have *said* he could keep flying on the side, as a hobby, but she would have found a way to take that from him too. The Cessna would have been downgraded from a tool of the trade to a toy, and she would have made him sell it."

Grayson shook his head. "And you're saying that was a reason for him to cheat on her?"

It *didn't* seem like a reason to give up on working things out, turn his back on his wife and three children, and walk out. But I was no expert on why men stayed or didn't stay. "All I know is what he told me. I'm just saying I've seen worse."

He smiled with no humor in his face. "You mean you've *done* worse?"

"No," I said loudly, "but that's what you thought when you asked me to come on to Alec, right? You think I open my legs all the time, for anybody. You've gotten this idea that I'm the airport whore."

He laughed shortly. "Mark was living with you."

"Only for a week, and it was actually my mom's idea."

"Your mom!" Grayson barked.

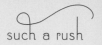

"Yeah." Most moms didn't want help with rent, and most teenagers had never heard of moms who did. I'd learned a lot from being friends with Molly. Sometimes it was better to change the subject. "And in that week . . . I won't say nothing happened between Mark and me, but what you're thinking must have happened didn't happen."

One of Grayson's blond brows shot up in disbelief. The expression was stern and effective. "What about before that?"

"Never with Mark," I said.

"With anybody?"

This was none of his business. But we were way past getting in each other's business tonight. Turning back toward the ocean and stretching both legs in front of me until my toes touched the dangerous waters, I said, "Once, when I was fourteen."

"Fourteen!" he exclaimed. "I couldn't tie my own shoes when I was fourteen."

"Yes, you could." I remembered Grayson at fourteen. We'd both been fourteen when I moved to Heaven Beach. My first glimpse of him was outside the Hall Aviation hangar, where he was rigging a bucket of water to fall on his dad's head when his dad opened the side door. Mr. Hall hadn't been amused. That was the day my crush on Grayson had started.

"How did it happen?" Grayson prompted me.

With difficulty I shifted my brain from my memory of Grayson to my memory of that lost boy who'd taken my virginity. "I was living in a trailer park very close to the Air Force base. At night some guys and I would lie down in the grass right outside the fence at the end of the runway, get stoned, and watch the planes take off over us."

Grayson laughed. "I'll bet that was cool. I would have been there with you."

*No, you wouldn't,* I thought. Grayson's mother would have been taking better care of him than that.

"One night," I said, "this guy didn't just steal a roach from his brother. He stole a roach *and* a condom. And we did it."

Grayson frowned. "And it was awful?"

"No, it wasn't awful. I wanted to do it again."

"But you didn't? There's more to this story than 'We did it.'"

"He was willing to do it with me again, but he couldn't steal another condom. I had to choose whether to do it without one, or not do it anymore. I walked away. Thinking back, remembering what I was like then, how angry and how lost, I can't believe I did that. Right before I moved here, I was smoking pot. Drinking the little I could get. The airport job ended all that, and your dad made me quit smoking and kept me off everything else by putting so much trust in me. He couldn't stop you, so he stopped me instead."

Grayson chuckled ruefully, like it was a joke.

Looking him in the eye, I told him, "I mean that."

He gazed at me somberly.

"But this one decision," I said, "I made for myself before I ever met your dad. My mom had me when she was sixteen, which means she did it when she was fifteen. My dad was probably some idiot exactly like that boy I lost my virginity to, a fifteen-year-old with a dick and nothing else. Nothing."

Grayson didn't respond. The crashing waves filled his silence. For the first time since he'd sat down, I remembered Alec and Molly, out there in the ocean somewhere. I hadn't heard their voices after they disappeared. Probably the current had moved them down the beach. I knew that much from my observations the few times I'd been to the ocean.

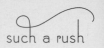

"I would have started a relationship with that guy," I said. "If he'd come back to me with a condom, I would have been willing. But right after that, my mom said we were moving to Heaven Beach. He went straight to my best friend and hooked up with her instead. Both of them acted like they'd never met me. That's when I realized that people use each other, Grayson. They define their relationships by what they're getting. The only good relationship I took away from my years in that town was with an airplane. Those beautiful, scary airplanes flying right over me.

"So, you blackmail me into dating your brother," I said bitterly, "and you think it won't be a big deal for me to kiss him. Mark thinks the path to my pants is smoothly paved and well traveled. Girls at school make comments about me constantly. But I hear this stuff and think, *Me?* I was headed in that direction a long time ago, yes. Now, no. I must *exude* something. Do I *exude* something?"

Grayson laughed. "Yes, you definitely *exude* something."

"What do I *exude*?"

"Super, super sexy."

In the moonlight, he was so sexy himself, his blond hair glinting, the shadows of his long lashes hiding his eyes. If I were his girlfriend and he had told me how sexy I was, I would have melted right there for him, just like I had last night. But he was my boss. We were having a matter-of-fact conversation about a business deal.

"A few days ago," I said, "Molly told me I exude that too. Only she didn't put it as politely as you put it."

"She wouldn't," he said. "You're lucky she's your friend. Most girls at your school hate you, don't they? That was clear at the party last night. But the boys like you a lot better. Patrick, for instance."

I laughed. "Patrick! We're just friends."

"Only because he knows you're looking for something else," Grayson said. "And if you've been holding all these boys off since you were fourteen, you've been working very hard at that. And then there are the male teachers."

"I never asked for anything special from my teachers," I said quickly.

"You don't have to ask. They can't help it." When he inhaled, I thought it was the wind picking up across the sand, but when he exhaled, sighing the longest sigh, I knew he was bracing himself for something. "Do you promise that you and my dad never . . ."

"Screwed?"

"Leah," he said reproachfully.

"You're saying it, not me."

"Okay." He folded his arms awkwardly on his chest. The self-conscious movement made him seem younger than eighteen, more vulnerable, and didn't match his strong arms and muscular chest. He asked, "But did you?"

"No!"

"Okay." He paused. "Did you want to?"

Though this line of questioning was rude, I didn't want to upset him. His dad was dead. Grayson really was trying to deal. He wanted to know this stuff. Maybe even deserved to know.

But I didn't think I should tell him the truth. I loved being around Mr. Hall because he was kind to me and we were friends. Other people around the airport—Mark, for instance—had insulted me when I was as young as fourteen, hinting that I was so worthless a person, Mr. Hall couldn't possibly be doing anything nice for me unless I was giving him blow jobs in exchange. When people implied this,

238

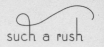

I understood where they were coming from. I knew how it looked. Otherwise, it never crossed my mind. Mr. Hall was much older than me, and honestly kind of asexual, at least as I saw him. Like a really good father.

I told Grayson another, simpler version of the truth. "If your dad had been the same person but my age, then yeah, I would have fallen for him."

Grayson watched me, arms crossed, in exactly the pose Mr. Hall had struck in that old photo of himself as a jet pilot, when he was only a few years older than Grayson. And they looked exactly the same.

I realized what I'd said.

The air between us was charged with electricity, the waves echoing the sound of it.

"Really?" Grayson asked.

"Really," I said.

Considering the ugly things we'd talked about tonight, my mind had doubted this moment would come, but my heart had known. Leaning forward until he was on all fours, he crawled one pace toward me. His lips met mine.

The rush was so intense that he was like a predator taking me by the throat. I opened my mouth.

His mouth wrestled with mine. He kept moving forward until he pushed me down on my back on the sand. His warm body covered mine, skin to my skin. His thighs hugged the outsides of my thighs, and his erection pressed against the center of my bathing suit bottoms.

I let him do anything he wanted, eager to find out what was next. At the same time, I was vaguely aware that we'd been archenemies a few minutes before, and now he had me on my back on the sand. I waited for him to realize what he was doing

and stop with a gasp of horror, just as he'd stopped himself in the basement of the airport office. But he kept kissing me. Finally I decided I'd better do something to end this, and it wasn't going to be pulling back.

I slid my hand down the outside of his bathing suit to cup him.

He did pause, and gasp. He didn't stop. His kisses grew more focused, more intense. His tongue forced its way into my mouth and swept inside me. He kissed my ear, licked my neck, and made his way down toward my breast, gasping again every time I stroked him.

Now I wondered where this was going to end. I hadn't wanted to do it without a condom at fourteen. Eighteen was not much of an improvement. My mind said, *Stop him*. My body said, *Let him*. I had never felt so good, not flying, not ever.

Molly giggled somewhere in the darkness. Grayson froze on top of me.

He gave me a deep kiss, then whispered against my lips, "I'm going in the water. If they see me like this, they'll know exactly what we've been doing."

"And that's not okay?"

He set his forehead against mine. "No."

I pushed his shoulders away so I could look him in the eye. "You still want me to go out with Alec?" I asked in disbelief.

"Yes!"

"Tell me why," I insisted.

"I can't," he whispered. "You'll give it away, even if you don't mean to. I can't let you do that. It's a matter of life and death."

I shoved him angrily. "Come on, Grayson."

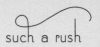

He rubbed his nose against mine, melting me all over
again. "Would I kid you about a matter of life and death?" He
pushed himself off me, his long body taking a while to make it
up to his full height. The moonlight outlined the blond edges
of his hair and made him seem to glow as he grabbed up his
surfboard and splashed into the darkness.

"No," I murmured, "you wouldn't."

In the end, my anger at him was wasted. For four days I'd
tried in vain to get him to tell me why we were playing Alec.
Less than twenty-four hours later, I found out.

# sixteen

For most of the next day, Grayson acted like he'd forgotten what had happened between us the night before. During my final break in the afternoon, Molly was putting together a banner for him out in the field. He paused on his way out of the hangar, behind Alec's back, and shot me one lingering, hungry look that sent vibrations through my body.

After he left, I sat in a lawn chair. Alec lay on the dusty sofa. He was grilling me about how a girl who'd lived in a beach town for three years could possibly not know how to swim. He and Molly had both asked me a hundred questions about it the night before. I was on the verge of cutting my hand across my throat to shut him up. But as Molly had pointed out, Alec wasn't like Grayson, and I doubted he would understand that blunt message like Grayson did.

Suddenly, underneath the lingering shivers I felt from Grayson's gaze on me, under the hum of the fan blowing

warm air around the hangar, something low and sinister shook the building. Alec felt it too. We frowned at each other.

"Someone's coming," I said.

"We have to get Molly," he exclaimed, jumping up.

We both ran for the wide-open doorway of the hangar. Way across the field, Molly was already dashing for the airport office. Luckily the banner she'd been about to hook up was still rolled in a heavy ball on the grass. If it had been stretched out, we would have been chasing it halfway to town on the breeze that the approaching helicopter was about to stir up. Grayson left his plane parked in front of the hangar and stalked in the direction of the airport office. In the sky, still too far away to be making that much noise, hung a Chinook.

Alec and I walked over to the airport office. Grayson stared up at the helicopter with his hands on his hips like he thought the Army had some nerve. Molly leaned over and shouted in my ear, "What *is* that?"

"Chinook." I stuck up both my pointer fingers and twirled them in opposite directions to represent the fascinating twin helicopter blades. Then I realized she had no idea what that meant, and I put my hands down. "Probably from the Army base."

The Chinook sailed low over the trees and set down on the runway, its gentle movements belying the head-splitting noise it was making. We all had our hands over our ears now. Everyone at the airport lined the unforested side of the tarmac— more people than I would have imagined, like ants escaping from a mound kicked by a malicious little boy. The pilots among us watched because it was a Chinook and we longed to fly one. The secretaries and janitors from the airport-based businesses watched because the Chinook shook the ground

and charged the atmosphere. Nobody could clean a floor or type a report, much less answer the phone, with that going on.

Camouflage-clad figures began to climb down from the helicopter. Two descended from the front door, three from another. The five of them met in the middle, yelled to each other with their headphones on, and walked toward us. One of them was a girl.

I wondered whether anybody was left in charge of the helicopter.

The lieutenant leading the group was a tall blond. I couldn't tell for sure since he was wearing mirrored shades, but I thought he was boyishly handsome, like Alec. He came straight for me because, dressed in a bikini top, I was obviously in charge of this airport. He grinned at me. "Got any vending machines?" he yelled, even louder than necessary. He was deaf from sitting in the helicopter with his headphones on.

I jerked my thumb over my shoulder.

"I'll show you!" Alec said, leaping in front of them and opening the glass door, ushering them inside the building. He followed them in, calling, "You guys from the Army base?"

Grayson stared at the Chinook, hands still on his hips, both fists white. He looked like he was about to explode.

"That's funny," I yelled at him conversationally. "They land their Chinook at our airport and act like they're driving on the interstate and pulled over at a rest sto—"

"You want to go with them too?" he bit at me.

"What?" I asked, realizing even as I uttered this word that Grayson was jealous. Of an Army lieutenant who had talked to me on his way to the snack machine. And then, even though I'd figured it out, I asked, "What do you mean?"

Because I wanted to hear him say it. If he was really jealous, he wanted me for himself.

244

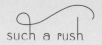

He opened his mouth. Inclined his head toward the door where the lieutenant had disappeared. Cut his eyes back at me. And then stalked through the door after them.

All the while, the chopper blades cut through the air and the gigantic motors throbbed. When it had approached, the Chinook had been loud. When it had landed, it had been absorbing. Now the noise became overwhelming but inescapable, a full-body vibration that shook me awake and insisted that something was about to happen.

"It's so beautiful, isn't it?" I yelled to Molly. "This massive piece of engineering that looks like it shouldn't be able to fly."

"What?" she shouted back.

The airport office door burst open behind us. Grayson hollered over the noise of the helicopter. I couldn't make out what he was saying. The four men and one woman in fatigues walked back across the tarmac with drinks and packs of crackers in their hands. They disappeared into the belly of the Chinook. It rumbled even louder and deeper for a few moments, just for good measure, then lifted as easily as a tiny Piper blown on a storm wind.

"What did you say to them?" Alec yelled at Grayson over the fading noise.

"I told him to get his fucking Chinook off my runway," Grayson said. "I'm trying to run a business here, and I'm not going to be held up and lose contracts just because these idiots think it's funny to land here."

"Did you say it to him like that?" Alec asked, horrified. "Grayson, you can't talk to him that way. He was a lieutenant!"

"I can talk to him any fucking way I want, Alec. I'm not in the fucking military."

"The Chinook's gone now," I pointed out.

Grayson looked around. He wanted to stay and argue, but he realized he was now being held up and losing contracts just by standing there. He walked toward the red Piper.

As an afterthought, he turned around and walked backward. "Molly," he barked. He pointed toward the rolled-up banner in the center of the field.

Molly saluted him and galloped toward the grass. The other spectators faded into the metal buildings they'd scurried from. Nothing to see here. The last rumble of the Chinook had faded. The airport was as calm as if the helicopter had never landed.

I turned to Alec. "What's Grayson's problem? I liked the Chinook dropping by. I thought it was neato."

"He's mad because I got admitted to the Citadel."

"What?" I exclaimed. "Alec, that's great!"

"He thinks I'm going into the military," Alec said.

"Oh." Now I saw. As Grayson started the engine of the red Piper and we watched him taxi past us toward the far end of the runway, I realized I didn't see the whole picture, but I understood the tiniest piece of why Grayson wanted Alec to be smitten with me. The Citadel was in Charleston, the city Grayson wanted me to keep Alec away from.

I asked, "*Are* you going to join the military?"

"I don't know," Alec said. "I can go to the Citadel without joining. I did think it was a great idea. I mean, I want to fly for a living. Where else are you going to get the chance to fly a Chinook? Or, gosh, an F-15?"

I nodded. An F-15 was what Jake had been flying in Afghanistan when he got shot down.

"I told my family a couple of weeks ago," Alec said, "and Grayson went ballistic."

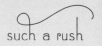

We both turned to watch Grayson take off, the tiny plane sailing without incident into the calm sky.

"He got my mom all freaked out," Alec said. "Then Grayson got this bright idea that we should run Hall Aviation, just like my dad. I'm thinking, *Hell no*. I couldn't imagine going into business with Grayson. Could you?" He turned to me, blond brows raised, wanting me to verify his answer.

"Before I saw it for myself," I started slowly, "I would have said no. But now . . ." I gestured toward the red Piper skimming low over the grass. Grayson passed the upright poles. The plane shot up at an impossible angle, nearly stalling the engine. Had he missed the banner? Had he missed it? Molly's banner stayed put on the ground way longer than it should have, it seemed. Then the plane stopped in midair, just for a split second, and kept going. The banner jerked on the ground and lifted gracefully: SUNSET SPECIAL 2 FOR 1 BEACHCOMBERS. It went sailing after Grayson into the sky.

"The business seems to be going okay," I continued. "I mean, gosh, Grayson knows how to do taxes."

"Right," Alec said. "He's putting forth all this effort *now*. He's throwing himself into this like he would have thrown himself into rock climbing before, this wall of energy with no understanding of the consequences, shoot now and ask questions later. That's just because he and Mom convinced me to try out the business with him over spring break and a few more spring weekends, since Dad already had the contracts. If it goes okay, they want me to come back and fly with Grayson over the summer, and consider it as a civilian career instead of ever going into the military."

"I get it," I said. I really did. Grayson had thrown himself into this business, for Alec. He had swallowed every bit of his

impulsive, irresponsible personality and redirected it toward a responsibility way too heavy for an eighteen-year-old boy, all for Alec. To fill out the contract schedule, he had needed me to work for him too, just like his dad had planned. To stack the deck, he had needed me to date Alec, so Alec would feel drawn to this place and wouldn't want to leave for Charleston and the Citadel at the end of the summer.

And when I had refused, Grayson had found a way to make me.

"What do *you* think?" Alec asked.

I blinked at him. He was wearing aviator shades, just like Grayson, but for some reason his expression was a lot easier for me to read than Grayson's ever was. Alec needed reassurance. "About what?"

"The military," he prompted me. "Versus flying tow planes, or some other civilian job. I mean, you've got this job now, and Grayson told me that Mark had been dicking you around about a job flying crop dusters for Mr. Simon. But you're not planning to stay here, are you? The military would be the perfect place for you."

I nodded. "Because I live in a trailer."

"That is not"—Alec paused in midsentence as he realized that's *exactly* what he'd meant—"what I meant," he finished weakly.

We both looked toward the Admiral's plane as he started his engine.

"I've never been in the military," I said slowly, "so I don't know for sure. I can only judge from what I've seen, living in trailer parks with mostly military families when I lived near the Army base and then the Air Force base."

Alec opened his hands, prompting me to go on. "What did you see?"

"I saw that the military treats people like dogs."

Alec's fresh face hardened. "If you lived in a trailer park with them, you probably mean single enlisted men. Privates."

"I mean the military treats its personnel like dogs," I insisted. "The military treats the personnel's families like dogs. The personnel start treating their own families like dogs because they've been treated like dogs themselves."

Alec's brows went down behind his shades. "I would have a college degree, though. I'd be an officer. I'd get a bigger housing allowance, and I wouldn't live in a trailer park."

"You would have no choice about what you did for your job," I promised him, "or where you did it. You wouldn't have a lot of say in where you lived. You would be a bigger dog."

Alec backed a step away from me. "You're awfully down on the military."

"Because I've lived with them!" I said. "That's what I'm telling you. You have no idea."

"I *do* have an idea," he insisted. "My father was in the military, and my brother."

We both fell silent. He was hearing what he'd just said, and I was waiting for him to hear it.

"Why did Jake join?" I asked him. "It seems like your dad wouldn't have wanted him to, honestly."

"He didn't want him to," Alec confirmed. "But Mom didn't want Jake to go into business with Dad. I think Jake finally joined up because he was so frustrated with both of them telling him what to do and trying to control his every move."

"He joined the military out of frustration?" I asked, incredulous. "I'll bet he regretted that."

Alec shrugged. "He never said he did."

"Of course he couldn't admit it," I said. "Not to your dad. He'd be admitting that your dad had been right all along. From what I've seen, that's not how your family works."

The whole scenario was making me ill. Jake joining up out of frustration. Regretting it the instant he got sent to Afghanistan. Mr. Hall knowing Jake regretted it, and feeling responsible because he'd driven Jake to that point in the first place. And then, when Jake died, Mr. Hall was in a dark place.

"So, if you're interested in joining," I said, "I wouldn't do it just because you thought your dad wanted you to. I'm sure he didn't."

Alec frowned at me. I realized what I was saying was none of my business. I went on anyway, because it was important. More important than making him like me. Actually, I was beginning to realize how closely connected all this was.

"Your brother died three months ago," I said, "and your dad died two months ago. So recently that you and Grayson and I hold our breath when one of us brings them up. You're grieving, and you're not thinking straight. Anything you do because Jake did it or your dad might have wanted it—that's suspect. You have no perspective. And especially something like this, a decision that will tie up your life for, what? Five or six years after college? The next ten years of your life? You should make that decision with a clear head. There's absolutely no need to jump into it now. You could wait six months and make the decision then."

Alec still frowned at me. "You sound like Grayson. Have you two talked about this?"

"No," I said honestly. I hoped I sounded honest. Really I was beginning to feel guilty. Now I saw exactly why Grayson had wanted me to seduce Alec. I'd been manipulating Alec all week without knowing why. Now I knew.

"Well, listen," Alec said, a small smile returning to his lips. "I'm going to miss you tonight, but I'm having dinner with my recruiter."

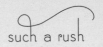

I blinked. "Your recruiter?" This *was* serious. "Alec, please think about what I said."

"I will," he promised. "But that means I won't see you to-night. We hadn't made plans, exactly, but we've all been going out together, and I thought you and I . . ." He took my hand and rubbed my palm with his thumb. "We haven't said we're dating exclusively or anything, so I don't mean to assume too much. I just wanted you to know where I'd be. And I wanted to explain it to you while we're alone. Grayson's going to have a fit that I'm seeing my recruiter, like it's any of his business."

Oh, it was Grayson's business all right. He'd made it his business. But all I said was, "Thank you."

Alec kissed me on the forehead. "And I'll see you tomorrow morning." He turned for the Hall Aviation hangar and walked back toward the yellow Piper, while Molly out in the field struggled to pull his banner along the grass and hook it up between the poles.

My last flight of the day was ruined. I loved that rush of takeoff, that sight of the world spread out below me. I hadn't played a lot of video games in my life, but I was sure threading the needle by pointing an actual plane toward two tiny poles to pick up a banner was more fun than any fake flying scenario ever invented. I loved fighting the engine, throttling down, nearly stalling, and negotiating a peace between the airplane and the sky.

That is, I loved flying when I could think about flying. But when my mind was filled with something else, flying was a chore. And right now my mind raced in circles, taking Alec and Grayson down a whirlpool with it.

I understood now why Grayson had blackmailed me. I believed that he believed what he'd told me last night: fooling

Alec was a matter of life and death. That didn't make it right. Showing Alec that they could make the business work was one thing. Adding me into the mix was evil. Now he was no longer convincing Alec. He was manipulating Alec.

In fact, the more I thought about it, the more I wondered whether Grayson had made up all those dire predictions about my crop-dusting job too. I wouldn't have put it past him, to make me do what he wanted.

I wondered whether last night at the beach had been just another method to keep me on his side.

This was what I was thinking as I dropped my banner and came around again to land. I should *not* have been thinking about anything but flying the plane, and Mr. Hall was scolding me in my head, but I couldn't help it. I analyzed every detail of what Grayson and I had done together on the beach. I'd never felt so good in my life. Was it possible that he had faked everything he felt? I didn't think so, but I didn't have a lot to compare him with.

I knew how my boyfriend had acted when we did it at the runway when I was fourteen. He hadn't been in love with me. I knew how Mark had looked when we made out. I was so confused now about his motivations that I had no idea what to think. How would he have acted when I kicked him out of my trailer if he'd really loved me?

That led me back to my conversation with Alec right before we took off. He'd asked me what I thought of his plan to go into the military. I'd told him. I realized now that what I'd said was all wrong. That's why he'd been frowning at me. If I had fallen for him, I would have hugged him and cried and begged him not to join up, and he knew it.

I'd blown that part of Grayson's scheme without even meaning to.

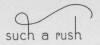

There was no help for it now. As soon as I landed, I was going to have a long talk with Grayson and convince him that if he wanted to change his brother's mind, no matter how important the issue, this was not the way.

That was my plan until I came in for my final approach. I should have been focusing on the runway, but my eyes drifted to the Hall Aviation hangar, where Grayson's and Alec's planes were already parked. Then to the lot beside the airport office, where my mother was stepping out of her boyfriend Roger's ancient Trans-Am, the door a different color from the body.

As I landed, taxied over to the hangar, and stepped out of the plane, I didn't see my mom anywhere outside. I scanned the hangar as I walked inside, but she wasn't there, either. Grayson, Alec, and Molly were talking in front of Mr. Hall's Cessna, all of them looking grim. Probably this was a very important discussion of the Chinook and the lieutenant and what Grayson had said to him, but none of that mattered right now.

I walked up and put my hand on Grayson's chest. He stopped talking and looked down at me in surprise over the top of his shades.

"My mother is here," I told him, "and you're my boyfriend. You've been my boyfriend for three and a half years, except for my week with Mark."

"What?" he yelped, panic in his eyes that I'd ruined my fake relationship with Alec.

"I can't explain it right now," I said impatiently. He wasn't the only one engineering fake relationships around here. Couldn't he see that? "I actually don't work that many hours at the airport office, and when I'm not working there, I'm spending time with you."

"But—"

I cut him off, turning to Alec. "You and I aren't dating. Okay? Just for right now."

"Okay," Alec said dubiously.

I turned to Molly. "You . . . haven't met my mother. Just keep your mouth shut."

I turned to the side door of the hangar, which my mother would come through any second. "She's at the airport office," I said, keeping my eyes on the door. "Leon is telling her I'm working here instead this week. If he tells her I'm flying, I'm screwed. If he doesn't offer that detail, I'm just your secretary, do you understand?"

I slipped my arm around Grayson's waist and stared at the Cessna for two seconds until, out of the corner of my eye, I saw the hangar door open.

I was astonished at how she looked. She seemed the same as always, and it had only been ten days since I'd seen her—the night she told Mark he could move in. What surprised me was how much she looked like that girl in Mark's truck, the one he'd taken to the beach, except that my mom was fifteen years older.

I walked over to her, calling, "Hey, Mama!" I hugged her. "Hey, Roger," I said over her shoulder as he came in the door.

She beamed at me. "Baby, I've got some news."

Since she'd just come back from the Indian casino, the first idea popping into my head was that she'd won fifty thousand dollars. But if she had, she would have spent it all on the way home. She and Roger would have rolled up to the hangar in a sparkling new club cab pickup instead of his Trans-Am.

"What is it?" I breathed.

"We're moving to Savannah!" my mom announced. "Roger's cousin says he may be able to get him on at the backhoe plant."

I went cold in the broiling hangar. My brain tried to process this information. It did not compute. The backhoe plant, or for that matter any factory in the United States, would require three things of its employees that Roger did not have and could not get: a clean drug test, references, and the ability to drag his ass into work more than two days in a row. But in my heart I knew it would take a couple of weeks for my mother to figure this out, if she even cared. By that time we would be living in Savannah.

In a trailer park next to the airport.

And I would have to start over.

# seventeen

"It's beautiful in Savannah." My mom made a vague waving motion that seemed to indicate Grayson, Alec, and Molly. "Your friends can come and visit," she told me, as if she was feeling very generous, and this would make up for everything. "So come on back home, Leah, and get your stuff together. We're leaving tonight."

"Tonight?" Grayson asked sharply, sending a cold chill down my neck.

I turned to them. Alec and Molly whispered with their heads bent. Grayson watched my mom in disbelief. In his world, families didn't move to a different town on the spur of the moment. They didn't need to. And that's when I realized what must be going on.

"What's wrong?" I asked my mom suspiciously. "Why were you suddenly hell-bent on driving to the Indian casino last week?" Usually it took at least a couple of days for her to hatch

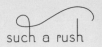

that plan. A sudden turnaround reeked of desperation. Like, she needed a lot of money fast.

"Nothing's wrong!" she exclaimed, her cheeks two spots of pink, and not from a day at the beach. "I just wanted to have a little fun. It's spring break!"

Spring break was for students like me, not unemployed waitresses like her. I wondered whether she still qualified as an unemployed waitress. She'd gone so long without working that at some point she'd stopped being an unemployed waitress and became just plain unemployed.

I put my hands on my hips. "How far behind are you on rent?"

"That's not why we're moving," she snapped. "Roger's cousin says—"

"That's why we moved from Golden to Equality," I said. "That's why we lived in every shithole in Equality at least twice. That's why we moved from Equality to the Army base, and from the Army base to the Air Force base, and from there to Heaven Beach."

"That is *not* why we moved here," my mother yelled back at me. "Billy told me he was going to get a job for me. He didn't do it, but that's what he told me."

Grayson was speaking soothingly in my ear. I didn't care what he said. I wasn't done.

"That's right," I shouted. "At least half those times, your boyfriend's brother's boss's cell mate thought he might be able to get your boyfriend on at the bullet factory. And y'all broke up fifteen minutes after we moved. But it took me longer than fifteen minutes to adjust, Mama. Moving doesn't fix everything for me like it does for you. I'm graduating from high school in six weeks and I'm not moving again!"

"—wouldn't be moving at all if it wasn't for you!" My mom

was yelling back at me now. "We can't pay the rent with what you make. If you would work more hours, we'd be fine." She turned to Grayson. "Aren't y'all back together? Isn't she working for you now? Can't you give her more hours?"

Grayson and Alec and Molly all must have been doing the math in their heads. They knew I'd been lying to my mom, holding out on her. They knew I was working every hour I could at the airport office. But I needed so much money to keep flying. There was no way I would let that go now.

And I was absolutely horrified that my mom was exposing herself as exactly the bad mother Molly had implied she was that night at her parents' café, in front of Alec and Grayson. Molly had been right, and I was wrong.

I shouted, "I'm in school, Mama. You want me to get a second job working third shift when I'm still in high school? That's not fair when you're not working at all!"

"It's not fair I pay the rent when I don't even stay there!" She turned and headed for the hangar door, pushing Roger ahead of her. In the doorway she called back over her shoulder, "We're leaving for Savannah in a minute, and you can come or not." She slammed the door behind her. The noise echoed like a Chinook around the metal walls.

Grayson's arm slid from around my shoulders. That's when I realized he'd had his arm around me the whole time—but not anymore. He was firing questions at me, and so were Molly and Alec, stupid shit that rich people would ask, and I kept saying, "I don't know. I don't know." I was puzzling through what was about to happen. "I think in the next few days I'm going to get evicted." I hadn't gotten the telltale business-size envelope in the mail, but maybe my mom had been staving off the landlord by phone. Until now.

"How is that possible?" Grayson demanded. "And why

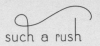

does she think I'm your boyfriend?"

"And why did you want her to think he's *still* your boy-friend?" Alec added.

I looked to Molly for help, but she watched me with her eyes wide, just as curious as the boys were.

"I've been telling her for a long time that Grayson was my boyfriend." After I'd said this, I realized it didn't explain any-thing, and in fact made the whole situation sound worse.

I said, "So, I'm going to follow my mom and make sure she doesn't take the refrigerator. Or the air conditioner." I walked out the hangar door.

I was thinking so hard that I didn't realize I'd walked the entire length of the airport until the pit bull cussed me out. Through the trees and across the gravel road, Roger was sit-ting in the Trans-Am with the motor running. The door of the trailer was wide open like a crime scene.

My mom had checked the mail for once. On the kitchen counter was a pile of junk mail and a business-size envelope. I unfolded the eviction notice and read it. Even after we moved out, we would owe all of the back rent, or we would be re-ported to a collection agency.

I found my mom pawing through her closet, stuffing clothes in a garbage bag. "We have two weeks before we're evicted," I said dryly. "Why are y'all in such a hurry?"

"His cousin in Savannah is having a party in a couple of hours." Her head was inside the closet, her voice muffled by the clothes. "Sure you don't want to come with us?"

"No, I want to stay here and finish high school."

"You could just get your GED," she said.

"Mama!" I yelled at her. "That doesn't make any sense!"

She straightened then and put her hand on my shoulder. "Baby, if you want to stay here by yourself, that's fine with me.

You're eighteen years old, and you'll be fine. Grayson is such a hunk! You did good on that one, much better than Mark. I didn't trust Mark."

The obvious question, *Then why did you invite him to move in with me?*, only tickled the edges of my brain. I might ask this if I could use logic to persuade my mom of something. I might be indignant or outraged if these emotions would have an effect on her. But I didn't bother. For all she cared, she was standing in a trailer by herself.

"Just ask Grayson to give you more hours," she was saying. "Or move in with him if you need to. Come here, girl. I'll miss you." She set her garbage bag on the bed and pulled me into a hug.

The Admiral's Beechcraft swooped low overhead, engine growling, coming in for a landing. She pulled away from me and looked up at the stained ceiling of the trailer, like she could see through it to the little white plane grazing the treetops. "I won't miss those fucking airplanes, though," she shouted. "I don't see how you and your boyfriend stand working over there."

I followed her to the doorway and watched her from the cement-block steps as she and Roger drove away. I blinked against the hot cloud of dust.

And continued to stand there in the doorway. I couldn't go out. Where would I go? I couldn't go in. That would mean the trailer was mine. I stood there for a long time, listening to the pit bull, with the expensive air-conditioning seeping out around me, the life leaving me as well. I hadn't felt like this since I heard through the grapevine at the airport that the Admiral had found Mr. Hall's body.

I stood there so long that the pit bull got tired and, with a final whine, lay down.

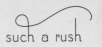

The trailer park was so quiet that I could hear someone's TV several trailers over, and cars swishing by out on the highway.

Then the pit bull jumped up and barked ferociously again, and Grayson appeared through the palm trees.

His shades glinted in the late-afternoon sun as he crossed the dirt yard without hesitation and climbed right up the cement-block steps. He stood in front of me on the top step, looking down at me, perspiration darkening the blond curls that peeked from underneath his cowboy hat. He said sternly, "We have to talk. Let me in."

"No."

He sighed impatiently, his hand making a fist and releasing. "Okay, Leah. Why won't you let me in your house?"

"Because it's not a house," I snapped. "It's a trailer."

"It's temporary." His voice was soothing as he stepped closer to me. I looked way up at him, but all I saw was my reflection.

"Eighteen years isn't temporary." I meant to say this sarcastically, but it came out hoarse, and I found myself backing through the open doorway as he leaned even closer.

"It's temporary from now on." He took another step forward, forcing me to take another step inside. "Let me in, Leah."

"Why? So you can search for beer again? There isn't any. If there had been, my mom would have taken it. That's probably the first thing she checked."

"No," he said. "This is important."

"Let me guess." I tried to sound cocky, but my heartbeat sped along and I sounded breathless as I said, "You've come to tell me that my fake relationship with you has screwed up my fake relationship with Alec, and I should keep my hands off you from now on. Well, sorry, but my mother is headed

to Savannah and she's not coming back to check on me, much less pitch a fit at the airport because I forged her name years ago. You can't order me around anymore. I never would have helped you in the first place if I'd known you were trying to control Alec's life. He told me about the Citadel and the military. What you're doing is wrong. Our agreement is off."

"I don't care what you think." Grayson took another step toward me. We were both inside the trailer now. He kicked the door closed with a flimsy metal crash and kept walking toward me. I kept backing up until I felt the hard kitchen counter behind me.

"I just want to know where Alec went," Grayson said.

"Now?"

"Tonight. Are you two going out? I went in the office to write your check and cash it. When I came out, he and Molly were both gone, and he's not answering his cell."

"He said he was going out with his recruiter."

"His recruiter!" Grayson ripped off his shades and his hat, tossed them both on the counter, and ran his fingers back through his damp curls. "God*damn* it, Leah. Why didn't you stop him?"

"Because I'm not your brother's keeper!" I exclaimed. "He said he was going out with his recruiter, Grayson. He didn't say he was signing up for a six-year stint tonight. And I did tell him what a bad idea I thought that would be."

Grayson shook his head at me, jaw set, nostrils flared, eyes hard, like this was all my fault. "There are two possibilities, and both of them are awful. The first is that he's lying to you. He doesn't want to spend time with you, and he's made an excuse so he won't have to go out with you again. Maybe he even has a date with somebody else, like a girl we went to middle school with that he ran into at that party."

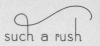

"Why is that so awful? I don't like him romantically either."

"It's your *job* to make him like you, Leah. Have you completely forgotten about that?"

"Not anymore," I protested, "because I—"

He put his hands on either side of me on the counter, leaning close and boxing me in. He interrupted, "The other possibility is that he wasn't lying. He really is meeting his recruiter. On a Thursday *night* on spring break in Heaven Beach. Which means they've gotten to be buddies. The recruiter will pal around with him to draw him in, and the next thing you know, Alec has signed his life away. Alec can do that, you know, anytime he wants to!"

"Yes, I know!" I was so exasperated with Grayson. I wished he could hear himself. "It's his life and his decision, and it's none of your business!"

"How dare you say that," Grayson said. It was such a funny-sounding, old-fashioned response. Maybe that's why it rang so true and sent a shiver down my spine. "You have no idea," he said. "None. How many brothers do you have?"

I swallowed. "None."

"How many dead brothers do you have?"

I squinted to keep from tearing up, then put my hands up on his shoulders, lightly, tentatively. "Grayson. Just because he joins the military doesn't mean he's going to die. The Admiral spent his entire career in the Navy, probably the first twenty years of that flying, and he never got wounded. Your dad never got wounded."

My words slowed to a halt as I heard how ridiculous they sounded. Grayson didn't need multiple friends and family members to die to make him fear for Alec's life. Jake was enough.

I'd realized this and I didn't need Grayson's lecture, but he was so upset that I let him give it to me anyway. "Alec's already a pilot, Leah."

"Okay."

"The second he graduates from college, they're going to send him to flight school. Hell, if he signs up for the reserves and there's a military emergency, they'll pluck him out of college and send him to flight school. It could happen this summer, Leah. It could happen in June. He'll be number one on that flight line. You're thinking that maybe he'll dodge a bullet, literally. I'm thinking that flying an airplane while people are shooting at you is never a good idea. In June he could be dead."

"I told him what I thought." I patted Grayson's shoulders once more and moved my hands together to his chest, placing my fingers gently on his neck. "You told him what you thought. I don't know where he went, and that's all we can do right now."

His hard gray eyes started to soften, and his body moved in, caging me more tightly against the countertop. "To answer your question, yeah, you screwed up your fake relationship with Alec today. Why did you tell your mom that you were dating me instead of him?"

I knew what was coming. My heart beat faster in anticipation, as if a plane were rounding from the taxiway to the runway and revving its engines, readying for takeoff.

"That started a long time ago," I admitted. "I didn't want to give her all my money. I told her that part of the time I was at the airport, I was actually spending time with my boyfriend, not working."

He put his hand up to my cheek. The broad pad of his thumb stroked across my lips. The engine revved so high that the roar filled my ears. "And why was I the boyfriend you picked?"

"It's easier to remember your lies if they're close to the truth," I whispered. "Wishful thinking."

He kissed me. So softly, gently, slowly.

I heard my own gasp, felt myself warming, sensed the trailer going darker around him as he leaned in until his forehead touched mine. He had backed me against the counter. I had no way to escape him, and I wasn't sure I wanted to anymore.

His voice sent shivers up my arms and his lips brushed my cheek as he spoke. "If I remember right, last night when we were interrupted at the beach, you had this hand here." He found my hand pushing weakly against his T-shirt and placed it on his hip. "And this hand here." He pulled my other hand to his other hip and slid my fingers into his waistband. "Then I did this." He moved one arm around my shoulders. "And I wanted to do this." His other hand moved down to my hip, the warmth of his palm soaking through the thin material of my shorts.

He pressed his lips to mine and paused. Maybe he was waiting to see whether I would push him away. Maybe, like me, he savored that precarious moment perched at the top of a climb. We could have fallen backward to Earth, pretending we'd been teasing each other and it was all a mean-spirited joke. Or we could have continued forward and pitched over into a weightless and euphoric free fall. In that moment of decision, his warm hands on my skin and the cold air around me confused my body. Electricity surged through my middle. The only sounds were the low hum of the refrigerator and Grayson sighing sexily.

I shifted my hand in his waistband, shoving my fingers farther down and flattening my palm against his bare skin.

That was it: we went over. He kissed me hard on the mouth, my stomach was gone, and we sped toward the ground. I stopped thinking. Nothing was left but the rush, the high, the sensations of his tongue in my mouth and his body underneath my hands.

After we had kissed like this for a long time, he scooped me up and sat me on the counter. I didn't protest, didn't even consider resisting when he slid his hands between my legs.

I wasn't expecting much. I let him touch me there because he wanted to. The boy who'd taken my virginity had touched me there too. But he'd been satisfying his own curiosity. Grayson was satisfying me. He watched my eyes and kissed my neck as he explored. Long minutes later when we rested with our foreheads together, panting into each other's mouths, he reached behind me and untied both strings of my bikini top.

We were back to the place with each other where we'd been at the beach. I wanted him desperately, but nothing would make me go through with this if I couldn't handle the consequences later. I nudged his blond curls aside with my nose and whispered in his ear, "Do you have a condom?"

"I do," he whispered back, his voice a sexy grind. But the mood cooled now that we needed to think. He fished his wallet from his pocket, placed it beside my thigh on the counter, and peered into the various compartments. "I thought I did." He removed a crumpled receipt. "Oh God, please."

I watched his long fingers search his wallet and slide inside to check for hidden condoms. Then I watched his face. He bit his lip, so concerned that he wouldn't find this condom and we wouldn't get this experience together after all. So eager and hot for me. I'd crushed on him for years and fallen in love with him over the past few days. But as he paused and frowned at me, then looked past me as if searching his mind for where else he might have left some of his things, I fell further.

Scowling at his wallet again, he slid out his pilot's license and his driver's license and the Hall Aviation credit card. "Come on now. Ha!" He grinned at me and held up two packets. "Two."

"Impressive."

"Oh." He laughed nervously, and a blush darkened his cheeks in the dim kitchen light. "Yeah, this all seems overly confident of me, doesn't it? Like I go around with condoms all the time just in case." He looked into my eyes and said, "I had a girlfriend. Before Jake died. Then I lost her because I was an asshole to her."

He sounded apologetic. I didn't know what to say to this. Of course he'd had a girlfriend. Of course he'd been hard to get along with after Jake died. I felt sorry for him and for this girl. If she had any sense, she was brokenhearted that they hadn't been able to hold on to each other until the worst passed.

Though Mr. Hall had died then. Maybe *this* was the worst, right now.

I could be this girl for him. I could be exactly what he needed. He was so full of life, but unsteady, and I would be steady for him and help him through.

He was squinting at the condoms. "They might have expired. No, that one's okay." He put one packet down on the counter. "That one's okay too." He gazed at me again. "Maybe we shouldn't do this."

*Oh no.* I'd wanted this with Grayson so badly for so long, way before I knew I wanted it.

But that was selfish of me. I swallowed and nodded, trying to understand. "Because of the condoms?"

"Hey." He gave me a long, chaste kiss on the lips, then one on the forehead. "No. They're really okay."

Now I knew. "Is it that girl you were dating?"

His brows arched in surprise. "What? No!"

I huffed out a little sigh of relief that he wasn't pining for his lost girlfriend. But now I was confused. "Why, then?"

"Because I'm your boss. And I'm taking advantage of you by coming over here when I know your mom has split."

"Is that all? You're realizing this a little late." I cupped his face in my hand and stroked my fingers down the blond stubble on his cheek. "We're both eighteen. What's really bothering you?"

His soulful gray eyes looked deep into my eyes as he said, "My dad would kill me."

He likely was right about that. But his dad wasn't here. And we were.

Slowly I slid off the counter, down his body. When I reached the floor, I looked way up into his eyes. I took his hand and led him down the hall to my bedroom.

# eighteen

Afterward he lay on top of me. His cheek pressed against my neck, but I didn't want him to move. With all of him pinning me, I felt oddly comfortable. I only tried to slow my panting, quiet my breathing, to the point that I could hear he was breathing hard too.

He propped himself up on his elbows, blinking at me, his long, blond eyelashes and the edges of his blond hair lit only by the streetlight through the tiny window. "God, I'm sorry, Leah," he whispered. "I was crushing you."

"Maybe a little," I said.

He smiled at me then, not an embarrassed smile, and that put me at ease. He had a look in his eyes I recognized from times when he'd pulled a prank on Mr. Hall, or he'd landed after a series of touch-and-go's when he was first learning to fly. Unlike a lot of people, he wasn't drained by a rush of adrenaline. His expression said, *I want to go again.*

I laughed. After that adrenaline rush of a flight, I'd come back to Earth now. But just like with flying, I was already looking forward to the next time too.

He couldn't, at least not yet. Boys had to recover first. I knew that much from TV and dirty talk on the school bus. He reached to my bedside table and fumbled with the alarm clock. The radio shut off for the first time since he brought me back from the airport basement two nights before. Normally silence would have descended on the room like a shroud. With Grayson here, the quiet was bearable. Even nice. I didn't mind the idea of a long, empty space.

He rolled to his side and settled on one elbow with his chin in his hand, watching me. "This is going to be kind of a downer after that, but I want you to know something. When we were at Molly's café the night of the party, you said something that got me thinking. You said sometimes people have problems, and they get stuck." He raised his eyebrows, asking if I remembered.

I nodded. I'd been talking about my mom.

"That's exactly how I've felt for the past two months," he said, "since my dad died. No, for the past three months, since Jake died. There have been moments—actually, a *lot* of moments—when I've thought I'll never be happy again. But I'm happy right now. You make me happy."

"Good," I said, smoothing a hand across his bare chest and trying to act natural. It was Grayson, I kept telling myself, Grayson whom I'd loved from afar for so long. But he was different in the flesh. This man's body would take a lot of getting used to.

"And whenever you and I are talking—" he went on.

"—or doin' it," I broke in, because this was getting so heavy.

He laughed. "Or doin' it," he agreed, but then his smile faded. "I'm serious."

"I know," I said, feeling like the worst friend, the worst person. I'd thought making a joke would help him out of this, but he wasn't ready to go yet.

"When I'm with you," he began again, "it's like . . . I still don't feel normal. But I can *see* normal at twelve o'clock on the horizon." He pointed past me, through the windshield of an imaginary airplane. "At least I know normal is still out there. I've spent the last three months not sure of that at all."

On a sigh he brought up his hand and used one long finger to brush a dark curl away from my face. With the saddest look in his eyes, he said, "A girl needs to be held right now, and comforted, and told that everything is going to be okay. I'm sorry I can't do that for you. I don't have any of that left."

"I have a little," I said, "and I'll lend it to you."

He kissed my lips twice more, wrapped his arms around me, and nestled his head under my chin. I worked my fingers through his blond curls. They sprang up and tickled my cheek.

He said low, "One down, one to go."

I laughed.

"I didn't want you to bed down for the night and get comfortable and think we were done."

"Thanks for warning me. That is so sexy." There really was nothing about the sex we'd just had that was sexy at all, except Grayson himself. The air conditioner was running, but the pit bull was faintly audible over the roar. My mom had bought the comforter on my bed at a thrift store when I was seven. It depicted a cartoon girl who hadn't been on TV in two decades.

And on the wall opposite from my pink bed, where I could see it first thing every morning, was a poster of US

Airways flight 5149. Captain Sullenberger had taken off from LaGuardia Airport in New York City one January afternoon, his Airbus headed for Charlotte, North Carolina. A flock of geese hanging around the runway flew into his plane and took out both engines. He managed to land perfectly in the Hudson River that ran along Manhattan Island. The poster was an iconic photo of the plane floating in the river, with the skyline of Manhattan behind it. All 155 passengers and crew stood precariously on wings, in business shirts rather than overcoats on the frigid winter afternoon, surrounded by icy water, waiting for boats to take them back to the wharf for hot chocolate. Afterward, Captain Sullenberger was acclaimed as a hero. He wrote a book and did the talk show circuit. And then it all became a joke. Movies made fun of the crash and said people in New York were so protective of this captain's heroic status, but modern automation meant those planes flew themselves.

We pilots knew Captain Sullenberger was a bad-ass. He could have crash-landed that plane and taken out half of Manhattan. But he kept calm, and the outcome was perfect.

Grayson's eyes had fallen on the poster too. "Hey, where'd you get that?" He nodded toward the poster. "My dad—"

"—had a poster like that," I interrupted him. "I know. It's his. After he died, I used the key the airport office had for your hangar and I took it, but that's all I took, ever. I'd gotten used to seeing it every day and I just wanted that one thing to remember him."

I must have sounded really strange, because he propped himself up on both elbows to look at me. "Leah, it's okay." He sank down with his chin on his crossed arms, watching me. "He's a good hero to have."

I wondered whether he meant Captain Sullenberger or his dad. As my heart raced, dragging my mind with it, I decided it

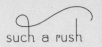

was best to come clean before I got caught again. "The poster is the only thing I took, but I already had this."

I rolled away from him and felt around on my bedside table for *The Right Stuff*. The paperback had been well worn, with a cracked white spine and missing corners, when Mr. Hall loaned it to me years ago. I'd read it a million times. When the cover had come off, I'd secured it to the book with a rubber band from the airport office. I handed the frayed bundle over to Grayson.

"Oh!" he said through a laugh, recognizing the book. He removed the rubber band and opened the front cover, setting it next to the book.

At the top of the inside cover, Mr. Hall had written *Brian Hall*. His name was crossed out, and underneath it, in a different handwriting, was *Jake Hall*. This too was crossed out. A third handwriting proclaimed, *Alec Hall*. A fourth, by far the messiest, claimed the book for *Grayson Hall*. Then *Alec Hall* again. The last *Grayson Hall* was the only name in the column that didn't have a line through it.

Grayson touched the cover in the space between *Brian Hall* and *Jake Hall,* then swept his fingertip down the page. "Dad tried so hard to get us to read it. When Jake finally did and told Alec and me how good it was, we fought over it. I guess buying your own copy of a book doesn't occur to you when you're twelve." He bit his lip.

And then, without moving his head, he brought his eyes up to meet mine. His look was hard to read. I'd known him for years, yet I'd had so little face time with him that his expressions were practically a stranger's. The basic look of chagrin I recognized. The subtleties were lost on me. I couldn't tell whether he was embarrassed that he'd accidentally accused me of freeloading, or he was accusing me on purpose.

And asking for his book back.

"You should have it," I said quickly.

Now his lips parted in surprise. "No! Of course not. You should have it. You were the last one to . . ."

He took a breath, and so did I. Neither of us wanted to delve into Mr. Hall's death right now. That much I understood about Grayson. We'd shared something that had to do with him and me, not Mr. Hall, not Alec, not Jake, just the two of us. We wanted to enjoy the afterglow and we were trying our best to bond, but it was difficult with so many people between us, even though most of them were ghosts.

He exhaled, and I did too.

"We're very tense," he said.

"Yeah."

He chuckled and touched my lips. "We weren't tense a few minutes ago."

I smiled. His finger followed the curve of my mouth. I watched him watching me. We'd shared tender moments like this in the past few days, but I had difficulty shaking the image of the distant Grayson I was used to. His fingertip on my cheek was warm and welcome but strange, because I knew his mood wouldn't last.

But if I hadn't understood his background, I would have thought he was a carefree eighteen-year-old with tender feelings for his girlfriend, experienced enough with sex to know what he was doing, inexperienced enough to act thrilled. His hand moved into my hair. Stroking my curls, he smiled as he said, "It's cool that I've scored a pilot."

I laughed, relieved at the joke. "I think so too."

He wound a curl around his finger, then unwound it, watching my hair rather than looking into my eyes. And sure enough, his chuckle faded into a frown. His blond brows

knitted. He seemed to be concentrating on the puzzle of my hair. I knew he was sliding away from me already. Now the unexpected sweetness that made him Grayson was fading, and he seemed like any other guy out there. Like Mark.

"If we hadn't done it tonight, would you want another girl on the side?" I asked.

I had his attention again. He untangled his finger from my hair and looked me in the eyes. "Like, if you and I were dating but weren't having sex, would I want a second girlfriend to have sex with?"

"Yes," I said, relieved that he got it.

"No," he said angrily. "Would you do that to *me*?"

"Of course not," I said self-righteously. I'd never really thought about it before, but I was way more loyal than was good for me.

"Then why did you think it was okay for Mark to do that to *you*?"

I gaped at him for a moment, speechless with astonishment. When I found my voice, I asked, "How'd you know I was talking about Mark?"

"I understand Mark pretty well," he grumbled. "I was headed down that path, only thinking about myself, when I wrecked the Piper. Something like that makes you rethink what you value and what you want. I wish it had happened to me a few years sooner, when I had more than a few weeks left with my brother and my dad."

He tapped my lips with his fingertip. "I know Mark. I know what he would do just to get a rise out of you. I want you to promise me that if you and I ever break up, you won't go back to him."

I sucked in a long breath around his finger, trying not to show how surprised and overwhelmed I was at the idea

that Grayson and I were a couple now. If we decided not to be anymore, we would have to go through the formality of breaking up.

Like any normal girlfriend and boyfriend.

My arms and face tingled with the rush.

Then I had to say on a sigh, "I can't make you that promise, Grayson. It's not that I'm planning to run back to Mark. But I determine what's best for me. I'm not making promises to other people about that. I've done that only once."

His eyes searched mine. "Even if it's for your own good?"

"Your dad earned the right to tell me that."

Grayson nodded, understanding. "You're right. I haven't. I just . . . worry about you." His fingertip moved down my cheek to trace the line of my jaw. He seemed so serious, heavy with responsibility, utterly unlike the crazy boy I'd crushed on years ago. I knew the old Grayson was in there—I'd seen him when he kissed me, when we made love—and I hoped he didn't count me as one more weighty responsibility that killed his spirit.

"Are you sorry that we were together?" I whispered.

His whole face changed like an idea was slowly dawning on him. He cradled my cheek in his palm. "Leah, of course not."

"You seem sorry," I said, feeling small again. I'd thought I didn't need his comfort. I'd thought *I* could comfort *him*. But out of nowhere, here was that waiflike girl he'd said would want to be held, a girl who'd taken what we'd done too seriously and needed him to pretend it had meant something.

"Hey. I told you. Lately my brain isn't working right. I feel one thing, but I act a different way and it surprises me. I don't know where my words are coming from half the time. But you . . ." He kissed my cheek. "Gosh . . ." He kissed my lips,

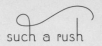

then backed away to look at me again. "You know what? Let me show you how I feel."

I gasped as he trailed kisses down my cheek, down my neck, across my breast and farther down, and then he showed me.

He crawled across the bed until he hung off the side. Dragging his shorts from the floor, he found his phone in the pocket. "I'm starving. Pizza?"

"Great. My treat."

He looked around at me and opened his mouth. And I took a breath to explain my situation. My refrigerator was empty and I always ate like it was my last meal because I had no phone and no car to get food, *not* because I had no money.

He closed his mouth and swallowed his protest, already flipping through search screens on his phone.

I rolled closer and watched over his shoulder. "Not that one. They don't deliver to this trailer park because they've had so many problems out here."

He gaped at me again. "What do you mean, they—"

I chopped my hand across my throat.

He closed his mouth and showed me the screen for a different pizza place.

"Perfect," I said.

An hour later, we were full of pizza, and I loved him a little more. I'd figured things would get awkward when we sat down on the pitted couch to eat with no TV in front of us. What were we supposed to do for entertainment, stare at my second-grade photo?

But we talked airplanes. He told me about his dad taking him and Alec and Jake to Sun and Fun in central Florida, to which everybody flew their planes instead of driving, and the

biggest fly-in in all of Oshkosh, Wisconsin, where he'd seen his first Harrier. He said the noise of a Harrier put the Chinook to shame. I'd never heard a Harrier.

We put away the pizza, he stepped into the bathroom, and I snuggled back into bed. I felt comfortable with him here. The only person who'd ever been in my bedroom, besides me and my mom, was Mark—and only that first night, when I thought we were going to do it and he fell asleep instead.

My mom had issued the invitation for him to live here, and when he passed out drunk, it was like she'd invited her life to become my life and lie useless beside me in my bed, the most private of spaces, and I wasn't allowed to get rid of it. Most nights after that when he'd stayed here, he'd gone out with his friends to get plastered, and I'd locked myself in my room. I knew from experience with the trailer that he could easily have kicked the door in if he'd wanted to badly enough, but he'd been too drunk to care that deeply. He'd only knocked on the door, then yelled threats at me, then passed out on the couch in the den. I'd stretched to take up both sides of my bed, relieved.

Funny how my feelings about Mark and Grayson were night and day. I'd thought I liked Mark at first. I'd tried hard to like him, but I just couldn't. I'd never wanted to like Grayson. I just did. And whereas I would have cringed at seeing the silhouette of Mark reentering my bedroom in the moonlight, my heart sped up when I saw Grayson coming back. To say good night, maybe. That was better than nothing. Or just to slip on his clothes. The promise of making love again seemed too good to be true.

He slid through the sheets next to me and nuzzled my neck until I giggled. He reached out. With one gentle hand, he turned my face to his so he could kiss me long on the lips. No

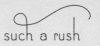

urgency this time, just a lazy exploration of my mouth with his tongue.

After a few minutes, he said, "The floor in the bathroom is spongy."

He paused, allowing me to explain.

When I didn't say anything, he went on, "Like the pipes have had a slow leak for decades, and the water has disintegrated the floorboards. That thin layer of linoleum on top is all that's preventing you from falling through."

He paused again.

When I just glared at him, he instructed me, "You should call the landlord. He's required to fix stuff like that, even if you'll only be here a few more weeks."

This time when he stopped running his trap, he realized from the look on my face that he'd said something wrong. He bit his lip. "What."

"My mom *did* call the landlord," I said self-righteously. "Years ago, right after we moved in. He said the floor had been like that for twenty years, it had been like that when my mother signed the lease, and if she hadn't been too good for the trailer when she signed the lease, she wasn't too good for it now."

"Leah. Okay," he said soothingly, a soft contrast with my voice, which had risen to a shout. He touched my lip with two long fingers, shushing me. "I've hit a nerve and I don't know what it is. What are you trying to tell me?"

"I am trying to tell you to shut? Up!" I was so angry that my brain was flooded with it and I couldn't even see him anymore. Everything was ruined now. I had known better than to let him into the trailer.

"Why didn't you do like that?" He chopped his hand back and forth across his throat. "I thought that was the signal."

I chopped my hand back and forth across my throat in turn. "Because I would be doing this all night!"

"Great," he muttered. "Now I have to start all over." He rolled out of bed, dragged me after him, and threw me over his shoulder.

"Hey!" I yelled. He was laughing, a sound I'd longed for so deeply that, despite myself, I laughed too.

He set me down on the counter in the kitchen and kissed me again.

I knew he was making a point of working his body over my body in exactly the way he'd done it when he first arrived. I knew he was being sweet and accommodating my hang-up. I tried to get into what he was doing. But my mind was still on the bathroom floor with the leaking pipes, the slow rot, the landlord who thought that's exactly what my mother and I deserved.

In my mind I put Grayson back where he belonged, at his shack by the beach, furnished with nothing but a futon and a surfboard. Instead of the counter, he kissed me on the sand, and I rose to meet him again.

The radio startled me awake. Grayson must have set the alarm accidentally when he turned the radio off. I hit the button and nuzzled against him, glad to have another hour in bed with him, another hour of sleep. But he slipped from the bed. The streetlight through the window lit the edges of his hard muscles as he felt around on the dark floor for his clothes.

"Leaving?" I asked, trying not to sound disappointed.

"I have to get back to the other side of town before Alec wakes up so he doesn't guess where I've been." Grayson sat on the edge of the bed and put his hand over my hand. "I know

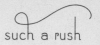

this sucks, but I need you to keep dating Alec for me. Now that you know why, you'll do that for me, right?"

I couldn't believe what I was hearing. I slid my hand out from under his hand. But I managed to keep my voice ironically pleasant as I asked, "What if he tells me tomorrow that he feels like we've gotten really close, and he wants to take it to the next level? What if he wants to come back here with me alone? What if he wants to go all the way? Should I let him? Can you stop by the store and buy me a new pack of condoms just in case?"

He closed his eyes like I'd slapped him. His face was three horizontal lines: two eyes, grim mouth. "That's not going to happen. Either he doesn't like you very much and none of this has worked, or he'll see this week as just the beginning, and he'll ask you to our prom next weekend."

"Your *prom!*" High school stuff seemed a million miles away, especially for Grayson and Alec's foreign town that really was eighty miles from here. "I hope you don't expect me to go to Alec's prom with him."

"If he asks you, yes."

"Then what if he wants to make prom night super-special?"

He looked out the window, his high cheekbones and long nose lit by the moon, and seemed to be considering it.

"That's it," I snapped. "You have officially lost your mind. I put up with this shit when I thought it was only going to last a week, and I didn't know I was going to get tangled up with you. Now I'm through. Get out."

He balled his fist and held it in front of his mouth. "Leah. We're both mad, and it's late, and we're tired, and we just . . . we just—"

"What? You don't even have a word for it, when you're still trying to get me to screw your brother."

He jerked up to standing then. He'd pulled his shirt over his head and was halfway across the dark room when he turned and said, "You don't have to fake anything with him anymore. Just don't tell him that I asked you to in the first place."

"Oh! Thanks, Grayson, for clarifying that. You know, I'm beginning to wonder whether you only slept with me to get me to do what you wanted."

He gaped at me. In the still dark, we could hear another man and woman outside a trailer up the road, screaming at each other.

Grayson's hands were shaking as he touched one of his pointer fingers to the other. "I would not do that, Leah. To *anybody*." He touched his middle finger. "And I especially wouldn't do that to *you*. My God!" He extended his hand. "What *was* tonight, anyway?"

I could see tonight had meant as much to him as it had to me. And he was willing to throw every bit of it away in order to manipulate Alec, just like he'd always planned. I'd played this game when I thought I was the only one getting hurt. But I wouldn't continue to play Alec. Why couldn't Grayson see this was wrong?

"So you won't do *some* immoral things to keep Alec out of the military," I pointed out. "*Other* immoral things to keep Alec out of the military are perfectly fine."

Grayson spread both arms wide, exasperated. "Yes!"

If Grayson didn't see my point, I would make him see. "I'm going to tell Alec."

"You are not," Grayson growled.

"I'll be at work at seven," I warned him. "I'll give you until then to tell him. If you don't, I will."

He balled both fists.

Put one to his mouth and one on his hip.

Seemed to be holding his breath.

Finally he stomped out of the room, down the hall, and out of the trailer. The pit bull became hysterical, but the aluminum door did not bang shut.

Staring at the poster of the beautiful Airbus floating in the Hudson, I knew I was right. I knew I would go through with my threat. Yet I wanted to call Grayson back. He was under so much pressure, but he hadn't slammed my door.

I walked up the path and emerged from the trees onto the bright airstrip as usual. Nothing else was as usual this morning. Mark must have had an early night, because he was in Mr. Simon's hangar, checking the fuel level in his Air Tractor. He whistled at me as I passed. I ignored him.

Molly was already out in the grass, unrolling a banner for Alec. But all the Hall Aviation planes were still there. First I swung around the doorjamb of the office and faced Grayson, grim behind the desk, his blond hair wet from a shower. I fought down the urge to go to him and embrace him and smell him. What I asked was, "Did you tell Alec?"

He glared up at me with pure hatred in his eyes. "No," he said curtly.

"It was kind of late when we talked last night," I said loud enough to make him cringe and look through the doorway to see whether Alec was listening. "Maybe you're kind of fuzzy on this. I said I would give you until I got to work this morning to tell him, and then *I* would tell him."

He squeezed all the blood out of his fist. His jaw went white too. He said very slowly, "I'm going to give you every opportunity not to do that."

I flounced out of his office. Alec stood in the open doorway of his airplane, peering into the gas tank on top of the wing, just as Mark had been.

I called, "Alec, can I talk to you for a minute?"

"Sure thing." He hopped down from the doorway and leaned against the strut. "What's up?"

He was so handsome, grinning, round-faced and blond and blue-eyed and innocent, that I found myself faltering. What if he really had fallen for me, and my revelation crushed him?

"Wow," I said. "I wanted to tell you something because I think you deserve to know, but this is a lot harder than I thought."

He never stopped grinning. He didn't even sound particularly sarcastic as he said, "You've only been pretending to like me? Grayson blackmailed you to do that, hoping I would cling to you instead of joining the military?"

"Yes," I said on a huge sigh of relief. "He *did* tell you."

"Molly told me," Alec said, and now I could hear the bitterness in his voice.

"*Molly* told you!" I exclaimed, glancing past his airplane to the field, where Molly stretched tall to hang a banner on the upright poles. "When?"

"Sunday night."

Sunday had been the day Grayson first came to my trailer. Sunday night, Molly had taken me for a drive. "Alec, you hadn't even met Molly on Sunday night."

"I've known her for a long time," Alec said self-righteously. "Sort of known her, but it seemed pointless to try to start something with her when I wasn't in town that often. I knew I would be here this week, so Sunday morning I asked her out. That night she called me to say my brother was forcing her best friend to pretend to like me."

My stomach twisted. No wonder Molly had acted so strangely all week. And when I felt like she'd betrayed me by dragging me to Francie's party, that hadn't scratched the surface of what she'd done to me.

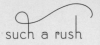

"So you knew all along?" I murmured. "And you played along with it? Why, Alec?"

"Molly asked me to, for one thing," he said. "She told me I could never let you know she'd spilled the beans. But it was all typical Grayson anyway. Underhanded. Breaking the rules. He convinced our mom that he'd changed. I realized Sunday night he hasn't changed at all. I was curious to see how far he'd take it. And he's been in love with you since the day you first walked onto this airstrip three and a half years ago. I thought it would be fun to make out with you and see how he liked getting double-crossed by his own brother."

His voice rose as he said this. The louder he got, the faster my heart raced. I thought it couldn't pump any faster, and then he told me Grayson had been in love with me for years.

But that didn't fix any of this, or take away from the fact that Grayson had been manipulating us all.

"Alec," I said, "I didn't mean to hurt you. And Grayson only—"

"It doesn't matter what you *meant*, Leah," Alec shouted. "I found Molly two years ago. I finally asked her out. But because of all this bullshit, it's ruined now. She and I spent last night alone together, and she's so convinced something happened between you and me that she's not even talking to me now. Thanks for that." He opened the door of his cockpit and climbed back up to look at the wing.

I didn't want to leave things like this between Alec and me, but I wasn't going to stand there and look at his feet.

I headed back down the tarmac. When I drew even with the upright poles, I waded through the long grass to Molly.

"Hey, chick," she sang. She dropped the heavy end of a banner she'd been struggling with. A cloud of bugs lifted into the air. "What's up?"

"Why did you tell Alec?"

As I watched, her face transformed from innocent teenager playing bad girl to a look of malice. I'd seen it on Francie's face a few nights before. The only time I'd seen it on Molly was when she first confronted me about stealing Ryan from her two years ago.

"What you were doing was wrong," she said, "and I was trying to warn him."

"You knew *why* I was doing it," I reminded her, "and when you told him, you were jeopardizing my whole flying career."

"Well, maybe you *don't* deserve a flying career," she snapped. "Did you ever think about that? Maybe you *don't* have good moral character. You forged your mother's name. You shacked up with Mark. One day later, you tried to fool Alec into thinking you had feelings for him. You knew Ryan was dating me and you tried to steal him from me."

"Is that what this is all about?" I demanded. *"Ryan?"*

"You're supposed to be my best friend, but you scope out the ones I really like and steal them! Can't I have *anything?"*

"I did *not* steal Ryan from you," I said firmly. *"He* came on to *me.* I turned him down, and he spread it around school that he'd been with me anyway."

"Then why didn't you tell me that in the first place?" she exclaimed.

"Because you like the upside down," I said. "The opposite. You think it's cool to tell your friends that you go slumming with a poor girl. It makes you feel different and proud to lift me up from the ghetto." I should have added the truth. When she thought I'd stolen Ryan, that had given me power and daring in her eyes. All I'd ever wanted from Molly was not to lose her. But I couldn't tell her this. Not after everything she'd thrown at me.

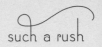

"That's what you really think?" she asked. "And you lied to stay friends with a bitch like me? It just proves I was right. I *couldn't* trust you with Alec. You *don't* have good moral character. You're a liar."

She was about to bend down and work on the sign again, like the conversation was over and I wasn't standing there, but something over my shoulder caught her attention. I turned around.

Grayson waded through the grass after me. As he reached me, he held out a wad of bills and coins and dumped them into my cupped hand.

"I don't want your money," I told him. "I quit."

"That's for yesterday," he said. "You're fired."

I turned and walked through the grass along a new trajectory, a diagonal that would spit me out on the tarmac closer to my trailer. Along the way I dropped a quarter in the grass and did *not* stoop to pick it up. Grayson and Molly had already lost interest in me and were screaming at each other, but I didn't want to risk having them glance over at me and see me groveling in the dirt for a coin. Then it occurred to me that there was no reason for me to go home. There was nothing there to eat, nothing to read, no way to get out, and in two weeks I would be homeless.

In the shadows of Mr. Simon's hangar, Mark was sitting in the cockpit of the crop duster, watching me approach.

I put a little extra swing in my walk and stepped over the threshold into his hangar. Sliding up to the open door of the cockpit, I whispered into the darkness, "Did I hear you whistle at me?"

"Normally you'd have quite a ride to the farm of the day," Mark said into his mike as we bumped along the tarmac toward the end of the runway. "We spray farms as far away as

three hundred miles. But since we're taking the Stearman and you're getting your feet wet, we'll just buzz the folks near the airport. Do you really want a rush?"

His voice sounded strange in my headphones, precisely because it didn't sound strange at all. He spoke the same as always. He wasn't imitating Chuck Yeager or making any effort to sound like a cool, collected pilot. That's when I had second thoughts about going up with him. But I couldn't ask him to stop, taxi back to the hangar, and let me out just because his voice didn't sound right. Not when this was the only chance I had left at a job flying.

"Yes," I said.

He stopped at the end of the runway and ran up the engines, like he was supposed to. But he didn't touch each instrument in the panel with his finger. He didn't work his feet to make sure the rudders moved the way they should. I'd always felt a little silly going through these motions so methodically, the way Mr. Hall had taught me, like the rudders were suddenly going to quit working. Then I heard Mr. Hall in my head, reminding me that if something went wrong in the air, I couldn't pull over. Clearly Mark had never received this warning. Or he didn't care.

*Aren't you going to test the rudders?* kept forming on my lips, and I kept brushing it away like an annoying bug. I had a vision of myself trapped in the back of this crop duster like a sardine in a can while Mark slung us all over the sky. But I'd never seen how he flew on a job. He was probably perfectly safe. I tried to picture what Grayson would do in this situation. If he needed a job flying a crop duster, he wouldn't second-guess Mark's prep at the end of the runway.

Of course, he wouldn't walk up to Mark in the hangar and ask whether Mark had whistled at him, either. But Grayson

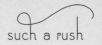
such a rush

would never need a crop-dusting job. Grayson and I were so far apart that we had nothing to do with each other. Thirty years from now, if a rumor ran around the airport that we'd had a one-night stand, we would still be so far apart that nobody would believe it.

Mark announced our departure over the airport frequency in his usual lilting tone, laughing at the end. His voice sounded louder as he released that button and talked only to me. "Get ready for the ride of your life, Leah. Later tonight, that is. The flight will be fun too."

My head jerked back against my seat as he accelerated suddenly. My stomach turned over and over as I processed what he meant: we would have sex later because he'd taken me flying. I wished I hadn't marched straight from an argument with Grayson and Molly and Alec into Mark's hangar. But what else was I going to do, go home?

The plane sped past the huge hangars on that end of the runway, past Mr. Simon's hangar. Alec had joined Grayson and Molly at the upright poles in the middle of the field. Grayson and Alec shouted at each other. Alec shoved Grayson. Molly tried to separate them, her ridiculous heavy work gloves hovering between them. They all stopped and watched the Stearman take off.

Mark took his hand from the stick and waved to them. There was no cabin in the biplane. Goggles and a small windscreen were the only things separating us from the open air. So the boys might have heard Mark as he shouted, "I've got your girlfriend, fucker!"

And then we were in the sky, zooming upward at a banner-towing angle. When I piloted a tow plane, I needed to fly at this angle to get the banner off the ground quickly. There was no reason for Mark to be flying this way, unless—

289

"I wanted you to feel some G's!" he said into the mike. "Now, step one. Survey the area for tractors, combines, cows. We don't want to hit anything when we're down near the ground. Cows will fuck you up. Take a look."

I was surprised he wanted to give me this demonstration so close to the airport. Other planes would be taking off and landing. But this was what I'd wanted, right? To feel a rush? I sat straighter in my seat and craned my neck to see past the lower wings. Rows of cotton flashed beneath us fast as strobe lights, unbroken all the way to the forest. "I don't see anything," I said.

"Step two," he said, "dive dive dive!"

My stomach stayed at five hundred feet as we plummeted toward the ground. I gripped the sides of my seat and was very glad he couldn't see me in the seat directly behind him. I realized now that he'd asked me to look for obstacles just so I would be scared when I saw the ground rushing to meet us.

"The switch to release the chemicals will be here," he said, pointing to the instrument panel with one hand. I wished he would keep both hands on the stick, at least while we were plummeting. "You'd flick it right about here, then pull up."

At the very last second before we tunneled into the dirt, he jerked the controls. The plane flattened its trajectory. We skimmed along five feet from the tops of the plants.

"Mark." My voice sounded shaky in the mike.

He chuckled. "Yes, Leah."

"Do I need to get this low," I asked, "or is it just you?"

He laughed more loudly. Maybe it was the effect of the headphones, but he sounded a touch insane. "It's not just me. You've got to stay near the crops so the chemicals don't drift. It's weird but when you spray herbicide on people, they call my uncle's office to complain. And now you're probably thinking I need to pull up again before I hit those trees."

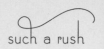

I was, in fact, thinking this as the dark forest rushed toward us.

"This takes practice, Leah. We're going to die now, right? That was the last second we could have saved ourselves and we missed it, right? Count to three."

"Onetwothree!" I shouted.

"You counted too fast."

I kept my eyes open as the forest loomed. I didn't want to die with my eyes shut.

"And *now* we pull up."

I was in the midst of a reflex to cover my face with my arms to protect myself from the impact when he nosed the plane up, tracing the outline of an oak tree.

The plane soared in a circle over the forest. Broken pieces of his cackle came through the headphones as his voice triggered the mike to switch on and off. After he'd collected himself, he asked, "Sick yet?"

"Yes," I said. "Mark, I've changed my mind. I'm really sorry but I don't want a relationship with you. I just wanted to fly. And if I can't have one without the other, please take me back and put me down."

Static sounded in my headphones, then silence. Static, silence. He was breathing hard.

"Mark."

"What did you say?" he asked, voice dripping sarcasm. "That you're ready to go again? I heard you the first time." He dropped the plane to zoom way too close along the highest branches of the trees.

I felt faint. All the warnings I'd heard about Mark over the past week rushed to my mind. That he was crazy. Dangerous. Used his plane as a weapon. Shouldn't be trusted to fly with passengers. Had fallen in love with me and didn't want to let me go.

"Mark, please," I said, pilot voice cracking.

"I *said* we'd go again, Leah." His words were so loud that I reached up to pull my headphones away and save my hearing. "Let me straighten her out and then—"

I was glad I didn't get the headphones off. The next second, the front of the plane exploded, the noise earsplitting even through the headphones. I ducked under the debris coming at me: the top of a tree, part of the propeller. I heard it crash across the tail behind me.

We'd cleared the trees now, but the terrifying noise hadn't stopped, only changed. With part of the propeller gone, the huge, heavy engine knocked around up front, threatening to tear the plane apart.

"Mark!"

He said nothing.

The plane was sinking fast.

"Mark!" I shouted. "My airplane!" Fists shaking, I pulled back on the stick, gaining as much height as possible so I'd have farther to fall. That way I'd have more choice about where I crash-landed.

I couldn't move much because I didn't dare take my hands off the controls, and I was unprotected in the open air. But I leaned as far forward and to one side as I could, twisting to look at what had happened to Mark. He was slumped over in the front seat—too far over. On the front instrument panel was a bright smear of blood.

I was on my own.

# nineteen

"Mayday mayday mayday." I announced over the radio that I was making an emergency landing. That was just a courtesy message telling other planes to get out of my way. Nobody answered, of course. There was no tower, no authority, no one to save us.

The engine vibrated dangerously. The controls were sluggish and the plane was hard to steer. I pointed the nose for the airport and hoped I would make it. All the while I was looking around for places to land—a field until we passed it, a straight stretch of two-lane road until we passed that. Puffy white clouds gathered over the ocean, a stereotypical heaven scene from a movie.

"Leah," Grayson said over the radio. He recited the number of the channel Hall Aviation used.

I switched to that channel. "I'm here."

"What are you doing?" We were both using the Chuck

Yeager voice like his dad had taught us, but even through the radio, I could hear he was breathless.

"Mark hit a tree. He's out cold. Controls are mushy. Part of the prop is gone and I'm about to shut the engine down. Call 911."

The plane dipped suddenly before dashing up again. I fought the controls to steady it. Static sounded in my ears. I realized it was my own gasp, which had triggered the voice-activated radio as if I'd said something.

I turned the engine off so at least the controls would work better and I could fly the plane like a glider. The propeller came to an ominous stop. The silence in my trailer had never been as awful.

"Make a pass and let us see the damage before you try to land," Grayson said.

"Negative," I said. "I can't stay up that long."

"Then skip the airport and go for the ocean."

"Negative. Mark will drown before they get to him." I couldn't swim, either, but if I survived the crash, I could probably cling to a piece of the airplane until the Coast Guard rescued me. Mark would be lost.

"That fucking—" Grayson's voice cut off suddenly as he remembered we were on a public frequency.

I knew what he meant. This was Mark's fault. But it was my responsibility now. I reminded Grayson, "What matters most is other people, then me, then the airplane, then the banner." I didn't have a banner this time, but Mr. Hall's rule still applied. No matter what Mark had done, he now fell in the category of "other people," and I wasn't going to lose him if I could help it.

I heard static in my headphones again as I breathed a sigh of relief. The runway had come into view, and the long row

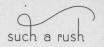

of hangars. Flying closer, I could see that people lined the tarmac—not as many as had watched the Chinook, because it was still so early in the morning, but I was the show of the day. In front of the Hall Aviation hangar, Molly folded her arms like she was cold. Alec's hand was on Grayson's back. Both Grayson's hands were on his cowboy hat. I couldn't see them well at that distance, but I knew them from what they wore and the way they stood.

Grayson put one hand to his mouth and spoke into Mr. Hall's radio. "Leah, you're missing your left gear."

"Roger." Looking over the side of the cockpit, I saw the left front wheel of the tricycle underneath the plane had been sheared off. That meant when I landed, the left side of the airplane would have nothing to touch down underneath it.

I'd better keep my wing tip up as long as I could, then, until I slowed down.

Static sounded in my ears. Then again. I wanted to move the microphone farther from my mouth so I couldn't hear my own breathing, but I didn't dare take my hands off the controls.

Underneath me, dark grass flashed past, then lighter gray pavement. I was over the runway, speeding just above the asphalt. Now that the broken engine and propeller weren't throwing the plane off balance, I could have been landing an undamaged airplane. I held fast to that denial, because it kept me calm. Too late it occurred to me that I probably should have been praying.

The plane vibrated as the right landing gear touched down.

Way ahead of me in the grassy strip between the tarmac and the runway, Grayson and Alec and Molly were running. Grayson's cowboy hat flew off. I wished they would stay away, because if the metal ground against the asphalt on landing

and kicked up one spark that lit leaking gas, the plane would explode.

I pitched the left wing up a little to keep the plane level until we slowed, but the Stearman was old and heavy and it was no use. The wing kept sinking, astonished that the landing gear wasn't there to support it, feeling for its place on the ground.

The wing screeched, screamed, skidded across the asphalt. Slammed to the ground and bounced violently upward.

Sparks and pieces of the wing flew over my head.

The plane veered sharply to the left. The trees loomed in front of us.

I gripped the controls. The trees came fast and I was about to slam into them. In my mind I was taking off again, in control of my airplane, sailing over the trees and over the ocean and into the clouds.

I let one sob escape. I heard it in my headphones.

I was close enough to the tree about to kill me that I could tell from the bark it was the same species of palm as the one outside my bedroom.

My stomach left me. Every atom in my body was forced forward and jerked back.

The plane stopped with a noise so loud that it sounded like nothing.

No, the noise was static in my headphones, and now my own screaming. My eardrums would burst. I reached up to push my headphones off.

Warm hands fumbled across my head and in my lap. Arms wrapped around my chest and pulled.

"Leah! Open your eyes."

I blinked at Grayson. We were standing safe outside the

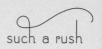

mangled plane, under the trees at the edge of the runway. But I couldn't catch my breath, gasping from screaming so long.

He tossed my headphones away. He took my goggles off. He put his hands on either side of my face and peered at me. My double reflection in his sunglass lenses was weird and convex, my dark curls wild, my eyes huge.

"Are you hurt?" he asked me.

"Is Mark dead?" I croaked.

"No. The treetop he plowed through got him in the head. His arm doesn't look right either." Grayson nodded toward the wreckage. The plane had come to rest against the trees, almost like I'd parked it there on purpose, except that the prop was mangled, the wings were torn, the tail was torn, the left gear was gone, and the whole thing listed to the side. Alec and Molly and the airport mechanic crowded around Mark in the front seat.

Grayson put his hands in my hair. "Your head okay?"

"Yes," I breathed.

"Neck okay?" He slid his hands down to my shoulders. "Anything sore?"

"No."

"Is she okay?" Molly shouted.

"She's okay," Grayson shouted back.

"Grayson!" Alec's voice was strained. "A little help!"

Grayson pointed at the ground and told me, "Sit down." He put his weight on my shoulders.

I didn't have a choice. I sat where he put me, flattening the tall grass under me.

"Don't move." He ducked under a half-broken branch hanging onto a tree by a few splinters. He took his place beside the others to help pull Mark free.

Way off in the distance behind me, sirens wailed. Above them I could hear the rope clanging against the flagpole.

• • •

The paramedics kept me in the back of the ambulance for a long time, like they couldn't believe there was nothing wrong with me. When the police wanted to question me, the paramedics left to help with Mark. The police left and the paramedics came back. Finally they helped me down from the ambulance, into the arms of Grayson, who had stood at the bumper the entire time, watching me.

When Alec saw I'd been set free, he walked over and hugged me under the trees. "Remember how my dad said 'You have to be better than me'? You are." He let me go.

Then Molly hugged me for a long time, squeezed me, and kissed me on the cheek. Below the lenses of her blinged-out sunglasses, her face was streaked with mascara and tears. "You scared the fuck out of me."

Her hand stayed on my back until Grayson led me away, through the grass to the tarmac. Behind us, a tractor was already towing the wreckage of the beautiful Stearman out of the trees. The runway needed to be cleared quickly so the rest of the businesses at the airport could fly.

Grayson didn't say a word until we reached my trailer. Neither did I. For some reason my mind was stuck on that last moment before the left wheel should have touched the runway, when I realized I'd been in denial. He held out his hand for my key, unlocked the door, and led me through the trailer, back to my bedroom. He sat me down on the edge of the bed and settled close to me, leaning over me, knee to knee with me.

He kissed my lips. "Are you really okay?"

"I will be."

He kissed my cheek, moving along my cheekbone until he was whispering in my ear. "We forgot that whatever kind of

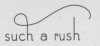

drama we've got going on when we're on the ground, we can't let it affect what happens in the sky." He kissed my earlobe, then backed away to look me in the eye. "I love you."

I took a long breath, meeting his intense gaze. "I love you too."

"I wanted to tell you on the radio," he said. "But we don't do that."

"Your dad would kick your ass."

Laughing, he pulled his phone from his pocket. "I'm leaving this here for you. Call Molly if you need anything."

"O . . . kay," I said. Crashing an airplane didn't fix the fact that Molly had called me a liar. Or that I was one.

"She's expecting you to call," Grayson said. "You rest. I'll be back to check on you." Watching my eyes, he kissed my hands, and then he was gone. I could trace his path through the trees by the pitch of the pit bull's bark.

I lay there for a while, but that moment in the airplane played over and over in my head. Thinking that the flight seemed normal, despite the fact that Grayson had told me the left wheel was gone. Setting the aircraft down on one wheel, feeling only by degrees that the other wheel was really missing.

Finally I got up, took a shower, and walked back to the airport. As I passed the office, Mr. Simon was coming out the door in his usual baseball cap and overalls, despite the heat. He waved me over. He hadn't been around that morning for the crash. Now I suspected that's why Mark had been willing to take me up: he really hadn't been allowed, but his uncle hadn't been there to say no.

I didn't want Mr. Simon to yell at me, but I figured I owed him the opportunity since I *had* crashed his airplane. I walked into the shade of the porch.

He said, "I want to shake your hand, little lady."

299

I didn't have a lot of experience shaking hands. I probably hadn't done it since I met Sofie, but I extended my hand to Mr. Simon. His grip was too strong at first, and suddenly so weak that I could hardly feel his hand at all, like he'd remembered he was shaking the hand of a girl. *Little lady,* he'd called me, so disrespectful even as he showed me respect by shaking my hand. Being a pilot had always been like this for me, and it always would.

He let me go and gestured to a rocking chair. I sat down. He eased into the rocking chair on the other side of the door, where Grayson had sat last Sunday when he tried to convince me to work for him in the first place.

"That was some fancy flying you did," Mr. Simon said. "Saved my nephew." He turned to gaze at the tree line, a few trunks showing bright scars where the crash had stripped them of bark. "Saved what's left of my airplane."

*Saved myself,* I thought.

"I've got contracts to fill," he said. "Mark's grounded. Permanently, as far as I'm concerned. I need a pilot."

Mr. Simon hadn't actually asked me to be his pilot. I knew that's what he wanted. I also knew assuming too much and voicing this first would give him the advantage in the negotiation. I'd learned a lot by listening to men on this porch.

And I didn't really care anymore, because I had my own agenda. "Mark told me a couple of weeks ago that you were willing to hire me even while he was still flying for you. Was that true?"

Mr. Simon's eyebrows went up. He shook his head. "No. First I've heard of it. He told you that?"

I nodded, stomach twisting.

I didn't show surprise.

And I waited him out, rocking slowly in my chair like I could sit here in the shade all day.

Finally he said, "I am sorry for it. His mama didn't teach him right."

*My mama didn't teach me right, either,* I thought, *and I don't act that way.* I kept rocking.

"But now I've got that opening," Mr. Simon said. "And I'd like you to fill it. You'd need training, but it's clear you've got the stuff."

"Would you train me for free?" I asked.

He kept rocking too. "If that's what it took, yeah."

Now I should ask about the pay. Otherwise he might lower my salary to make up for the cost of crop-duster lessons. I'd learned a lot from Grayson this week too.

But there was no reason to keep playing this game. "I've got a job for the summer," I said. "I'm going to keep flying for Hall."

He turned to look at the Hall Aviation hangar. I followed his gaze. The red Piper was parked there, and Grayson walked toward us across the tarmac, carrying boxes.

"You think they're going to stick around?" Mr. Simon asked me.

"I do," I said, "at least for the summer. Next year I don't know what I'll be doing. Maybe you and I can talk again then."

"Fair enough." We both stood. He shook my hand again, this time covering it with his other hand. He looked straight into my eyes with watery blue eyes and said, "I do thank you." He ambled off the porch and headed for the huge crop-duster hangar at the opposite end of the airport.

Grayson sat down in Mr. Simon's chair, then set what he was carrying on the floor of the porch beside him: two

eco-friendly recycled paper containers from Molly's parents' café, and an eco-friendly drink cup.

I could tell he had something important to say. Just as on the first day we'd talked here on the porch, I could feel the weight of it around us in the hot, humid air.

He stood and held out his hands to me. He tugged me up to standing. Wrapping his arms around me, he pulled me close for a long hug.

Slowly I relaxed. Despite a couple of hours in bed, staring at the ceiling of the trailer, I hadn't known how tense my muscles still were from the crash until I melted, boneless, into Grayson's embrace.

He relaxed too, his tight hug fading into a shoulder massage. Finally he held me at arm's length and looked into my eyes. At least, I thought he did. We were both wearing aviator shades. Despite the fact that I couldn't see his eyes, this time I knew he was sincerely concerned as he asked, "Are you okay?" His voice broke. He cleared his throat.

"I'm fine," I said. "Are *you* okay?"

"Now I am. It took me a while. I was getting worried about you, though, and I was just coming to look for you. Sit down."

I didn't want him treating me like an invalid when I wasn't hurt at all. But he'd been through a lot that day, so I didn't argue with him. I sat down.

He sat beside me. Frowned at me. Reached over, took my chair by both armrests, and dragged it closer to his own chair. "There." He put his hand on my knee.

We both looked toward the far end of the runway as the orange Piper revved up its engines for takeoff. That must be why my knee was tingling, then—the vibration from the plane. I had thought at first it was Grayson's touch. But after the plane left Earth and angled into the air, its engines fading into

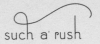

a tinny buzz, I still felt the vibration up my thigh from Grayson's hand on my knee. Then he squeezed my knee though he still watched the plane, as if he wanted to make sure I was still there.

"Who's flying?" I asked. "That's my plane. I guess you *did* fire me. You replaced me already?"

He groaned. "What was I thinking? Please come back. The Admiral's only flying for me the rest of the day."

"The Admiral!" I exclaimed. "Grayson, he's not going to tow banners for you, is he? You shouldn't have asked him! I don't care how good a pilot he is. If he hasn't been taught how to do it, he'll kill himself."

Grayson squeezed my knee again, this time to reassure me. "He volunteered so I could make my contracts and you wouldn't have to fly. This is how he learned to fly in the first place, back when he was a young damn fool idiot. That's what he said."

I laughed. "That sounds like your dad talking."

"There's a reason they were friends." Grayson tapped his finger on my knee. "Don't tell the Admiral's wife, though. That was a condition of his employment. He said she would shit a brick."

"Get him down and send me up. I was just headed over to the hangar to tell you I'm ready to fly."

"No," Grayson said. "I was just headed to your trailer to bring you breakfast and lunch." He gestured to the boxes from the café.

"I'm fine."

"No."

"I want to fly."

He pulled his hand off my knee. "Leah, no. You crashlanded an airplane this morning. I'm not sending you back up

the same day. If you feel okay tomorrow, you can fly tomorrow and Sunday."

"I need to get back on the horse *now*." I said this lightly like I was kidding, but I meant it. I wasn't scared. I knew what had happened that morning hadn't been my fault. But I didn't want to *get* scared because I'd waited too long and had too much time to think. "I'm embarrassed."

"Of what?"

"Screaming."

His left eyebrow lifted clear of his shades. "You think you should have crashed with more flair?"

"More composure."

He smiled. "After I crashed the Piper last year, I went into the woods and threw up, as you know. I got over it. You'll get over this too. You can get over it tomorrow. It would be irresponsible of me as your employer if I let you go back up today. End of discussion." He sliced his hand across his neck.

I frowned at him and sliced my hand across my own neck. "We use that too much."

"We need it," he said. "Neither of us knows when to shut up." He took both my hands in his. "*You're* about to tell *me* to shut up. I have something to say to you, and something to ask you."

"Okay." I should have been used to Grayson planning things out, but years of knowing him died hard, and it seemed odd that he'd thought ahead to a confession, and a question.

He rubbed my hands with his thumbs, steeling himself.

"Wow!" I exclaimed. "What could be so awful, Grayson?" I took off my shades and set them in my lap, then reached forward and took off his shades.

His eyes surprised me as always, because I seldom saw them: his irises a strange light gray, his lashes blond and long.

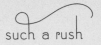

Usually when I'd seen his eyes, he'd narrowed them at me. Now they were big and worried, and he bit his lip.

"Tell me," I said.

"I should have told you earlier, but I was busy blackmailing you. I have to tell you but I don't want you to break up with me."

"Tell me." I didn't want to know. It was too soon for us to be over. But I couldn't stand being in the dark.

"My dad left you the Cessna."

I gasped. "The Cessna?" The white four-seater that Mr. Hall had used to give lessons. The first plane I'd ever flown. "Why didn't somebody tell me in the last two months?"

"My dad, in his infinite wisdom, made Jake the executor of his will. Since Jake's gone, the will is tied up in court. But I'm sure you'll be getting a call in the next few weeks. Or you would, if you had a phone."

I gaped at him. I couldn't believe it. Mr. Hall had left me the Cessna.

Grayson shifted uncomfortably. "See, it didn't make sense to me that he would will an airplane to a flight student, unless you were a lot closer than he'd admitted. That's why I was . . . unkind to you at first this week. It wasn't until that night we ate at Molly's café, when you talked about flying, that I began to understand. You might never have come out and told my dad how you felt about flying like you told us, but he saw that in you. He knew. And then, as you and I talked and . . . did more than that . . . I got it. I felt guilty for suspecting you. It's just that there was this *airplane*!" He spread his hands, indicating the thirty-six-foot wingspan, twenty-seven feet propeller to tail, and thousands upon thousands of dollars.

I owned a Cessna. I still couldn't believe it. "Has Alec known about this the whole time?"

"No. I was the one who talked to the lawyers. I just told Alec about it this morning."

"But he was going to find out," I said, "and you knew that. How could you go ahead with this plan to get him and me together?"

He held out his hand. "I didn't care about him finding out," he said as he touched his thumb. "Or you finding out." He touched his pointer. "Or him being mad." He touched his middle finger. "Or you being mad." He touched his ring finger. "All I cared about was keeping him alive."

I nodded. I understood that.

I still couldn't believe I owned a Cessna.

"I can't accept it," I said.

"I figured you'd say that. You think you don't deserve it. But Dad gave it to you because he loved you. Love isn't something you have to deserve."

He sounded like he was reading a cue card. I looked at him, puzzled.

He grinned. "I learned that recently." His grin faded. "At least, I hope it's true." He looked toward the Hall Aviation hangar. We couldn't see the white Cessna inside, but we knew it was there. "I was thinking you could sell the plane and use the money to live on and pay tuition until you graduate from college, if you're careful. Of course, then you wouldn't have a plane, and knowing you, you'd rather have a plane to fly than a place to live."

I laughed, because it was true.

"Some people sell shares of their airplanes," he went on. "A retired doctor around here would love to buy half an airplane that my dad kept up the maintenance on." In his voice I heard his pride in his dad. "You could still fly it half the time and pocket the profits for the other half."

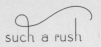

I sat back in my chair on a sigh, overwhelmed at the whole strange idea of owning an airplane. "Wow."

"I know," he said. "This changes everything for you, and I should have told you. If I'd told you, though, it would have been a lot harder to make you do what I wanted. So if you want to walk away from me now, I would completely understand, and—" He took off his hat, ran his hand back through his blond curls, and put his hat back on. "That's actually not true. I would grovel at your feet."

I giggled, but I didn't tell him I forgave him. Not right away. He'd put me through a lot. I understood why, but it might be nice to see him grovel a little. I wasn't sure yet. "What did you want to ask me?"

"Oh." His cheeks turned bright pink. He cleared his throat. "Will you go to the prom with me?"

I cackled so loud that my voice echoed against the Hall Aviation hangar and back to us. "The *prom*!"

"Yes!" He grinned.

"In Wilmington?"

"Yes, next Saturday."

I looked over my shoulder at the airport office door. "I would have to ask off work."

"It's at night, when the airport is closed."

I nodded slowly. "I would have to wear a prom garment."

"It doesn't matter what you wear. You could wear that bikini top you fly in, and every girl I ever dated would . . ." He grinned at me. "And all the guys . . . I know I've ribbed you for being beautiful and taking advantage of it, but you've got to give me my turn."

"Well, if you frame it like a revenge plot from middle school, how could I refuse? I've never been to a prom before. Mine was a few weeks ago and I never thought about going."

"We'll make sure this one is good."

Still thinking this through, I asked, "Would you drive down and get me? I would hate for you to come all that way and then bring me back. That's a lot of driving."

"I would come get you," he said. "You would stay at my house, in the guest room, and my mom would make sure I didn't touch you inappropriately. While she was looking. Or . . ." He held up his finger like he'd just gotten a bright idea. "You could fly up to Wilmington in your airplane."

I stared at him for a moment without understanding what he was saying. And then realized he was talking about Mr. Hall's Cessna. Which was now my Cessna. "Can I do that?" I asked. "It's not technically my plane yet."

"Right," he said. "It belongs to Hall Aviation for a few more weeks, until I sign it over to you. But you're insured to fly planes for Hall Aviation. It's all good. You can go wherever you want."

"*Really.*" I pictured flying to the prom in Wilmington. Flying anywhere I wanted, anytime. I pictured rising above the ground to a thousand feet, where I could see, and pointing the plane in every direction. The whole Atlantic coast, the whole country was suddenly mine.

Grayson chuckled. "I thought that would make you smile. It's taking a few minutes to sink in, but now you see."

"Yes," I said. "Now I can see."

"The only thing is, Alec's asking Molly to the prom too, so it would be nice if you made up, and you could bring her with you."

On cue, the yellow Piper dove low over the grassy strip and dropped a banner. The fabric sank straight down and settled on the grass. The wind was calm.

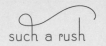

Watching the plane sail away, I said, "I hope things won't be awkward between you and Alec because of all this."

"Oh, it'll be awkward all right," Grayson said. "When we were so mad at each other this morning, before you went up, he called our mom and told on me."

"Told on you!" I exclaimed. "He never tells on you. And I thought your mom knew you were running the business and trying to get him to stay."

"She knew about that," Grayson acknowledged. "She didn't know about *you,* and what I made you do. On Sunday night when we get back to Wilmington, grief counselors are getting called in. And uncles."

If he'd said all this bitterly, I would have worried about what he had in store. But he said it lightly, like he didn't mind the idea too much.

"Maybe it will be good," I said carefully.

"Maybe. But whatever happens, Alec and I are brothers. We've been through hell and back together. We can handle awkward." His eyes followed the trajectory of Alec's plane as he circled back around to land. "My dad would hate that you and I are together. He would think I'm bad for you."

"He would be wrong," I said. "I would tell him so. That day last December when you crashed . . . You had a handle on it at first, even in that high wind. You set that plane down and your dad said, 'Perfect.'"

Grayson smiled. "And then I crashed, and he said something else."

This was true. "Well. He thought you were perfect for a second. And you really were. I could hear in his voice how proud he was of you. Like you had conquered something, so he had conquered it himself."

"Thank you, Leah." Grayson leaned forward until his rocking chair tipped down. He kissed me on the mouth, putting one hand up to my cheek to hold me there gently while he caressed me.

With a deep breath, he backed away and motioned over his shoulder. "I've got to get to work."

"Let me come with you," I said. "I promise I won't try to fly. I'll just sweep the hangar or, Jesus, beat the dust out of the couch. Something."

He gave me such a stern look that I backed out of the suggestion myself. "O-*kay*," I said with my hands up.

He bent down and picked up the boxes and the cup from Molly's parents' café. "Here." He nodded his head toward the airport office. "Go inside and steal your newspaper like you do. Go home. Relax. Molly's coming over after work to talk to you. Don't make that face. And then I'll come pick you up and take you to dinner, to the grocery store, and wherever else you need to go."

*To buy a prom dress,* I thought. But that's something I could do one night next week with Molly.

If we were speaking by then.

He tried to hand me the boxes and the cup, probably thinking that if he just pressed them toward me, I would take them automatically. When I didn't, he asked, "What is it? You're resentful at being jerked around?"

I nodded, already feeling better because he understood where I was coming from.

"You're not used to having a lot of family and friends," he said, "giving you advice and telling you what to do and sticking their noses in your business. That's what we do because we care about each other. Get used to it. You've joined the club." He poked the boxes at me again. When I took them, he kissed

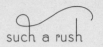

me on the forehead, slid his shades back on, and turned for the
Hall Aviation hangar.

With the stacked boxes in my hands, I did slip into the office. I called a hello to Leon. He called back from somewhere
in the depths of the office. So it was safe to snag the newspaper
from a side table in the waiting room. I also went back to the
break room and grabbed an apartment finder magazine from
the rack of brochures for local attractions. When I leaned
against the glass door to open it because my arms were full,
Grayson was just turning around to look for me at the door in
the side of the Hall Aviation hangar. He waved. I moved my
elbow in response. He went inside the hangar, and I turned for
the trailer park.

On second thought, I paused. Looked up to the sky above
the runway and the trees. An airplane motor buzzed up there
somewhere, but I couldn't see the plane.

I whispered, "Thank you. For everything."

I continued on my way, my flip-flops slapping on the pavement until I reached the end of the tarmac and waded through
the long grass. As I left the field and entered the forest, the pit
bull lunged at me, as usual. This time his growl cut off short,
though. He stood at the end of his chain, eyed me silently, and
sniffed the air. He smelled the food.

Inside my trailer, standing at the kitchen counter and suddenly starving, I investigated the contents of the boxes. I ate
the chocolate croissant first—not warm anymore but still
Molly's dad's chocolate croissant—and then a big portion of
the sandwich for lunch, and carefully packed the rest away in
the refrigerator for another day.

Then I settled on the pitted sofa with the apartment finder
magazine. I planned to borrow Grayson's phone tomorrow,
call the landlord, and find out exactly how many months my

mother had been pocketing the money I gave her instead of paying the rent. Ever since Mr. Hall had let me fly for free, I'd stashed my salary for college. I didn't want to part with it now, but I had plenty to cover the cheap rent for a few months.

Back rent was all I would pay the landlord, though. I was on my own now. I had choices, and I chose not to live in this trailer a second longer than I had to. Paging through the apartment finder magazine, I felt panicky, like I had last Sunday when Grayson told me Mark had made up my job with Mr. Simon. The cheapest apartments were twice as much as the trailer, and they were on this side of town, possibly in more dangerous neighborhoods. Because I'd been reading the newspaper for years, I knew exactly where all the shootings and stabbings had occurred.

The apartments on the nice end of town were, predictably, much more expensive. Now that I wasn't supporting my mother, I could afford one. Then I couldn't walk to the airport. I could ride the school bus to the airport, I supposed, and then ask the Admiral to take me to my apartment when he landed for the day, which was about the time I got off work. But like Grayson had said, I hated to rely on someone. And I had only six weeks of school bus left before I graduated. It was time I learned to drive. And bought a car.

The apartments on the nice end of town also required a credit check. I had no credit. I had a job, though. I'd held my job at the airport for three and a half years, and Grayson could vouch that he would employ me for a lot more money through the summer. Or I could find a roommate who'd rented apartments before, maybe one of the college kids Molly's parents hired to work at the café during the summer. I could see this imaginary girl now. She would usually be hanging at the apartment when I got off work. She would almost always be there

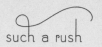

when I woke up in the morning, because she lived there too. We would go out together sometimes. She would be worldly and fun like Grayson and Alec and Molly. She would have a TV.

This fantasy, as delicious as the chocolate croissant, had only one drawback. Knowing my mother, she would show back up in a few weeks, dumped by Roger in Savannah. Or she would have stayed with him long enough to figure out he really wasn't getting hired on at the backhoe plant, and she would get a ride back to Heaven Beach to mooch off *me*. She wouldn't find me here at the trailer.

Thinking this made me feel a twinge of guilt. After all, she was my mother, the only relative I knew. But if she really wanted to find me, all she had to do was come to the airport. Maybe now that I wasn't her responsibility, she'd find the strength to stand on her own. In that case, I would like to see her sometime. I just didn't necessarily want her to know where I lived.

The trailer seemed to tremble with new energy. Looking around, I thought it seemed brighter than normal, with more sunlight filtering through the palm fronds and streaming into the tiny windows. Then I realized the vibration was from a plane overhead, a Piper. I jumped up and leaned out the door just in time to see Grayson in the red Piper flying through a small circle of blue sky in the treetops.

Then I looked out into the "yard," which Grayson and Molly would be walking through later. One of the plastic chairs lay on its back where Molly had knocked it with her car Sunday night, and I was pretty sure the margarine tub still held cigarette butts. My mother didn't live here now, but I did, at least for another two weeks, and this mess was my responsibility. I took a wet rag outside, wiped everything down, threw the

margarine tub away, and even considered cutting back some of the underbrush around the trailer with the only garden tool I had, some craft scissors, before I got depressed and decided I wouldn't live here long enough for yard maintenance to be worth my effort.

The inside of the trailer *was* worth the effort. I went back inside and looked around with new eyes—not the eyes of Grayson, but my own eyes, in my own home, not my mother's home that I happened to be living in too. First I took down my sad school photos on the wall where the TV had been. I would keep the photos, but I separated them from their cheap frames, which I would give away.

That got me started packing. I didn't box up my toiletries or my summer clothes, since I'd need those until the end of the month. But I cleared out every closet and put much of what I found in garbage bags to give away. I started to put what I wanted to keep in garbage bags too. But that reminded me of how Mark and my mother treated their worldly possessions. I took my belongings out of the garbage bags and put them in a pile, which I would transfer to an organic produce box I would snag from Molly's parents' café.

Finally I moved to my mother's room. At first I just stood there in the dark space, unbearably hot because I'd had her door closed to save on air-conditioning since she left. I was afraid to touch anything. But she was gone, and I was leaving. I dragged her clothes out of her closet and her dresser. I started to put those in garbage bags to give away too. But she might show up at the airport and demand them back. She would be very angry that I'd given them away. I kept them in the garbage bags. I would store them in the cellar at the airport. There they would remind me of her only when I took a box of files down for storage, or I sought shelter there with Grayson.

I got so absorbed in the chore that I didn't realize how much time had passed until a knock sounded on the aluminum door. The knocking wasn't hard enough to make a noise like a gunshot and alarm me, but it did follow the beat of Molly's favorite rock song.

I opened the door wide. Molly balanced there on top of the shaky cement-block staircase. In her face I saw relief that I was okay. Love for me. Anger and betrayal and loss and hurt. We had a lot to talk through and a lot of apologies to make to each other.

"I have *never* thought of you as my charity case," she said.

"Okay."

"I didn't want to be friends with you just because you were an edgy girl with the guts to steal my boyfriend, either."

"Okay."

"But I can see why you would think that," she wailed. "How did we get to this place where we had to be tough all the time and never said how much we loved each other?"

"Shhh." I wrapped my arms around her and let her rest her chin on my shoulder. "I'm the one who had the plane crash today, but *I* will comfort *you* because I love you."

As she straightened, laughing, her eyes were full of tears. "Can I come in?"

I pushed the metal door wide for her. "Yes, chick. Come in."

# twenty

The next Saturday, a few hours before the airport office was scheduled to close, I handed over the phone and the keys to Leon. In the restroom, I scrubbed my hands to make sure they didn't smell like avgas, redid my hair and makeup carefully, and slipped on strappy sandals and the adorable sky-blue prom dress that Molly and I had found at the consignment store. The restroom didn't have a full-length mirror. Standing on the porch of the office, I checked my look in the glass door. With the airplanes behind me in the reflection, I looked like a model from a fashion magazine spread that showed fine clothes against a gritty background of asphalt and machinery. A couple of guys whistled at me from several hangars down, and I waved to them.

By the time I crossed the tarmac to the Hall Aviation hangar, Molly's car was parked outside. She stood by patiently in her heels and hot-pink dress while I rounded the Cessna slowly, running my hands over the wings. She didn't comment

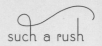

when I climbed the stepladder to check the gas level. She only took pictures of me with her phone and probably posted them online.

But when I asked her to help me push the plane out of the hangar, she absolutely refused. She would trip in her heels. The rivets would snag her dress. The plane was too heavy. I could prove her last assumption wasn't true by showing her how the plane rocked back and forth on its wheels when I shoved it. Still, I thought I was going to have to hunt up Leon or the Admiral or someone to help me when she finally relented. She pushed the strut while I hauled on the guide holding the wheel. The airplane was outside in the breeze scented with meadow flowers.

I closed her into the cabin and showed her how to put on her headphones. She didn't protest. But when I taxied to the end of the runway and turned the plane around, I finally realized why she'd been so obstinate before. Her hands were shaking.

"Scared?" I asked her.

She looked over at me. Even her glittering eye shadow was unable to draw attention away from the panic in her wide blue eyes. "What do *you* think? But I said I would go with you."

"Haven't you ever flown before?"

"Not in a plane this small."

"Oh, that's right." I nodded. "You only fly to Europe."

"First class," she agreed. "I can close the window blind and pretend it isn't happening. Flight attendant!" She snapped her fingers. "What do I have to do to get an appletini around here?"

I rolled my eyes. "There are lots of things that can go wrong," I acknowledged, "but I won't let them. And the plane is our friend. The plane wants to fly. Watch." I powered the

engine up and sped away from the trailer park, then took my hands off the yoke. "Look, I'm not doing anything and the plane lifts into the air when we hit a certain speed. That's just how it's made."

*"Put your hands back on the steering wheel,"* she shrieked in my headphones.

To placate her, I grabbed the yoke. As we rose above the trees, I made the gentlest turn I could manage so the cabin wouldn't tilt. To give her the smoothest ride, I pointed us toward the ocean, where the water would temper the air and there would be less turbulence. I wished for the airline pilot's uniform that would give people confidence in me.

I would get it soon enough.

"It's beautiful up here," she murmured. Auburn updo smashed against the window, she watched the late-afternoon sun glinting on the ocean.

"Yes," I said, "it is."

The longer we stayed up, taking in the scenery, the more she seemed to relax. But soon we had to come down. As the North Carolina swampland passed under us and the skyline of Wilmington came into view, I neglected to point out that we were landing at an airport much larger than ours, with actual airlines and an air traffic control tower. I'd done plenty of touch-and-go's at large airports during lessons with Mr. Hall. Besides, the airstrip wasn't busy late on Saturday afternoon. Still, Molly was so nervous, head pressed against the glass, freshly manicured hands gripping both sides of the seat until her fingers turned white. I used my Chuck Yeager voice to radio my request to land and sailed on in, feeling like an airline pilot already.

I taxied where they pointed me, toward the terminal. Ten teenagers in prom dresses and tuxedos stood grinning behind

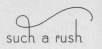

a railing, with Alec and Grayson in front. The instant I told Molly it was safe, she snatched off her headphones, unstrapped her seat belt, and bailed out of the plane with her overnight bag. She skipped across the tarmac and threw herself into Alec's arms.

I went over my checklist in my head, made sure I wasn't forgetting anything as I shut the plane down, and slid out of the cockpit slowly. The guy with my airport job, who looked college age, brought out the chocks for my plane. He glanced at me and then did a double take. "You are the prettiest pilot I ever saw."

"Hey." Grayson walked forward. "Do you see me standing here in a tux? Get in line."

"Dude! Sorry." The guy couldn't back away with his hands up because he had to put the chocks down first, but he did round to the other side of the airplane.

Grayson slid his arms around me. I caught a whiff of his sexy cologne and wanted to inhale him. "You're the prettiest pilot *I* ever saw." He pulled me close for a long, slow kiss. Behind us I could hear some of the girls say, "Awww."

Grayson laughed against my lips. But as he broke the kiss and looked down at me, his gray eyes were serious.

"What's the matter?" I whispered. "Did it spook you to see your dad's plane coming in?"

"No," he said in surprise. "I wasn't thinking about that. I just missed you. A lot." He kissed my cheek, then turned. "Let me say hi to Molly."

He passed Alec, who hugged me. I hugged Alec back, pretending it wasn't weird that I had made out with my boyfriend's brother. Maybe one day soon it wouldn't be. He kept one hand on my shoulder as he asked quietly, "Did Molly do okay on the flight?"

I made a grim face and shook my head no.

He leaned forward and said in my ear, "I was afraid of that. Between the two of us this summer, maybe we can break her in."

I grinned and nodded as he walked back to her. If he was planning to fly with Molly this summer, that meant he planned to help Grayson keep Hall Aviation open. Grayson must be so relieved that Alec wasn't rushing to join the military anymore. At least Alec would give the family business a shot.

Grayson found me again. With an arm around my bare shoulders, he faced his friends. "So, here she is. I told you so. Some of you owe me money."

They burst into laughter. A girl stepped forward with her hand stuck out for me to shake. "Leah, it's nice to meet you. I'm Nance. And when Grayson told me he was bringing a beautiful pilot to the prom, I said he was making you up. We all had to see it to believe it."

"Let's go eat!" a boy shouted from the back of the group. "Classy," a girl said, and suddenly all of them were moving into the terminal. Molly kept walking with Alec as she turned around and waved at me, smiling like her face would break. I'd never seen her so giddy about a guy.

Grayson took my overnight bag. He led me by the hand to the office where I had to register my plane, and he leaned against a pillar to wait for me while I filled out the paperwork. I couldn't help glancing over at him a couple of times, so tall and handsome and strange in his black tux and bow tie, without his shades or his cowboy hat. Dressing up suited him. Several groups of passengers turned to stare at him as they walked by. Then they looked around for the other half of the prom date, saw me, and smiled. They knew we were together, and that made me happy.

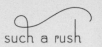

I held out my hand as I walked toward him. He took my hand in his, and we swung them between us as we walked through the lofty terminal with mile-high ceilings. "I'm sorry about the huge group date," he said.

"It seems like fun."

"Well, they wanted to do it because we're graduating soon. And I haven't been a good friend to them lately, but they've been good to me." He opened the door to the parking lot for me and held it as I blinked in the sunlight on the other side.

"We're going to dinner," he said. "Then there's the prom. Then a party at my friend Ish's house, and then, if you're up for it, a better party at my friend Steve's house." He stopped and turned to me in the middle of the wide brick stairs. "But I promise, Leah, I vow to you, that sometime in there, we will be alone." He raised his eyebrows suggestively and grinned. The edges of his blond hair glowed golden in the sunlight. A jet high in the atmosphere passed behind his head, silently streaking white across the blue sky.

That's when I knew. The pressures of business and the sadness of death remained with him. But he could forget them for one night, for prom night, and worry only about how to get me alone, like a normal high school senior. Grayson would be okay.

I smiled and squeezed his hand. "I can't wait."

The prom theme was "Up, Up, and Away!" Instead of Superman decor, blue streamers looped through the rafters of the gym to look like sky. Sparkling white clouds hung down, plus cutouts shaped like hot air balloons, blimps, and airplanes. Even the prom photo backdrop had a 1950s aviation theme, like the inside of an airport bar in Hawaii. I had a weird feeling of déjà vu. It all seemed a little too perfect, like the prom had

read my mind. Then Grayson explained that Alec was the student council president and the head of the prom committee. Of course he was.

I hoped someday I would look back at my prom photo with Grayson, vintage airline posters in the background, and laugh at how it had predicted such great things to come.

Late that night when the crowd started to thin, moving on to other parties, Grayson whispered that we would leave soon, but there was something he needed to do first. I sat on the bottom row of the bleachers, directly under the silhouette of a 737. Glad to get off my high heels for a minute, I happily watched Molly and Alec slow dancing and making out. They both half grinned as they kissed like they were *really* enjoying it. This was not how Alec had kissed me at all. He'd been holding out on me, which made me smile too. I was glad what he and Molly had found together was something special.

As I scanned the shadowy crowd, I spotted Grayson. He was dancing and talking with an elderly lady. Someone had told me earlier she was their high school principal.

"Leah!" Nance exclaimed, sliding onto the bench beside me and dragging her boyfriend, Ralph, with her. "You're all Grayson's talked about this week. I can't believe he left you alone!"

I nodded to the dance floor. Nance slapped her hand over her mouth. Ralph laughed and swore.

"I take it Grayson and the principal aren't close?" I asked.

"Not hardly!" Nance exclaimed.

"They've spent a lot of quality time together over the last four years, if you know what I mean," Ralph said. "He's gotten sent to her office at least once a month. To see them dancing together is truly bizarre."

As he said this, the principal and Grayson laughed together

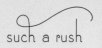

like friends, as if all of Grayson's transgressions had happened a long, long time ago, when he was a child.

"Speaking of bizarre," Ralph said, "Nance and I have been dying to ask you something."

I eyed them warily. "Okay."

Ralph held both hands out flat, like he wasn't sure how to put this. "Ever since their brother died, and then their dad died, Alec seemed to hold himself together pretty well. Grayson didn't."

"He's been lost," Nance added, watching me sadly.

"Depressed," Ralph said.

"Gone," Nance said.

"And now he's back." Ralph extended his hand toward me. "How did you do that? What did you do?"

"Listened." I shrugged. "Understood."

The song ended and a new one started. Couples shifted on and off the floor. Despite the movement, Ralph and Nance continued to stare at me like they were waiting for the rest of the story, but I'd told them all I knew.

"Well, please keep doing it," Nance said finally, "because he's like a new person."

Grayson came toward me from the darkness. As he stepped out of the crowd, colored lights played across his wavy hair and handsome face, disappearing against his black tux. With a grin like a promise, he reached for me.

As I put my hand in his and let him pull me up, I murmured to myself, "So am I."


"Seven-thirty-seven," Grayson said. "Yours someday."

My heart pounded and I squeezed his hand as the massive airliner seemed to head straight for us. But it was pitching into the sky by the time it screamed overhead, giving us a glimpse

of its white underbelly. We both turned around in our lawn chairs to watch the gorgeous plane until it disappeared into the dim early-morning sky. We could still hear it.

After Ish's party and Steve's even better party, Grayson had driven us here to the industrial complex near the Wilmington airport, at one end of the runway. In the dead of night, in the cab of his truck, we'd finally gotten our delicious time alone. I was still smiling at the thought of it.

He'd planned ahead. Now we sat in our chairs in the truck bed, holding hands under a blanket against the wet chill, watching the first flights take off.

He sighed with satisfaction and relaxed his hand around mine. He'd gotten as much of a rush from the plane as I had. Then he nodded toward the horizon. "Sunrise."

An intensely pink sun, striped by purple clouds, peeked over the trees. It was so small and weak that I hadn't noticed a change in the light yet, but I knew it was coming.

"Uh-oh," I said. "I shun the light. I probably look like I've been fooling around in my boyfriend's pickup."

"No, you—" He turned to smile at me. His eyes lingered first on my crumpled prom dress, then my hair. "Well, maybe." He let go of my hand under the blanket, wrapped his arm around my shoulder, and pulled me closer. "I hope we stay together for a long, long time. I'll never get used to looking at you." He kissed me gently.

At first I had trouble kissing him back because I was smiling so hard. Then his other hand moved under the blanket, sliding across my dress. My body was right back where it had been half an hour before, giving itself to his and taking anything he wanted to give in return.

After a long kiss, he drew away, sighing again, sounding and smiling exactly like he had after the airliner buzzed us.

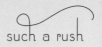

Then he looked up at the sky. The blue had deepened from the grayish hue of first light. "I wonder if Jake did this at the end of his prom night."

"Did his girlfriend like flying?"

He laughed shortly. "No."

"Yeah. I think this is perfect, but after prom night, most girls would rather watch the sun rise at the beach."

"That's so strange." His fingers traced a pattern on my bare shoulder. "I'm very lucky, and I will never forget that, I promise." In the middle of this declaration of love, his voice trailed off. He was distracted by the hum of a small airplane. "Cessna Corvalis."

"Where!" I exclaimed at the exact moment I saw the tiny airplane taking off toward us. It was the same make as mine, but the model was high-end: the Beemer of four-seater, single-engine planes. It roared over us, the noise nothing compared with the airliner's scream, but powerful for the plane's size. The underbelly was painted in racing stripes, which made me giggle. The plane looked happy.

We turned around in our seats to watch it disappear. "I wonder where she's going so early in the morning," Grayson murmured.

"She wants to get a head start," I said. "It's going to be a pretty day to fly."

# Acknowledgments

Heartfelt thanks to my brilliant editor, Lauren McKenna, for her enthusiasm; my incomparable agent, Laura Bradford, for making this book happen; my dad and my brother, both pilots, who patiently explained how to fly (and crash) an airplane; my partner in crime, Erin Downing, for reading it and getting it; and as always, my wise critique partners, Catherine Chant and Victoria Dahl, for their unwavering support.

## Such a Rush
Jennifer Echols

TOPICS AND QUESTIONS FOR DISCUSSION

1. Consider the opening paragraph of *Such a Rush*. What are your first impressions of Leah? Does this impression change over the course of the novel?

2. "I could not guess at Mr. Hall's motives, but I had liked him because he was kind to me and funny, not because he gave me something I wanted. I felt guilty for putting the loss of him and the loss of my flight time into the same depressing thought." Why does Leah equate the loss of flying with the loss of Mr. Hall? What do planes and flying represent to Leah? Is there anything else in her life that matches the feeling she has when flying?

3. Leah thinks to herself, "If Molly was going to force me to a party where the girls would call me trash, and Grayson was going to treat me that way, I would dress the part." How much of our personalities are defined by how others see us?

Do you think Leah's rebellion against how others see her is effective? Is it constructive? Do you think, given her circumstances, the "tough girl act" is her only means of standing up for herself? Have you ever been placed in a similar situation? How did you react?

4. Molly and Leah have a strong, but very unconventional friendship. In the end, both girls realize that neither one is truly being herself out of fear of losing the other. What assumptions do Molly and Leah make about each other? Why do you think it was so hard for them to trust each other? Does their friendship remind you of any relationships in your own life?

5. "I remembered what Mr. Hall had told me when I first asked him for a lesson: the kids who watch planes are destined to be pilots. I envied Molly . . . she wasn't driven toward a career that was out of her reach. But envying Molly was a dangerous road for me. I knew better than to go down it." Do you agree with Leah? Or do you think Leah is the lucky one, to have found what she loves to do even if she has to fight to hold onto it?

6. While having dinner at Molly's parents' cafe, Molly asks Grayson, Alec, and Leah why they each wanted to start flying in the first place. What do Leah, Grayson, and Alec's different answers reveal about them as characters? Do you think it is significant that both Leah and Grayson mention the "rush" that flying gives them, but Alec doesn't? Or that Alec mentions Jake and the family business, but Grayson doesn't? Compare, contrast, and discuss their answers.

7. Leah loves both the Hall brothers in very different ways. What are some of the characteristics Alec and Grayson share? What are some of their differences? Who do you think Leah should ultimately be with?

8. Grayson and Leah both see themselves as outsiders. Do you think that's why they are drawn to each other? What judgments do they make about one another? How do they learn to move past those judgments?

9. Discuss Leah's relationship with her mother. How does her mother's attitude toward men shape Leah's own attitude? Consider the following quote in your response: "Men always do that to women when they feel threatened. They tell everyone the woman must be giving out blow jobs because there's no way she could be successful otherwise." (pg. 232) Do you agree with Leah's statement? Do you think Leah accuses Grayson because this statement is true, or because of what she has learned from her mother?

10. Leah defends Mr. Hall to Grayson when Grayson gets angry about the fact that his father cheated on his mother and walked out on their family. Do you feel that sometimes we are too hard on the people we are closest to, because it is difficult to see them clearly or objectively? Do you think that Leah perhaps saw Mr. Hall for who he was better than Grayson simply because they weren't family?

11. "That's when I realized people use each other, Grayson. They define their relationships by what they are getting." Do you agree or disagree with Leah's assessment of relationships? Discuss how this perception shapes her decisions. Do you think Leah still feels this way about relationships at the end of the novel? Why or why not?

12. Leah, Grayson, and Alec's primary motivations are rooted in their family history and their backgrounds. Leah wants to escape her past and never wants to be like her mother; Grayson feels guilty over the way he behaved when his father was alive and is determined not to let him down; and Alec is searching for a way to make his father and brother

proud. Discuss the differences and similarities implicit within each character's motivations. Did you identify with any one character in particular? Were you surprised by any of the decisions these characters made?

13. Leah, Molly, Alec, and Grayson all keep important secrets from each other in *Such a Rush*. Discuss these secrets and why you believe each character chose to keep secrets from one another. Were you surprised to discover that Alec had known about Grayson's plan the entire time? Why do you think Molly didn't tell Leah the truth about her and Alec?

## Enhance Your Book Club

1. Is there something in your life that means as much to you as flying does to Leah and Grayson? What are your passions? What gives you that "rush" feeling? Do you love to cook, knit, draw, write, scrapbook, run, or snowboard? Have each member in your book club share their own passions with the group. How do these activities make you feel? Why do you think you are drawn to your particular passion?

2. Leah often borrows old copies of *Plane & Pilot* from the aviation office to take home and read. Visit www.planeandpilot mag.com to learn more about the magazine Leah describes as a "delicious luxury." Have each member choose an article to read and then plan to share an interesting fact or something you learned with the rest of the group.

3. Visit Jennifer Echols's website at www.jennifer-echols.com to read her "Frequently Asked Questions" and her personal blog. Consider reading another novel by Jennifer Echols, such as *Going Too Far* or *Forget You,* for your next book club discussion. How do the characters and plot relate to *Such a Rush*? Did you notice any similar themes?